DAWN OF WAR: TEMPEST

BATTLING TO SAVE the Blood Ravens' precious gene-seed, Librarian Rhamah is sucked into the Eye of Terror and crashes down onto a bizarre planet of alien libraries and museums – an ancient eldar world hidden in the tempests of the warp. His battle-brothers mourn the passing of this hero, but his fate is far worse than death...

When a detachment of strangely familiar Space Marines lands on the planet to plunder its forbidden knowledge, Rhamah finds himself embroiled in their confrontation with the planet's mysterious guardians. As the rest of the Blood Ravens begin their search for him, Rhamah struggles to discover his true identity – unaware that his allegiance could tip the balance to deciding the fate of this world and its secrets.

A WARHAMMER 40,000 NOVEL

DAWN OF WAR: TEMPEST

C S Goto

For Inquisitor Tsensheer and all your unappreciated work.

A BLACK LIBRARY PUBLICATION

First published in Great Britain in 2006 by
BL Publishing,
Games Workshop Ltd.,
Willow Road, Nottingham, NG7 2WS, UK.

10 9 8 7 6 5 4 3 2 1

Cover illustration by Philip Sibbering.

A CIP record for this book is available from the British Library.

ISBN 13: 978-1-84416-399-1
ISBN 10: 1-84416-399-7

Distributed in the US by Simon & Schuster
1230 Avenue of the Americas, New York, NY 10020, US.

Printed and bound in Great Britain by
Bookmarque, Surrey, UK.

See the Black Library on the Internet at
www.blacklibrary.com

Find out more about Games Workshop
and the world of Warhammer 40,000 at
www.games-workshop.com

IT IS THE 41st millennium. For more than a hundred centuries the Emperor has sat immobile on the Golden Throne of Earth. He is the master of mankind by the will of the gods, and master of a million worlds by the might of his inexhaustible armies. He is a rotting carcass writhing invisibly with power from the Dark Age of Technology. He is the Carrion Lord of the Imperium for whom a thousand souls are sacrificed every day, so that he may never truly die.

YET EVEN IN his deathless state, the Emperor continues his eternal vigilance. Mighty battlefleets cross the daemon-infested miasma of the warp, the only route between distant stars, their way lit by the Astronomican, the psychic manifestation of the Emperor's will. Vast armies give battle in his name on uncounted worlds. Greatest amongst his soldiers are the Adeptus Astartes, the Space Marines, bio-engineered super-warriors. Their comrades in arms are legion: the Imperial Guard and countless planetary defence forces, the ever-vigilant Inquisition and the tech-priests of the Adeptus Mechanicus to name only a few. But for all their multitudes, they are barely enough to hold off the ever-present threat from aliens, heretics, mutants – and worse.

TO BE A man in such times is to be one amongst untold billions. It is to live in the cruellest and most bloody regime imaginable. These are the tales of those times. Forget the power of technology and science, for so much has been forgotten, never to be re-learned. Forget the promise of progress and understanding, for in the grim dark future there is only war. There is no peace amongst the stars, only an eternity of carnage and slaughter, and the laughter of thirsting gods.

CHAPTER ONE: VAIROCANUM

THE HEAT WAS sudden and intense, as though I had been thrown from the coolness of gentle night air into the fury of a blast furnace. All at once, I could feel my senses coming alive: my skin prickled beneath the familiar ceramic touch of my armour, and my face burned as though it were on fire. There was nothing but light – radiant, searing and unbearable – piercing through to the back of my closed eyes, dragging me into consciousness like a beacon bringing a ship to shore.

Flicking open instinctively, my eyes merely filled my head with lancing agonies as the dazzling light crashed against my unguarded retinas. Still, I could see nothing, only the burning, red, bloody brightness of an intense sun that dominated my vision as though I were blind. My mind raced for images of darkness, trying to bring cool salve into my boiling thoughts, but the heat incinerated every thought, as though my head were an inferno in which nothing could survive.

Am I blind? The thoughts spiralled through the boiling convections, making me nauseous and dizzy. For a moment I thought that I was on my feet, but then my balance seemed to flip and turn, and the ground ran over my back like simmering water, scalding me through the panels of my armour, trickling through the joints against the scarred and leathery skin beneath.

No. Blindness is being lost in the darkness. Here I am surrounded by light. Without another thought, I lifted my left hand to my face and felt the darkness of a shadow fall over my blistered skin. The light against my eyes shifted and the temperature on my face dropped by a fraction of a degree. Cracking open my eyes once again, a burst of darkness cut into my mind as the silhouette of my hand burnt its image into my retina, like a moon eclipsing the sun.

My weapon! The thought exploded into my head, extinguishing the flames that wracked my mind like dynamite blowing out a forest fire. Nothing else mattered.

Reaching urgently around behind my shoulder, my hand plunged into a sea of burning granules as it quested for the hilt of my sword. *I'm lying on sand – this must be a desert!* But the hilt was not there. I rolled onto my side and felt the sizzling sand cascade across my back as I checked the sheath for its ancient blade. Nothing. It was not there.

Blood was pulsing through my neck, running close to the surface of the skin in an attempt to cool my body, and I could feel the labour of my secondary heart pounding in my chest.

Am I injured? I couldn't tell – all of my senses were swamped by the heat. I slumped back onto my back, folding my arm across my face to shade the exposed skin from the relentless assault of the desert sun.

After a few seconds, fragments of memories started to flicker past my eyes.

How did I get here? They were questions more than memories, but they implied memories: *I was somewhere else before – this is not where I am supposed to be. I am someone who belongs elsewhere.*

That single notion lingered in my mind, as though all trains of thought led directly back to it: *I – who am I?* It was like a black hole sucking everything else in.

There were no answers. The clearest image in my head was of an ornate and ancient sword, and I felt sure that the beautiful item was mine. It was important to me. Integral. It was part of who I was, and I felt its absence like an icy, physical wound. Instinctively, I reached again with my hand, letting the flames of the sun lap against my raw face once more, hoping faintly that I would find the hilt this time and, with it, find something of myself.

Nothing.

Without thinking, I snatched my right hand down to my thigh. *I should have a boltpistol in that holster.* The realisation was not quite a memory; it was more like an assertion about the proper state of my being.

I should have a sword on my back and a pistol against my leg: that was what it meant to be me. But the holster was empty and my bare fingers found nothing except the hiss of scorchingly hot ceramite, as my fingertips burnt against the armour fitted over my leg.

There must be something. I must have a weapon. A memory stirred and my hands darted to the fixtures and fittings that were moulded into the band around the waist of my armour. With my eyes still closed, my fingers danced across the surface with a muscle memory of their own; they knew what they were looking for. After a second, a wave of relief eased through me, like a wash of cool water. *A combat knife.* The metallic hilt burnt my fingers and the palm of my hand, but I gripped it with the certainty and strength with which a lame man might hold his cane.

Then the heat overcame me once again, and the searing light blinked into the darkness of unconsciousness.

THE SKY SWIRLED with purple clouds, spiralling into whirling nebulae against the heavy, deep red of the darkening atmosphere above. The air had cooled, and I could feel the crack of a thin layer of ice as I snapped open my eyes. Perspiration had frozen across my face, forming a delicate and brittle second skin.

It was freezing cold.

The sand beneath me crackled as I shifted my weight, flexing my aching shoulders to bring sensation back into the muscles that were sealed within the ice-encrusted shell of my armour. The servos that assisted shoulder movement whined for a moment, as though they had been frozen in place after a long period of inaction. The joints between the armoured plates had been sealed by ice after layers of sand had insinuated their way into the cracks.

Like bones crunching back into place, the armour broke through the pathetic resistance of the elements, and I could feel freedom return to my motions. The mechanical augmentation felt strangely natural. As my muscles flexed and power returned to the auto-reactive plates over my shoulders, warmth began to flood through the rest of my body. Something had shifted in my physiology, triggering a chemical release that raised my body temperature. *I should understand this process, but I have forgotten its name.*

As I climbed to my feet, splinters of icy shards exploded out of the joints in my arms and legs, but my body already felt warm and strong within its super-augmented shell. Only my face felt strange: cold and exposed, as though it had been stripped of its very skin. A sense of vulnerability made me reach for my head, but in place of icy ceramite I found the brittle and moist touch of ice-coated, blistered and scarred skin. An icy, metallic stud stood proud of my left temple.

I should have a helmet. That much I could remember. *Something is missing.* Then I remembered the missing sword and boltpistol. In my other hand, I registered the metallic touch of the hilt of a combat knife. Memories of searing heat and desert-blindness flashed back through my mind. *Where am I?*

Behind me, the desert stretched out to the horizon, barren and featureless, rolling with shifting dunes as the bitter wind toyed with incoherent clouds of dust. The scene was tinged with red from the dying light of three local stars, each just vanishing over the horizon and filling the sky with a wash of bloody light. The sand radiated an eerie paleness. I could not tell whether this was the natural colour of the desert, or a trick of faltering light, but I was certain about one thing. *This is a lost world.*

A narrow channel had been blown through the sand; it started in a crater about two hundred metres away and ended at my feet. From the look of it, it had been made by the impact and slide of a fast-moving, solid body. Perhaps it was the impact scar of a meteor. *Or perhaps the signature of my own arrival on this planet?*

Scanning the rest of the horizon and turning in the opposite direction, the desert dropped away sharply into a ravine. I was standing on the lip of a sheer cliff. Far below, the foot of the cliff-face was lost in deepest shadow, making it almost impossible to estimate the depth of the fall.

On the other side of the wide ravine, the landscape rolled and swept out into the darkness that shrouded the distant horizon, from whence the touch of the triple suns had already withdrawn. The dim, undulating dunes were punctuated with occasional tors and rocky protrusions, and great, jagged, black lashes through the sand suggested that other ravines broke the desert in the vaguely discernable distance. The icy wind scraped through the sand like the serrated breath of death itself.

Is this whole place dead? The thought had only just formed when a glint of light from the shadows at the base of the cliff caught my eyes. It was little more than a flash, just a flicker of reflected light, as though dancing in the eyes of a predator.

Did it move? I could feel my pupils dilate as my brain drew as much light as possible out of the surroundings, sucking it in like tiny, depthless black holes. In a reflex reaction, I squinted, and suddenly the light in the scene shifted, as though enhanced by something in my own brain. The bottom of the ravine zoomed up towards me, tinted in an overexposed, pale blue; it was as though my eyes were reeling it in. The sudden flush of nausea and vertigo lasted for only a fraction of moment, and then I realised that this was natural.

My eyes are the eyes of the Emperor. The words formed effortlessly in my mind, as though I had recited this thought over and over again until it had become part of me. But I couldn't make sense of it. *The Emperor?* Who was this man that strove to dominate my thoughts?

At the base of the cliff, half buried in the sand as though it had dropped directly out of heaven, my enhanced vision could discern the elegant shape of a sword. A large warpstone jewel glinted darkly from the pommel of the hilt, and intricate, alien runes glowed faintly as they snaked around the half

concealed blade. It gave off a barely visible green
light, as though it were a living entity that pulsed
with veins of energy in place of blood.

Vairocanum. It was my sword. Its name slid silently
into my thoughts, like burning oil, singeing incomp-
prehensible, runic shapes into the fabric of my
mind. It was calling for me, reminding me that it
should never have been forgotten, pressing its presence into my very being as though it were a
necessary part of me.

As I stared down at *Vairocanum*, watching the green
glow wax and wane as eddies of dust and sand
drifted past it, flickers of other images started to
pulse through my thoughts. The sight of the sword
triggered a flood of memories. They flashed like
visions being projected intermittently into my mind.
I could see other people. Giant, armoured warriors
like myself. They were battling something unimaginable. Vague, amorphous shapes were reaching out
of the walls, thrashing towards them and burning
with daemonic passions. The warriors fought and
then ran, turning towards me and charging. They
yelled, screaming, brandishing their weapons as they
stormed forwards. But before they could reach me, I
plunged the burning *Vairocanum* into the deck at my
feet, and everything vanished.

The darkness of my memory faded gradually into
the near-darkness of the desert. I found myself
unmoved and unmoving, still standing on the edge
of the cliff, staring down at the oddly enhanced
image of my once-lost force-sword, half buried in
the pale blue sands of an unknown, alien desert.

Vairocanum. The word sat comfortably in my brain. It felt like it belonged; I trusted it.

Self-consciously, I raised my hand over my shoulder and felt the empty sheath on my back. *Vairocanum*. It was one of the missing pieces, and it was as good a place to start as any. The cold, metal combat knife in my other hand felt lifeless and pathetic. *I need my sword.*

THERE WERE AT least three ways to descend the cliff: about a kilometre to the south I could see a rift in the structure of the ravine, and, given the geological composition of the landscape, I was sure that such a rift would be accompanied by rock falls and sand slides that would provide an easy path down to the valley floor. The deductions came naturally to mind, requiring no concentration or conscious effort. For a moment I wondered whether this strange landscape was familiar to me, but then I realised something quite simple. *I have been trained to understand terrain.*

The rift in the ravine held my interest for less than a couple of seconds. It would take me away from *Vairocanum* before bringing me back to her. I would lose sight of her very quickly, especially in the rapidly failing light. And the journey would not be a rapid one: the sand was loose and deep, and my heavy boots would sink significantly with each step; the going would be hard. I had no idea when I might have access to water or nourishment, so the exertion and the extra time would be wasteful and foolish. *Besides, I must not leave the sword – it is all I have.*

A better way down was more direct. The cliff beneath my feet was rocky and riddled with cracks. Tufts of vegetation had drilled their roots into the surface, suggesting that there would be handholds in the cliff, and that its composition was likely to be sedimentary – sandstone perhaps. *I should be able to hack out handholds with my knife, if I need to.* The climb looked challenging, especially in the icy dark, but I felt confident that I had made harder climbs before, even though I could not remember them. *I must not leave the sword.*

As I stood on the brink of the climb, a third possibility suggested itself to me like a secret revelation. *I might survive the fall.* Holding my hands out in front of my face, I studied the strong, heat-scarred fingers; the large combat knife looked tiny in my fist, even as it glinted with the last rays of the third red sun. The armoured panels that covered my arms were scratched and dented, but they seemed immovably fixed, as though they were somehow grafted to my body. The ceramite plates looked heavy and formidable, and yet I could not feel their weight at all. It was as though they were made of the air itself. *The armour supports its own weight. It does not sap my strength; it gives strength to me.*

Glancing back over my shoulder towards the last of the setting suns, I considered the deep impact channel that had been ploughed through the desert up to my feet. *If I survived that, the drop from this cliff would be nothing.*

As I watched, the third sun finally dipped below the horizon and the last of its ruddy light vanished from the surface of the desert. For a moment, a heavy dark shroud hung over the scene, obscuring everything beneath a veil. But then, as though activated by a silent and secret command, two pale red moons emerged from behind the roiling clouds; one massive like a fourth sun, and the other little more than the reflection of an eye. All at once the sky was alive with points of light, as the gently swirling clouds parted and shifted to reveal unknown constellations of stars and raging tempests of nebulae. *Where is this place?* The sands of the desert were cast into myriad colours, each grain a pale reflection of the glory of the stars above.

Vairocanum. The thought brought me back to the top of the cliff, prodding back into my mind like the pain of a phantom-limb. *I'm wasting time.* The one thing that I was sure about, the one thing that I knew had a place in my life, the one thing that I could name was at the base of that cliff. Everything else seemed vague and poisoned by conjecture, ignorance and disremembrance.

Resolution settled into my mind: *I am a warrior, and I must have my sword.* Taking a single step backwards and then two rapid steps forwards, I vaulted off the top of the cliff and down into the darkness below.

THE FROZEN DESERT rose up to meet me like a solid and impenetrable block of ice. As my feet punched into its surface I could feel the frozen structure crack and shatter beneath me. The ground frost exploded instantly, scattering shards of ice and fragments of congealed sand in all directions, as though they were being evacuated from a blast crater. With the ice-hard surface thoroughly ruined, my legs ploughed down into the softer sand beneath; it decelerated me rapidly as it compacted under the force of my impact.

I hardly felt that landing at all. The dynamism felt right. *I am the sword of the Great Father.* The phrase emerged out the darkness like a flaming torch in my brain; it was instinctive and I knew that I believed it instantly, but the words rang hollow like distant bells. *The Great Father?*

Vairocanum… The name pressed into my mind persistently and relentlessly. My eyes snapped to the north as I pulled myself out the sand and onto my feet. I could see the hilt clearly now, with the warpstone pommel glinting with dark complexity in the shadows of the night and the runes burning with eerie green power. After a couple of strides, I fell to my knees before the faintly glowing blade, bowing my head before it as though to an idol. It stood upright like a statue; its hilt and half its blade protruding up out of the sand, with the rest buried firmly in the frozen desert.

'I am the Sword of Vidya.' The words whispered from my lips automatically, as though they were the beginning of a mantra or prayer that I had taken inside my being and internalised so strongly that they had transcended even the shackles of memory. *I am the sword of the Great Father and my eyes are the eyes of the Emperor. When I gaze upon the unrighteous, I shall visit upon them the tempest of truth and lay waste to their souls.*

'For knowledge is power, and I will guard it with my life... and my sword.'

My words caught the frozen breath of the desert and drifted across the sand.

The snaking runes along the length of the blade seemed to beckon to me, luminous and sparkling in the icy night air. They curdled and swam through the metallic substance, as though the heart of the blade was composed of a fiery liquid, seductively confined in the shape of an ancient sword. The script slipped and flowed from one pattern to the next, inscribing a narrative and a history into my head in a language that I suddenly understood.

The runic characters became suddenly vivid, burning with an emerald passion that I knew I had seen many times before. It felt forbidden and exhilarating. I could feel the power pulsing into the sand beneath my knees. The sword called out to me, using a name that I could barely hear; it was as though the desert wind itself was eroding a word from the cliff-face by my side. *Rhamah.* I recognised it. *I am Rhamah – the touch of death.* It was clear and obvious all at once, like something that could never be forgotten.

With a sense of ceremony that I could not explain, I carefully tucked my combat knife back into its harness before reaching for the hilt of the great sword. Despite the freezing, arctic cold of the desert night, the grip felt warm to my touch, as though my fingers were closing around the thin neck of a traitor or a long forgotten lover.

At my touch, delicate tendrils of energy started to quest out of the warpstone pommel, questing over my hand and creeping towards my forearm. The intricate green flows prickled against my skin, filling my veins with an electric energy that I recognised at once. It was like life returning to me.

On my feet, I grasped the hilt in both hands and pulled to free it from the frozen clutches of the sand. But it didn't move. Half of the blade's length was submerged and fused into the desert, and the icy sand seemed reluctant to release it.

I pulled again, wrenching *Vairocanum* out of the ground and thrusting it into the air above my head like a prize. Heavy shards of frozen sand showered over me, peppering my armoured shoulders like hail stones. Looking up at last, I could see the pale red light of the moons dancing over the greening blade, swirling like clouds in the substance of the ancient sword.

A sudden and sharp pain lanced through my arms. *It's broken!* The thought was a dagger.

About a third of the blade was missing, broken off roughly on a jagged diagonal. For a moment I thought that I had inflicted this terrible wound myself, as I had prised the sword free of the desert. But there was no way that *Vairocanum* could be ruined by sand. *Something must have happened before we came to this place.*

Images and memories of the warriors charging towards me, flanked by the nebulous and terrible daemonic forms that were pouring out of the walls, returned to my mind. I plunged *Vairocanum* into the deck and the threat vanished. *Did I break her after all?*

Spinning the blade in an effortless and natural flourish, I returned it to its place on my back, feeling the reassuring and solid presence of the sword in its sheath once again. *Now I am ready for this world: I bring the touch of death, the sword of Vidya.*

THE NIGHT WAS as short as the desert was vast. I walked directly away from the cliff-face, using it as a point of reference in the continuously shifting landscape of dunes, but before the cliff had even vanished over the horizon behind me one of the suns had clawed its way into the sky ahead. I walked directly into its fierce gaze, trudging silently through the sand without pause, hesitation or rest.

As the first sun crested the horizon, the shift in temperature was sudden and extreme. In the distance, a strip of dust-cloud was whipped up along the line where the rapidly heating air touched the icy sand. It rolled and charged forwards, keeping pace with the daybreak, shattering the ice and the frozen desert in a relentless storm, ploughing up the sand behind the rapidly advancing morning light.

I glanced up at the scene, squinting my eyes against the distant but gathering wind. I might have dropped to the ground or flung myself behind a dune for cover, but something deep in my brain told me that there was no need. This was a storm that I could weather. As it thundered towards me, I simply raised an arm to shield my eyes from the maelstrom of sand, and walked on through it.

The temperature soared as the cloud broke over me. I could feel the air seethe against the skin of my face and hands. But the rest of my body seemed to register no change at all. Neither the wind nor the sand nor the heat penetrated my armour, and, after a couple of seconds, even the exposed skin of my face was regulated back to normality.

Pausing, I looked back over my shoulder at the diminishing image of the cliff-face behind me, with the storm wall rolling towards it. By my own calculations, I had walked about fifteen kilometres in twenty minutes, through a frozen desert in arctic temperatures, and yet I was not even breathing hard. I could not remember the last time I had eaten or drunk, and yet I felt strong and full of energy. The maelstrom of superheated sand had blasted past me, and I had hardly even noticed. And none of this felt strange to me. *I am the will of the Emperor, incarnate and terrible.*

A massive explosion sounded ahead of me and I returned my eyes to the horizon. The second sun had just lurched into the sky. It was vastly bigger than its junior cousin, and its impact on the desert was immeasurably more powerful. The horizon had erupted into a frenzy of sand storms, perhaps reaching a kilometre in height, which threatened even to obscure the sun as it rose rapidly into the sky. The massive tide thundered through the desert towards me, ripping the dunes from the ground and sucking them into incredible waves of convection.

In one movement I unsheathed *Vairocanum* from my back and dove to the ground, plunging the damaged blade deeply into the desert until it struck rock beneath the sand. As the infernal storm blasted into me and rolled over me, pressing me flat against the ground like a tidal wave pummelling me into the seabed, I gripped the hilt of my sword and trusted in its strength to anchor me.

The roaring of the wind pounded into my ears, but for a brief moment I thought that I could hear something else screaming through the air. Peering up through the turmoil of sand, the blood-red sky was almost obliterated by the abrasive air. Even so, I was certain that my eyes could detect the movement of a metallic flash skirting the billowing clouds in the lower atmosphere. It was akin to a tiny burst of light, refracted instantly through the entire colour spectrum. *My eyes are the eyes of the Emperor... I am not alone here.*

They are looking for me. The storm cleared as quickly as it had arrived, leaving the desert shrouded in a floating and gradually settling mist of searing sand. A delicate, wispy contrail was still faintly visible, disappearing into the clouds over the easterly horizon, vanishing behind a rugged, rocky peak that jabbed out of the desert and partly obscured the tardy, third sun as it started to rise. *That is the best vantage point.* Spinning the wounded *Vairocanum* back into its holster on my back, and ignoring the third sand storm as it barrelled over me, I set off for the mountain.

NIGHT WAS ALREADY falling by the time I crested the mountain. Dusk had settled over the desert like a ruddy blanket, transforming the scene into a sandy swamp of bloody images. The temperature was dropping rapidly, cooling from the blistering and inhuman heat of the day to the freezing, inhuman cold of the night. For a few moments, just as the suns touched the far horizon and their radiation burst into myriad shades of red, the temperature would have been bearable for an unarmoured human. But those moments passed quickly, and I paid them no mind.

Throughout the long climb, there had not been a single sign of the return of whatever craft had flashed through the lashes of the desert storm that morning. Part of me began to wonder whether I had actually seen a ship streaking through the troposphere, or whether my rapidly thawing brain had hallucinated it. However, such doubts were almost immediately overridden by a deep seated sense of certainty in my own senses; somehow I simply knew that I was not mistaken. It was neither intuition nor arrogance, but merely a certainty that the nature of my senses was not such that they could be tricked.

My eyes are the eyes of the Emperor. I turned the thought over and over in my mind as I climbed, feeling its weight and its peculiar gravity. This Emperor had power in my thoughts and over them, even though he had no form in my memory. If my eyes were his, then somehow I knew that they were beyond the trickery of mirage and fatigue.

But the Emperor was not alone in my thoughts. The name 'Vidya' kept returning to me, flashing through my mind like a comet, as though it were a sign that I should recognise. And then there was the battle in which *Vairocanum* was damaged. I could vaguely recall the blue-helmeted visages of the other warriors in that vision, as they charged towards me with their weapons crackling with warp light. I recalled a sense of resolve: I would not let the ship fall. However, my mind was not certain about whether the threat to the ship was the warriors or the nebulous snakes of warp fury that oozed through the corridor behind them. They blurred into a single, thundering force, charging at me as I plunged *Vairocanum* into the deck and... and then I had found myself reaching for my sword, blistered and cooking, lying in the midday sun in this Throne-forsaken desert.

I am the sword of Vidya. What did that mean?

On the summit of the mountain, I looked out towards the eastern horizon, which was already clothed in the midnight blues and purples of the gathering night. As far as I could see, barren mountains aspired into the sky, rippling out into the distance. The landscape was cut through with arid canyons and desolate valleys, each hidden in the deepening shadows of the mountains and cliffs that flanked them. There was no sign of a city, a base or an airstrip. There was no sign of the vessel that I was sure that I had seen. *It could be anywhere.* Any one of the ravines could hide a landing pad, a dwelling, an entire city.

Behind me, the desert rolled out like a red carpet, touching the horizon at the kiss of the largest sun. The cliff on which I had started the day had already disappeared from view, even from the vantage point offered by this mountaintop. In the space of one short day, I had walked further than the eye could see – further even than the enhanced and flawless eyes of the Emperor could discern.

Even as I watched, I could hear the crackling of ice as it started to form over the surface of the peak, expanding the moisture that had been dragged out of the clouds and trapped between the grains of sand during the day. Then the suns finally vanished over the western horizon and the mountain was almost instantly encrusted in ice. I could see a wave of frost sheen over the desert towards the still-glowing horizon, making the sand sparkle faintly in the emerging moonlight.

The whole world seemed to freeze as night finally fell.

But my thoughts were far from frozen. They raced, burning my mind's eye with half-forgotten and disremembered images, making me feverish. *I should remember more.* I could feel a sudden urgency, as though something in my soul was rebelling against my ignorance; it felt like an aberration, as though I was offensive to myself. My feelings lurched ahead of my thoughts, bringing me understanding that I could not rationalise. *This is not right… Knowledge is power, guard it well.* The phrase rang hollow, as though I was mocking myself.

Instinctively, I pulled *Vairocanum* off my back and held it up before me, feeling the solid reassurance of its familiar form and letting my eyes trace its contours against the deepening hue of the roiling sky. An ineffable calm seemed to flow out of the faintly glowing blade, filling my mind with cursive runes and ideas that were not yet properly formed. It whispered to me in a tongue that I should have understood, and in a tone so delicate that it was almost seductive, forcing me to quieten my thoughts in order to pay it the attention it craved. The warpstone in the pommel glittered darkly as I narrowed my eyes and stared into its depths.

I must quieten my mind – I am deaf to myself, and I know more than I think.

Turning *Vairocanum* end over end, I plunged it down into the rock at my feet. The ground cracked and flashed under the sharp impact, but it accepted the sudden violation, holding the blade of the sword upright before me like an altarpiece. Without taking my eyes off the warpstone pommel, I sank to my knees before this single physical connection with my past.

Kneeling alone on a freezing, moonlit mountaintop, stranded on an unknown, barren and alien world, I silenced my mind and let my thoughts plunge into the depths of the warp-jewel, searching it for images of the past, of the present, and of myself. *Knowledge is power, and in ignorance we are nothing more than beasts, offensive to the gaze of the Great Father.*

CHAPTER TWO: MIRAGE

DEEP IN THE impregnable heart of the *Litany of Fury*, suspended in a high orbit around Lorn V, the cavernous, hemispherical Sanctorium Arcanum resounded with the voices of priests, mystics and astropaths. The choir patrolled the circuits of the ambulatories that encircled the central altar, which was held aloft in a single beam of silver light that pierced down from the sky dome at the apex of the massive, curving ceiling.

A mist of incense wafted through the gently moving air, swirling into a spiral around the altarpiece, stirred into motion by the perambulations of the choir, and a deep resonant chanting pulsed through the space, sending visible ripples through the mist.

Directly above the altar piece, captured in the beam that shone down from the ceiling, was a sphere of luminous, pearlescent energy. Light danced and curdled over its surface, and it sheened as though slick with oil. Delicate tendrils of silvering light snaked up into the glowing pearl, feeding out of the blind, sunken and gaunt eye-sockets of a number of the peripatetic, green-robed astropaths. As the energy flows converged, the silvery pearl shimmered and pulsed, as though alive with the combined powers of the astropaths and the psychic chanting of the choir telepathica. Soaring sounds and radiant light seemed to congeal through the eerie, incense-veiled mist, forming the very heart of the ancient and venerable battle-barge.

Laid on the altar itself, like a holy relic, Korinth and Zhaphel could see a fragment of ancient metal. It was an elegant point, like the tip of a sword, but the thick end was jagged and broken, as though it had been snapped unceremoniously from the blade of a once-magnificent weapon. The two Librarians stood behind the altar, on the elevated podium of the apse that overlooked the ritual affairs of the Sanctorium. From there, they could observe the perpetual chanting of the pledged priests of the Adeptus Telepathica, as they orbited the relic on the altar, performing the rites of the Summoning of Exodus. The relic itself glowed with a faint, alien green light, as though feeding on and transforming the psychic energy that filled the dense, fragrant atmosphere.

Only specially inducted Librarians of the Secret Orders of Psykana were permitted to enter the Sanctorium, and the sight of it never failed to inspire a sense of awe into the souls of Korinth and Zhaphel. The last time they had taken up the podium, many years before, there had been four of them in the Ninth Company: Brother-Librarian Bherald had ascended into the light of the Emperor's gaze toward the end of the Cyrene campaign, leading a detachment of battle-brothers in support of the captain of the Third Company, Gabriel Angelos, Commander of the Watch, as he cleansed that forsaken world. Brother-Librarian Rhamah had fallen only days ago, standing with Korinth and Zhaphel against the warp daemons that had assailed the Implantation Chamber of the *Litany*, as the massive battle-barge had made its way through the warp to defend the Lorn system. The sword fragment that lay on the altar was all that was left of the once-magnificent warrior.

The Blood Ravens were an ancient and profound organisation, and they were unusually well-connected within the various institutions of the Emperor's Imperium. The Sanctorium and its associated rites were a product of one such relationship. In many ways, the Blood Ravens' position within the networks and matrices of the Administratum was rivalled only by that of the legendary Imperial Fists. However, whilst the Fists could trace the origins of their political acumen all the way back to their once and great originator, the Primarch Rogal Dorn, the Blood Ravens had no real knowledge of their origins. The identity of their primarch had been lost or obscured in the records of history many millennia ago, and their place in the

Imperium was now guaranteed only by their industry, labour and spirit, rather than resting on the laurels of a magnificent and half misremembered past.

Despite the angst of ignorance that struck into the soul of every Blood Raven, the Chapter was fiercely proud of the fact that its greatness was in the present, based entirely on the merits of its current deeds. In dark moments, the Secret Masters of the Chapter might acknowledge a repressed but seething resentment at the persistent renown of the Imperial Fists, when it was the Blood Ravens that had actually achieved most in the last couple of millennia; the Fists were so arrogant that they probably didn't even know it.

As far as Korinth was aware, the Sanctorium Arcanum was unique. He was certain, in any case, that even the magnificent *Phalanx* of the Imperial Fists had no such facility hidden in its monstrous form. Its existence was the result of an unusual and intimate connection between the Blood Ravens and the Scholastia Psykana. In many ways it was an aspect of the complementary natures of the Inquisition and the Blood Ravens, who shared an interest in esoteric and historical knowledge. Indeed, the Blood Ravens had a number of mutually beneficial relationships with certain branches of the Inquisition and Ecclesiarchy, particularly with the Adeptus Sororitas of the Ordo Dialogous.

Korinth's old mentor, Librarian Father Jonas Urelie, who was seconded to the outpost-monastery on Rahe's Paradise, had launched a number of joint research projects with the Sisters of the Lost Rosetta.

The arrangement with the Scholastia Psykana was of an entirely different nature. In the hidden lore of the Blood Ravens Secret Order of Psykana, it was theorised that the existence of the Sanctorium demonstrated that the Blood Ravens were actually a Chapter dear to the undying soul of the Emperor of Man. An ancient and revered document, known as the *Apocrypha of the Un-Founding*, allegedly penned by Azariah Vidya himself, the first recorded Father Librarian of the Chapter, argued that this was why the history of the Blood Ravens was so obscure. The authenticity of the document had never been substantiated, but its argument was whispered in the folklore of the Chapter.

The *Un-Founding* suggested that agents close to the Golden Throne had acted to obscure the history of the Blood Ravens. Azariah suggested that the Chapter's true origins were not actually absent from Imperial record, but deliberately lost, or hidden, perhaps even by psychic means. Hence, Azariah and the Blood Ravens searched for all kinds of knowledge in order to help them to see through this veil of ignorance.

The *Un-Founding* suggested that this quest would be heretical only if the knowledge were sought for the self-serving purpose of disseminating it throughout the Imperium, risking conflict with other Chapters. Azariah argued that the Emperor had never meant for the Blood Ravens to be ignorant of their own origins but had merely sought to hide them from his other sons, and Great Father Vidya had insisted that such knowledge was entirely appropriate as long as it remained within the secretive confines of the secret orders of the Chapter. *It is enough that we should know the face of the Emperor – for others it may be the face of insanity or death.*

Korinth was well-aware of these legends as he stared down at the shattered fragment of his battle-brother's sword, watching the telepaths and astropaths chant and perambulate, performing the Summoning of Exodus. He was also aware that the unusually high number of psykers in the Blood Ravens Chapter leant some support to those who argued that they were the Chapter closest to the nature of the Emperor himself: who but the Blood Ravens could really claim to reflect the psychic grandeur of the Emperor? In the not-too-distant past, the rogue Librarian Father Phraius had broken away from the leadership of Chapter Master Izaria, dragging a squad of Librarians into heresy as he declared his nature identical to that of the Emperor himself and thus free from the confines of the Chapter and the Codex. The formidable Izaria had unleashed his fury against the renegade Librarians and crushed them almost single-handedly. But Phraius was not a solitary example; a similar incident had happened more recently, involving the Third Company Librarian, Isador Akios, on the planet of Tartarus.

The chapel of every battle-barge in the Chapter was fitted with an immense Bell of Souls, which tolled one hundred times every day to commemorate the lost souls of fallen battle-brothers. It was said that the practice originated early in M.38 when the entire Fifth Company, under the leadership of the magnificent Librarian-Captain Lucius, had been lost in the warp storm of the Maelstrom. The present Fifth Company still wore badges of shame and penitence, which suggested that something other than an accident befell Lucius and his battle-brothers. No records of the events survived, but the Fifth Company became known as 'The Fated' thereafter, and the Secret Masters of the Chapter had seen to it that they had fewer Librarians than the other companies in modern times. Whispered rumours amongst the more puritanical Librarians of the Chapter implied that Lucius had led his company into the Maelstrom on purpose.

The sphere of energy pulsed and spun in the middle of the shaft of light, rotating above the altar and the last remnants of Rhamah's great weapon. It was traditional for the remains of a lost Librarian of the Secret Order of Psykana to be laid to rest on the altar of the Sanctorium for one hundred days. The pearl of psychic energy above the altar acted like a beacon for lost souls, and it was not unknown for the soul of a Blood Ravens Librarian to return to his body within the hundred days, as though guided by the Astronomican itself, summoned back from its exodus. A blade-fragment would not be enough; Korinth and Zhaphel knew that Rhamah was lost, despite the relentless efforts of the gothic choir.

The telepaths and astropaths of the choir worked in shifts so that the litanies and chants never fell silent even for a moment. As one group shuffled around the smoky ambulatories, chanting and pouring their psychic energies into the swirling and radiant pearl, another two cohorts were sitting in meditation along the pews beneath the elevated apse, preparing themselves for their exertions.

Each of the psykers had been recruited directly from the Scholastia Psykana on Terra itself. The Blood Ravens maintained a special relationship with the Adeptus Telepathica and a certain number of its most talented students were reserved for service in the Sanctorium Arcanum aboard the mighty *Litany of Fury*.

Indeed, like the Inquisition and the mysterious Grey Knights Chapter of Space Marines, the Blood Ravens drew a number of primary psykers from the Scholastia Psykana as potential Librarians; without a fixed homeworld, the Blood Ravens actively sought alternative sources of neophytes and, thanks to its excellent position within the Administratum, it was able to draw on powerful and unusual pools of talent. Korinth himself had once walked the hallowed corridors of the Scholastia on Terra.

However, the Blood Ravens held another unique contract with the Adeptus Telepathica, according to which they would also take a small number of secondary psykers from the Scholastia, some of whom would undergo the Soul Binding ceremony necessary to render them into astropaths capable of transmitting messages through the warp. These psykers were then sent to serve in the Sanctorium of the *Litany of Fury*, the battle-barge of the Blood Ravens Commander of the Watch.

Although their precise function aboard that venerable vessel was shrouded in myth, legend and apocrypha, the dominant theory within the Secret Orders of Psykana was that the psykers acted as a kind of mobile repeater station for the Astronomican itself, spreading the voice of the silver choir into the farthest and darkest reaches of the galaxy. But like so many rituals and technologies, the precise origins and function of the Sanctorium were lost in the tempests of history.

As Korinth watched the perambulations of the psychic choir, he could almost imagine the huge, hollow sphere of the Chamber of the Astronomican itself, carved out of the interior of a single mountain and filled with tens of thousands of faces of the Chosen, the astropaths who literally emptied their souls into the blazing beacon of light that riddled the psychic realms throughout the galaxy, anchoring the Imperium in the divine grace of the Emperor. Despite its own magnificence, the Sanctorium Arcanum paled in comparison – it was little more than a distant echo of that glorious monument, whether or not there was any real connection between the two. Nonetheless, Korinth knew the pride that flooded the hearts of the Librarians who had been inducted into the Secret Orders of Psykana in the Blood Ravens; even an echo of the Emperor's choir was an affiliation that no other Chapter of the Adeptus Astartes could claim.

In the centre of the chanting, the incense and the ambulatories, the simple metallic fragment of Rhamah's sword glowed a faint and lonely green.

Korinth and Zhaphel whispered silent prayers for their fallen brother, while the Blood Ravens and the Emperor himself called out for his soul. Even though there seemed no chance that the Librarian could have survived the rupture in the warp that had sucked him out of the *Litany of Fury*, there were very few places in the galaxy that could obscure the call of the Astronomican. If he was alive, there was still hope: neither the Emperor nor the Blood Ravens ever abandoned their own. The rites of the Summoning of Exodus would continue for one hundred days, but thereafter the choir telepathica of the Sanctorium would never cease their psychic beacon.

As THE FIRST sun broke the horizon, whipping up the sand into a rolling storm once again, the light burst against the jewel of warpstone that was set into the pommel of my sword. It split into an infinite spray of darkly sparkling refractions, dazzling me for a moment; I lifted my gaze from its complicated depths and cast it out towards the reddening sky. My mind was calm and my thoughts had found a measure of peace after the icy hours of meditation on the mountaintop. The voices and images that had plagued my brain had been brought under control, but only in the sense that ghosts and spectres appear tamed by the daylight. Although my mind felt my own once again, it was still pestered by more questions than answers, and doubts lurked just below the surface of my consciousness, lying in wait like sharks.

There were a constellation of facts of which I felt sure: first there was *Vairocanum*, my sword, which sang into my soul like an ancient companion; then there was the armour that encased my body, which was fused so closely to my skin that it might have been an organic outgrowth of my own genetic structure; and then there was my body itself, which seemed to function so perfectly and with such incredible strength and stamina. Of all of these things I was certain. They were undeniable, physical aspects of my being, and I had found my peace with them during the cold night. Of the other things that emerged into my thoughts, I was less certain. They had less physical presence, and I was less confident about their necessary validity.

The Emperor swam through my mind with the figure of a warrior that I named the Great Father, Vidya, the Seeker of Truth. I could perceive a number of resemblances between their images and myself, and from this I had deduced that either I had been made in their image, or that I had imagined them in mine. Either way, it seemed clear that my three physical certainties supported the image of myself as a warrior – it did not seem unlikely, therefore, that I was in the service of some greater power. Given the tremendous force of their images in my mind, I supposed that the Emperor and Vidya were either the greatest of my patrons, or my worst enemies.

Of the faltering and inconsistent memory of the battle in which *Vairocanum* had been broken, I had not been able to reach any further conclusions. My deductions appeared to be contingent upon my interpretation of the role and importance of the Emperor and of the Great Father since, like them, the warriors in my vision resembled me in a number of significant ways. This left an open question in my memory-frazzled mind: if I were to encounter others like myself, would they be friends or foes?

Another contrail! The air-vessel has returned.

Even after hours on my knees in meditation, my legs sprang easily and powerfully, pushing me to my feet as though my muscles were already warm and supple.

No, this one is higher than the other one, and slower. The previous flyer had skirted rapidly over the crest of the sand storms, flittering through the lower levels of the troposphere, like a fast atmospheric craft. But the new contrail was higher, perhaps even as high as the thermosphere. Specks of flame coughed out at the head of the line of wispy cloud, suggesting that the craft was firing powerful engines or still burning as it dropped down through the thickening air of the outer atmosphere. *It's descending. They're going to land.*

Tugging *Vairocanum* out of the rock and spinning her into my back-holster, I paused to calculate the trajectory of the landing craft and then vaulted off the peak of the mountain, jumping and sliding my way between the shelves that protruded from the sheer face of the east-facing side, skidding and skating my way through the rolling sand storm kicked up by the second and third suns as they crested the horizon.

The descent took only a matter of seconds. When I hit the ground, I was already running, hurdling the rocks and traversing the dunes, checking my bearings against the thickening contrail above me as the vessel dropped through the ozone layer of the stratosphere. The delicate white line of cloud behind the craft was developing a darker tinge, like an oily black lining. For a moment, I wondered whether the craft was in trouble. *That is no engine failure – someone inside that vessel is producing the darkness himself.* The realisation struck me suddenly, but I did not break my stride.

THE SOFT SAND of the rapidly heating desert quickly gave way to increasingly dense constellations of rocks and outcroppings. From a distance, the landscape had appeared like a smooth, sandy, gradually ascending slope, but as I moved towards the horizon, the smooth surfaces revealed themselves to be massive sandstone pavements, riddled with scars and fissures that cracked through the ground and aspired to undermine my footing. The ground in the fissures, between the slowly rising level of the stone-surface, remained at desert-level, thick with soft drifts of sand.

As I ran through the early phases of the slowly rising sandstone matrix, keeping the descending gunship in sight above me, I vaulted the smaller rocks, darting between the larger boulders and jagged stone protrusions until the lattice-like patterns of rock grew too dense and too high for me to move through efficiently.

Weaving and twisting to keep pace with the cloud-cloaked ship above, it began to occur to me that the increasingly solid and massive rock formations

would provide excellent defences against a ground
assault, since they would force even a small force to
slow down, almost to the point of completely losing
its momentum. A larger force with any kind of heavy
equipment or vehicles would simply not be able to
get through; nature was one of the very finest military architects. *Nature is the master of design, and
knowledge is the master of nature.* The thought was
self-evidently true; it resounded with pride and
power. *But nature has no will, and this landscape can
serve no conscious design; it defends nothing.*

After several minutes of scraping and squeezing
through the diminishing cracks and crevices
between the rocks that now towered over my head, I
stopped running. It was as though I were trying to
run through the cracked and fragmented foothills of
a massive mountain, driving myself through deepening fissures that had been blasted out of the
foundations by centuries of unchecked desert winds.
The forest of rocky walls grew massive around me,
and the clefts between them grew narrower and narrower as I pushed on, making the light dim, the
temperature drop, and the darkness draw in like a
mist. Looking up, I could no longer see the gunship,
only the sickly wisp of its thickening contrail cutting
across the brilliantly lit slit between the sheer stone
walls. I wasn't even sure whether I was running in
the right direction any more.

*I need to get above this maze; not even the Emperor's
eyes can see through stone.* But the sides of the rocks
were sheer and smooth, blasted into a featureless
sheen by the relentless erosion of the desert wind. I

ran my hands impatiently over the stone, feeling the slight unevenness of the sandblasted surface. My fingers clawed experimentally at the sandstone, testing its density to see whether I could rip out handholds or stab them through with my combat knife. The surface crumbled under the strength of my fingers, and I realised in frustration that even if I could cut a hold it would not support my weight.

High above, I could hear the decelerating whine of the gunship as it banked and started to drop. The distinctive hiss and burn of retros firing told me that the ship was preparing to land, but the sound echoed and bounced through the stones around me and I couldn't tell from which direction it was coming from. Looking up and training my eyes against the bright bloodiness of the sky, I could see nothing other than the whirl of sickly clouds.

The frustration crept up on me like a predator. I could feel it stalking around the dark recesses of my mind, whispering and murmuring like a ghost in the shadows. *I am better than this.* The whispering voices prodded and cajoled; they mocked me, telling me that a few rocks should not be an obstacle to an Angel of Death.

I am an Angel of Death! The surprising thought was immediately comfortable in my head, resonating with warmth and pertinence.

With a cry that rose from my stomach, I leapt into the air, reaching out with one hand above my head. I felt my fingers clasp the top lip of the stone, and I pulled, yanking my body up the rock face and flipping my legs over my head in a smooth arc. The ruddy, red light burst all around me as I cleared the rock-line and landed on top of the sandstone pavement. Instantly, my eyes scanned the sky and identified the distant, descending form of the gunship. Keeping my gaze fixed on the vessel, I started to run again, jumping and springing automatically over the wide cracks and crevices in the sloping ground.

I made that jump like it was nothing. The thought tumbled about my head as I ran, distracting me and jabbing me with its significance. *That rock was more than twice my height.* My skin still tingled with an unrealised power. *I could have gone higher.*

THE SPLINTERED, SLOPING, rocky pavement suddenly fell away at my feet, leaving me standing on a sheer precipice. With my eyes still fixed on the contrail of the gunship ahead, I skidded to a halt. Before me, a wide and roughly circular valley filled the foreground. It might have been cut down into the sandstone pavement, submerged from any ground-based line of sight, visible only from the air or from the very edge of the cliff that swept around the entire perimeter.

This rocky maze might be a defensive configuration after all. I had known it all along.

The wide, crater-like valley was filled with stone structures. Hundreds of towers and monoliths rose towards the sky, and hundreds more low-rise rocks were scattered around their bases. At first glance, the arrangement looked like a town or a city, with winding streets and broad boulevards twisting around the stone structures. But on closer inspection it was impossible to tell whether the rocky protrusions were natural formations or artificial constructions. Immediately, my mind ran back through the cracks and fissures of the rocky maze beneath my feet. *What kind of architecture is this – so perfect that it seems like nature itself?*

The stone city blended into the ground, like nothing more than an unusual pattern of rocks. Straining my eyes, as I had learnt to do, I could enhance the image before me, and I could see subtle details etched into the sides of the spires and towers. There were windows and balconies. Gargoyles and images etched in relief adorned the sides of the edifices. Rather than being straight or carved into a grid, the streets were winding and latticed, after a vision of cracked rocks. They were punctuated with small constellations of rock, and I could see now that those had been subtly fashioned into breathtaking statues and dry fountains of sand.

A burst of fire from the sky brought my thoughts back to me, and I realised that I must look vivid and incongruous standing on the lip of the valley: massive, shining and blue. About a quarter of the way around the perimeter of the circular valley, the gunship flared with flame as its thrusters fired and it started the last stages of its descent. If anyone in that ship were to glance over in this direction, they would be able to see me clearly.

I ducked low, dropping down into one of the crevices that laced the ground, catching my weight with fingers that gripped the edge of the surface while my feet found purchase on a narrow shelf that jutted out of the sheer drop. From there I could still see the billowing, purpling clouds that plumed around the gunship, but I was confident that I had fallen out of their sight.

The ship rotated on its axis, hovering heavily. *They had found a place to land*. Then another thought struck me: *They couldn't see this city from the sky*. They must have been looking for it; that was the only way to explain the erratic, inefficient and cumbersome hovering.

Such architecture and camouflage – who could have lived in this place. There was no sign of movement in the city. *Is the city as dead as the desert?*

With a natural confidence and an animal strength that still surprised me, I reached hand over hand and started to move, letting my body hang from my grip on the lip of the cliffs that formed the perimeter of the city, hidden within the matrix of cracks but heading over towards the landing craft.

PRESSED INTO A fissure in the rocks, I watched the heavy gunship manoeuvre; it was searching for the ideal landing spot amongst the rocky outcrops of the barren desert landscape, as the clouds in the sky above it started to thicken. The pale pinks and sickly purples began to swirl and billow into darkness, as though a pool of black ink had been dropped into the roiling mass, spilling out of the fire-enshrouded gunship.

The ship itself was a radiant mix of startling blues and dazzling gold, hanging in the air with heavy menace, pouring flames out of its thrusters just to maintain its position and demonstrate its disregard for the force of gravity. As the sky darkened around it, I could sense the defiance seeping down from it like black rain.

And then the rain really started to fall: great, solid, black droplets of acidic moisture fell from the gathering darkness, drilling into the sand and fizzing, staining it in random speckles.

As I stared up at the gunship, half hidden in one of the dense rock formations that jutted down into the sandstone around a wide, level clearing in which I presumed the ship was about to land, the rain scraped dryly across my face. *There is no moisture in this rain – it is dry as bones.* It didn't feel like rain at all.

The gunship hovered on its thrusters, blasting jets of furious heat down into the growing inferno of the barren landscape; the flames and the intricate golden markings glittered brilliantly against the sickly, swirling dark around it. It was like a massive, cumbersome and ugly bird of prey, and I realised in that instant that it was looking for something. The analogy of the predator stuck in my mind, and I withdrew deeper into the cracked rocks, pressing my body out of sight in an attempt to avoid becoming prey for the monstrous bird. I was not sure that it had not seen me on the opposite cliff-face.

In the absence of certainty, caution is a wise man's valour. The maxim emerged naturally into my mind, and I almost smiled at its appropriateness: the gunship could have been sent by my brothers to take me home, but it could also have been something else entirely.

Uncertainty is the seed of all knowledge – it is the catalyst of investigation.

The gunship's engines thundered and whined as the vessel dropped down onto the cracked, rocky pavement. Clouds of sand erupted from the down drafts, blowing a series of cavities into the soft sandstone beneath the flaring vents. Black rain sleeted down all around it, as though it were thickening the air itself to cushion the descent of the ungainly craft. Dark clouds billowed and roiled in nauseating patterns, pluming out of the armoured plating of the vessel as though sucked into the atmosphere by osmosis. A crackling, blue energy coursed over the surface of the gunship, defining its contours in a pulsating matrix of forked lightning. Shrouded in the commotion of darkness, the vessel was all but invisible as it touched down into the mist of sand.

As the engines cut, the turmoil of dust began to settle and the black rain eased, as though the air was relaxing its efforts. The crackling lines of energy flickered and snapped, fading slightly, as the clouds of dark mist thinned noticeably.

Leaning out from my hiding place in amongst the rocks, I could see the shape of the gunship emerging from the commotion.

It's a Thunderhawk. The name was lurking at the fore of my mind, waiting to be given a voice. *That means that there are Space Marines in there.* The knowledge was based on suddenly remembered experience; I had been in such vehicles myself, many times. The memories flooded back into my mind, riddling my brain with new images of blood red Space Marines and alien worlds. Thoughts of death and violence filled the scenes: *I am the sword of Vidya.*

As the desert wind gusted past the Thunderhawk, it blew a moment of clarity across the hull, revealing a vivid blue and gold crest that I did not recognise. Glancing down at the dirty, dented and scratched blue armour on my own arms, I tried to reconcile the memories of the blood-red Marines with the gold-tinted, blue crest on the Thunderhawk.

In my vision, the two warriors that charged towards me in amongst the daemonic fury were clad in blue power armour, but I could not tally their image with the golden dragon-serpent that swirled around the blue emblem on the gunship. Something did not feel right.

Until I have more knowledge about the intentions of these strangers, I will remain in their shadows. Knowledge is power.

The dark plumes of dissipating smoke that curdled more thinly through the waterless rain were tinged with an ineffable purple, and something in my soul stirred with primordial knowledge as I watched the unusual gases and energies intermixing.

The vapours touched something in my soul. I knew that I had seen patterns and phenomena like this before, and I knew that they represented something special or rare in the world. The oscillating purple veins seemed to whisper and hiss with esoteric knowledge, and I could feel them tugging at my mind like threads of thought. *I know this power; it is*

mine – it is part of me, just as Vairocanum is part of me.
I could taste it on my tongue and in my breath. An
unknown spice thickened the air and fragranced it
with something intoxicating. It tasted like… power.

Pressing myself back into the fissure in the rocks,
standing on a ledge above a steep drop, out of sight
of the landing craft and submerged in the heavy
darkness of deep shadow, I stared down at my
hands. They were only suggestions in the darkness,
dimly lit and almost imperceptible. Normal eyes
would have seen nothing at all.

I am the eyes of the Emperor. The thought rolled over
and over in my head, as though generating gravity
like a spinning planet. I inhaled deeply, calming my
mind and drawing a fine mist of purpling vapour
into my throat. Something in my mouth shifted and
I could feel my physiology change subtly, but only
after my lungs had seemed to lurch into flames and
my eyes flashed.

There was a tiny blue spark. It seemed to flare out
of the tip of my index finger. My eyes squinted
sharply, but my mind reeled back to calm, as though
something inside me had expected the startling
event.

The little flame vanished as soon as it appeared,
but I reached over and felt the fingertip with my
other hand. An instant later and a sticky thread of
blue energy arced across from the fingertip to the
back of the other hand, creating a pool of viscous,
crackling fluid that quickly grew and spread to cover
my entire hand. The submerged skin tingled slightly,
but it remained cool and supple. Clasping my hands

together, the invigorating energy instantly spread to cover them both, and it started to send shimmering tendrils questing up my arms. I could feel the power pulsing and growing as the light consumed my body; my eyes widened with a sudden realisation and appreciation of my nature. My soul thrilled in the heart of the gathering power and I could feel my eyes begin to flare with energy.

These are the Emperor's eyes. The thought fought for prevalence in my mind, forcing out another voice that urged caution and quiet. I could feel a certain mania descending over me, engulfing my senses and teasing me with promises and visions of the future, even as the purpling and noxious cloud started to fill the crevice in the rock. The power flooded out around me, filling the cleft in the rock with a pool of shimmering blue, banishing the darkness and the shadows and rendering the space radiant, like a fragment of heaven.

But I am not alone with these powers. The memory of the black and purple smoke-enshrouded Thunder-hawk jabbed into my mind, intruding on my reverie. Still dizzy from the unexpected and sudden rush of power, for a moment I could not work out whether the thought of a powerful psyker in the Thunderhawk held portents of rivalry or comradeship. Of one new thing I was certain: my world had become a much bigger and more fantastical place over the course of the last few minutes.

CHAPTER THREE: TALDEER

THE ICE-PLANET of Lorn V spun slowly like a massive comet, pock-marked and scarred by dirty patches of urban decay and huge impact craters. It was an unassuming planet, in many ways little more than a backwater. But the damage that had been stamped onto its surface suggested that its importance was belied by its unremarkable history.

As the *Ravenous Spirit* ploughed into the outer reaches of the Lorn system, Captain Gabriel Angelos of the Blood Ravens Third Company, the Commander of the Watch, stood on the bloody and fire-damaged control deck and gazed out at the floating debris that littered the sector. Tumbling chunks of splintered asteroids raced past the strike cruiser as it advanced towards the central planets, as though they had been thrown out from the heart of the system by a massive explosion.

In his mind's eye, Gabriel could still see the smoking remains of Rahe's Paradise, upon which he had ordered the Exterminatus shortly before. The rain of ruined rock that clattered against the *Spirit's* armoured plating echoed the hail of destruction that had befallen that ill-fated world.

Intermixed amongst the rubble and the asteroids, Gabriel noticed the crude and cumbersome hulks of ork space vessels. They were little more than massive wrecks even when fully operational, and they floated like gargantuan pieces of refuse, aimless and wretched. Huge holes had been blasted through a number of the craft. Others bore the distinctive imprints of more precise destruction: rows of small puncture wounds around the engine blocks and command decks, or delicate gashes where surgical strikes had excised the essential systems from the vast floating corpses.

Standing at the captain's side, the Father Librarian Jonas Urelie stared with undiminished awe at the scene. The veteran Librarian had been based at the outpost monastery on Rahe's Paradise for over four decades before it had been annihilated, and he had not seen destruction on this interstellar scale for even longer. Somewhere in his soul he had hoped that he would meet the end of his days delving into the forgotten history of the Blood Ravens on that isolated, volcanic and desolate world. The slower pace of life had suited him, as the atrophies of old age had started to work their decay on his ambitions as much as on his abilities. It was not a dishonourable posting: the research had been important – more important than he could possibly have imagined – and Rahe's Paradise had provided a reliable if small stream of recruits for the Chapter. However, over the last few days, Jonas's world had been exploded, quite literally.

'These are not just ork wrecks, Gabriel.'

The captain nodded. He had already seen the broken and twisted forms of damaged Imperial pattern vessels and Furies. Here and there, he even thought that he could make out the distinctive shapes of salvageable Cobra fighter gunships.

'It seems that the situation in Lorn was more serious than we had imagined,' confessed Gabriel, turning slightly with a smile of resignation on his scarred and tired face. He knew that the Blood Ravens would have been blamed if the Imperium had suffered a loss in this system, and he also knew that any such loss would have been his responsibility. No matter what had happened at Rahe's Paradise, Gabriel had taken the *Ravenous Spirit* and most of the surviving Third Company halfway across the galaxy on a blind hunch. Captain Ulantus of the Ninth Company, with whom the Third shared the magnificent battle-barge *Litany of Fury*, had been right to disapprove of his departure, and a defeat for the Blood Ravens at Lorn would certainly have proven the straight-laced captain's point.

'There are eldar ships amongst the detritus, captain. Did you notice?'

Gabriel shook his head slightly and frowned, fatigue creasing his features. 'No, old friend.' He turned back to the large viewing screen that dominated the front wall of the control room. 'But it does not surprise me at all. Those devious aliens always seem to be one step ahead of us.'

Jonas heard the weariness in his battle-brother's voice and let his own eyes drift off the viewscreen to inspect his comrade's face. The captain looked tired and exhausted; his normally sparkling blue-green eyes were dull and lifeless, as though there were no soul enlivening them from within.

'It is not your fault, Gabriel.' Even to him the words seemed hollow and inadequate.

The captain breathed the suggestion of a smile, and his eyes squinted with what might have been pain. 'Perhaps not, father.' His tone betrayed his thoughts.

The Librarian hesitated for a moment. Although he was one of the oldest and most experienced Marines in the Blood Ravens, he was no Chaplain and he knew his limitations; he was not sure that he was properly equipped to offer counsel to his friend, even if Gabriel had asked for it... which he hadn't. The Commander of the Watch had been through more than most could bear, and Jonas was well aware of how heavily he had leaned on Chaplain Prathios for support and guidance over the last few years. On top of everything else that had happened, Gabriel now had to deal with the fact that Prathios was returning from Rahe's Paradise in a sarcophagus, entombed in the chapel of the *Ravenous Spirit*. He was not entirely dead, but he would never see normal service again – the best he could hope for would be to serve the Great Father and the Emperor in battle as a dreadnought. He was certainly of no use to Gabriel's conscience any more.

In the distance, in a close orbit around the fifth planet of the system, the massive and glorious shape of the *Litany of Fury* began to appear. It looked like a small, malformed moon cresting the horizon of Lorn V. The radiant, blood-red insignia was emblazoned across the prow and the sides of the hull; the black raven's wings were spread broadly around the glistening droplet of blood at their centre. It was a sight to warm the hearts of all aboard the *Ravenous Spirit*. All around the battle-barge, dusty detritus and shards of scrap metal spiralled down into the upper atmosphere of the planet, speckling the world with a rain of fire. It was like a victory salute, or a symphony of welcome.

'It appears that Captain Ulantus was victorious,' offered Jonas, meaning the observation to console the troubled Commander of the Watch, but conscious that it may have the opposite effect.

'Yes,' replied Gabriel, his jaw clenched as he stared out towards the magnificent vessel. 'Ulantus is an admirable Astartes.'

Jonas flinched inwardly, conscious of the note of self-reproach that struck through the captain's words; his attempt at consolation had failed completely. 'You did what you had to do, Gabriel. Had you not gone to Rahe's Paradise, we cannot know what horrors would have been unleashed on the galaxy. You did your duty, just as Ulantus did his.'

With slow determination, Gabriel turned his face away from the viewscreen, bringing his eyes to meet those of Jonas.

For a second, Jonas thought that the captain was not going to say anything, but then his eyes narrowed and flashed with a violent, electric blue: 'You will notice, father, that Lorn V continues to revolve around this star, devastated though it may be... The same cannot be said of Rahe's Paradise.'

There was poison and violence in Gabriel's voice; Jonas took an involuntary step away from the captain. He felt the furtive glances and the sudden tension amongst the serfs in the control room. Sergeant Kohath, who had been given command of the strike cruiser for the voyage to Lorn, snapped into alertness at the far side of the command chamber.

'You did what had to be done, Gabriel,' pressed Jonas calmly. His voice was lowered almost to a whisper. 'Ulantus would have done the same, had he been in your shoes.' The veteran Librarian watched the captain carefully, searching for signs that his aggression was fuelled by something other than self-reproach. The fierce blue stare held him like a magnetic field.

'He was not in my shoes, Jonas,' said Gabriel, finally dropping his shoulders and turning back to the viewscreen. 'That is entirely the point.'

Kohath and Jonas exchanged a concerned look. Neither of them were ignorant of the venerable captain's recent experiences; both of them had heard the whispered rumours about his state of mind. They shared the awkward moment in silence, turning their attention back to the space graveyard that was scrolling past the main viewscreen. Something caught their eyes almost simultaneously.

'That's a Space Marine frigate!'

'No. But the pattern is close. It looks heavily modified,' corrected Kohath efficiently. He nodded to Loren, one of the command-deck serfs whose name he had taken the trouble to memorise, but the man was already poring over a glowing terminal, checking the vessel's signature.

The main viewscreen flickered and changed, bringing up a magnified image of the side of the frigate. The heraldry was clear and instantly recognisable to everyone aboard the *Ravenous Spirit*: an emerald green, three-headed hydra. Next to the icon was the many pointed star of Chaos, with the words *Hydra Dominatus* etched crudely through its heart.

'The Alpha Legion,' muttered Kohath, giving a gruff voice to the thoughts of the others. 'Typical.'

'Did Ulantus mention anything about the involvement of Alpha Marines?' Jonas turned his question towards Kohath, since Gabriel's fixed jaw had offered no response to the discovery.

'No, nothing. But he also failed to mention the Ultramarines...' Kohath's voice trailed off as he nodded towards the spinning wreckage of the Chaos frigate. The legendary blue sheen of a battle-scarred Ultramarines crest tumbled into view as the vessel rotated. In immaculate, cursive, High Gothic, the name *Dominatus Regalis* was emblazoned beneath the Chapter icon.

There was a long silence as the significance of this discovery gradually made itself felt. The three Blood Ravens gazed at the Ultramarines frigate and tried to imagine what could have happened to permit a detachment from the cursed Alpha Legion to board and take over the vessel. It was not inconceivable that the *Dominatus* had been taken in a previous engagement between the two forces, but the emerald hydra glistened with such brightness that it might just have been painted that day.

In the back of his mind, the veteran Librarian could vaguely remember reading a secret and forbidden text, buried in the deepest vaults of the great librarium of the *Omnis Arcanum*, the near-mythical Librarium Sanctorum. It was an Inquisitorial file written by the infamous witch-hunter, Inquisitor Girreaux. As far as Jonas was aware, the copy of the file aboard the venerable fortress monastery was the only copy outside the hallowed halls of the Ordo Hereticus; having such good relations with the Inquisition had a great many benefits.

The file was a record of the charges against the Ordo Malleus Inquisitor Kravin pressed by Girreaux himself after the Ikrilla Conclave, at which the impassioned Kravin had warned that, unlike the other traitorous Chaos Marines who had fled into the Eye of Terror, the Alpha Legion was recruiting neophytes from within the Imperium, just like the loyal Space Marine Chapters. Girreaux had charged Kravin with heresy, arguing that the once-respected inquisitor was in league with the Alpha Legionaries, and that he was attempting to sow the seeds of panic and suspicion into the Imperium.

More important, however, was the fact that Kravin was the only Imperial researcher to have made any significant headway into the secretive history of the Alpha Legion. Indeed, it was on his research that the Inquisition and the Blood Ravens based their understanding of the origins of that mysterious Chapter. If Girreaux was right, then the Imperium's understanding of the Alpha Legion would have to be reconsidered.

Interestingly enough, one of the only possible sources that could corroborate Kravin's stories was the extensive archives of the Ultramarines. Despite the renowned scholarship of the Blood Ravens, however, not even they had access to the archives of other Chapters of Space Marines.

In his early work, Kravin had postulated that the Alpha Legion and the Ultramarines had been at loggerheads right from the start. Alpharius, the youngest of the primarchs, had felt patronised by the righteousness of Guilliman, Primarch of the Ultramarines, even before the Great Heresy, and he had rejected the teachings of the *Codex Astartes*. Whether or not this was true, it was indisputable that Alpharius deliberately sought out Guilliman in the Eastern Fringe during the galactic civil war that followed Warmaster Horus's great treachery.

The epic battle of Eskrador was depicted on frescos and murals all over the system, since it was there that Guilliman finally slew the traitorous Alpharius. However, the battle was certainly not a victory for the Ultramarines, who were driven from the planet by the cunning of the remaining Alpha Legionaries, suffering immense losses. In some tomes of Imperial history, Eskrador was counted amongst the greatest ever defeats visited on the Ultramarines, since they were bested by superior strategy rather than greater numbers.

As the ruined and mutilated frigate tumbled, free-floating amongst the debris on the viewscreen, Jonas sighed slightly. Given their particular history, it should be no great surprise to learn that the Ultramarines had rushed to confront the Alpha Legion on Lorn V, but he knew that this would be no consolation for Gabriel. The Blood Ravens also had a long history of conflict with these Chaos Marines; Gabriel himself had recently done battle with them on Tartarus. The Librarian could imagine the chagrin of Ulantus if he had arrived too late or if he had been forced to share the field with the Ultramarines because the *Litany of Fury*'s battle company – Gabriel's Third – had vanished off to the other side of the galaxy. Gabriel would blame himself for any such shame.

'Send a message to Ulantus,' said Gabriel, breaking the silence and turning away from the screen. 'Tell him that we will be there presently, and instruct him that I will expect a thorough debriefing on arrival.' He paused for a moment. 'Also, inquire about the status of our young neophyte... We need all the recruits we can get,' he added under his breath. 'If I am needed, I will be in the chapel with Prathios.'

THE NOXIOUS AND pungent gases swirled into an eddy as the heavy doors to the Implantation Chamber hissed open, admitting Captain Ulantus into one of the most sacred and secure parts of the *Litany of Fury*. A harmony of chanting broke over him, as a wave of litanies washed out from the Chapter Priests who were ensconced within the ritually purified space. The captain paused in the doorway, touching his fist to his heart and bowing slightly at the shimmering, blood-red, stylized raven that shone down from the apex of the portal on the far side of the chamber. A clutch of automatic defence cannons clucked and whirred as they tracked his motion from their mountings amidst the archaic runic script that ran around the portal's archway.

Ulantus inhaled deeply, taking the poisonous gas fully into lungs without concern for its toxicity. He had long since learned to trust in the functioning of his multi-lung, which filtered all the toxins out of the air before it was infused into his bloodstream. After all, it was not long ago that he had watched the apothecary insert this organ into the crammed chest cavity of Ckrius, the young neophyte who still lay broken and horrified on the surgical table in the centre of the chamber.

The youth was undergoing the most brutal transformation imaginable – the transformation from boyhood into one of the Adeptus Astartes, one of the Emperor's own Angels of Death – and he was being pushed through the process at an incredible, unnatural speed. The Blood Ravens could no longer afford the luxury of waiting years for their neophytes to grow into their implants. Their numbers were getting dangerously low, and they had to take the risk of a number of short-cuts, despite the terrible dangers inherent in such a move. Young Ckrius was an experiment in more than one way.

As the captain entered the sacred space and the door clanked shut behind him, the apothecary looked up from his work and nodded a brief acknowledgement. Although the Blood Ravens observed strict discipline at all times, apothecaries were always excused from the formalities of salutes and official greetings while they were at work; even the smallest hesitation or error might result in the death of their patient. In this case, the young man lying on the tablet was certainly more important to the Chapter than any ritual courtesies – he was a future Blood Raven. The shrouded and cloaked surgeon was a cacophony of chattering augmetic arms and chinking, glittering instruments.

A black, hemispherical Melanchromic organ was clutched into one of the apothecary's real hands while a series of mechanical forceps and automated scalpels chattered across Ckrius's scarred and bloody chest. The cluster of little incisions must have been painful, but the neophyte's face showed no signs of discomfort; next to what he had been through already, this was nothing. However, the apothecary suddenly stabbed a large metal blade into the youth's chest and swept it into a broad arc, defining a semi-circle from shoulder to waist.

Another metal hand reached down and peeled back the perforated skin, revealing the rapidly developing musculature of the would-be Marine's chest. Ckrius scrunched his eyes against the sudden, tearing pain, but did not cry out.

With smoothly choreographed motions, the apothecary pressed the Melanchromic hemisphere down into the neophyte's chest whilst drawing out threads of nerves from its slick surface. With incredible precision and dexterity, the numerous augmetic limbs positioned and fused the nerve endings into the underside of the skin-flap, hardwiring the organ into the youth's epidermis. In the future, the Space Marine's skin would act as a sensitive radiation sensor, triggering changes in the pigment and colour shielding of exposed skin to protect the Marine from atmospheric radiation, thus shielding him from the poisoning and cancers caused by solar activity or dirty weapons.

The very instant that all the nerves were fixed, the apothecary slapped the skin back over Ckrius's chest, nodded briskly towards Ulantus, and then turned away, shuffling into the shadows, leaving the terrible torn skin to heal by itself. If Ckrius could not survive this wound, he was of no use to the Blood Ravens anyway.

Captain Ulantus watched the apothecary disappear into his sanctum through a hidden door to one side of the Implantation Chamber. None except the apothecary were permitted to enter the Sanctum

Medicae that adjoined the sacred room, and Ulantus found himself wondering about what the hidden space contained. He was aware that there were a number of secrets hidden within the massive structure of the *Litany of Fury*, and he permitted himself a faint smile at the irony that the investigative and scholarly Blood Ravens were expected to respect the open secrecy of these places. He knew, for instance, that two of his Librarians, Korinth and Zhaphel, were even then involved in a secret ritual in the Sanctorium Arcanum, into which none but specially initiated Librarians were permitted access. Ulantus knew that the ceremony had something to do with the fall of Librarian Rhamah during the difficult trip through the warp on the way to the Lorn system, but he had not asked any further questions.

Librarians occupied a special and revered place in the Blood Ravens, and Ulantus knew better than to pry too closely into their affairs. He knew the dangers of getting too close to the Librarian Fatherhood, and he had his suspicions about the insidious effect that such proximity was having on the Commander of the Watch. He had heard the whispered rumours about Captain Angelos's state of mind. There were so many Librarians in the Blood Ravens that Ulantus often wondered whether the Fatherhood tended to forget the potential evils and contagion of the unharnessed warp. If he had needed any reminder, then the journey to Lorn was more than sufficient, as Rhamah had sacrificed himself defending the Implantation Chamber from the daemonic forces of the warp.

The doors hissed open abruptly, sending a shaft of light piercing through the smoky fumes from the battle-scarred corridor outside. Sergeant Saulh stood imposingly in the doorway. He had arrived back from Rahe's Paradise aboard the *Rage of Erudition* only hours before. Ulantus had sent him to bring the cavalier Commander of the Watch back to Lorn to assist in the fight against the greenskins and the eldar. Unfortunately, neither Saulh nor Gabriel had made it back in time to be of any help; but Ulantus had not even asked for a debriefing from his sergeant about the events that had waylaid them at Rahe's Paradise. His patience with the celebrated captain had worn thin, almost to the point of breaking completely.

'Sergeant?' Ulantus turned his head to greet Saulh, and the light burst into reflected stars off his grey eyes.

'The *Ravenous Spirit* has entered the system. Captain Angelos sends word that he will be here presently. He inquired after Ckrius, captain.'

Saulh's tone was unusually formal. Before his recent mission to rein in the flighty Captain Angelos, Saulh had shared Ulantus's distrust for him. However, he had returned from Rahe's Paradise with a new-found respect and faith in the Commander of the Watch: Gabriel had been right about the threat to that distant world, after all. Despite his position as Ulantus's favoured sergeant in the Ninth Company, Saulh felt his sympathies beginning to shift away from the straight-laced Captain Ulantus and towards the flamboyant Captain of the

Third Company. Heroism had a knack of obscuring suspicion.

'Very good, sergeant,' replied Ulantus curtly. He turned his attention back to the youth that was strapped to the ceremonial tablet in the centre of the room. 'Inform the good captain that the neophyte is still alive. Tell him…' He trailed off. 'Never mind.'

'Is there something else, sergeant?' Saulh had not moved.

'Yes, captain. The Commander of the Watch has requested an immediate debriefing on his arrival.' Saulh delivered his line like a messenger, conscious off the effect that the order would have on Ulantus.

The captain's jaw clenched and his eyes fixed on the suffering of the neophyte. He could not believe the arrogance of Gabriel: after everything that had happened since he went gallivanting off to Rahe's Paradise, leaving him to command the *Litany* against orks, eldar, Alpha Legionaries, and even necron at severely reduced strength and without a battle company. Although he would hate to admit it, if it hadn't been for the timely arrival of a detachment of Ultramarines, the day might yet have been lost. Whatever it was that had occupied Gabriel and his Third Company at Rahe's Paradise, it had better have been nothing short of Armageddon.

'Of course, sergeant,' he said smoothly. 'Inform the captain that we will be ready for him.'

As THE *Ravenous Spirit* advanced through the Lorn system, closing on Lorn V and the glorious form of the *Litany of Fury* that hung in a low orbit around that central planet, Jonas and Kohath remained glued to the main viewscreen on the control deck. The space debris grew thicker as the cruiser pushed deeper into the system, and the two Blood Ravens were increasingly surprised by the scale of the conflict that could have left so much wreckage and destruction in its wake.

In amongst the metallic debris and the tumbling rock, Jonas could identify chunks of greenskin vessels, Cobra fighter gunships, Fury fighters and eldar Shadowhunters. However, there were also fragments of darker material glittering like shadows in the starlight. Even as they watched, the mysterious debris continued to disintegrate and dissolve into the void.

'Kohath, can you identify that material?'

The sergeant nodded briskly, realising that the unknown shards of darkness could present a security threat. He flicked a signal to Loren, who was already performing the necessary cogitations at one of the terminals.

'We have encountered this before, sergeant.' Loren's voice seemed thin and sibilant in the company of the Space Marines. 'In the battle of Rahe's Paradise, the necron Dirge-class fighters were made of something like this.'

Knowledge was one of the Blood Ravens' great advantages: their Space Marines and serf pledge-workers were each fully educated in the vessel classifications used by the Adeptus Astartes, the Imperial Navy, and their major enemies. After the battle of Rahe's Paradise, Captain Angelos had made sure that the crew of the *Ravenous Spirit* were thoroughly drilled on the various known classes of necron vessels, including the Dirge fighters that had given them so much trouble in the battle. The material from which these fighters were constructed had eluded all attempts at analysis, a fact that was noteworthy in itself.

Kohath and Jonas turned as one.

'Are you saying that the necron have been here too?'

'That is what the data suggests, sergeant. Yes.'

The Librarian and sergeant shared a look with one another before turning back to the viewscreen, their minds racing with questions. They had gone decades without even hearing rumours about the ascension of the necron, and now it seemed that the Blood Ravens had encountered them twice in two simultaneous battles on opposite sides of the galaxy. Coincidence was the last word on their minds.

'We should inform the captain,' said Kohath, citing due process as much as opinion.

'I'm not sure that we need to disturb him now, sergeant,' replied Jonas, letting his voice deepen with the implication of significance. 'He is in the chapel preparing for his arrival on the *Litany of Fury*. He may… need a little time.' In the absence of Prathios, Jonas felt a certain paternal kinship towards Gabriel – somebody had to look out for him at this difficult time.

Sergeant Kohath turned to face Jonas, meeting his eyes and staring evenly into them. Procedure was very clear in situations like this: any evidence of a new threat or information that changed the strategic orientation of a situation should be reported to the commanding officer at once. However, despite his own straightforward nature, Kohath had to concede that the *Ravenous Spirit* was no ordinary Blood Ravens cruiser. Under the leadership of Captain Angelos, the venerable vessel had witnessed the massaging of a number of conventions and procedures. The idiosyncrasies of the captain were echoed in the operations of his strike cruiser.

'Very well,' grunted the sergeant. 'We are well within range of the *Litany of Fury* and we may assume that hostilities in this system have been neutralised already.'

'Indeed,' said Jonas, flicking his eye brows to indicate the viewscreen once again. Emerging from behind the distant and monstrous, glowing gas-giant of Lorn VII, half hidden by a cluster of asteroids and ork war-wrecks, was the sleek and beautiful shape of an eldar cruiser. The long, slender craft bore the green and white markings of the Biel-Tan. Its elegant, great star-sloop, which swept out of the stern like a massive dorsal fin, was holed in three separate places, including a yawning rupture that had torn a third of it clear away. However, the worst damage had been reserved for the breathlessly curving prow, under which could still be seen the remnants of the pulsar lance and other weapons batteries. The whole front end of the vessel had been blasted away, as though it had been pummelled into submission and then destruction by a relentless and impossibly powerful barrage of fire.

'What could have caused such damage?' asked Jonas as Kohath turned to inspect the distant and improbable wreck.

The sergeant didn't answer. He just screwed up his face in consternation. Whatever had happened here, he was certain that the *Ravenous Spirit* should have been part of it. No matter how much good they had done at Rahe's Paradise, they should never have left Ulantus and the *Litany* to deal with this kind of enemy on their own.

Something was moving on the other side of the wreckage. Tiny threads of purple and blue energy flickered and glistened like droplets of water cascading down a pane of glass. For a moment, Jonas wondered whether a group of powerful psykers had survived the wreckage of the eldar cruiser, shielded in some kind of miraculous psychic bubble. But as he watched, it became clear that the arcs and streams of energy were not coming from within the husk of the eldar cruiser but from behind it.

'Loren,' said Jonas calmly, remembering the name that Kohath had used. 'Can you enhance and magnify image-sector 18.K?'

The viewscreen panned and zoomed, clicking into focus once again. The image enhancers dragged the cruiser closer, pulling it in from the far side of the stellar system, and looking through the massive rupture in its dorsal fin, framing the screen with the ragged edges of the hole.

'Can we get any closer?' asked Jonas, taking a step towards the screen and peering at the poorly resolved picture. The energy trails swirled faintly, and the fabric of space itself seemed to shift and stir slightly in the surrounding area, as though something were moving just under the surface of reality.

'What do you see, Jonas?' Kohath was looking from the viewscreen to Jonas and then back again. His expression betrayed his confusion: he could not see the odd warp patterns eddying on the far side of the eldar vessel.

'I'm not sure, sergeant,' answered Jonas honestly, as Loren tweaked the focus and pushed the magnification even further. 'But it is possible that we are not entirely alone in this system… Perhaps it is time to alert the captain after all.'

One the nameless serfs jumped to attention and hurried from the control room to find the Commander of the Watch.

Even as Jonas spoke the words, an explosion of power erupted on the screen, as though massive engines had suddenly awoken and ignited. At the same time, the curdling tendrils of warp power spun suddenly into a giant and hypnotic spiral. A bulky Astartes frigate lurched out of the distant shadow of the eldar cruiser and plunged into the spinning whirlpool with its engines pouring power into its wake. For a moment it began to roll with the motion of the warp vortex, spinning along its axis like a bullet. But then, as abruptly as it had appeared, the ship seemed to explode into a rain of light and darkness. The vortex flared violently and then vanished, leaving the bright haze of light to fade gradually from the overexposed viewscreen, returning the scene to a star-riddled blackness once again.

'What in the name of the Great Father was that?' Kohath spun and started to bark orders around the control room, making sure that the *Ravenous Spirit* would be ready for battle if necessary.

'I don't know, sergeant. Loren?' Jonas turned hopefully to the serf.

'It only registered on our sensor arrays for a fraction of second, Father Librarian. Its signature was an approximate match with a Nova-class frigate.'

'Not one of ours, surely,' muttered Kohath in restrained disbelief.

'No, sergeant. The match was very rough. Whoever was in that frigate has modified it heavily.'

'Alpha Legion?' queried Kohath, looking to Jonas.

'No, I don't think so, sergeant,' answered the Librarian. 'Did you notice the psychic halo? Whoever was in that frigate managed to generate a massive warp field just before the ship exploded. I have never heard of Alpha Legion sorcerers with that kind of power. In any case, the markings on the hull were blue and gold, from what I could see.'

'Are you sure that it exploded?' Kohath sounded sceptical of the old Librarian. The sergeant may not be a psyker, but he knew space combat and he knew that no frigate in the galaxy would explode like that. 'I also noticed the touch of blue, Jonas. Perhaps it was a stolen Ultramarines vessel, like the one we saw earlier?'

THE HATCH-DOORS cracked open and released a hiss of steam into one of the landing bays of the *Litany of Fury*. The door detached and lowered like a ramp, clanking solidly against the deck, revealing the smoke-shrouded figure of Captain Angelos standing in the shuttle's hatchway. He paused, surveying the dock; it was much as he had left it before running off to Rahe's Paradise. Like then, there was nobody there to honour him; except for a few servitors, the landing bay was almost completely deserted.

'I'm sure that Ulantus has a great many things to attend to, captain,' said Jonas, pressing his hand reassuringly onto Gabriel's shoulder.

'I'm sure he does,' answered Gabriel matter-of-factly. He turned back into the transportation bay of the shuttle and inspected the assembled honour guard. It was a glittering and glorious ensemble of red and gold. The towering form of Tanthius, the imposing Terminator sergeant, dominated the interior, making it seem cramped and poorly designed. His ancient armour had been polished to the point of radiance. He was flanked by Veteran Sergeant Corallis, whose bionics gleamed brilliantly down the right side of his abdomen. Behind them was the spidery shape of Techmarine Ephraim, whose augmetic arms were glistening like silver. And finally, there was the young scout, Caleb, one of the few survivors from Jonas's Paradise squad. His chest was thrown out with a fierce pride that spoke of the honour that Gabriel had bestowed on him by including him in the escort.

There was one person missing, reflected Gabriel, setting his jaw with concentrated and stoic strength. Each of the four Space Marines had a hand clasped around one of the poles that ran along the length of an ornate sarcophagus that hovered between them. The casket was sealed against the atmosphere so that its internal environment could be carefully controlled, and the broken body within could be preserved.

This was the last homecoming of Prathios, Chaplain of the Blood Ravens Third Company.

Gabriel hesitated, forming words in his mind, wanting to say something about the scale of their loss. But there was too much. Prathios had been his friend for longer than he could remember. He had been a guide and a battle-brother, the guardian of his soul in times of darkness.

It had been Prathios, many decades before, who had first recruited the young Gabriel Angelos into the Blood Ravens, setting the great captain's feet on the road of service to the Emperor. Aside from the Great Father and the Emperor himself, there was nobody to whom Gabriel owed more. His eyes glinted as he turned back to the hatchway, and then they narrowed in disgust at the discourtesy done to the valiant chaplain by Ulantus's absence. The return of a great hero should be marked with ceremony and honour, even in a time of strife. Ulantus should have sent an honour guard, at least.

Silence filled the transportation bay and flooded down the ramp into the dock of the *Litany of Fury*. Gabriel let the silence prevail, realising that it was more eloquent than any words that he could craft. After waiting for a long moment, he strode down the ramp with Jonas, their boots resounding against the metal. Behind him, he could hear the solemn progress of the others as they carried Prathios back into the *Litany* once again.

As GABRIEL PUNCHED the door and strode into the Apothecarion, Captain Ulantus lifted his head and turned to face him. The two Marines held each other's gaze for a second, before Ulantus nodded slightly and then turned away again. He was busy with a patient on the far side of the hall, stooping over them attentively and shielding their form from the newcomers in the doorway. Meanwhile, Gabriel twisted his head to the side and made a signal with one hand, bringing Jonas into the wide, low chamber alongside him. The others remained outside, standing in a guard of honour around the sarcophagus that bore Chaplain Prathios.

Looking around the medical facility, Gabriel could understand the kind of action that Ulantus had engaged in his absence. There were Marines held in a number of the suspensor harnesses, most of the beds were occupied, and the apothecary himself was rushing from one case to the next, barking quiet instructions to his staff of serfs and servitors. With the Third Company on the other side of the galaxy, the Ninth had certainly been pulling its weight in the Lorn system.

After a couple of seconds, Apothecary Medicius saw Gabriel and hurried over to greet him, striding in between the beds and suspensors with accustomed ease. Without his long black shroud and heavy hood, Gabriel would hardly have recognised the unusually shaped Marine, in his bone-white armour with dozens of chittering mechicanical augmentations protruding from various parts of his abdomen. His accomplished and confident manner was quite at odds with the dark and severe persona that he adopted during his work in the Implantation Chamber. Ritual and ceremony had a powerful place in the life of the Blood Ravens.

'Captain, it is good to see that you have returned undamaged.' Medicius bowed. 'As you can see, we have more than our fair share of damage already. The space battle was costly to all sides, captain, and we should be grateful that the planetary assault was all but over by the time we arrived. I am not sure that the Ninth could have absorbed any more casualties.'

'I can see that you are busy, Medicius,' answered Gabriel, noncommittally, but Jonas could sense the unease in his manner. 'We too have some injuries that will require your attention in due course. However, we also have a special case for you, which you will deal with before all others.'

Gabriel's tone was not lost on the apothecary. 'As you wish, Captain Angelos.'

Raising his hand, Gabriel beckoned to the Marines waiting outside. With slow solemnity, Tanthius and Corallis led the sarcophagus through the doors of the Apothecarion. All eyes turned to observe the procession. Even Captain Ulantus looked up from his business and turned to face it. After a moment, he straightened himself up and marched across the hall to join the group. Saying nothing, he simply bowed his head in respect as the sarcophagus was manoeuvred into position in the midst of a complicated array of instruments and terminals.

'Chaplain Prathios has been badly injured. The damage was beyond the skill of Techmarine Ephraim, but he was confident that it would not be completely beyond your own expertise, Medicius. Even if his body cannot be saved, his soul and geneseed remain strong. He deserves the honour of fighting in the Emperor's service once again.' Gabriel spoke as though delivering a report: stiff and formal, without emotion. The tone was incongruous in the setting, and unbefitting the closeness of the relationship that they all knew he had shared with the chaplain. For once, the captain's defences were transparent to everyone.

'Of course, captain.' The gravity of the task was clear and heavy; Medicius bowed deeply. The Blood Ravens were beginning to suffer from a serious lack of recruits, and Medicius knew better than most that they could not afford to let Marines slip out of service if there was any way to save them. It had been nearly a decade since he had performed the Rites of Enshrinement – the irreversible process that implanted the ruined form of a Space Marine into an ancient and glorious Dreadnought, wherein he would live out his days as the half-living incarnation of the Emperor's warhammer. If there was a Marine that deserved this great honour, it was Prathios.

There was a long, respectful moment of silence before Tanthius spoke. 'And what of young Ckrius, Medicius?' The half-suppressed anxiety in his voice was stark in comparison with the massive form of the Terminator armour. 'Has our small friend made it this far?'

Medicius smiled slightly and nodded to Tanthius. The apothecary had been touched by the concern of the mighty Terminator ever since he had brought the neophyte aboard the *Litany of Fury*, saving him from the smoking remains of Tartarus all that time ago. He liked Tanthius; despite his massive size and formidable power, he was a genuine and compassionate human being.

'Ckrius is doing well, Tanthius. The Melanchromic organ has just been implanted; all the other zygotes have taken perfectly. He heals quickly, and his body has not rejected any of the implants. I am most hopeful about this one.'

Despite the solemn atmosphere of the Apothecarion, Tanthius grinned. 'That is the best news we've had for a long time, Medicius.'

'We have a number of candidates for the implantations from Rahe's Paradise,' Jonas added, remembering the youths that had fought alongside the Blood Ravens on that ill-fated planet. There was one in particular, a boy called Varjak with startling green eyes and blond braids; he might make a Librarian one day.

'Very good, father,' answered the apothecary. 'The Great Father knows that we need them.'

'We all know that we need them.' Ulantus's voice was flat and heavy, and it crushed the life out of the conversation. He was standing just to one side of the group, paying due respect to the entombed chaplain. 'Prathios was a fine Marine, Gabriel. He will be missed. I am sorry for this loss. However, we have lost many fine battle-brothers over the last couple of days, and this may not yet be the time for grieving their passing.'

Gabriel turned slowly, dragging his eyes from the sarcophagus to cut into Ulantus's face. 'Thank you for your kindness, captain.'

The others felt the tension between the two captains like a storm cloud gathering around them.

'You are right, of course, that this is not yet time for grief or for honouring the dead. Perhaps it is at least time for debriefing, however. I would like to be made aware of events in Lorn during my absence.' Gabriel's voice was taut, and Jonas watched his eyes closely as he spoke, searching them for ill portents.

Gabriel?

Something flickered in Gabriel's face, as though a sudden thought had struck him.

'Captain? Are you alright?' Jonas's concern drew the attention of the others.

Ulantus eyed him suspiciously. 'Are you having another vision, Gabriel?' His question dripped with sarcasm, and it bordered on insubordination. The massive form of Tanthius flinched visibly at the slight to his captain.

'It's alright, Tanthius. I'm fine… I just thought–'

Gabriel? Is that really you?

Gabriel looked around the faces of his companions, but it was clear that none of them had heard the voice. Jonas and Tanthius returned his inquiring look with expressions of concern; they had seen

Gabriel like this before, and he knew it – he also knew how it must look to them, let alone to the straight-laced and bitter Captain Ulantus.

Gabriel. Macha? Where is Macha?

Pushing the perplexed Ulantus gently aside, Gabriel walked slowly across the Apothecarion, oblivious to the confused and concerned eyes of the others burning into his back. Without realising it, he was retracing the path that Ulantus himself had taken when he had strolled over to pay his respect to Prathios. Finding himself standing over a low, white-sheeted bed, Gabriel peered down at the slender body obscured under the covers. It didn't look like a Space Marine's body.

With sudden realisation, the captain grabbed the corner of the sheet and yanked it off the bed, casting it aside into a billowing parachute. Lying on the bed, barely clothed and shivering, was the bruised and bleeding body of an eldar female. Her depthless, dark green eyes shone like pools of ocean in her pale face, while her long, fair hair cascaded roughly over her pallid shoulders. She looked petrified and wracked with agony.

Gabriel!

The thought was like a scream in his mind, deafening and painful.

'It's alright, I can hear you,' he said; his voice was calming, little more than a whisper. 'It's alright now, I'm here.'

Back on the other side of the Apothecarion, the others looked at each other and then back at Gabriel. They could not hear the thoughts of the eldar witch, and the Commander of the Watch appeared to be talking to himself. Without knowing that she was there, he had walked directly over to the alien sorcerer, as though he had been drawn to her by some invisible force.

Ulantus watched Gabriel carefully before addressing the others. He nodded slightly, as though something had just been confirmed to him. His voice was low and serious, as if he were making a concession or a confession. 'She has been asking for him ever since we picked her up. His name is the only word that we have been able to get out of her.'

CHAPTER FOUR: PRODIGY

'SHE APPEARED ON the *Litany* just as her own vessel was finally destroyed. You must have seen the wreckage of the Dragonship around Lorn VII, Gabriel? That was her cruiser. It suffered terrible damage, and we think that she was the only survivor. I'm not sure how she got aboard the *Litany*: none of the intrusion detectors sounded. Korinth found her in the Sanctorium Arcanum, when he went to prepare the sacred chamber for the rituals to mark the passing of Librarian Rhamah. The astropaths were not disturbed, and the beacon continued unblemished, but the farseer was broken and unconscious on the floor next to the central altar. He took her directly to the Apothecarion, and she has been there ever since. She has said nothing that made sense to our ears...' Ulantus hesitated, as though unsure of how his next words would affect the Commander of the Watch. 'Nothing except your name, captain.'

Gabriel nodded thoughtfully. He was kneeling at the altar of the *Litany of Fury*'s chapel, gazing up at the iconography that transformed the place into a testament to the glory of the Blood Ravens and to the divine grace of the Emperor himself. The visage of Azariah Vidya, the Great Father, stared down at him from the dimly lit heights above the altar, peering into his soul and searching for the faintest fragments of doubt or moral failing.

'Do you spend much time in here, Ulantus?'

The open, confessional tone took Ulantus by surprise. He had been expecting a wall of resistance and defiance from the commander. At the very least, he had expected the great captain to respond to what he had said.

'I pay my respects and chant my prayers, as is my duty. Of late, there has been less time for the observances than I might have liked, but I am not remiss in my reverence, despite the toils of war.' Ulantus measured his answer carefully, unsure of whether he was being tested or entrapped.

Gabriel nodded again, keeping his eyes elevated. He didn't look at Ulantus, and it was almost as though he was talking to himself. 'And what does the Emperor tell you, Captain Ulantus? What strength does he give to you in return for your humility and obeisance?'

Standing behind the captain of the Third Company, Ulantus looked down at him. 'I'm not sure that I understand your question, Gabriel.'

'When you pray to the Emperor, or to our own Great Father, do they answer you, Ulantus? Do you hear them speak to you, as you hear me speaking now?' As though to emphasise the point, Gabriel lowered his eyes and turned, glancing up into the face of his comrade. 'What do they give you in return for your humiliations?'

'I do not offer humiliation, Gabriel. I offer service. When I drop to my knees before these figures, I do not do it out of fear or expectation. I do it out of gratitude and duty. Neither the Great Father nor the Emperor owe me anything – they have already given me purpose. They have put light into my life, and I strive always to be worthy of their sight in that light.' Ulantus paused, unsure of the purpose of this exchange; Gabriel had ordered a debriefing in the chapel, and this was unlike any debriefing he had ever known. 'What is this about, Gabriel?'

There was a long silence. 'I have never knelt in this chapel without Prathios, Ulantus. Never. Not once in my whole life have I been aboard the *Litany of Fury* without my chaplain.'

'We have all suffered loss, Gabriel. All of us. It is part of our burden.'

'I understand loss, captain. Better than you could ever know.' Staring up into the startling, ruby eyes of Great Father Vidya, Gabriel could see the tortured faces and screaming souls of the people of Cyrene – *his* people. He could see the life flickering out of the eyes of his friend, Librarian Isador Akios, as he withdrew his own blade from the dying body. He could see the smoking remains of three planets misting over his conscience like a dense fog of remorse and suffering. First Cyrene, then Tartarus, and finally Rahe's Paradise. He had put them all to the sword. 'I am the sword of Vidya,' he muttered, almost unconsciously.

'As are we all,' intoned Ulantus, nodding with understanding. He was not unaware of the controversial deeds of the Commander of the Watch, and he could only imagine the inner turmoil that such things could cause. If ever a Space Marine was in need of a chaplain, it was Gabriel.

'So, you hear nothing?'

'I hear the echoes of my soul, and that is enough guidance for the pure of heart.' Ulantus's answer was crisp and perfect. He might have been reading from one of Prathios's own sermons. 'For my soul is bathed in the light of the Emperor, and through it I hear his words as though they were my own.'

'You always know what is right, Ulantus? Is the will of the Emperor and the Great Father always so clear, so unambiguous to you?'

'Yes, Gabriel. Always.'

'Are there no other voices?' Gabriel stared intensely into Ulantus's eyes as he asked the question, transforming it into a challenge or a plea.

'No. There are no other voices,' answered Ulantus with level calm, meeting Gabriel's challenge without flinching.

Nodding with a forlorn silence, Gabriel turned his attention back to the altar. 'That is as it should be, captain,' he muttered almost inaudibly. 'Now, tell me of the battle of Lorn.'

'As you wish, captain,' replied Ulantus, shaking his head slightly as though to clear it and pulling himself to attention. 'Shortly after dispatching the *Rage of Erudition* to inform you of the situation, the *Litany* entered the Lorn system. It was immediately clear that the fifth planet was besieged by the greenskins. A force from the Imperial Navy was engaging its orbital fleet, and Imperial Guard Commander Sturnn reported that that ground battle was turning a corner. It seems that we were not the first of the Adeptus Astartes to reach the scene, captain.

'Of course, the *Litany* laid in a course for Lorn V to provide assistance. Before we could clear Lorn VII, however, we were caught by a fleet of eldar fighters. They engaged us at range and prevented us from closing on the planet. It seems that they were concerned that we should not reach Lorn V.'

'Did they attempt to communicate with you?'

'No captain, they simply opened fire.'

'Continue.'

'As suddenly as they had appeared, the eldar fleet disengaged. At the same time, a report came from Commander Sturnn that the greenskins had been routed and that the battle was won. It seems that the Imperial Guard had recovered a Dominatus-class titan – a rare and almost unknown class of titan – and a squad of Ultramarines under the command of Chaplain Varnus had air-dropped a crew for it. The titan had fallen centuries before in defence of the capital city of Talorn. As you might imagine, the titan changed the tide of the battle.'

'I see,' said Gabriel, rocking back on his heels and standing to his feet. 'Your account leaves a number of questions unanswered, captain. In particular, I should ask about the eldar farseer in the Apothecarion. I would also like to know about the involvement of the forces of Chaos – we identified a number of Chaos wrecks in the outer reaches of the Lorn system.'

'With due respect, Captain Angelos, my report is not yet finished. We do not yet know the reason or extent of the involvement of the Chaos forces. Intelligence suggests that the Alpha Legion were active on the planet's surface, but little has been confirmed.

'At the instant that Sturnn's report came in, we identified a new threat emerging from the dark side of the planet. The eldar fleet engaged it immediately, without hesitation. On the planet's surface, Sturnn reported that a new enemy was decimating his positions. After a few moments, we identified the new assailants as...' Ulantus hesitated, as though afraid that his words might not be believed. 'They were necron, captain.'

'And you fought them in co-operation with the eldar fleet?'

'Yes, captain. It seemed the only way.'

'Indeed, it probably was the only way to ensure victory.'

'You don't seem surprised to hear this news, Gabriel.'

'We also met the necron menace at Rahe's Paradise. I am not surprised to hear that you have encountered them, but I am concerned to hear that the Blood

Ravens have now fought them twice, simultaneously on opposite sides of the galaxy and in alliance with the Biel-Tan eldar. In what circumstances did the farseer gain access to the *Litany*?'

Gabriel's thoughts raced back to the image of Farseer Macha, the eldar witch-queen with whom he had unearthed the necron on Rahe's Paradise. He wondered whether she had anything to do with this. Despite the distance and the impossibility of the timing, he would not be surprised to hear that she was here.

'The space battle was fierce, and the eldar fought with an intensity and passion that even we could not match. The necron were destroyed, but the cost was great: nearly every eldar vessel in the fleet was destroyed. Just at the point of the destruction of the flagship, the eldar farseer somehow transported aboard the *Litany*. Since then, she has done nothing but ask for you.'

'You have not yet been down to the surface of the planet?'

'No, captain. There has not yet been the time or the need.'

'Did Sturnn report any archeological activity?'

'He has made no such report, but we understand that he has been in communication with the Ordo Xenos in this sector. Why do you ask?

'On Rahe's Paradise, Father Jonas stumbled across a necron tomb under the outpost monastery as he was excavating. The eldar intervened in an attempt to prevent the ascension of their ancient enemies.'

'It appears that they did not succeed, captain.'

'Indeed not. However, I wonder whether something similar was happening here.'

'Perhaps, but the coincidences would be too staggering. We are scholars, Gabriel, and this sounds like sloppy thinking. We must research the possible connections between Rahe's Paradise and Lorn...' Ulantus let the thought slide; the most obvious connection between them was standing directly in front of him. 'Besides,' he added, 'your explanation would suggest that the affair was over now that the necron had been defeated. Why then would the farseer have boarded our vessel, and why would she be calling for you? There must be some other explanation.'

THE PHANTOM RAPTOR'S engines lay dormant as the heavily modified Nova-class frigate floated in the massive, sleek shadow of the eldar Dragonship. The dirty, las-scarred and impact-pocked vessel drifted freely, almost indistinguishable from a huge chunk of space debris in the vast space graveyard of the Lorn system.

Only on very close inspection did it become clear that the dirt, grime and damage that seemed to coat the vessel were actually intricate and winding litanies, etched into the armoured plates in ancient and near-unintelligible runes. Deep blue and golden fins and flaps extended from the hull, breaking up the outline and signature of the vessel, designed to frustrate the sensor-arrays of the false Emperor's space cruisers.

A dull psychic field shimmered around the hull, masking the psychic resonance of the once-human forms within; the entire ship was effectively a warp-blank, all but invisible to psykers. The only deliberately distinguishing features of the vessel were the perfect, circular ocean-blue crests that sported a golden dragon-serpent chasing its own tail; there were three of them spaced around the hull. No attempt had been made to hide or obscure the icons. Indeed, they appeared to be the only parts of the hull that had been recently cleaned and properly repaired.

The space around the *Phantom Raptor* seemed to shiver, as though repulsed by its presence. Icy threads of burning warp energy danced imperceptibly through the muggy vacuum of real space, questing for a touch from the ancient and potent vessel. Something was being drawn out of the immaterium towards the powers that curdled and roiled in the hidden chambers within the frigate. It was causing the fabric of space around it to buckle and twist, like the clashing of tectonic plates beginning to push up ranges of invisible mountains.

Enshrined in the Cyclopean Hall of Sorcery, hidden in the depths of the *Phantom Raptor*, the mightiest of sorcerers, Ahriman the Unchanging, held his hands out to the stars and beseeched them to fall into the chamber. Power crackled between his outstretched arms, filling the profound darkness of the spherical chamber with an eerie invasion of purpling light. Ahriman himself floated, cruciform, in the centre of the sphere, with energy coursing from his limbs and spiralling around him in the darkness, holding him in the epicentre of the psychically conductive space. All around him, the Cyclopean Hall seemed to open out to the heavens: although the chamber was constructed at the very heart of the *Phantom Raptor*, protected behind dozens of metres of armoured plating and hidden within a labyrinth of spiralling corridors that swept around it in ever decreasing circles, it was as though there were no walls at all.

The stars glittered directly into the Great Cyclopean Eye as Ahriman revolved slowly in its centre. It was as though he were suspended directly in space, the *Phantom Raptor* little more than a ghost around him, merely a psychological comfort. He could see the wreck of the eldar Dragonship looming massively, dominating the view from one side of the chamber but somehow within it. Beyond it, despite being blocked by the form of the alien vessel and out of sight, the sorcerer could see the shape of an Astartes cruiser, emblazoned with a blood-red raven.

He knew that they could not see him – he was a phantom in the darkness, at one with the tempest of warp and space that roiled around him, just beyond visibility. He knew that the arrogant Space Marines would think the *Phantom* was little more than another chunk of space junk – they had neither the wit nor the intellect to understand or recognise his presence, let alone his scheme. Like the Emperor himself, all those millennia ago, his intellectually-stunted, retarded Marines knew nothing of the true power of the warp.

Ahriman's eyes widened and burned. Flames of warpfire flickered and lapped from his eyelashes before streams of energy burst out of his eyes and mouth. The thickening, lashing tendrils of fiery power quested and thrashed like high voltage cables in a storm. They latched onto a shape in the unseen dimensions of the immaterium, grasping it and crackling around its form, digging roots into it like daemonic maggots into pallid flesh.

The effort of the sorcery tore at Ahriman's soul, searing his mind with symphonies of agony. He roared with terrible ecstasy, letting the pain fill him, ripping gashes into his very being and riddling him with the daemonic substance of the warp itself; he was becoming one with the immaterium. At the edge of hearing, he could just discern the dull, rhythmic chanting of his cabal of sorcerers, who knelt in a deferential and dedicated ring around the hall, invisible in all but voice to Ahriman in its heart.

Their voices swirled and congealed, stirring through the Eye like a wisp of colour in an iris, giving strength and stamina to the master sorcerer as he fought with the currents of the warp. He could see the galaxy shift around him as the stars started to spiral in towards the Cyclopean Hall – the Great Eye of Ahriman.

His tendrils of warp energy were now firmly secured around their target, and Ahriman wailed with effort as he dragged the edifice through the immaterium, tugging and yanking and hauling it towards the material realm. He could feel its resistance to his power. The eldar had rooted it with artistic precision, and he strained against its incongruous solidity in the immaterial environment. It felt like a burning poker in his hands, and he could feel the outpouring of power from his body begin to singe and blister his skin.

Beyond visibility, daemonic creatures started to swim and writhe, responding to the sorcerer's whispered prayers, promises, and threats. They descended on the ancient eldar aberration, tearing at it with unreal claws and pummelling it with their feral forms. The realms were merging around him, even as he floated and revolved, imperial and impervious, untouched and majestic in the Cyclopean Eye.

All at once, the chorus from the cabal soared to new heights and Ahriman thundered his defiance, throwing the last reserves of the culminated power of the Prodigal Sons through the rupturing interface between the realms. The daemonic beasts of the warp brayed in symphony, conjoining with the supreme effort of the master sorcerer. In the fury, Ahriman felt the webway portal give way, twisting around under the pressured onslaught, and he roared with the very last of his strength, bringing the portal closer and closer through the immaterium until he could see it flickering on the edge of reality just beyond the prow of the *Phantom Raptor*.

Consciousness started to ebb from Ahriman's mind. He could feel his grip on the arcane, alien structure beginning to slip. But he held it fast, supporting its ethereal weight on the shoulders of millennia of research, scholarship, wisdom and sorcerous power. He gasped the last words of ancient and agonising incantations, bringing the daemonic host to a final level of frenzied devotion. He grasped the eldar structure with his unbreakable, disciplined will, and anchored it for a fraction of a moment with the gravity of his overburdened and dark soul. He had waited for this for too long. He had searched for centuries for this chance. Nothing, not the eldar, not the necron, and certainly not the stunted Adeptus Astartes, would take it away from him.

As his eyes flared and his mouth poured rivers of cacophonous power into the unreal space of the Cyclopean Eye, he felt the *Phantom*'s engine come on line. In his mind, he could see the flowing lines of the sensor arrays from the Astartes cruiser flash round to scan the sudden energy source. But then the *Phantom*'s engines fired and roared, and it lurched forward into the flickering, shimmering webway portal that Ahriman held open with the raw power of his will, supported by the teeming daemonic host that pleaded for his touch. As the frigate plunged through the rupture in the material realm, it seemed to explode in all directions at once, and Ahriman watched the show like a spectral shower, grinning in the heart of his own Great Eye.

THE YOUTH WAS almost unrecognisable from the energetic and overconfident Guardsman that Tanthius had met on Tartarus. His eyes had lost the glistening sheen that had characterised his desperate fight for survival against the greenskins on his homeworld. Tanthius smiled as he recalled the way that the impetuous and foolhardy boy had dropped down off the roof of a tank onto the back of an ork, determined to drive his pathetic knife into the brute's neck. Such passion. Such courage.

He had seen the glint in Ckrius's eyes even then, but now it was gone. Instead, those eyes sparkled with a deeply buried suffering; he was old before his time. His body, once strong and fit like the best of young men, was now scarred and broken, run through with implants and augmentations. A web of tubes and wires was punched into his abdomen, limbs and head, pumping him full of chemicals and toxins, some designed to enhance his development, others designed to test his defences against poisons. He could die at any time, and he probably wanted to. Without the hypno-conditioning that was pouring constantly into his mind, his brain would have given up the fight ages before. Meanwhile, his muscle bulk had grown beyond normal proportions, but the growth was not yet even, so he appeared malformed like a mutant or freak.

His transformation was happening very fast, which heightened the risks of mutation and implant-rejection. Uneven muscle development was the least of Ckrius's worries.

As Tanthius watched in silence, the apothecary carefully cauterised the wound that he had opened up under Ckrius's jaw, where the little neuroglottis had been implanted. Thinking that the neophyte was making good progress, Medicius had decided to introduce the poison-detector at the same time as the oolitic kidney, since the two organs worked in combination and inserting them together made it less likely that they would reject each other later on.

Nonetheless, making two implants at the same time was unusual, particularly at such an advanced stage of the neophyte's transformation. It was even more than usually traumatic for the patient. In the early stages, organs such as the ossmodula and biscopea implants were sometimes introduced at the same time as the secondary heart, but such a process was as much a test of the resilience of the neophyte as a surgical necessity.

At the start of the process, the apothecary just needed to know whether the aspirant had the constitution to see it through. Towards the end, however, a new tenderness and compassion entered Medicius's manner: not only had he caused and witnessed the incredible suffering of the neophyte, and hence had developed a measure of compassion for the youth, but also the loss of an aspirant Space Marine at this late stage of the process would be costly both in terms of resources and time. It took time to grow the implants. It took skill and effort to implant them. Very soon, the progenoids themselves would be implanted; this was no longer a time for needless waste.

Medicius checked the wound one last time and then, satisfied that it had healed already, he turned and left the Implantation Chamber, leaving Tanthius alone with the semi-conscious Ckrius.

'Do you wish you were dead?' Tanthius's voice was low and gravelly. He whispered in through the ceremonial, noxious gases that wafted around the chamber, letting his words reach Ckrius without shocking him. But even from the edge of the chamber, the Terminator sergeant could see the neophyte's eyes widen at the sound of his voice. This was probably the first time that anyone had addressed him directly since he was first strapped to that tablet. Since that fateful day, when Tanthius had deposited him on the *Litany of Fury* as the rubble of Tartarus hailed against its massive hull, Ckrius had merely been an experimental body, little more than a slab of meat.

Taking a couple of steps closer to the tablet, Tanthius repeated himself. 'Ckrius, do you wish you were dead?'

That was his name. He remembered it now. They had called him Ckrius once, before it had all begun. Would they call him that again, once it was all over – if it was ever all over?

'I know you can hear me, son. I remember the voice that I heard when I was strapped down on that tablet. It is a voice that I will never forget, though it is now forever silenced… forever only in my memory.'

'I… I can hear you.' The voice rasped, like glass being dragged through sand. 'When will it… end?'

'It will not end, young Ckrius.' There was no point in lying to him now. 'Do not trust to hope that the pain will stop. But one day you will learn to embrace it. It will burn into your soul in every waking moment, reminding you that you are alive, and that you live for only one purpose. You are being remade to serve that purpose fully, with your entire being, as an Angel of Death.'

'I… I… can't.' The wretched voice grated and hissed as blood gurgled in his raw, sliced throat. As though to demonstrate his desperation, Ckrius attempted to flex his bulging arms, but they merely shuddered and convulsed, like a corpse twitching with electric current. He had no control, and his body was not yet formed. He could no longer even strain at the shackles that gripped his wrists and ankles.

'Do you wish you were dead?' asked Tanthius again, taking the last step to bring himself next to Ckrius's feverish face. 'I can end it now, if that is your wish. I can end this suffering.'

The massive Terminator sergeant loomed over the neophyte, staring calmly down into his crazed eyes. 'We are not savages, Ckrius. You give yourself willing to us, or we do not take you at all. Know this: this is the last choice we will ever ask you to make. Service is a matter of choice, but it offers no choices.'

Ckrius's eyes twitched and shook in their sockets as hysteria wrestled with his reason. The sergeant had seen this before, and he could remember the frenzy of thoughts that were assailing the youth's tortured, damaged and mutilated mind. At this point, the neophyte was beyond rational thought – the human brain can only withstand so much pain and suffering before its grip on reason and sanity grow too weak to be meaningful. But it was not a rational answer that Tanthius was waiting for; he was waiting for a cry from this boy's soul. He wanted to hear the word of the Emperor touch this youth's lips. With all of the architecture of rational thought stripped away, Tanthius wanted to know who young Ckrius really was after all.

All Blood Ravens were asked to make this decision at this point in their transformation. In was called the 'Constituo Fatum' – the fateful choice. Long and tortuous justifications and rationalisations of this principle filled hundreds of shelves in the Librarium Sanctorum aboard the glorious fortress monastery of *Omnis Arcanum*. The orthodox treatise, penned originally by the Great Father Azariah Vidya himself, argued that this moment of choice represented the only instant in a human being's life when his soul could be subjected directly to the light of the Emperor.

Stripped of dignity, physical integrity and mental fortitude, the only thing left for a mind was truth. According to tradition, the question should be posed by the veteran Blood Raven with the closest bond with the neophyte. In most cases, this meant the chaplain. However, Tanthius had discovered Ckrius on Tartarus; he had brought the youth aboard the *Litany* and had watched over his progress. The Terminator sergeant was the closest thing to a father that Ckrius had in the Chapter.

If Ckrius's soul was found wanting, despite the gene-compatibility and resilience of his body, Tanthius would kill him. In the past, a number of Librarians in the Blood Ravens had argued that this was a waste of an able neophyte. They pointed out that most Chapters of the Adeptus Astartes require no such choice from their aspirants – indeed, some Chapters actively coerced gene-compatible neophytes, effectively forcing them to become Marines, by which time their fates were sealed. To discard a neophyte at Ckrius's stage of transformation was costly, foolish, and unnecessary.

But the Great Father had been clear and adamant. No matter how low Blood Ravens' numbers became, and no matter how desperately the Chapter needed to recruit new battle-brothers, they should never compromise on the purity of their neophyte's souls. It was subsequently suggested that Vidya had been so adamant about this because of the special nature of the Blood Ravens: they were scholars and researchers, who spent much of their time immersed in the forbidden and secret teachings of ancient times or alien species. Only the purest of heart would be able to keep the grace and light of the Emperor always in mind, even in the face of the greatest temptations and the most powerful of knowledge. Vidya's 'Constituo' helped to ensure that the Blood Ravens would not slide into heresy.

'Well? Shall I end it for you now?' Tanthius's eyes glistened with a mixture of pity and resolve.

There was a long silence, broken only by the gurgling, rasping breath of the neophyte. 'No! The choice is not mine to make. I am the sword of Vidya.'

A faint smile of relief creased Tanthius's features. 'As you wish, young Blood Raven.'

THE SAND STORM had thinned to little more than a shifting mist of dust since the Thunderhawk had touched down onto the cracked, rocky slope. The gunship's thrusters had been cut, leaving only the wind to whip the sand up from the desert, disturbing the layer that shifted constantly over the barren rock. Even the wind was broken by the ring of tors and boulders that surrounded the landing site, offering the vessel a little cover from the elements and from any prying sensors that might have been trained around the outskirts of the strangely deserted, alien city that dropped away into the bottom of the circular valley to the east.

The rocky cleft in which I had pressed myself offered me some measure of cover, and I was reasonably sure that whomever was inside the Thunderhawk would not be able to see me directly. Whether or not they had sensors that would be able to detect my presence, I had no idea.

If they are looking for me, then I will be found. On the other hand, if they were here for some other reason, then I was confident that they would not notice.

It is only the rare mind that notices the unexpected.

The maxim was just sitting there in my thoughts, like the face of an old friend. As soon as I saw it, I recognised it as the first truism of the Scholastia Librarium, where I was once trained in the ways of knowledge and scholarship. Images of great columns aspiring into majestic, illuminated vaulted ceilings, soaring above endless rows of document stacks blossomed into my mind.

A pang of nostalgia gripped my heart, and I realised that the librarium was important to me, as though it was an essential part of my being. *Strip away the confusions of knowledge and you are left with only one thing: the truth.*

A flicker of genuine pain troubled my soul at the thought of having forgotten even that place. It was like forgetting home. *Home?* I had forgotten that too.

A loud metallic crack drew my attention back to the gunship in the clearing. The prow of the Thunderhawk had shifted forward, revealing a wide joint all the way around its nose. A ring of smoke or steam hissed out of the gap, circling the vessel like a vertical halo before dissipating the wind. The nose creaked and then tilted back, pivoting along the roof-line, revealing the mechanical grind of a ramp dropping down to the ground from within. It was like watching a massive metal beast snarling.

As I watched, a dark, sickly, nauseating cloud of emotion seemed to plume out of the interior of the vessel. It was hardly visible, except as a slight haze disturbing the sand-filled mist. But I could feel it emanating briefly from the open prow of the Thunderhawk.

Instinctively, my mind jumped into an alertness that took me momentarily by surprise. *I have defences against this thing.* The realisation was accompanied by a new clarity in my sight, as though my mind was somehow filtering out the chaotic whirl of sickening energy that ran out of the gunship like an ocean spray.

Striding down the ramp in the wake of the invisible energy flows, his heavy boots resounding solidly against the metal, was a magnificent and formidable figure. He must have stood over two metres tall. Like me, he was adorned in an ornate and breathtaking suit of blue power armour. Like me, he had no helmet, although a great gold and blue crest rose out of his shoulders framing his head from behind. Nonetheless, like mine, his face was exposed to the abrasive sand. However, from my hiding place in the rocks, it seemed that the mist of sand parted around him; not a single grain appeared to touch his oddly shifting skin.

I strained my eyes, employing the trick of optical enhancement without giving it a second thought. However, despite being only fifty metres or so away from the stranger, I could not make out his facial features. It was as though he didn't have a real face at all. His skin seemed to shift and swim before my gaze. It was at once both pale as porcelain and dark as ash. It gave him an immense gravity, as though the entire planet was suddenly drawn into orbit around him, but it also made him seem entirely translucent and insubstantial. More than that, however, I found that I simply couldn't look at his skin for long enough to see it properly; my eyes kept slipping off his form, drawn into his own eyes like matter into dying stars. And they were such eyes! I could see no eyeballs; there were only complicated, intense blue infernos, flickering and spitting like shards of warp fire.

As the awesome sorcerer reached the bottom of the landing ramp, he paused and looked around, surveying the landscape as though he were drawing it all into his thoughts, mapping the scene in his head, possessing it like a creation of his own. Behind him, in the shadows of the interior of the Thunderhawk, I could hear the clattering of other people preparing to disembark. Then, after a few seconds, a squad of blue- and gold-armoured warriors strode down the ramp, each carrying assortments of heavy kit and arcane equipment. Like the awesome sorcerer himself, each of the Marines sported elaborate crests, which plumed up behind their exposed heads. None of them appeared to have helmets, but there was something disconcerting about all of their faces, as though they were lingering on the very edges of reality.

The squad parted around the sorcerer, like a stream rushing around an immovable boulder, and then set to work erecting machinery and emplacements in front of the Thunderhawk, as though establishing a camp. Meanwhile, those inferno-eyes continued to scan the surroundings. As I watched them sparkling and sweeping the rockscape, a realisation struck me. *He's looking for me. He knows I'm here!*

As soon as the thought leapt into my mind, the sorcerer turned his head directly towards where I was hiding, bringing his flaming blue eyes straight into mine until I thought that I could feel the heat of his warpfire burning into my irises.

I stepped back instantly, pressing my back harder against the rocky resistance of the interior of the cleft behind me, dropping my face into the shadow of the crevice. Although the spitting fires of his eyes had seemed to settle on me, I was not sure whether he had seen me. Something in my mind stirred, telling me that he knew I was near, but I could not tell whether he had yet spied me with the mundane realities of sight.

The trained mind sees things that cannot be seen: the Emperor's eyes are beyond nerves and flesh.

My mind raced: should I reveal myself to these strangers? There was something familiar about them, but my soul did not rejoice in their image. There was no sense of nostalgia, no sense of homecoming when I had finally seen the magnificent sorcerer striding out of the Thunderhawk. My intuition told me that these were not my brothers, even while my reason railed against me, telling me that I could recognise at least something of myself and my nature in the stature of these impressive warriors: if there was nobody else on this lost world, then I would be foolish to let these strangers pass. *But there are things more important than finding a home: finding truth. It is better to perish in truth than to live in delusion.*

I peered out from the crevice once again, still unsure about how to proceed. What had I expected to do once the gunship had landed? Suddenly the whole enterprise seemed foolish and ill-considered. Why had I followed the landing craft if I had not wanted to make contact with its occupants? If only my mind would clear and return to myself – I needed my memories now, perhaps even more than I needed *Vairocanum*.

The towering figure of the sorcerer was striding away from the rapidly constructed camp, marching directly towards my position but leaving his battle-brothers behind him. His eyes flared ineffably, like miniature galaxies swirling hypnotically as he approached.

Hidden in the shadows of the cleft, I carefully drew my sword from its holster on my back, clasping it into both hands in readiness. I would not go out to meet this sorcerer, but I would be ready for him if he made the mistake of trying to root me out like an animal. *I am the sword of Vidya.*

Even as I watched, I saw a sudden flicker of red light over on the other side of the clearing, beyond the approaching stranger. The sorcerer stopped instantly, turning his head away from my position, back around towards the apparition. Another light appeared, shimmering like a multicoloured flame. It danced for a second and then vanished. By now, the rest of the sorcerer's squad had noticed the unusual patterns of light; they were abandoning their work on the camp and reaching for their weapons.

With emphatic slowness, the sorcerer turned his warpfire eyes back in my direction. For a long moment, I thought that he was staring straight into my face. But then he turned briskly and strode back through his camp, hefting a long, heavy black staff from an ornate case that had been laid across a makeshift altar for him. As soon as he clutched it into his hands, the staff burst into life, sizzling with unspeakable energies. The other warriors fell in behind their leader, and they broke into a run towards the location of the multicoloured, flickering lights. After a second or two, they all opened fire with their weapons, unleashing a relentless and furious barrage into the rocks, shredding them into explosive hails of shrapnel and masonry.

The strange, unearthly flickering lights vanished almost immediately.

Taking advantage of the distraction, whatever it was, I eased myself out of the crevice and darted across to the cusp of the valley, sheathing *Vairocanum* before dropping off the cliff and spinning to catch myself on the lip with my fingertips. Quickly spotting a ledge beneath my feet, I let go of the cliff and dropped a few metres onto the stone shelf below. The impact of my boots rang hollow, as though there was nothing beneath the stone ledge but air.

Cut into the cliff-face under the shelf was a shallow cave, obscured completely from above by the ledge itself. Gripping the lip of the ledge, I kicked into a handstand and let my weight roll me over in a slow somersault. Pivoting around my grip, I spun down into the cave, hitting the uneven rocky ground and rolling to stop against the back wall.

He will not look for me here. Safety embraced me like a cloak of shadowy anonymity. As I sat back against the dry wall of the cave, hidden in the sheer cliff-face that dropped down into the strange, circular valley, my mind leapt back up to the mysterious sorcerer in the clearing above me. *What caused those lights? Their timing was too perfect – they were designed to give me chance to escape.*

Looking out of the cave mouth, I could see the ancient, alien city below me. It may have been a trick of the light, as the three suns started to drop once again over the distant horizon and their beams were refracted into spectrums by the rock formations around the crest of the valley, but I thought that I could see a faint flickering of multicoloured lights dancing into the outskirts of the city. For a moment, the flickering motion paused, and I thought that I could discern the nearly-human shapes of a group of lithe figures. They appeared to be checking behind them, perhaps to ensure that they were not being followed into the city. Then they vanished into a blur of lights once again.

Perhaps the sorcerer and I are not alone on this planet after all. It seems that I was not the only one tracking that Thunderhawk.

IT HAD BEEN many years since Father Librarian Jonas Urelie had walked through the ornamental portal of the Sanctorium Arcanum. Indeed, it had been several decades since he was last aboard the battle-barge *Litany of Fury*. Before entering the sacred chamber, he paused under the lintel, on which was engraved a single raven's wing, its tips dripping with blood.

Inhaling deeply, he tasted the incense-clouded air and let it ease into his bloodstream, allowing the rhythmic and elevated chorus of astropaths, telepaths and mystics to intoxicate his senses for a moment. During his time on Rahe's Paradise, the father Librarian had neglected the ceremonial aspect of his nature; in relative isolation, it had been all but impossible to maintain the range of rituals that defined the routine of the Blood Ravens in normal circumstances.

There had been a time, long ago, when Jonas had relished the ritualistic significance of this hallowed space. Indeed, when he had first been elevated to the rank of father Librarian, he had been given responsibility over the rituals and ceremonies of the Secret Orders of Psykana. In many ways, this was a homecoming for the aging Blood Raven, and his deep breath on the doorstep filled him with mixed emotions.

Smiling faintly, the Librarian stepped into the Sanctorium, letting the portal drop shut behind him. He heard the once-familiar grinding of heavy bolts clanking into place, and he knew that a complicated array of purity seals was also clicking into position around the perimeter of the door. The Sanctorium was almost impregnable to physical and psychic attacks; not even the Implantation Chamber itself, where the Blood Ravens stored its precious gene-seed, could boast defences of the same magnitude.

However, its best defence was its secrecy: potential enemies of the Imperium would have no idea that such an unusual and important chamber existed hidden within the depths of an Adeptus Astartes battle-barge. They would not be able to detect its presence with any kinds of sensors or psychic channels. Only the all-seeing eyes of the Emperor himself could see the gleaming, silvering pearl of energy that rotated in the centre of the hemispherical chamber.

Jonas knew that the purpose of the pearlescent Beacon Psykana was far from certain. It was one of the many innovations of the Great Father, Azariah Vidya, who had arranged for it to be built several millennia before. Like so many of Vidya's designs, however, their real purpose and meaning had been lost in the ensuing centuries, buried beneath piles of treatises and tracts by lesser scholars who thought that they could interpret the actions of their Great

Father. One of the great travesties of the Blood
Ravens Chapter was the over-profusion of mediocre
and confusing scholarship that obfuscates more
than it reveals. Such was the price the revered Chapter paid for its emphasis on the importance of
scholarly pursuits.

Jonas himself had taught a number of young
Librarians that the pearl of pure psychic energy in
the Sanctorium Arcanum was linked in some way to
the Emperor's silver choir: the Blood Ravens had
been entrusted with a sacred and unique mission to
spread the pristine symphony of the Astronomican
throughout the farthest reaches of the uncharted
galaxy.

During his time of contemplation and research on
Rahe's Paradise, Jonas had begun to realise that this
explanation was probably unfounded. In a long and
heated debate with Sister Senioris Meritia, of the
Order of the Lost Rosetta, Jonas had realised that
the effectiveness of the Astronomican rested on the
fact that it was absolutely stationary – or rather than
its position marked the absolute point of the centre
of the Imperium at any one time. The Astronomican
called out to all the souls of the Emperor's chosen,
guiding them back into the sight of the Emperor
himself. If the Beacon Psykana was really a booster
for this signal, then its constant and relentless perambulations around the galaxy would destroy the
purpose of the Astronomican completely.

Nevertheless, it remained true that Vidya had
sealed a number of unusual and highly privileged
contracts with the Adeptus Telepathica in order to

maintain the beacon. Whatever it was, it was obviously something that the very highest authorities on Terra itself wanted to see maintained.

One theory that Jonas still found plausible was that Vidya had designed the Beacon Psykana to provide a light for the lost Fifth Company – the so-called 'Fated' – who vanished into the Maelstrom three thousand years before. However, the Fifth Company had been lost nearly a thousand years after the death of Vidya. Any such purpose for the beacon would therefore require a foresight so immense that it seemed unlikely that even a great Librarian of the immense learning and power of Vidya could have planned for it. Unlikely and impossible are allied, but they are not identical.

Like so many things that Jonas had encountered in his long and honourable career, he had to confess that the truth of the Beacon Psykana had probably been lost to the Blood Ravens long ago. Perhaps the Master of the Adeptus Astra Telepathica on Terra would remember its real purpose, but Jonas suspected that even he simply placed his faith in the ongoing echoes of historical brilliance: in the end, historical scholarship was about repeating and maintaining the practices of the past, and the Beacon Psykana was exactly one such practice.

In the absence of certain knowledge about its real purpose, everyone worked to maintain it as though it were of essential and vital importance for the Chapter and the Imperium. Meanwhile, the Librarians of the Blood Ravens concocted numerous hypotheses about its value and function.

It was another disadvantage of a scholarly nature that Jonas and the Blood Ravens more generally found it harder to accept conventions on faith than just about any of the other Chapters. During the epic battle of Geadion Secondus, in which the Blood Ravens and Black Templars had repelled a massive force of Thousand Sons Chaos Marines, Jonas had been amazed and repulsed by the mindless, unquestioning and simple way in which his allies had embraced the Imperial dogma. He had nearly come to blows with the Templar Chaplain Broec when Broec had accused him of heresy with his persistent questions and doubts. The self-righteous and unreflective chaplain had gone so far as to accuse Jonas of being little better than one of the Thousand Sons themselves, searching for arcane knowledge with no respect for the higher callings of faith or belief.

'Father Urelie.' The familiar voice made Jonas look up towards the elevated apse on the other side of the altar. 'You are most welcome here, once again.' It was Korinth. The Librarian, who had once been a student of Jonas, was standing on the apse in support of the choir for the ceremony of the Summoning of Exodus. Jonas recognised the positions immediately; he had conducted this ritual himself many times. Too many times, he reflected.

Korinth was not alone. A second Librarian stood next to him, deep in contemplation and reverence, long grey hair cascading over his shoulders. Jonas did not recognise him, but presumed that he was Yupres Zhaphel, one of the most recent additions to the cadre of the Orders Psykana. Despite his youth, his reputation was already formidable. Jonas had heard the rumours of the unusual force-axe that Zhaphel used in combat – it was said that he had recovered it from a research expedition on the planet of Dorian Prime, a world that had been lost for millennia behind the veil of a vast warp storm and whose residents, once normal human citizens of the Imperium, had become stunted and malformed by the bizarre gravitational effects of the storm. Their metalwork was beyond compare in the known galaxy, but the planet had been lost to the warp once again before their resources could be properly exploited by the Blood Ravens.

'Librarians Korinth and Zhaphel,' nodded Jonas, greeting them as old friends in the intimate manner appropriate to fellow initiates into the Order Psykana. The veteran Librarian made his way around the ambulatories, circumventing the silvering pearl of energy in the heart of the chamber, and climbed the polished stairs up to the apse, where he bowed briefly to the Librarians. 'The Summoning of the Exodus does you both honour,' he said, startled slightly by the mismatched eyes of Korinth, one ruby red and the other black as pitch; every time he looked into them, it was like the first time. 'It demonstrates your regard for your battle-brothers.' In the back of his mind, Jonas wondered whether this was the only value of the ceremony and whether it was in fact all that Vidya had in mind when he instigated it.

'It honours neither of us,' replied Korinth, returning the bow. 'The honour belongs to Librarian

Rhamah, who was lost defending our heritage. The ceremony is for him, not for us.'

Jonas nodded in acknowledgement; that was a suitable response. 'How did he fall, brothers?'

'During the warp jump into the Lorn system, the *Litany* was assailed by daemons. Somehow they breached our Geller field and penetrated the hull. Rhamah fell defending the Implantation Chamber and our gene-seed. It is to him that our survival is owed.' Korinth's report moved from pride to hesitancy.

Jonas nodded solemnly, showing his appreciation of the deed of Rhamah. 'You have reason to believe that he can hear the Rites of Summoning?' As he asked, the father Librarian looked down towards the altar and saw the sword fragment that lay on it, glowing an eerie shade of green. 'Is that all that remains of him?' It was certainly unusual to have so little, and to be left with something that seemed so alien.

'The manner of his fall was... singular,' replied Korinth carefully, studying the features of his former teacher. 'We believe that he is lost, but not that he is dead.'

Jonas raised an eye-brow and turned back to Korinth.

'At the moment of greatest peril, Rhamah plunged his blade into the fabric of space and tore it asunder, opening a breach into the warp through which he fell, dragging the thirsting tendrils of daemons with him. When the tear sealed itself behind him, the daemons had vanished and that blade fragment was all that was left of our brother.'

Jonas gazed evenly at his one-time student. 'As you say, his fall was indeed singular. Let us place our faith in the Great Father that his soul can still hear the call of our beacon.'

DARKNESS CROWDED THE Apothecarion, drawing in around the beds like heavy curtains of privacy, leaving the wounded and the sick to suffer without humiliation. Whenever Medicius and his staff of specialist servitors were not busy at work, the lights were dimmed to the point of darkness for the sanity and recuperation of the patients. Rest was not something that came easily to Blood Ravens, whose ability to sleep was thwarted by a defect in their catalepsean node. Hence, peace and darkness was as much as they could hope for, even whilst recovering from injury.

Gabriel picked his way between the beds carefully and silently, trying not to alert anyone to his presence, and doing his best to avoid the motion sensors that would trigger the glow-globes in the low ceiling. Despite the darkness, Gabriel's well-honed eyes could make out nearly everything in the expansive room, and he recognised many of the faces in the beds that he passed. So many Blood Ravens had been injured in the battle of Lorn. None of them were sleeping, but most had closed their eyes. Even so, Gabriel could see their reactions twitching as their sensitive ears detected his motion in the room – they would assume that he was Medicius.

A few of the open eyes were startled when they saw who it was that was creeping in between them; none had expected to see the Commander of the Watch slipping so stealthily through his own ship. One or two attempted to climb out of their beds to stand to attention, but Gabriel calmed them, pressing his hand to their shoulders and making them lie down again. This was not the time for such ceremony.

Gabriel!

The thought was like a shout in the dark, but Gabriel knew that he was the only one who could hear it. He found the eldar witch's bed and crouched down next to her pillow. She was writhing in pain and sweat, only half covered by the blood-soaked sheets that had been twisted and wrung with moisture. Casting his eyes over the suffering body, Gabriel realised that she was not receiving the level of care that he would have expected from Medicius; she lay neglected and pain-wracked, and the apothecary was clearly waiting for her to die.

'I am sorry for your pain,' whispered Gabriel, although he understood why Medicius would not waste his time or resources on an alien, especially when so many battle-brothers required his attention. It was a minor miracle that the eldar had not simply been killed when she was discovered. His name had saved her.

Gabriel! You are here. Macha was right. You are here. Macha. Gabriel. They are coming. They are rising. They were here. They are gone. Defeat. Victory. The beginning and the end…

The seer was delirious and feverish. Her head was snapping back and forth, and her eyes were wild as though stricken with panic. Gabriel reached over and took her jaw in his hand, guiding her face around to meet his own.

'I am here, eldar,' he whispered. 'What can you tell me?'

The old enemy. They return – the cry of the banshee is heard.

'We have heard it too, eldar,' muttered Gabriel, recalling that phrase from the ancient tablet on Rahe's Paradise. It foreshadowed the appearance of the necron there, but victory had belonged to the Blood Ravens and the Biel-Tan eldar under the guidance of the troublesome Farseer Macha. 'But the threat has been defeated.'

Perhaps, but we must be certain. The portal may yet have been destroyed.

'Portal?' Gabriel realised that they were talking on cross-purposes. 'There was no portal at Rahe's Paradise.'

The portal is here, human. Lorn houses a gateway to the ancient webway, an access point to Arcadia, the planet of law. The Yngir seek to close all such doorways, to cut off the Sons of Asuryan from our roots and our power; only then can they complete their terrible purpose and bring darkness perpetual.

'The necron were here for your portal, eldar?'

Yes, but does it survive? So many died. So much blood has been spilled. So many waystones have been lost to into the mire of sha'iel. But does it survive?

'The necron are gone. Your battle was won.'

The Yngir cannot die, human. They can be merely confined. Our battle is lost if the portal is gone. All that death for nothing. Without it and the others, the balance

*of the galaxy will shift, and the Yngir will return. Macha
knew this too – she should have been here. Why could she
not see this? Ash-ruulnah – the blindness of sight.*

'We know nothing of your portal, eldar.'

*You must take me down to the surface of Lorn. There
we will verify the condition of the Arcadian Gate.*

Gabriel stared into the twitching and shifting eyes
of the bloody and sweating eldar seer. She lacked
focus, and he feared for the condition of her alien
mind. Were she a human, he would dismiss her
words as the rantings of the insane. But she was no
human, and his experiences with the eldar had
already taught him the folly of treating them as people. Macha, the farseer from Tartarus and Rahe's
Paradise, had revealed much about the eldar of Biel-
Tan, and Gabriel knew better than to ignore their
warnings now. Ulantus would not understand, but
Gabriel would do as this alien desired.

'Who are you, eldar?'

*I am Taldeer – servant of Biel-Tan, of the court of the
farseer.*

CHAPTER FIVE: SOLITAIRE

TUMBLING THROUGH THE freezing vacuum of deep space, the Wraithship *Eternal Star* spiralled and twisted out of control. Energy bled from a terrible wound that had been punched into its hull, hissing out into the void and spinning the vessel even more violently. The characteristic, ethereal sheen of the Wraithship fluctuated and oscillated, as though its life-force was ebbing away in the uncontrolled turmoil of the fall. Its massive star wings fluttered and twitched, like those of a dying bird, but they could not restore stability to the tumbling ship. Deep within the heart of the ship, the injured and bleeding Farseer Macha sat in meditation, trying to restore order to her racing thoughts and to her errant ship.

Flashing along in its wake sped the sleek and dark form of the Ghost Dragon, *Avenging Sword*. The

Biel-Tan Exarch of the Dire Avengers Aspect Temple, Uldreth, stood silently on the control deck of the cruiser, willing it to greater speeds in pursuit of his farseer. As his eyes flared with emerald fires, his mind eddied and gyred through a confusion of emotions.

Watching the tumbling, uncontrolled flight of the *Eternal Star* ahead of him, Uldreth could not suppress the feeling that it was all his fault. In the back of his mind he could hear the gloating voice of the old Fire Dragon Exarch, Draconir, taunting him with accusations.

Uldreth could not deny the words that he had spat with such venom into the midst of the Court of the Young King, back on Biel-Tan before all this had begun. He had challenged the court, insulting the older, slower and more pedestrian exarchs. Draconir had warned him then, but he had not listened; the passion of his youth and the arrogance of his aspect had blinded him to the wisdom of the old dragon. And there had also been something else: if Uldreth were honest with himself, he knew that his anxiety about catching the Wraithship contained more than simple concern for the farseer of Biel-Tan – there was a personal investment in Macha that he refused to acknowledge but that fed oil into the fires of his soul.

Had this infernal affair involved anyone other than Macha, Uldreth might well have listened to reason. The realisation filled him with resentment and self-loathing, and he toyed instinctively with calling off the chase and letting the *Eternal Star* tumble into oblivion.

His own words haunted his memory. He had stood
in the Court of the Young King on Biel-Tan and told
the other exarchs that he did not believe in Macha.
He had swung their views away from her and forced
them to embrace the visions of lesser seers. Instead of
sending support with the senior farseer to
Lsathranil's Shield – the cursed planet that the
mon'keigh called Rahe's Paradise – he had twisted
their wills, and the Swordwind army had been dispatched with Taldeer to Lorn. The young seer Taldeer
had seen an ork invasion of that once-majestic
exodite world; she had requested that the
Bahzhakhain be dispatched to repel this terrible
insult to the heritage of the Sons of Asuryan.

Uldreth had laughed at the choice. He had
laughed, stating that there was no choice to make:
the threat to Lorn was substantive and real; Macha's
visions of Lsathranil's Shield were vague and formless. He had scoffed about the role of the Seer
Council on Biel-Tan, provoking the exarchs with
challenges to their identity as warriors: *We do not need
the anachronism of the seer council – we are warriors, for
Khaine's sake!*

He had been so certain that Macha was wrong – or,
at least, he had been so determined to prove her
wrong – that he had voiced a test. He had challenged
her and the Court of the Young King together, removing all hope of a real choice and trapping them into
the wrong course. 'Let us devise a test,' he had said,
thinking to humble Macha once and for all. He had
protested that the actions of the Court should make
no difference to the patterns of the future if the

visions of Farseer Macha were really as potent and formidable as Draconir and the others seemed to claim.

He had railed that there should be no need to act on her insight, since the battle that she had seen raging in the murky and mysterious future of Lsathranil's Shield should happen whether or not the Court of the Young King decided to send army to fight it; otherwise her vision was little more than an impotent and fanciful daydream. Hence, Uldreth had ordered the Bahzhakhain – the Swordwind of Biel-Tan – to follow Taldeer to Lorn, leaving Macha to set sail for Lsathranil's Shield with only the support of that cursed and damned Dark Reaper, Laeresh. 'I propose that we decide to ignore Macha's vision,' he had said, filled with vitriol. 'If we end up fighting for Lsathranil's Shield anyway, thenceforth I will bow to your greater wisdom, Draconir of the Fire Dragons.'

And there had been such a fight for Lsathranil's Shield; even the long-lost eldar gods of old would have gloried in the confrontation with the ancient foe. Uldreth's test had riddled his own soul with guilt and failure: Macha had been right after all. If he ever made it back to Biel-Tan, Uldreth would have to concede that Draconir, the old Fire Dragon exarch, had been right to place his faith in the archaic institution of the farseer.

Uldreth Avenger – I know that you can hear me.

The thoughts pushed easily into his head, breaking him out of his self-indulgence.

Farseer! His mind raced with intense emotions of relief and anxiety. Although Macha was ensconced in the glittering *Eternal Star*, which tumbled and spun through the void ahead of Uldreth's *Avenging Sword*, he recognised her thoughts and his soul leapt at their touch.

Uldreth, the blame is not yours. She had known the Dire Avenger for longer than most could remember, and she knew what would be in his mind. *The future is a roiling intermixture of pathways and possibilities, and this one opened more inevitably the further down it we progressed. Your decisions did not make this worse, they just made it into what it was. Even without your choices, the future will unfold; you cannot escape from time. Without you, the Swordwind may have descended on Lsathranil's Shield... but I may have spun off into oblivion forever. Besides, even without the Bahzhakhain the victory was ours: your choices brought you here, and the Yngir were defeated in this system.*

Staring out the main viewscreen of the control chamber, Uldreth watched as the *Eternal Star*, a brilliant fiery wing in the darkness, stabilised suddenly and then dropped its speed to almost nothing. In immediate response, the *Avenging Sword* cut its engines and came to a near-halt, instantly matching the velocity of the startling Wraithship as though the two ships were organically fused.

It does not matter who was right, Uldreth. It only matters what we do about our mistakes. Pride is the affliction of our kind, Avenger, and it defines your own calling. Enact vengeance for your errors, but do not visit it upon yourself. Your conscience is clear, since you are here revealing the very future that you professed to deny. We are judged by our actions, and yours have already done you credit – beyond our emotions we can find the truth of our selves.

Macha's tone was deep and insistent; Uldreth had heard it before, and he resented its patronising undertones. He was not some simple courtier that would be cowed by the words of the farseer; he had known her before she had become embroiled in the greatness and awe of her position. He knew her. She had no need to patronise him. And yet her words soothed his troubled mind and brought a measure of calm to his anxiety. Part of him snarled at the fact that she could affect him so much, despite his resistance and his consciousness of what she attempted.

I am sorry, Macha. I should not have doubted you, he replied.

You are wrong, Uldreth Avenger: it is your place to doubt and your duty to question. Without challenges and tests, the complacency of our people grows into a tyranny of its own. You should not apologise for saving us from ourselves.

But my doubts brought us so perilously close to disaster, he thought back.

Yet your pride did not prevent you from coming to my aid.

You knew that I could not desert you, Macha. Despite the circumstances, Uldreth could not hide the genuine affection in his tone.

Yes, I knew it. Macha had affection too, but its nature seemed maternal and condescending and it infuriated Uldreth, who instantly regretted his moment of weakness. There was silence.

Whatever the past, muttered Uldreth dismissively, *the enemy is defeated now.*

We should not find our conclusions so frivolously, Uldreth of the Dire Avengers, Macha replied. *Victory and defeat are not such convenient categories in the myriad nodes of the future. Even the Old Ones could not find victory in their wars against the ancient enemy. They found only a momentary peace. I fear that we have found even less than that. The Yngir do not ascend without contingencies – there may be ripples in time and space that we have not yet seen. There may have been ripples even before the ascension. Perhaps those are what Taldeer saw in the Lorn system. Perhaps, my reproach-ridden Avenger, you were yet right to send the Tempest of Blades to Lorn. We both know what lies just under the surface of that ancient, exodite world.*

THE DESCENT DOWN the cliff face to the valley floor was a simple matter, but finding a route that kept me continuously hidden from any eyes above me was harder. There were numerous ledges and overhangs, and I dropped beneath them as rapidly as I could. I was learning the limits of my physiology as I went, and I soon discovered that my body could withstand long drops and that my arms could catch my weight even after a fall of a dozen metres.

From time to time, when I thought that I had missed a ledge, or that I had caught myself too late and that I would tear my shoulder out of joint, I felt the electric pulse of an unknown energy gather strength in my body, reinforcing my shoulder or guiding my weight suddenly onto a shelf. In my mind, I muttered words of thanks and litanies of power, praising the Great Father and the Emperor for my body, armour and mind.

Once I had reached the valley floor, I turned and inspected the townscape that filled the basin. It was even more unusual than it had appeared from the top of the cliff. The buildings around the circumference were low-rise and wide, sweeping around the outskirts of the city in both directions. They seemed to be made of stone, but it was as though each had been carved out of a single piece.

The doorways and window-holes had been cut out of the unbroken lines of the walls, and there were no joints between the walls and ceilings, nor between the walls and the ground. Each aspect of the buildings flowed naturally into the next, as though the shapes had emerged out of the rocky landscape all by themselves.

I made a mental note about the skill of the architects that had designed and built these structures: *If they have mastered buildings in this way, what would their skill have produced as weaponry?*

Further in towards the centre of the city, the buildings grew higher and more impressive, sculpting the skyline into a massive cone or pyramid, aspiring to the sky in the very heart and dropping away to ground-level at the edges. Looking up, however, I could see that the very highest structures in the downtown area were actually the same height as the cliffs that surrounded the town on all sides. There was nothing that stood proud of the valley; everything was contained and hidden in the circular basin. I marvelled at the genius of the urban design: *A good defence is not to be seen, but better still is to be hidden in plain view.*

The streets were empty and deserted, and yet they seemed pristine and perfect, as though people had been navigating them only hours or even minutes before. Something about the atmosphere in the city made it seem as though it had only recently been abandoned, if it had been abandoned at all.

For a moment, my mind flickered with memories of other towns that I had been in: they were deserted and evacuated. People's belongings were left strewn in the streets and psychic wisps of pain hung around street corners; abandoned vehicles burned, overturned on the pavements, and others were crashed and exploded in the carelessness of haste; smoke, flames and cries riddled the town; the resonant, metallic thunder of siege engines rumbled through the ground.

But this city was different: an ancient and implacable calm hung in the air like an invisible, tranquilising cloud. A faint breeze drew itself through the streets like a wave of natural air-conditioning, presumably pulled into the town by the cracked rock formations of the surrounding cliffs and by the perfectly designed street plan of the city itself.

What manner of city is this? It was unlike any town that I had been in before.

Even as I paused to consider the city, the sparkle of myriad lights caught my attention once again. The multicoloured flutterings that I had seen around the sorcerer's camp and again on the edge of the city had continued at irregular intervals through the streets. They flickered like a refraction spectrum, glittering against the pale stone walls, always just at the limit of my vision.

Darting into a narrow side-alley, I broke into a run. It was already clear to me that the lights were leading me (or were they luring me?) towards the centre of the town, so I swept through the complex of streets and alleys, endeavouring to emerge back in the main street ahead of the sparkling constellation.

The best way to avoid a trap is to spring one of your own.

Even the side-alleys were pristine and clean, as though they had just been sandblasted and white-washed. There were no obstacles for me to jump over or duck under, the alleys were just wide enough to accommodate my broad shoulders, and the run through the city was so simple that it aroused my suspicions. Why would a city so well designed for defence be so easy to navigate?

As I emerged out into the main street once again, I found the clutch of shimmering lights still ahead of me, as though I had no made up any ground at all. The lights flickered momentarily, as though beckoning to me or waiting for me to catch up, and then they were gone again.

I am not tracking these things; they are leading me somewhere. Thinking back to the way that the lights had intervened in front of the sorcerer's Thunderhawk on the cliff-top, I decided to assume that whatever these lights were, their intentions were probably benign.

Trust is the preserve of the unwary.

Following the bizarre light formations through the widening streets and boulevards of the alien city, I quietly drew *Vairocanum* into my hands. No matter how benign the light clusters might seem, I would not be taken unawares in this strange place.

The lights directed me through a twisting and circuitous path, taking me off the main thoroughfare and back onto it, circling around sections of breathtaking beauty and leading me through the plainest and least ostentatious of the streets.

The route was confusing and labyrinthine, and it took me some time to realise that we were heading gradually towards the centre of the city, in ever decreasing spirals. I wondered whether the tortuous route was designed to hide parts of the city from my eyes, but it also occurred to me that it might have been designed to protect me from the dangers that lie in wait in some sections of the town.

My mind could not settle in the alien atmosphere of the streets, and I found myself unable to determine the motives of whatever was leading me. Doubt was not something that sat comfortably in my thoughts, and I felt increasingly anxious as I drew closer to the heart of the city.

After an age of walking, I emerged into a wide plaza. The buildings on each side of the elliptical space soared into the sky, aspiring like spires. The speckle of lights had vanished about half an hour before, leaving me to wander the last few streets unguided and unmolested. And such streets they were: wide and sweeping like the great boulevards of

Qulus Trine, the wealthy merchants' world that was protected on all sides by massive orbital fortresses, manned by a private army but overseen by the Emperor's gaze in the form of the Blood Ravens Eighth Company, whose glorious battle-barge *Ominous Insight* had made the Qulus system into its home.

A succession of images of that prosperous and vainglorious world cycled through my memory, triggered by the grandeur of my surroundings: I had been to Qulus Trine more than once, it seemed. But I had never been in a city like this before: there was no bustle of business and no pompous processions of wealth, not a single soul stirred through the gorgeous streets or in the windows and doors. It was like an imitation of a town, more like a ghost or a pristine memory than a real city.

On the far side of the piazza was a giant domed building. A tall, conical spire erupted out of the centre of its curving roof, with its tip pushing up amongst the tallest towers of the city, like a giant tree crowning the canopy of an immense forest. Following the line of the cone back down to the ground, I noticed that there was a dark opening in the front of the dome. It was positioned at the top of a flight of steps, which were proportioned almost perfectly for a humanoid to ascend them with ease. Somewhere in the shadows within, I thought that I saw the glittering of movement.

I sprang up the last of the steps and pressed myself against the frame of the arch which opened up into the cavernous interior of the massive dome. Edging inside, I found that the circumference of the circular hall was defined by a single, sweeping ambulatory, which was separated from the main domed space by a row of columns. It was akin to a large, domed cloister. The central space was completely empty, although a single beam of red sunlight lanced down from the apex of the dome, defining a circle in the very heart of the hall, like a droplet of blood.

Judging from the position of the beam, I guessed that it was focussed directly down the entire height of the spire above. Such precision in the design and on such a scale – the architects of this place were clearly superior artists.

Scanning my eyes around the shadows that swept the edge of the hall, deepening behind each of the pillars, I could see no signs of movement or life. In fact, there was no sign that life had ever touched its magic fingers into this place. It was so quiet that I could hear the perfectly channelled and controlled breeze easing over the steps outside.

In such an atmosphere, I would not have been surprised to see the floor plume with dust as I stepped out towards the centre of the room. Yet there was not a speck of dust or dirt on the ground in the hall. It was immaculate, and I left no footprints. This was not simply a recently cleaned hall, it was a place that had never known dirt. What is dirt if not matter misplaced? Yet there is nothing misplaced in this city. The thought made me pause. If everything was so perfectly positioned, if nothing was out of place, then I had been engineered into this place at this time.

The realisation sent a sudden shiver through my spine. Now that the thought had occurred to me, it seemed so obvious that I couldn't believe my own stupidity. As I unsheathed *Vairocanum*, I cursed the ease with which I had been distracted by the beauty and elegance of the city.

At exactly that moment, as though responding to the shift in my own mood, the patterns of light that had lured me into the domed hall started to flutter and flicker against the curving wall opposite the entrance. The moments of light were brighter than before, and their colours more vivid as they danced and flashed in intricate patterns. I lowered my sword out in front of me, holding it into a guard between myself and the swimming fragments of light. As I did so, the lights suddenly blurred and spread, multiplying around the hall until the walls of the entire ambulatory were ablaze with flecks of colour and motion.

Spinning on the spot and moving reflexively into the spotlight at the centre of the hall, I tried to keep myself equidistant from all the walls. In my hands, *Vairocanum* started to glow with renewed vigour and heat, spilling flecks and flashes of green light into the down-blast of blood red in which I had posed. The alien runes along the blade pulsed with life, as though coming alive in response to the threat that encircled us. With a flourish, I swept the sword into a circle around me, whipping it out and around my head in a spin.

Rather than deterring the light, this action seemed to urge the dancing fragments into greater frenzies of motion. The flecks moved faster and with more energy, burning brighter than ever. As I watched, a number of flushes of light congealed and brightened; they started to form into more solid and familiar shapes. The more I moved in the spotlight, the more intense and vivid became the motions of the light-shapes, until I began to recognise flashes of rapidly moving arms and catch glimpses of dancing legs. The shadowy ambulatories around the chamber were alive with spectres of light.

I turned faster and faster, trying to keep the whole of the perimeter under surveillance at the same time, but my motion only inspired even greater movements from the emerging figures. Stopping abruptly, I stepped out of the red spotlight and lurched forward towards the archway that led back out into the piazza outside.

As I took the steps, the light-forms whisked around the hall and collected in front of me, as though to block my route out. With *Vairocanum* in front of me, I held my ground as the light-forms advanced towards me, gradually resolving into more solid forms. After a couple of seconds, the blur of multicoloured light that had sheened over the archway, obscuring my view of the plaza outside, had transformed into three ranks of humanoid creatures. Each of them was dressed ostentatiously in fantastical colours, and each carried some kind of weapon – swords, staffs, whips and glaives.

They were inhumanly tall and elegant, and their faces were paler and more perfect than the city itself. Their eyes burned like distant stars, and their ears drew up into graceful points. And they moved. They moved perpetually and without apparent effort, dancing and drifting and swaying as though not entirely of this realm.

The relentless motion gave the fantastical troupe the air of the ocean, and I could feel its hypnotic effects on my mind, like an intoxicant or a sedative. Although I cut out with *Vairocanum*, lashing across in front of myself as I staggered backwards towards the spotlight of blood, my mind was already racing and confused and I struck nothing but air. Piercing and discombobulating sounds started to echo around the dome, and I realised instantly how lethal the acoustics in that hall could be. I stumbled back under the sudden sensory assault just as plumes of varicoloured gases exploded from grenades all around me, partially obscuring my view of the elegant, sickly, dancing aliens that closed in around me.

The scent of the gas conspired with the tumult of noise and the whirl of lights to confuse my senses utterly. In a matter of seconds, I felt *Vairocanum* fall from my hand, as though in slow motion, and then I lost my balance completely, falling backward and crashing to the ground in the spotlight at the very centre of the theatre. Stunned and startled, I looked up into the blinding shaft of bloody light and lost consciousness.

ON THE ALTAR in the desert, in front of the open nose of the Thunderhawk, there shimmered an image of a book. It was laced with an eerie green-blue light and it oscillated gently, as though caught in a soft breeze.

The squad of Prodigal Son Chaos Marines were fanned into a crescent around the altar, facing back in towards their gunship, and Ahriman himself stood before the altar, his arms outstretched to the triple red suns above, his eyes burning with warpfire.

Glaring up into the heavens as though defying the power of suns, the great sorcerer muttered a series of inaudible words. All around him, the rest of the Prodigal Sons leaned in slightly, trying to discern what their magnificent leader had said, but the wind dissolved the sounds and carried them out of earshot. Besides, Ahriman had not meant them to hear; there was not one amongst them who did not seek Ahriman's power for his own.

In the distant past, Ahriman had sought the knowledge of the galaxy for himself and for his brothers; he had stood proudly at the side of Magnus himself, bathing in the swirling pools of information and knowledge unearthed by the misguided primarch and his Thousand Sons.

But there came a day when Ahriman's knowledge challenged even that of Magnus, just as the power of Magnus had once rivalled even that of the False Emperor of Man: as prodigal sons are fated to overcome their fathers. The key was knowledge itself, and Ahriman had learned quickly that he should be more cautious than his old master about with whom he shared his knowledge: unlike Magnus, Ahriman would not be cast aside by one of his own Prodigal Sons. There was no Book of Ahriman to be stolen from him, as he had once acquired the Book of Magnus.

Even as they dispersed and evaporated, the words ascended into the sky, like puffs of smoke signalling to some far off power. The sky darkened noticeably, almost at once. With his gaze unbroken, Ahriman could see the triple stars deepen their colour and dim, as though responding to his commands. At the same time, the cloudless sky began to condense and vaporise. From horizon to horizon, the air started to swirl in a massive, slow vortex, as though the atmosphere itself were being unscrewed from the planet below. Wisps of purple and gold cirrus clouds started to appear, pulled into long, thin strips by the atmospheric motion.

Ahriman stood motionless at the epicentre of the furore that was gathering around him, his arms beseeching the unseen powers of heaven while his whispered and sibilant words provoked agents beyond the comprehension of normal men. He was a powerful psyker, and it suited his purposes for his Space Marines to believe the rumours that he rivalled the power of Magnus and the Emperor himself.

In truth, however, most of Ahriman's power came from the allies that he could enlist. Over the long centuries and millennia, the unmatched sorcerer had learnt the keys that unlocked many secrets: he could call upon the aid of daemons without exposing his soul to their thirst, binding them to his will and his purpose; he could seduce service from the lithe and terrible daemonettes, promising them pleasures that he would never have to fulfil; and he could speak the hidden words that stirred the warp itself, bringing the raw, depersonalised power of the empyrean into his service for short periods of time.

He had required all of these assets to break the moorings of the portal into the eldar webway at Lorn, and yet his Space Marines grasped only that he had accomplished it with his own power. The irony of cultivating such stupidity in these ostensible searchers of truth was not wasted on Ahriman, but the preservation of his own power was a still higher imperative: if they had his knowledge, they would have his power too. If they learnt too much, Ahriman would kill them himself. If knowledge was power, then Ahriman, Sorcerer Lord of the Prodigal Sons, was its ultimate guardian.

The sky darkened until it seemed that night was falling prematurely on Arcadia. However, the searing and insufferable heat of the day persisted, as though the shroud over the triple suns was nothing more than an illusion. With a slow movement, Ahriman looked down from the sky and placed his gaze onto the glowing image of a book on the altar. He muttered some more inaudible words, asking the local powers to show him the location of the sacred tome. His Marines watched expectantly, but nothing happened.

Silence fell, as though the desert wind itself were holding its breath. In his mind, Ahriman smiled: he knew that nothing was more glorious and suggestive of power than a dramatic, tension-riddled pause. He waited for a couple of seconds, and then completed his incantation.

The rocks under the altar started to tremble and quake, making the altar shake and shift with increasing violence. At precisely that moment, Ahriman nodded a signal to the Sorcerer Obysis, his sergeant, who started to chant the Litany of Placation. His voice was joined immediately by those of the other Prodigal Sons, who each knew the possible consequences of their failure to contain the eruption of power. The choral sound swept around the altar in the ritual crescent, presenting a barrier of sound and will.

With a groan of cracking rock, the altar convulsed with a sickly energy and then exploded, sending shards of stone and metal raining out over the Prodigal Sons, leaving the holographic book hanging momentarily in the air before it flickered and vanished.

In place of the altar, a vertical stream of electric blue fountained out of the ground into the sky, like a fiery pillar reaching for the heavens. It would have visible for dozens of kilometres in every direction, searing out of the desert like the finger of god. At the same time, the rocky ground started to crack and crumble away. The collapse started at the point that used to support the altar, then spread like a growing cave-in, clawing away the ground in a wide crescent, stopping at the boots of the Sorcerer Lord and his Prodigal Sons. In place of the rock, sand bubbled and seethed to the surface, like oil gushing up from a drill-hole. It bubbled and frothed at the surface, overflowing the hole and lapping at the feet of the warriors who chanted and muttered the words necessary to hem it in.

Glowering with his blazing eyes, Ahriman barked a sudden command at the roiling mass of sand, making it flinch and ripple as though repulsed by his words. But then the chaos of sand started to form into vaguely recognisable shapes, each held together by the unearthly bonds of warp and the unspeakable, glittering will of the empyrean.

After a moment, the forms resolved into a three-dimensional map of a circular, almost conical city. Then it exploded into turmoil again. Suddenly there were buildings and streets, market places and great, towering cathedrals. The shapes shifted and reformed, as though guiding Ahriman through an unknown city, showing a route to him that would lead him to what he sought. As the sorcerer lord was shown a wide plaza with a vast domed hall dominating one side of it, the holographic book suddenly reappeared in the mire of sand. It pulsed and glowed with a vague green presence, only half visible through the sandy walls of the dome.

Ahriman let the suggestion of a smile play over his lips as his inferno-eyes burned into the image of the book: *The Tome of Karebennian*. The book was a mythical guide to the location of the fabled Black Library of the ancient eldar; even the foolish old Magnus the Red had never believed that the book was anything more than a legend. But Ahriman had always been a finer scholar than his primarch, and centuries of research had finally paid off. Since his expulsion from the Planet of the Sorcerers, Ahriman had taken his cabal on a rage of erudition, plundering ancient tombs, acquiring forbidden tomes, unearthing magical artefacts, and discovering the most talented of psykers. Even Magnus would not have thought it possible, but he had found Arcadia, and now he would find *Karebennian* too. After that, there was nothing that could keep him away from the Black Library, the impossibly ancient repository of the wisdom of the eldar.

The image of the book sizzled and glittered in the sandscape, but then the shimmering light shifted slightly, as though it had been blurred. Other flecks of light danced through the sand, sparkling and whirling like fireflies or refractions through a prism. After a fraction of a second, one of the Prodigal Sons stopped chanting and unsheathed an ornate force-sword, brandishing it and flourishing it into defensive stances. Then another Marine tugged twin bolters from holsters against his legs, snapping them back and forth at targets that never quite seemed real. Suddenly, all of the Marines had abandoned the Litany of Placation, and the sandscape erupted into a massive, diffuse mist that covered them all. Meanwhile, the Prodigal Sons had braced their weapons and Ahriman himself had his infamous Black Staff poised ready for combat.

Fleet, multi-coloured shapes danced through the sandstorm with incredible speed and grace, never pausing long enough to present a definite target for the Prodigal Sons. But it was clear that the shapes were not simply tricks of the light: the flashes of arms and legs, the glint of bright eyes, and the eerie songs of battle betrayed a humanoid threat.

Without waiting to identify the mysterious assailants, Ahriman grinned, letting his mouth open to reveal burning blue teeth, like rows of warp shards. His eyes flared with the sudden thrill of combat. Taking his Black Staff by one end, he spun it around his head, letting a stream of crackling energy lash out into a circle around him. A couple of his own Prodigal Sons shrieked in pain, but Ahriman's infernal grin broadened as he poured more and more power into his spiralling inferno.

'I WILL NOT ask you again, General Sturnn. The captain is not accustomed to being kept waiting.' Scout Sergeant Corallis held the general's eye for a moment, making sure that he was aware that the Blood Ravens did not fall under the same command hierarchy as the Imperial Guard. With his one remaining eye, Sturnn glared back at the partially reconstructed, half-mechanised sergeant, making sure that he was aware that he was not intimidated by the Adeptus Astartes. He had seen them before.

'We fight for the same Emperor, sergeant. I mean no obstruction to your captain.' The officers behind him smiled nervously, proud of their general's composure but anxious lest he had gone too far with his pompous manner. 'The problem – if we can really call it a problem – is that we were not expecting to see you, Blood Raven.'

'And why is this a problem? Many Guardsmen will go through their entire lives without seeing a Space Marine–'

'And others will become Space Marines themselves, sergeant. Do not lecture me about the nature of the Adeptus Astartes. I did not become a general in the *Imperial* Guards without becoming familiar with your functions and practices.' Sturnn cut off Corallis in mid-sentence, and there was something about his tone that the sergeant didn't like: he knew that the Guard were fiercely proud of their name and the association it implied with the Emperor, but Sturnn had bitten down on the word 'Imperial' as though it were a bullet. 'The Adeptus Astartes and even the Blood Ravens themselves are not unknown to me. I am not as uninformed as you may think.'

'It is gratifying to know that our reputation precedes us, general,' nodded Corallis with a show of graciousness. 'Then you will appreciate the imperativeness of cooperation.'

'Is that a threat, Blood Raven? You would do well not to threaten one of the Emperor's generals.' The theatrics betrayed the fact that only days before Sturnn had been a captain; his promotion was a field-promotion only, but his officers knew that field-promotions were the ones that really counted.

Corallis was taken aback. He had certainly not meant to imply a threat with his words, but only to indicate the likely importance of their presence on Lorn V.

Why would Sturnn interpret him with such a lack of charity? What had the general heard about the Blood Ravens?

'Forgive me, general. It was not my intention to appear hostile. Please explain your problem, and we will see what can be done to solve it.'

Sturnn regarded him for a moment. 'Very well, sergeant. You are not the first of the Adeptus Astartes to have made landfall on Lorn V in the last few days. The first squad called themselves Ultramarines and claimed command of our forces, turning our own plans into ruin.

We killed them – does this surprise you?'

Corallis stared at the general in horror. He glanced back over his shoulder towards Gabriel and the figure of the eldar farseer who was slumped in between the captain and Librarian Jonas.

'You laid hands on the Ultramarines!' Disbelief fought with the violence of restraint in Corallis's voice, and his hand twitched over the holstered bolter on his leg.

Sturnn tilted his head, as though assessing the sergeant's reaction. 'We killed the Marines in question. We surrounded them in the command tent and then blew them to pieces. Dozens of our own men sacrificed themselves so that the traitors would not suspect the plan.'

'Traitors? I cannot believe that the Sons of Guilliman were traitors to the Emperor or the sacred tenets of the Codex Astartes.'

'Have you heard enough then?' said the general.

'What?'

'Have you heard enough? Do you condemn Lorn and the Cadian 412th already?' The general was goading him.

'Who were those Marines?' snapped Corallis, unwilling to believe the report.

'Ah, that is the right question, Sergeant Corallis.' Sturnn smiled as though relieved. 'I do not know who they were, but it seems that they were merely disguised as Ultramarines to deceive us and usurp our command structure. These are the markings that were borne on their shoulder plates after we scratched the blue paint from their dead forms.'

Sturnn flicked a signal and one of the officers behind him threw a shoulder guard onto the ground in front of Corallis.

The Blood Raven stepped aside so that Gabriel and Jonas could see the evidence: they recognised the green hydra immediately – it was the insignia of the Alpha Legion. This was not uncharacteristic behaviour by the deceitful traitor Marines.

'As I say,' continued Sturnn, 'we identified them quickly and then eliminated them.'

'They were traitors – Alpha Legionnaires – they do not follow the Imperial creed. You were right to turn on them, general.' Corallis paused as a realisation sank in. 'And you suspect the same of us?' He flinched as he spoke, with genuine repulsion written across his face. The story made sense, and it explained the wrecked Ultramarines' cruiser on the edge of the system, which had crude Alpha Legion markings hacked into it.

'No. The battle here is won, as you can see,' said Sturnn, sweeping his hand out towards the smoking remains of the ice-encrusted battlefield. 'But the Ultramarines did come. They brought us a control team for the Dominatus titan. It seems odd to me that the Blood Ravens should arrive now, damanding access to the site where the titan was found.'

'I see,' nodded Corallis, not quite sure what might be the point of this exchange. 'But I fail to see your problem.'

'I never said that there was a problem, sergeant. In fact, I explicitly said that I should not call it a problem.' Sturnn smirked. 'I said merely that we had not been expecting you, and that we know enough of the Blood Ravens to understand that your arrival is not always... fortuitous.'

Sturnn had chosen that word carefully, and Corallis picked up on the deliberate ambiguity. What had this man heard about the Blood Ravens, he wondered. Perhaps more importantly, how had he heard whatever he had heard? It was possible, supposed Corallis, that this General Sturnn had some connections with the Inquisition – Ulantus had implied as much.

It was certainly the case that a number of factions within the Ordo Xenos would be interested in keeping track on the movements and activities of the Blood Ravens Third Company, especially after the affairs on Tartarus when one of their own inquisitors was lost whilst under the Blood Ravens' protection. Hence, it was not altogether impossible that Sturnn had been briefed before their arrival.

It was also possible that one of the officers of the Ultramarines contingent was similarly connected, and that he had passed on dubious information to the general when they learnt that the Blood Ravens were en route. Chaplain Varnus was certainly well-connected.

Whatever the case, the pointed nature of Sturnn's comment implied that he had little faith in the judgement or honour of the Blood Ravens. This was the only way to explain the way that Sturnn tried to test Corallis's response to the Cadian 412th's treatment of the alleged Ultramarines: would the Blood Ravens wait for an explanation or simply blow the place and leave?

Corallis fought back the urge to kill the general on the spot for slighting the honour of his Chapter. 'We do not seek a role in this conflict, General Sturnn, and it is clear to us that you have secured the theatre already. Nonetheless, we must request access to the site of the excavation of the Dominatus titan. There is reason to suppose that there is more to that site than even that venerable machine.'

'I can assure you that my men examined the site thoroughly. What kind of reason would you have to doubt this?' As he spoke, Sturnn let his eyes fall past Corallis and alight on the sickly, broken shape of Taldeer.

'We have our reasons, and they need not concern you, general. Will you give us access or... not?' Corallis could be ambiguous too. His patience was wearing thin.

WITH TALDEER HANGING off his shoulder, limp and almost weightless, Gabriel pushed through the cordon that marked off the excavation site. Jonas and Corallis followed behind, with Sturnn striding along between them, making a show of being escorted by the massive Space Marines. The encampment was ringed by a series of Hellhound tanks, gunnery emplacements and several full squadrons of Armoured Fist troops. Given that the titan had been removed days before, the security around the site certainly suggested that Sturnn knew something else of value remained within the cordon.

After a few steps, the ground fell away into a wide pit. Mounds of earth and piles of rock around the

perimeter suggested that the cavity had been excavated only recently. The bottom of the crater was
uneven and skewed; to one side a wide, low tunnel
had been hacked out of the wall of the pit, leading
off under the ground. Even from the rim of the crater,
Gabriel could see the half exposed runic markings
that poked through over the apex of the tunnel
mouth. They had not been fully uncovered, as
though a decision had been made to ignore them.
Gabriel bristled at the casual disregard for knowledge
acquistion that the site demonstrated.

'You located the titan inside that tributary?'

'No captain. The titan was uncovered in the main
pit.' Sturnn gestured around the crater, implying the
great size of the titan and the impossibility that it
could have been pushed through that tunnel.

'Of course,' answered Gabriel. 'And what of the tunnel?'

'Our engineers unearthed it when they drilled the
trial hole in this area. We made it about one hundred
metres along its length before a second team found
the titan in this area in front of the tunnel's mouth.'

'I understand. Did your men finish excavating the
tunnel even so?' Gabriel's tone suggested that he
doubted that the Guardmen would have understood
the importance of such exploration.

'We pushed the tunnel through into a large chamber under the ice, but it appeared empty... We were
at war, captain. It was not the time for searching for
trinkets.'

Gabriel just nodded. He understood Sturnn's position on this, and he knew that it would be shared by

most men in his position. However, Gabriel's view
was radically different.

'Did you establish why the Dominatus titan was
preserved at the mouth of this tunnel?'

'We supposed that it was guarding the inner chamber,' conceded Sturnn, realising the direction of
Gabriel's questions.

'And you yourselves are guarding the tunnel
entrance now? It seems that you suspect the chamber holds more than mere trinkets, general.'

Nodding slowly, Sturnn sighed. 'The ice of Lorn V
is riddled with caverns and tunnels, captain. A number of them resemble this, and some are marked by
that foul alien scrawl. Legends suggest that the eldar
once lived here, long ago, before the ice and the
wrath of the Emperor purified this world.' Sturnn's
eyes twitched to the eldar farseer and discomfort settled over his face. 'I am sure that you would know
more about this, Captain Angelos.'

'Perhaps,' replied Gabriel as Jonas and Corallis
vaulted down into the pit to investigate the arch over
the tunnel, leaving the captain alone with Sturnn
and Taldeer. 'Have you set up cordons around all of
these sites?'

'No, captain. We do not have either the time, the
resources or the inclination to do so. This is the only
site that we are defending.'

'Why this one?'

'Because of the titan, captain. Even to a lowly general in the Imperial Guard, a titan guarding an eldar
artefact seemed unusual. I notified Inquisitor Tsensheer of the Ordo Xenos, and then established the

cordon while we awaited his arrival. I have had dealings with Tsensheer before,' Sturnn added significantly. 'He is a good man with a strong and far-reaching interest in these things.'

The mention of the Ordo Xenos made Gabriel flinch slightly; he had bad memories of a Xenos inquisitor, Mordecai Toth, on Tartarus, and he did not need to think about the events of that troublesome campaign now. 'I am sure he is, general. And has your inquisitor arrived yet?'

The general watched Gabriel's reaction carefully, noting the discomfort that lingered just below his features. 'No, captain. He is not here yet. We expect him imminently.'

'I see,' replied Gabriel, relieved. 'You were right to guard this site in preference to the others,' he continued, his mind snapping back to Rahe's Paradise, where an Adeptus Astartes outpost had been constructed over the remains of an eldar facility. 'The signifiance of an Imperial guard over this site should not be underestimated. You were right, also, to summon the inquisitor.'

'Thank you, captain.' Sturnn's tone suggested that he didn't feel as though he needed the approval of the Space Marine.

'Nonetheless, general, I'm sure that you will permit us to investigate this before Inquisitor Tsensheer arrives.' Gabriel nodded down towards the figures of Jonas and Corallis, who had already uncovered the rest of the archway around the tunnel and were busy translating the ancient eldar text that spidered across it.

'I am not sure–'

Before Sturnn could finish his objection, Gabriel stepped off the lip of the crater, skidding and jumping down its sheer sides, cradling the farseer in his arms.

THE TUNNEL WAS straight and direct. Its sides curved smoothly into a perfectly formed tube through the ice, and a pale eerie light suffused through the passageway.

I have been here before, Gabriel.

Taldeer used the captain's name as though she knew him well. The effect was destabilising at first, but Gabriel was quickly getting used to the presumptuous manner of the aliens.

Long ago, before the ice. This world was verdant and brilliant. A pearl in the ancient eldar empire.

The farseer's thoughts were weak and wispy, like breaths of smoke in Gabriel's mind. As she muttered, the captain carried her through the tunnel and emerged into the cavernous ice-chamber of which Sturnn had spoken. The floor was polished to a sheen, as though it was cleaned and maintained every day. The huge domed ceiling was similarly pristine; the pale blue ice was unblemished, uncracked and unmarked, even after thousands of years of neglect.

This is the place, Gabriel. This is the location of the portal.

As her thoughts formed in his head, Taldeer struggled out of his arms and stood onto her own feet on the ice.

'Jonas. What do you make of this place?' asked Gabriel.

As he surveyed the echoing bubble of ice, Gabriel could see nothing of significance. He wondered whether the eldar witch was too sick to really understand what she was doing, and whether the gruff, military-minded Sturnn was actually right about this place.

The Librarian was gazing around the chamber with wonder written over his face. He was clearly awed by something invisible to Gabriel. 'It's amazing Gabriel.' His eyes twinkled with wonder. 'It's amazing.'

A gentle melody flowed into the ice-cave. It was quiet at first – little more than a whispered and melancholy song. But the acoustics of the chamber turned the notes back on themselves, boosting them, shifting them and enhancing them, bringing echoes into harmony with themselves. The solitary voice of Taldeer rapidly built into a chorus, as though the cave were filled with eldar seers, each chanting and singing with exquisite beauty. After a matter of seconds, the ice itself hummed and resounded with the ineffable, alien music.

Stand back.

The thought pushed through the music into the minds of each of the Space Marines, making them step back away from the centre of the cavern. As they did so, cracks of light flashed through the ice-dome, riddling the massive curving ceiling with intricate patterns of energy. Runes wrote themselves across the dome, appearing and vanishing as though written in the sands of a wind-swept desert. Then the runes ran into images and pictures. Maps and star-charts spiralled around the vast cavernous chamber, searing through the ice in flashes of blue and green.

Abruptly, the images blinked out, leaving the cave empty and cold once again. But Taldeer's chorus continued to ring out. After a few moments, columns of electric blue started to rise up around the domed roof, each aspiring towards the apex of the dome. As the columns converged, power trickled down from the apex in a gentle shower of warp energy. The trickle became a stream and then a torrent. In a matter of seconds, the whole hall was a storm of warp fire, swirling like a tempest.

The polished ice of the walls and floor acted like mirrors, reflecting the maelstrom off to infinity in all directions, until the Space Marines felt their balance failing, standing in the heart of an infinite warp storm. In the centre of the floor, a structure started to appear through the rain. It was an arch, a giant gate that stretched almost to the ceiling. The archway was inscribed with burning runes, and the whole structure flickered and spat as though it was struggling to find resolution.

Taldeer's voice reached new heights amidst the tumult. Tearing his eyes away from the spectacle that was raging before him, Gabriel stole a glance at the farseer. He could see her strength failing and her skin beginning to shrivel. The effort was killing her, but her eyes blazed with concentration and determination, all thoughts for her own survival vanished.

It's no good. The eldar's thoughts were breathless and exhausted. *The portal is ruined. Your stupid Sturnn has destroyed it. It reeks of mon'keigh, as though you had ripped it from its very moorings. The Yngir need not complete their Great Work, if you will complete it for them, human!*

The effort was finally too much, and Taldeer collapsed down to the ice. The chorus of echoes continued for a few seconds after the singing stopped, but then a gradual silence unfurled itself into the cavern. The warp fire flickered and blinked out of existence, and the ghostly, incomplete portal itself remained for only a second. At exactly the instant that the portal vanished, a solitary figure walked directly out of its centre, stepping into the freezing air of the cave and striding down a flight of invisible steps to the polished ground.

The eldar warrior was unlike any that Gabriel had seen before, and instinctively the three Space Marines reached for their weapons.

Taldeer's eyes widened in shock and fear, and she struggled to drag her body back over the ice, pulling herself away from the newcomer as though repulsed by his very presence.

Karebennian!

The word slammed into Gabriel's mind, and he could sense the terror that flooded out of Taldeer. In response, Gabriel braced his bolter and took aim. The eldar Solitaire cocked its head to one side, as though curious about what the Space Marine was going to do. Unphased, Gabriel squeezed the trigger and let a volley of bolter shells fly.

No! Taldeer's protest came too late.

With a smooth and incredible movement, the Solitaire spun around the shells, letting one pass to his left, another to his right, and he bent backwards under the last, letting it flash over his face and impact into the ice-wall behind him. Finishing the spin with a flourish that resembled a bow, Karebennian grinned at the prostrate farseer. He paused for a moment, as though letting the drama of his entrance seep into the consciousness of his audience, then he produced two long-bladed weapons. One in each hand, he started to dance with them. He vaulted and flipped, spun and spiralled, sometimes flashing into a multicoloured blur, at other times falling into abject stillness. In the ice-mirrors of the cave, the solitary Harlequin appeared as a troupe of thousands; the farseer and the Space Marines looked on, captivated.

CHAPTER SIX: HERESY

A SENSATION OF stony cold pounded against the back of my head, making my eyes squint even before I opened them. The dull, monotonous ache of a concussion resounded in my brain, muddling my thoughts as my senses gradually swam back into coherence. Before any other thought, my hand swept up to my shoulder, searching for the metallic comfort of a hilt: *Vairocanum*. My sword was exactly where it should be, strapped into its holster across my back, but the instant of relief was immediately followed by a wave of confusion.

I dropped her. I could remember it clearly. In the misty and confused images of my short-term memory, the moment at which *Vairocanum* had slipped from my fingers and clattered to the ground shone like a beacon of certainty. *She had been glowing intensely, as though surrounded by invisible but familiar energies. Then I dropped her.* The pain of loss hit me suddenly, like an icy blade between my ribs. The memory swam: I had fallen almost straight afterwards, nauseous and staggering like a drunken youth. The kaleidoscoping lights had penetrated my brain, exciting neural nodes that I had thought long dormant, leaving me stunned and unable to function. It was as though I had succumbed to a fit. *What could have done this to an Angel of Death?*

Embrace your questions – they will bring you to power in the end.

My eyes snapped open instantly; those were not my thoughts. There was a silent and only half-repressed menace lurking in the words as they pressed into my mind, cold, heavy and non-negotiable.

'Who are you?' I tried to roll away from the kneeling figure, reaching around for my sword as I turned. But pain lanced into my head, making my body lurch into rigidity, as though a massive electrical charge had been suddenly passed through my muscles. *Vairocanum* was only half-unsheathed when my fingers involuntarily released her once again. I slumped back onto my back, staring up at the face of death.

Rest.

There was no malice in the word, but it offered no space for doubts or questions. I would rest; it was simply a statement of what would happen, as though the mind from which the thought emerged was certain of what the future held for me.

Narrowing my eyes in an attempt to bring the face into proper focus, I nodded slightly, letting the looming figure think that I would not challenge his vision. No matter how hard I concentrated, however, I could not bring the face into focus – it remained blurred and ill-defined, as though it were not entirely present, or perhaps present in a different way from the rest of the warrior's magnificently armoured body. The phantoms of the warrior's face echoed those of the formidable sorcerer that I had seen emerging from the Thunderhawk in the desert. *They have found me.*

'You didn't answer my question.'

I did not offer to give you answers, came the logical reply. *I merely told you to embrace your questions.*

'What use are questions without answers?'

You misunderstand the priorities, Son of Ahriman. Answers are of no use without questions, but questions are most helpful when we do not yet have their solutions.

Son of Ahriman? 'What did you call me?' The name rang a distant and deep bell in my mind, but I could not resolve the memory.

Did you recognise yourself in what I said?

There was a note of satisfaction in the thought, I could tell.

I called you a Son of Ahriman. We are brothers, you and I.

There was the suggestion of a smile on the spectral face. It was the first time that I had seen the features of the face move, and a thick feeling of nausea rippled through my stomach. The warrior's lips did not move as he spoke his thoughts into my head, and this flicker of emotion took me by surprise, making my eyes widen slightly.

'Brothers?' It was too incredible to believe.

*Of course. How else can you explain our presence here?
We were searching for you – you were lost to us. It has
been many years since we have seen another brother.*

As I stared up at the malformed and eerie face, it
occurred to me that it was unbelievable to think that
this warrior and I would be just coincidentally on
this forsaken alien world at the same time. Inspect-
ing his armour, I realised that it was not entirely
dissimilar from my own: it was predominantly blue
and covered in a series of esoteric, runic seals; it
appeared to have been constructed out of the same
materials, and its structure was broadly the same. It
seemed clear that the designer of both had been trying to solve the same problems; it was not
impossible to believe that they had been designed
and built by the same people.

Do not fear the weapon, fear the soul of its wielder.

The maxim prodded into my thoughts from somewhere in my subconscious; it rang like a caution or
a warning. The mysterious warrior's ghostly face did
not shift, but I could tell that he was peering through
my eyes, trying to see into my thoughts. I had not
seen my own face for a long time, and I could not
remember what it looked like, but I remembered the
blistering pain of sun-burn in the desert, and I could
not imagine that this warrior's face was affected by
any natural forms of heat.

And there were differences in our armour as well:
his was a slightly darker blue, and was touched with
gold. It had a fiery serpent etched into one of the
massive shoulder guards; and behind his head was a
tall crest that stood nearly half a metre proud of his

shoulders. My own armour was paler blue, although still with lines of gold, and it was bedecked with glorious wings on the shoulder guard. There was no crest framing my face.

'I will keep that question in mind, friend. Since it seems that questions are more useful than answers at this point.' I pushed myself up into a sitting position and stared at the warrior that knelt implacably at my side.

As you say. The face grinned, as though unable to contain its glee.

THE EVENTS ON the planet's surface swam through Gabriel's mind as he knelt in quiet contemplation before the altar in the chapel of the *Litany of Fury*, letting the atmosphere of reverence and stillness flow over him. He needed the space for thinking, and he needed a little emotional stability. The last few months and years had drawn him thin, like a ghost of his former self.

No matter how many times he told himself that these doubts and pains had no place in the mind of a Space Marine captain, his thoughts kept falling back into the basic and inalienable humanity of his condition. He was simply unsure that he could cope with the responsibility of killing entire planets, watching his family fry, and putting his own friends to the sword.

Nobody, not even a Blood Ravens captain, should have to do these things. Prathios used to tell him that the Emperor was really the guardian of his soul, sending out lances of immaculate brilliance from the Astronomican to show him truth and radiance in the darkness. Without Prathios, Gabriel found these ideas increasingly hard to stomach: did the benevolence of the Emperor really excuse him from responsibility for his own actions? He was one of the Emperor's Angels of Death, but he was still Gabriel.

The captain had no way to understand the events that had unfolded down on the surface of Lorn V. Part of his soul screamed out to him that it was a blessing that the eldar portal had been destroyed – the deceitful and manipulative aliens were not to be trusted.

He, of all people, was well aware of the machinations and subtlety of the elegant race. He knew that Ulantus would consider the matter finished: the necron had been defeated and the eldar were dead. It was the perfect conclusion to a trying battle. But the universe contained more complicated problems than merely life and death. It was not simply light and darkness. There were shades of grey and spectrums of colour spread out between the infinite stars.

If Taldeer was right about the consequences of the portal's destruction, then Gabriel had a responsibility to act on that knowledge. By the grace of the Great Father, he was a Blood Raven, if he could not act on new knowledge, then he was a traitor to himself and his forebears: knowledge is power. He had to consider the source of the information, of course, but he had learned something of the ways of the eldar and their connections with the necron on Rahe's Paradise. In his heart, he believed Taldeer. He believed her with the kind of certainty that he had once believed in the immaculate light of the Astronomican. He simply *knew* that she was right about this.

Staring up at the awesome images of the Great Father Vidya above the altar, Gabriel felt his soul shiver. What would he have done in my position, wondered Gabriel, his eyes beseeching the icon for an answer. In the ancient texts, those supposedly penned by the Great Father himself, there could be found detailed treatises on the nature of knowledge and the various merits accumulated in its pursuit. However, as far as Gabriel could remember, Vidya never went so far as to concede that the good could be served from heretical sources.

Nonetheless, these grey areas, and the colourful extravagance represented so perfectly by the eldar Harlequin on Lorn, were of little concern to Vidya. For him, there was only the light of knowledge itself and then the dark of ignorance. His work and his example offered little in the way of guidance or comfort to Gabriel. Would following the pleas of the eldar witch mean betraying the Emperor and the Imperium? Was Gabriel right to believe that there was a greater good to be done than the defence of Lorn against the aliens? Was this battle over, or just beginning?

'If only Prathios were here,' muttered the captain, talking to himself in the darkness. 'He would know the right words.'

Hanging his head in a moment of despair, Gabriel's thoughts shifted to his one-time friend and battle-brother, Librarian Isador Akios. The two of them had been through so much together, even performing in the Blood Trials together on Cyrene, all those long years before.

Gabriel had learned to trust the erudite and wise Librarian, placing his life into his hands on many occasions. And then, on Tartarus, Gabriel had been forced to execute his friend. Isador had succumbed to the thirst for forbidden knowledge, craving the power that was the product of knowledge rather than the knowledge itself. There was a line that Gabriel recognised instinctively, and Isador had been lured over that line by the temptations of daemons and their servants.

On Tartarus, Gabriel had shown no confusion, and he had executed his oldest friend, believing implicitly and unquestioningly that he was acting as the Sword of Vidya. He had seen the light of the Astronomican, and he had *known* what to do.

And now it seemed that Gabriel had lost sight of that perfect, indelible, moral line. Yet his soul still cried out for it, beseeching the darkness around him for guidance. He *wanted* to do the right thing, but he was no longer certain what that was. The weight of his deeds pressed down on his conscience, curdling his certainties and compressing his thoughts into doubts.

'I do not seek the power of the eldar,' he whispered, reassuring himself as he looked up into the impenetrable eyes of Vidya. 'I do not seek to place their knowledge into my soul. But...' His muttered words trailed into silence as he struggled to find the crucial end of his sentence; everything depended on that 'but.' 'But... I *know* that the eldar witch is telling the truth about the portal and the necron threat. By acting on her knowledge, I am defending the Imperium. The battle for Lorn is not yet won. Sturnn and Ulantus are acting out of ignorance, and I would sin against my nature, against you, and against the Emperor himself if I did not attempt to act within the light of superior knowledge.'

He paused, letting his breath calm and permitting the dark silence to enshroud him once again. 'But... they will not believe me. My method is poor and my conclusions are based on instincts, not on reason. I would not believe me.'

Lowering his gaze, Gabriel closed his eyes and knelt in the private darkness of his own head. He let his thoughts swim and shift, watching them pass through his consciousness like ships on an ocean, waiting for them to settle into some kind of equilibrium. Then, somewhere deep in his subconscious, he saw a flicker of light. It was faint, like the merest suggestion of a distant reflection. But it trembled and shivered with a living nature. At the same moment, a quiet, barely audible note pierced the darkness. It was like the sound of silver. After a few seconds, the light began to pulse with energy in his mind, and the single, silvering note grew into a lance of sound.

Focussing his thoughts, Gabriel drew the light closer to his mind's eye, opening himself to it, dropping his innate resistance to the presence of this intrusion. He had seen it before, many times, but always in moments of crisis. He knew that it was the light of the Emperor himself. This was the Astronomican reaching for him, reassuring him with the brilliance of the Imperial faith, confirming his righteousness. He had seen it on Cyrene. He had seen it on Tartarus. And he had even seen it on Rahe's Paradise. It was the beacon that drew him towards the good.

The single, pristine tone became a harmony. It was a chorus, filling his head with platinum light and angelic music, leaving his senses in rapture. He opened his soul in relief and release, letting the symphony consume him. But then something shifted in the music. A tone fell flat, and another spiked into sharpness. Dissonance oscillated through the chorus, shattering the pristine sound like a spray of bullets through a pane of glass. The voices trembled and broke, breaking away into separate melodies that devastated the harmony, each aspiring to subsume the next.

Faces started to flicker in the light, flashing like strobed memories. Peaceful at first, the faces gradually grew ugly and contorted, twisting into daemonic images of fury and rage. They screamed, releasing infernos of pain into Gabriel's head, and for a moment he saw the face of his father burning in the fires of Cyrene. Isador's death rattle spat through the sound, reverberating like the chiming of a great bell.

It was a tempest of emotions and thoughts, and Gabriel threw himself forward, trying to drag himself out of the heart of the maelstrom. He lurched and crashed his head against the chapel's altar, cracking a gouge out of his already scarred forehead. The blood rushed out over his eyes, turning the phantom, mental lights momentarily into floods of blood, before the Larraman cells in his enhanced blood clotted and sealed the wound. The impact jolted him free of the vision and left him lying prostrate at the foot of the altar, sweating and panting for breath.

'Prathios...' he muttered, with his cheek pressed against the cold flagstones. 'What should I do?'

'BY THE THRONE, Gabriel, I can't believe that you're even considering this!' Ulantus stood in the centre of the control deck, his face white with fury and disbelief.

'And I, for my part, Captain Ulantus, cannot believe that you are challenging my authority aboard this vessel.' Gabriel's eyes flashed with restrained indignation. 'The last time I checked, it was Gabriel not Ulantus who was Commander of the Watch.'

'This is not a game of ranks, *commander*. I can hardly be blamed for voicing my concern about this plan. The *Litany of Fury* may be the base for our exalted Third Company, but you are not alone on this venerable old vessel. I know my position, and I know that you are overstepping your authority here.' Ulantus held his eyes on Gabriel, deliberately not casting around for the eyes of the other Space Marines on deck.

'Is this really a question of authority, Ulantus? Or is there something else bothering you?'

The Captain of the Ninth Company smiled in despair, finally looking around as though appealing to the control crew and the command squad for sympathy. 'Are you really going to make me say this, Gabriel? Do we really need to go there?'

'Yes, captain, I think we do.'

'We all know what the problem is here, captain,' began Ulantus. He hesitated slightly, as though weighing the gravity of his next words. 'The problem... the problem is not your authority... the problem is your judgement.'

'So there it is,' replied Gabriel quietly, narrowing his bright eyes into slits of reflected light.

'You wanted me to say it. So it is said.'

The silence on the control deck was intense and solid, as though the chamber had been flooded with an ocean of white-noise. Behind Gabriel, Jonas and Corallis stood shoulder to shoulder; their jaws were clenched and their hands lingered over the hilts of weapons. Behind them towered the massive form of Tanthius, still resplendent in his Terminator armour, completely blocking the only way in and out of the room. The strategy was obvious and bordered on heresy aboard a battle-barge: if this was going to come down to violence between battle-brothers, Gabriel had his back covered. He knew that he could trust his friends, even in a potential conflict with another ranking Blood Raven – that was why they were his friends.

'What *exactly* do you find offensive about my judgement, Ulantus. And, more importantly, why should I care about it?'

The expression on Ulantus's face betrayed his emotions; he simply could not believe that he was having this conversation. The issues seemed to be as obvious as a supernova. For a moment, he found himself wishing that there was an inquisitor present to make the obvious allegations; he had never wished for such a thing in his life before. How could Gabriel be so blind? It was as though the eminent captain was actually challenging Ulantus to make some accusations.

'The specifics are of no matter at this time, captain,' replied Ulantus, trying to evade the issue.

He did not want the rift between them to grow any wider. He could not believe that Gabriel was so far gone down the slippery road to heresy that he would actually take control of the battle-barge by force, but then he had also not believed that the good captain would try to force him to accuse him of heresy in front of an array of witnesses.

'You are wrong, captain,' replied Gabriel. 'The specifics are entirely the point. If you are going to refuse to let me take the *Litany*, then both I and the other Masters of this Chapter are entitled to understand the reasons for your… reticence.'

'*You* accuse *me* of having questionable motives!' The anger spilled out at last. 'How dare you, Gabriel! How dare you? Who was it who vanished off to Rahe's Paradise with no good reason, leaving me to pick up the pieces on Trontiux III and then engage multiple enemy forces here in the Lorn system? Who was it who subsequently demolished Rahe's Paradise altogether, without even a word of consultation with the Chapter Masters? Come to that, Gabriel, who was it who exterminated all life on Tartarus and Cyrene…'

As soon as he had said the words, Ulantus knew that he had gone too far. It was not his place to challenge the strategic decisions made by another commanding officer in the field, especially not those of a senior officer and the Commander of the Watch. He knew as well as anyone that decisions had to be made quickly and assertively, and that the burdens of command carried punishments of conscience as well as privileges.

'All I am saying, Gabriel,' he continued with a hint of contrition, 'is that you need to be a little more forthcoming about your reasons for taking this vessel back out into deep space. It is needed here to ensure the security and stability of Lorn V. Without good reasons, I cannot condone this course of action, and I will oppose it as best I can.'

As though on cue, two of Ulantus's sergeants rose out of their seats on the control deck and turned to face the group.

Saulh, who was standing just behind Ulantus, planted his feet a little more securely against the deck.

'How do you propose to oppose me, Captain Ulantus?' Gabriel's eyes shone with daring. He was goading the junior officer, forcing him to reveal how far he was willing to go. If Ulantus acted now, it would be mutiny, and everyone knew it.

'By the Father, Gabriel! Why do you think that General Sturnn distrusted you so much? He has his own contacts in the Inquisition... This Tsensheer of the Ordo Xenos... Even this field officer of the Imperial Guard is now suspicious... about your record. No wonder he didn't want to co-operate with you! Can't you see, Gabriel? Can't you see what this is doing to the Blood Ravens themselves? By the Throne, we're talking about the Inquisition, Gabriel!' Ulantus sighed, as though realising that he had nothing left to lose. 'Gabriel – you should have seen the reaction of the Cadians when the Ultramarines arrived. Sturnn welcomed them as saviours–'

'Sturnn was mistaken about them, wasn't he.'

'That's not the point–'

'It's entirely the point. Sturnn is not a reliable standard of judgement. He welcomed the fraudulent Ultramarines, and he was suspicious about us. Why should I care about this?'

'You should care about the reputation and conduct of your Chapter, Gabriel. You are a Blood Raven before all else. Your actions reflect on all of us. I cannot let you behave as though you are somehow independent of us – you are not. This ship is not yours, it is given in trust to the Commander of the Watch. You cannot simply make it the base for your personal crusade against the eldar... or for the eldar, or whatever the hell it is that you think you're doing with those cursed aliens.'

In the next second, Corallis and Saulh both lurched forward, tugging their bolt pistols out of their holsters and levelling them, Corallis at Ulantus and Saulh at Corallis. Accusations of heresy demanded action, even if that action might also look like heresy.

'You will not talk to Captain Angelos in this way,' grated Corallis through gritted teeth.

'And you will not level your weapon at Captain Ulantus on his own bridge,' countered Saulh.

Gabriel made no attempt to make Corallis stand down, and he ignored Saulh completely. He was sure that he was standing on the right side of the law. 'Exactly what are you saying, captain? Are you accusing me of being in league with a defiled alien species? Are you accusing me of heresy, Ulantus? Is that what is happening here?'

LYING ACROSS THE altar under the swirling pearl of the Beacon Psykana, the sword fragment flared and pulsed with darker energies. A deep green light emanated from its heart, rising and falling rhythmically like the breath of a sleeping beast. It was its own kind of beacon, radiating an eerie green silence into the Sanctorium Arcanum, sullying the sacred space with an unspeakable and unidentifiable pollution.

From the elevated podium in the apse, Korinth and Zhaphel looked on as the choir telepathica continued its ritual chants. The green-robed astropaths shuffled around the ambulatories with their gaunt, blind faces staring blankly ahead of them. Streams of psychic radiance streamed out of them, converging on the perpetually spinning gyroscope of the Beacon Psykana, which revolved beautifully and impossibly in the air above the altar.

The Summoning of the Exodus had been performed countless times in that ritual space, and the
Librarians of the Secret Order of Psykana were always
there to oversee it.

Even though this was only the second time that
Korinth and Zhaphel had played such a central role,
they were certain that things were not developing as
they should. The first time had been the ceremony for
Brother-Librarian Bherald, who had passed out of this
world at the end of the Cyrene campaign. Korinth
and Zhaphel had placed his helmet onto the altar and
had watched over it for one hundred days, observing
the rites and privileges afforded to a Librarian of the
Order Psykana.

Despite the professed purpose of the Summoning,
they had not expected Bherald to return to them, and
they had performed their duties as exercises in respect
and meditation. After the requisite period of time had
passed, the Brother-Librarians of the Order had committed the helmet to rest, and Bherald's name was
finally entered on the Wall of Accolades as a honoured Blood Raven lost to Chapter.

With Rhamah, things were different. They had no
bodily remains; they had only this shattered fragment
from his sword – the famed *Vairocanum*, that had
once been the weapon of a mighty eldar warrior. It
was the first time that an alien artefact had even been
brought into the Sanctorium, and the Librarians were
uncertain about the possible consequences of having
done so. In the backs of their minds, they had
wondered whether they were performing a kind of
sacrilege. But they had little choice: neglecting or

refusing to perform the Summoning of Exodus would have been tantamount to insulting the eternal soul of Rhamah and damning it to remain forever out of the Emperor's sight. They reasoned that it would be better to commit a small evil in order to achieve a greater good, so the ceremony had gone ahead.

As the shard of metal pulsed and glowed, surrounded by the swirling chants and energy flows of the choir telepathica, Korinth could see an elegant thread of silver being pulled down out of the Beacon Psykana. It grew with slow determination in tiny increments, expanding gradually down towards the sword fragment on the altar beneath the pearlescent sphere. It was as though something in the metallic shard was calling out to the pristine psychic signal and drawing it in, like a spider reeling in its web to reach its prey. And all the time the green glow in the blade fragment grew brighter and more intense.

'I do not trust this alien material, Zhaphel. It responds with its own energy, instead of conducting that of the Beacon towards our lost brother.'

Zhaphel nodded slowly, his gaze absorbed completely by the scene before him. His lips whispered a continuous thread of litanies into the prayer-riddled air and his eyes glistened as though looking upon a distant light. 'I share your concerns.' He was a man of few words.

The wizened and aging Librarian Jonas Urelie, once one of the keepers of the Order Psykana, had also expressed his surprise about the presence of an eldar relic on the altar when he had visited the Sanctorium to pay his respects. He had not offered any opinion about the appropriateness of it as a connection with the lost Librarian, but had simply noted that it was an unusually small item around which to conduct the ceremony. In hindsight, Korinth realised that his old mentor's response had been guarded; it was no longer his place or his right to challenge the rites of Summoning – he had been away in isolation on Rahe's Paradise for many years – and he was a dutiful Space Marine. Perhaps Jonas also had concerns about the alien relic.

As they watched, the silver thread that extended out of the bottom of the beacon gradually thickened into a stream, with energy coursing down towards the sword-shard, which pulsed and ebbed with a swelling life of its own. The stream broke into a river, pouring the pristine silver energy out of the spherical beacon in such quantities that it appeared to be draining it completely. Then, without warning, the orb convulsed and spluttered and a tidal wave of energy crashed down out of the beacon, flooding over the oscillating energy field of the sword fragment and engulfing it in a torrent of mercurial silver.

Korinth and Zhaphel stood transfixed, unable to process what was happening. In all the centuries of its existence, they had never heard of anything like this having happened before. As far as they knew, the Beacon Psykana had burnt undimmed and unbroken since the days of Vidya himself, fuelled by the minds and souls of the brightest and best that the Scholastia Psykana could produce. And now, under their stewardship, it spat and ran thin like a viscous fountain.

For their part, the circling astropaths and the choir telepathica continued to chant and process around the turmoil of energy, with threads of silver still running from their blind faces up into the spluttering, misshapen orb.

They continued for a while as though nothing had happened, splashing through the ripples of energy that ebbed and flowed over the floor, like a tide lapping at their feet. If anything, their chant grew louder and the amount of energy that they were sacrificing into the beacon swelled. After a few seconds, other telepaths and astropaths emerged from the shadows beyond the ambulatories, where the reserves rested before it was their turn to take over in the service of the beacon. But rather than replacing the procession, the newcomers joined it, swelling its ranks and adding their voices to the harmonies and their wills to the flood of energy that struggled to keep the beacon alight.

The two Librarians looked down from the elevated podium in the apse with horror dawning onto their features. The beacon was still burning, but it had ruptured utterly, and as much energy spilled out of it onto the altar as was thrown into it by the heavily reinforced choir. It took all of the reserves of the entire choir telepathica just to keep the pearl of energy flickering with life.

In the midst of the torrent, the sword fragment glowed and radiated life, but it hissed and fizzled under the flood of silvering energy, as though the two energies were rejecting each other. The downpour from the beacon bubbled and blistered as it struck the alien shard, and it seemed clear to Korinth that Rhamah's unusual weapon was the cause of the tumult. He took a step back away from the edge of the podium before darting forward and vaulting off the lip, splashing down into the waves of energy that lapped across the floor of the Sanctorium. Pushing in between the ambulating astropaths, the Librarian strode towards the altar spinning his staff into readiness.

'No, wait!' bellowed Zhaphel from the podium as Korinth brought his staff back in an arc, ready to smash it into the shard of metal on the altar.

Korinth hesitated, looking up at his battle-brother for an explanation.

'Look,' stated Zhaphel simply.

Turning back to the roiling, curdling confusion of energy on the altar, Korinth let his eyes focus more deeply into the myriad reflections. There were other colours hidden in the depths – not only silver and alien green. Flecks of red and blue swam in random patterns, questing for coherence in dizzying whirls. As he stared into the mire, Korinth watched the colours swim into recognisable shapes; after a few seconds his eyes widened in recognition. It was Rhamah. The lost Blood Raven was prone in a desert, surrounded by crackling and impenetrable energy fields. His helmet was missing, and Korinth could see his battle-brother's face blistering in the heat.

As he watched, Korinth saw the eddying swirls of ineffable energy lance and spike into Rhamah's eyes, bursting them open into a maniacal gleam. The eyes expanded suddenly until Korinth could see nothing else in the mess of mercury, and he had to avert his own eyes from the chaotic intensity of the massive stare.

'I REMEMBER LIGHTS... They danced and riddled my mind.' I struggled to find the words to express the memories that rushed back into my head. There was a mixture of humiliation and intrigue in my thoughts as I realised that whatever had caused those lights was probably an even greater threat to me than the stranger who knelt at my side.

Yes, brother, there were lights. The aliens lured you into this trap, tempting your soul down from the cliff-top and into this forsaken city. We found you just in time.

Once again I stared into the Space Marine's face, trying to find the inexpressible comfort of familiarity in his implacable eyes. They shone back at me without light, as though sketched in by a clever but soulless artist. Every time I looked at him, I felt as though I was looking upon a different man, as though myriad souls were competing for expression on his face; all the time, a seething sea of souls simmered below the surface.

'I was like this when you found me?'

Yes, brother. We found you already unconscious, with your blade drawn and discarded. The aliens filled this hall, dancing their decadence and profanation into the fabric of this theatre. The shadows themselves conspired against you as the alien sorceries worked their magic on your broken mind. They gave you answers to questions that you had never thought to ask... which is why you were so vulnerable to them. You need to ask more questions, Son of Ahriman. The boundaries around your thoughts make you weak.

'And, what happened to the aliens?' I asked, trying to assimilate the information that the stranger kept pushing into my head.

I was not comfortable with this kind of communication, and I found it difficult to take possession of the thoughts that ran through my mind. I needed to feel that they were mine, that I had interrogated them and indigenised them before I could let them settle back into my memory, otherwise it would be as though this strange Marine were simply giving me knowledge and memories that I had not considered – he would be changing me from within, making me into somebody else.

Stay out of my mind! It was a subconscious impulse; the thought fired out of my head like a volley from an automatic defence cannon. The stranger had gone too far, and my primal instincts suddenly kicked in where my will had failed me.

The Space Marine's face twitched slightly, like a candle flickering in a sudden draft. His eyes narrowed in marked displeasure. 'The aliens are dead, friend. Look around.'

As he spoke, the Marine gestured with a glittering, golden gauntlet, indicating the circumference of the circular hall.

For the first time, I noticed the slick patterns of red blood that coated his fingertips, and I saw the destruction that had been wrought around the once-beautiful hall. There were slim, humanoid bodies, snapped and broken, slumped into bloody piles around the perimeter of the chamber. Each of the corpses wore brightly coloured and immaculately fitted armour. One or two of the aliens had made it to within a few strides of my position, but they lay prostrate on the ground at the end of a sliding wake of blood, their bodies shredded with bolter fire and ripped open with energy gashes. Their hands were outstretched before them, as through they had been reaching for me when the fire had punched into them.

'Come,' said the Marine, rising to his feet at last. He had watched carefully as I had taken in the scene around me, and something in my reaction had brought him to a decision. 'The Great Lord will want to see you now. He left clear instructions that you should be brought to him when you awoke. It has been so long since last we encountered a brother on our travels. You will come with me, now.'

The Great Lord? Did he meant the Great Father? Are we brothers after all? Taking a final look at the blood-drenched scene around me, I clambered to my feet and stood before the Marine. Our physiques were comparable; we were of similar height and build, and our armour gave us both the same air of formidable strength. Despite facing each other directly, neither of us stepped back. In both of our minds, this was a moment of test.

'Where is this lord?' I asked, challenging him to turn and lead the way.

BEDECKED IN HIS ancient and glorious Terminator armour, Tanthius stepped past Gabriel to flank

Corallis, positioning himself between the raised weapons and his captain.

'Lower your weapon, sergeant,' he said to Saulh, his voice low and rumbling like a landslide. But Saulh's resolve did not waver and his gaze did not shift from Corallis. 'Sergeant,' he repeated. 'This is mutiny and it is heresy. You were there at Rahe's Paradise. You saw what happened. You know that Captain Angelos was right then, and you must suspect that he is right now. Lower your weapon.'

Saulh eye-checked his own captain, looking for direction, and Ulantus nodded slowly. With a complicated mixture of deliberate slowness, reluctance and relief, Saulh lowered his pistol to his side. He did not holster it. How had it come to this?

For his part, Corallis showed no signs of having noticed the release of tension, and he remained alert, his eyes burning with intensity and his pistol trained on Ulantus's head.

'I do not question your intentions, Gabriel,' said Ulantus, letting his eyes reveal the desperateness of the situation. 'But you must see this from my point of view.'

'Must I? Again you seem to fail to appreciate your position on this ship, captain. There is very little that I *must* do for you, short of preventing you from being flushed out into space. The Chapter Masters have faith in my judgment, which is why I am Commander of the Watch and you are not. Are you questioning their judgment too, even if not their intentions?'

'It is not my place to question such things,' conceded Ulantus, feeling the teeth of the trap snap closed around him. 'Explain what you need, *commander*, and I will see what can realistically be done to support you without compromising the position of the Blood Ravens in the Lorn system. This is my warzone, Gabriel, and I will not permit the Ninth Company to be left short.'

'Very well,' said Gabriel calmly, nodding to Corallis to lower his weapon. 'It is imperative that we return to the place in the warp where you lost Librarian Rhamah. It seems likely that there is a rupture in the fabric of the eldar webway at that point. I intend to enter the webway and follow its course. I am given to understand that its terminus is an ancient eldar world of knowledge, and it would be unwise to permit it to fall into less well-intentioned hands.'

Despite his scepticism, Ulantus was still a Blood Raven, and the mention of a world of lost eldar knowledge made his eyes sparkle with interest. 'You have said this much already, captain. I assume that the source of your information on this topic is the injured alien witch?'

'Taldeer, yes.' Gabriel was unphased; they had dealt with this question already, and Ulantus knew better than to start that argument again.

'And how will we find this rupture? Our Navigator made no mention of seeing the webway during the trip through the warp. Indeed, I can recall only myths and legends of any such sightings – are you sure that it is even possible for a Navigator to see this devious alien structure?'

'Taldeer will navigate the ship.'

A stunned silence gripped the control deck. Even Corallis and Tanthius slowly turned their faces towards their captain, staring at him in disbelief; they had not heard this part of the plan. It was bad enough that Gabriel insisted on giving the creature a name, but giving her a ship was beyond belief.

'She is the only one capable of locating the rupture and manoeuvring the *Litany* into place. Without her guidance, this mission comes to nothing,' explained Gabriel, ignoring the incredulity and outrage of his battle-brothers.

'You would rest the future of this venerable vessel in the mind of an alien witch, Commander of the Watch?' Ulantus's eyes had narrowed into slits of disgust.

'I believe that she is trustworthy in this regard. It is not in her interests to lure us into a trap. Her fleet engaged the necron in this sector in order to prevent them from closing the webway portal unearthed by General Sturnn – that portal was the entrance to the route that we must find. The eldar know this ancient enemy, and they know that it fears their control over the immaterium more than anything else. You must also have read the legends, Ulantus? And you are aware of what happened on Rahe's Paradise. The presence of the eldar and their esoteric lore is the key to the suppression of the necron.'

Ulantus hesitated. 'Was the portal destroyed?'

'Yes, but not by the necron.'

'Then by whom?'

A deep, slow voice from behind Gabriel made the group turn. 'We saw a Chaos frigate amongst the wreckage as we passed through the Lorn system. It was not an Alpha Legion vessel, and it was shrouded in psychic energy. We have reason to believe that a powerful sorcerer aboard that vessel may have ruptured the webway and somehow disabled the portal.' Jonas's tone was even and heavy with the authority of scholarship.

'Father Librarian Urelie,' nodded Ulantus, showing his respect for the aging Librarian. 'Forgive me for asking, but what reason do you have to suspect this?'

'We saw the vessel vanish into a warp rift. What we witnessed would be consistent with the explanation provided by the Harlequin,' explained Jonas.

'Harlequin?' Ulantus stared; this was getting worse all the time. 'Harlequin, captain?'

'When we went down to the surface of Lorn, General Sturnn showed us the webway portal that his men had excavated. Taldeer attempted to activate the portal, but the attempt failed because the portal was damaged. She assumed that the necron had been successful. However, an eldar Harlequin emerged from the ruins of the portal–'

'Do you really expect me to believe all of this, Gabriel? Can't you see how incredible this story is?'

'These are incredible times, Ulantus. Taldeer interpreted the Harlequin's dance to mean that a group of Chaos Marines had already made landfall on the ancient eldar world – they shattered the portal as they wrenched it from the planet's surface. The fear is that these Marines will make use of the untold esoteric knowledge hidden on that world. We cannot permit this to happen, Ulantus.'

Ulantus shook his head slowly. He had heard of the Harlequins. There were one or two tomes dedicated to them in the great librarium of the *Omnis Arcanum*, but nobody really believed that they were real. All of the evidence had been collected from fragments of forbidden eldar texts, assembled and reconstructed by agents of the Ordo Xenos in times long ago.

It was widely accepted amongst the most learned of the Blood Ravens Librarians that the Harlequins were part of eldar mythology – little more than characters from folklore that appeared in children's stories. They were supposed to be the guardians of the mythic Black Library – the eldar's grand repository of wisdom and erudition. They were the sentinels that stood guard over the timeless knowledge of the ancient race. But nobody had ever actually *seen* one.

'What do you expect me to say, Gabriel? Do you expect me to let you take the *Litany of Fury* out of a warzone, under the guidance of an alien witch, in pursuit of an unknown alien planet and an enemy that was identified by a mythological creature?'

'Yes,' nodded Gabriel. 'That is what I expect.'

'Why? Why should I do this?' Ulantus looked at Gabriel as though he were insane. 'I cannot do this, Gabriel. You *must* see it. This is not a question of your authority or even your judgment. This is a question of your sanity!'

With crisp efficiency, Corallis snapped his pistol back up into Ulantus's face. 'You will watch your tongue, captain.'

The control deck teetered on the brink of the abyss of heresy once again.

At the same moment, Saulh's pistol was levelled at Corallis, and Tanthius darted forward, forcing himself between the two sergeants and swatting Saulh's pistol with the palm of his gauntlet.

'I understand your concerns, Ulantus,' answered Gabriel, letting his mind drift momentarily back to his visions in the chapel. 'But you must understand that I do not need your approval, I merely demand your compliance.' He made no attempt to make Corallis or Tanthius stand down. 'The best solution here is a compromise: I will record your objections, and I will take my strike cruiser, the *Ravenous Spirit*, on this mission, leaving you with the *Litany* to consolidate this field of victory. Your should be aware, Captain Ulantus, that your actions in this matter will not pass unnoticed.'

'You should also be aware of this, Captain Angelos. But it will be as you say.' With that, Ulantus strode past Tanthius and off the control deck.

Saulh flicked his eyes from Corallis to Tanthius, as though looking for something hidden in their purpose, and then he marched off after his captain, leaving the officers of the Third Company in command of the bridge.

THE SPACE MARINE pushed the massive double-doors, leaning into them to shift their immense weight. They cracked open and then gave way, swinging away from us in a cloud of dazzling dust, as the brilliant red light of the triple suns poured out of the ancient room beyond.

I should wait to be summoned. Something in the air told me that I should be careful of the man who waited for me beyond those doors. It was not merely the seriousness of the deference that was suddenly and completely affected by the Space Marine who had escorted me from the grand, circular hall twenty storeys below; there was a subtle power in the air itself, as though it were charged with unspeakable energies just beyond the confines of this reality. It felt as though an electric anticipation was oozing out of the immaterium and into this realm, permeating the very air that I breathed. Whoever waited in the room ahead, he was surrounded by an incalculable field of power.

No, you should merely enter. Unless... unless you are afraid of me.

For the second time, I was shocked to feel the presence of another's thoughts where I anticipated only my own. I chastised myself silently, feeling the weakness of my control and the vulnerabilities of my mind. Whoever this was, he should not be able to read my thoughts so easily, and he should certainly not be able to plant his own into my mind so effortlessly.

I will not fear what I do not know. Ignorance is the spark of curiosity, not of fear, I replied

Noble sentiments, indeed. You have come to the right place, friend of Ahriman.

The thoughts were of an entirely different quality from those of the Marine that had knelt with me in the hall. These were heavy and light all at once. It was like having chilled mercury poured through my mind. The words were icy and yet liquid, viscous without being sticky, substantial but sparkling with reflections.

It was not an alien voice. It didn't even feel external to my head. It felt as though it entered my mind from some forgotten place in the depths of my soul, rather than trying to prod and force its way in from outside. It felt comfortable and nauseating all at once, like too much rich food.

In front of me, the Space Marine stood with his back to one of the doors, holding it open. He nodded with his spectral, eerie head, gesturing for me to enter the room.

I held his shimmering eyes for a moment, and then walked through the door way, my strides filled with resolve and confidence.

The doors clanged shut behind me, with the Marine on the outside. I did not look round.

'Welcome.'

For a moment I could not locate the origins of the deep, resonant voice. It seemed to echo around the room, as though refracted and reflected from thousands of mirrors. I turned with slow deliberation, letting my eyes scan over the hundreds of aisles of books and scrolls that filled the room. Great shafts of red light poured in from the circular window cavity that dominated the far wall, casting the thousands of shelves and millions of books into a bloody hue.

There was movement beyond the window opening, presumably from a balcony outside, and an impressive silhouette appeared into the blaze of red light, obliterating the suns. It paused without entering the room.

'You are welcome here, friend of Ahriman. Do you bring questions with you?'

I squinted against the flood of light that the figure wore as an aura, raising one hand to shield my eyes.

'Yes, I have many questions.' The name of Ahriman suddenly seemed to make a connection in my memory. I knew that name. It meant something to me. I had heard it before, or read it in some forgotten manuscript. My mind coated it in a sense of urgency, as though it knew that the name itself was important or dangerous, but I could not remember what it meant.

'You wish to know who I am?' The figure in the light did not move, but his voice seemed to shift freely around the room – at once behind me, beside me and in front of me.

'You are Ahriman,' I replied, realising that it must be true even as I spoke.

'And you?' There was a new quality in the strangely disembodied voice, but I could not tell whether it was surprise or pleasure. 'Are you a friend of Ahriman?'

'You have said so. I am better at questions than answers today.'

'As you say, so it is.'

He's testing me, checking my responses. Is he playing? No, this is too serious: he suspects something.

What do you think I suspect of you, friend?

'As I said, I am not good at answers today.' I cursed inwardly for letting the stranger into my mind.

I must keep my guard – I do not trust this one. He is more subtle than his Marines. His thoughts carry death in their undertones.

'Where is this place?' I asked, taking my eyes off the silhouette and looking around the librarium.

There was a pause, and I imagined a smile on the indiscernible face. 'You have many questions, I'm sure.'

'That is not an answer.'

'What makes you think that I have any answers for you?'

'Did you bring me here to ask *me* questions? I have no answers for you, Ahriman. I don't even have answers for myself.' *I don't even know who I am.*

'You are Rhamah, a lost brother of Ahriman.'

I nodded. *Yes. He has some answers after all.*

'This place is part of the fabled Arcadian Librarium, one of the most extensive repositories of knowledge in the galaxy.'

Ahriman stepped into the room as he spoke, emerging from his own silhouette as he moved away from the flood of light in the window. The golden details on his deep blue armour shone with life, bursting into ruby radiance as the light of the triple suns bounced off the purity seals. The armour was inscribed from boots to shoulder guards in intricate, cursive scripts, only some of which were recognisably human, and only a few of which I could understand. I realised immediately that this was the sorcerer that I had seen in front of the Thunderhawk in the desert. 'And this room,' he continued, waving a casual and encompassing hand, 'is perhaps the most valuable room on the entire planet. It is the resting place of the *Legend of Lanthrilaq*.'

Ahriman strode over to a heavy stone desk between the book stacks. It was covered in piles of manuscripts, tomes and scrolls. The great sorcerer tossed a few volumes aside, checking their spines casually, and then he pushed a whole pile off onto the ground, disregarding the ancient tomes as though they were little more than irrelevances.

Picking up one of the remaining books, he turned and offered it to me, holding it out like a gift. 'You have heard of this book, I'm sure.'

I shook my head and took a step towards him, reaching out my hand to take the book. 'I do not remember.' But something stirred in my memory; the name meant something to me, although I could not yet recall its significance. I knew that I could not resist the offer to touch such an ancient text. Its lure was sufficient to momentarily overcome my suspicions about the mysterious sorcerer.

As my fingers closed around the edge of the book and I began to pull it out of his grasp, I felt Ahriman resist me. For a moment, we stood alone in the blood-lit librarium, our fingers only centimetres apart as we both gripped the tome. Delicate tendrils of energy arced between our hands, dancing over the dusty cover of the book. I wondered whether Ahriman had suddenly changed his mind and decided not to let me hold the book, but then I looked up into his face and saw the truth.

It was a face unlike any that I had ever seen.

With a faint smile, the features tensed suddenly and then relaxed. At the same moment, the book slid from Ahriman's grasp and I withdrew it, taking a step back to put some distance between me and the sorcerer, holding his inexplicable gaze all the time.

'Lanthrilaq the Swift was one of the great eldar warriors that once did battle with the star god, Kaelis Ra. It is said that he wielded one of the hundred Blades of Vaul in that epic duel.'

I carried the book over towards the circular window, holding it carefully into the flood of ruddy light. The cover glittered with runes and images that had been etched delicately into the dark material. I could make out the phonetic ideograms for Lanthrilaq – the swift one. They were run through by the image of a glorious blade, striking diagonally across the cover. The blade was damaged and chipped; its tip was missing completely, but it was decorated with a breathless whirl of alien characters that seemed to charge even its image with life and energy. On the jewel of the pommel there was a single runic symbol: Vaul – the smith-god of the ancient eldar.

'In times long ago, before even our Emperor drew breath in this galaxy, it is said that the Death-Bringer brought portents of the eldar's demise,' continued Ahriman. He was speaking slowly and with affected drama, watching me study the book, waiting for a response.

What does he want me to say? He mentioned 'our Emperor,' but his words were chilled and tinged with

something other than reverence – or, perhaps, with
something in addition to reverence. Who is this Ahriman?

'None could stand before the might of this star-god,
for it carried the scythe of death itself. The blood of
entire systems could not slake its thirst, and the greatest of eldar heroes fell under its blade. But the ancient
eldar were cunning, and they knew that there was
more than one way to humble a god – this is their
first great teaching to us, my friend: even gods can be
shown humility.

'Through their whispered cunning, the eldar turned
the c'tan against themselves, and they watched as the
galaxy degenerated into unholy feasts of star-flesh.
But Kaelis Ra saw the plan and turned his own wrath
against the c'tan that betrayed his cause. The Nightbringer butchered its own kin, laying waste to the
stars themselves in order to bring the necrontyr back
into line.

'Meanwhile, the eldar were not idle. Their greatest
warrior, Kaela Mensha Khaine consulted with the
Laughing God and his Harlequins, receiving wisdom
and advice. Then he struck a bargain with Vaul, the
smith-god, commissioning him to forge one hundred
blade-wraiths – swords of such glorious
craftsmanship and power that they could slay the
gods themselves. These were the legendary Blades of
Vaul.

'With rage incandescent in his soul, Khaine led one
hundred of his finest warriors in a final stand against
Kaelis Ra. Each of the eldar faced hordes of silvered
necontyr so vast that the horizon glittered like the
heavens in all directions. Yet, armed with the

blade-wraiths, the eldar warriors knew no dread and no fear. They formed into a sweeping circle, each defending the back of another, and they fought like mythical heroes for seven days and seven nights, never tiring or falling back.

'But then the ring was broken. Lanthrilaq the Swift grew suddenly tired and drained of energy. His face turned pale and his features became gaunt. In an explosion of darkness, his blade-wraith cracked, falling from his hands into the corpse-strewn earth.'

I could feel Ahriman's eyes on me as he spoke, but I did not look at him. My attention was captured by the image of the broken eldar blade on the cover of the book, and saw that it resembled the now mutilated form of *Vairocanum*. I realised that the sorcerer could see the association growing in my mind.

'Vaul had tricked the eldar; one of his blades was imperfect and flawed. The energies that pulsed and glowed within its mystical structure were imbalanced and unstable. Vaul had tricked Khaine, leaving him vulnerable to the wrath of the Nightbringer. Lanthrilaq fell and Khaine's formation was ruined. What followed was little more than a slaughter – the eldar heroes fell one after the other, valiant in their desperate and futile fight, as the thousands of silvering necrontyr overran their position. Their blades were shattered and ruined, falling into the rivers of blood as sparkling shards.

'Only Khaine himself stood above the fray, his spear flashing like lightning. On the point of his own exhaustion, Khaine came face to face with Kaelis Ra. At the last, as the Nightbringer's scythe sliced toward his neck, Khaine remembered the words of the Laughing God and he danced inside the blow, thrusting forward with his lightning spear and skewering Kaelis Ra just as his form solidified in order to land his own strike. The star god screamed and exploded into a rain of silver. The scattering essence of the Nightbringer shredded the teeming necrontyr, vaporising them and rendering the world into a mercurial flood, leaving only Khaine standing, howling his costly victory to the heavens.'

'Why are you telling me this story, Ahriman?' I asked, finally looking up from the book. The sorcerer was leaning against the stone desk with a heavy book in each hand, casually glancing at the pages as though mildly indifferent to the ancient knowledge that they contained. His manner sent a chill through my spine.

Is he suggesting that I am a weak link, like Lanthrilaq? Perhaps he implies that I have been cheated by those whom I have trusted?

'What do you find in that tale, friend?'

'Is this a test?'

'Everything is a test. There are treasures hidden in all our words and in every story. The test of our power is whether we can identify and find those treasures.'

'The story is about Lanthrilaq's blade,' I concluded quickly.

'How so?'

'We know that the other ninety-nine blades were destroyed, but Lanthrilaq's fell from his hands whilst only damaged. The story does not say anything about what happened to it after the battle. We might suppose that it still exists in some form.'

Ahriman's face shifted into a smile. 'Very good, friend Rhamah. What is not told is often more important than what is pushed into our faces.'

'You suppose that this blade is here?'

'Supposition is bad scholarship; I would not presume. But its location is certainly worthy of investigation.'

'Why would you want to find this blade? Do you seek to wield it for yourself, Ahriman? Should we not exercise judgement about the types of treasures that are appropriate for us to possess? Some types of knowledge are too dangerous, no matter what their potential power.'

'Why should we be deprived of such things? We are not responsible for the mistakes of others, nor for the existence of any artefacts. We are responsible only for what we choose to do: knowledge is never dangerous on its own, friend Rhamah. Despite its imperfections, this is clearly a weapon of immense power, fashioned by the hands of a god. Certainly this is a blade worthy of Ahriman. I would be as blind as a fool not to recognise this. At the very least, we have a responsibility to investigate.'

I watched the sorcerer's eyes light up as he talked about the lost blade. He cast the two books from his hands, sending them skidding across the floor, and his face glowed with a sudden and maniacal flush of life. Just talking about the ancient eldar artefact seemed to animate him, and a shimmering energy field flickered into life, oscillating around his body like an aura. But there was something about his attitude that disturbed me. I shared his excitement about the possibility of discovering more about ancient and forgotten lore, but I felt an instinctive sense of scepticism about utilising one of Vaul's blades: it was a treacherous and alien artefact, with no place in the hands of one of the Emperor's angels.

Knowledge is power.

Exactly so. The thought was Ahriman's but it resounded in my mind as though it originated there. I had only just met this charismatic sorcerer, but already he was inside my mind, planting the seeds of a thirst for new knowledge and wisdom.

'Knowledge has many guardians,' I began, studying the sorcerer's unreal features as they shifted and moved over his face. I wondered whether we understood this role in the same way. 'Should I assume that the dead eldar in the hall downstairs were the guardians of this librarium?'

'That would seem to be a sensible conclusion.'

As Ahriman spoke, a flicker of blue flashed between the shafts of red light. A fluttering of green danced between two of the book stacks, and a blur of darkness streaked past the window. Instinctively, I tugged *Vairocanum* from its sheath and turned, tracking the vague and indiscernible movements. Out of the corner of my eye, I could see Ahriman lift his force staff from the desk, a broad grin cracking through his shimmering face. He turned, bringing his staff around in an ostentatious flourish, and then stepped back towards me. As the swirling colours started to solidify all around us, crystallising into the recognisable shapes of eldar Harlequins, I found myself standing back to back with Ahriman, surrounded by a ring of alien menace.

'Knowledge is power!' I yelled, hearing my words echoed from the mouth of the great sorcerer behind me. Then I sprang forward towards the Death Jesters, bringing *Vairocanum* around in a punishing arc.

CHAPTER SEVEN: RUPTURE

ANY RUPTURE IN *the webway is like a magnet for all the daemonic energies of the warp. To begin with, it might be little bigger than a man, perhaps torn out of the fabric of the timeless maze by the blaze of a force weapon, or perhaps it might grow from the tiniest of imperfections in the structure itself, gradually eroding and expanding throughout the millennia by the persistent and desperate thirst of the chaotic powers.*

Time passes strangely in the warp, if it can be said to pass at all, but that does not mean that it is a static or changeless realm. The real character of the immaterium is Chaotic; it contains time and space, but not in the ordered and predictable ways that they are contained in the material realms.

In the ancient texts of the eldar farseers, now hidden in the depths of the fabled Black Library, it was once hypothesised that the warp was an expression of the terrible responsibilities of the farseers themselves. It contains images, echoes and reflections of the myriad time lines that penetrate reality, swirling and congealing around possibilities that seem satisfactory according to the natures of whatever unspeakable beings could be satisfied.

In the story of the Great Fall of the eldar, it is told how the daemon of Slaanesh was given form in the warp because of the lascivious, decadent and thirsty turn in the consciousness of the eldar themselves. As soon as the daemon roared into existence, it had suddenly always been there, and the farseers of the eldar people suddenly realised that they had always known that it was there, lurking on the fringes of their vision, waiting to emerge into a fully shaped nightmare.

The webway itself is only partly contained within the warp, although it has no existence outside the immaterium. It is an artefact from the golden days of the eldar empire, criss-crossing the galaxy like an intricate, dew-dappled spider's web. It is a maze and a labyrinth. It is a network of tunnels and passages, some as small as a man and others so large that a great space fleet could pass through unconstrained.

Like the foresight of the farseers and the emergence of Slaanesh, the webway is a testament to the profound and intimate connections between the eldar and the warp itself. The project to harness the spaceless and timeless warp was the greatest of the ancient eldar's achievements. To travel through the webway is to traverse the warp itself, insulated and protected by the golden passages of material space that the eldar managed to stabilise.

The ancient and glorious fleets of the Sons of Asuryan could blink across the galaxy in an instant, dropping into the webway in the eastern rim and emerging almost instantaneously in the cusp of the western arc; the trip through the warp was literally timeless when perceived from the material realm.

In the impossibly ancient past, at the time when the wars between the Old Ones and the Star Gods raged, the webway was the salvation of the eldar and the bane of the c'tan. The terror of the night, Kaelis Ra, vowed to return and destroy the structure that riddled the universe with the psychic curse of the eldar. Although the Nightbringer fell under the shining spear of Khaine, its vow remains to be fulfilled.

(Extract from *The Quest for the Black Library*, author unknown. Fragments of the original text recovered by Librarian Jonas Urelie of the Blood Ravens, and stored aboard the *Omnis Arcanum* [Librarium Sanctorum, 23.1274:c.xvi])

A RED LIGHT PULSED on the bridge, and a harsh klaxon pounded out an intrusion alert. Something alien had penetrated into the very heart of the Third Company's strike cruiser.

The *Ravenous Spirit* streaked through the timeless dimensions of the warp, ripping through the tempests and storms of uncontrolled energy that roiled and lashed around the venerable hull. The control deck was strangely silent, as the crew sat transfixed, staring at their terminals like an audience watching an intricate performance. The vessel was being controlled from elsewhere, and there was nothing that the serfs could do but watch. Aside from the persistent alarm, nothing in the chamber suggested that the *Spirit* was in peril; the crew appeared calm and there was only one Blood Raven officer at his station. Sergeant Kohath stood immovably in the centre of the deck, his eyes fixed on the dizzying kaleidoscope of colours that whirled and smeared across the main viewscreen. Yet there was something inexplicable in the air, a tension that held the scene on the cusp of a flashing red hysteria.

'Loren?' growled Kohath without shifting his gaze. 'Anything?'

'No, sergeant. Nothing that I can detect... But these sensors are not designed–'

'–to work in the warp,' cut in Kohath irritably. 'Yes, I know.'

Loren nodded silently, understanding the sergeant's brusque manner. None of them liked what was happening, but it was certainly not the place of a pledged-serf to question the plans of the Commander of the Watch. He knew the meaning of his pledge, and he was proud to be in service. However, he had never anticipated that pledging service to the Blood Ravens and the Emperor would place him under the power of an alien witch. The serf was accustomed to feeling powerless: his function was to follow the orders of the commanding officer without question, hesitation, or error. But this was an impotence of an entirely different nature: the *Ravenous Spirit* had been placed under the control of an alien consciousness, and even the Blood Ravens themselves had lost their usually implacable sense of control. It was like being in free-fall, waiting for the final impact.

In the klaxon-punctuated silence, the image on the viewscreen shifted and changed suddenly. A thin streak of gold lanced across the monitor, a band of radiance cutting through the quagmire of sickly colours and swirling darkness. Whilst all the other shapes and images seemed to swim and morph freely in nauseatingly chaotic patterns, the tube of gold appeared solid and material. As they watched, the golden tube thickened and grew larger until it dominated the screen.

'Loren?'

'I guess that's it, sergeant. The regular sensors are still non-functional.'

Kohath watched for a few more seconds, noting the way in which the curdling tendrils of colour in the void around the lance of gold lapped and licked at its structure. Momentary flashes of light revealed the ghosts of beastly figures clambering over the golden surface, clawing at its integrity with a violent hunger. The eldar witch had done something to the imaging system; it projected the visions from her mind's eye. They were seeing what she was seeing.

'Captain,' said Kohath, clicking the *Spirit*'s vox-relay to open a channel to the Navigatorium. A blast of static fed back into the control room. 'Captain Angelos,' he repeated, 'it appears that we have found the webway.'

THE ELDAR SEER was tiny in the massive throne, held high on a pedestal in the centre of the vast

Navigatorium that domed up out of the top of the *Ravenous Spirit*. Her figure looked almost impossibly slight and fragile, and her pale complexion had taken on the hue of death. A maze of wires, pipes and connections studded her limp body, trailing off into the walls and into the ceiling, and plugging directly into the labyrinthine structure of the throne itself. She was hard wired into the very soul of the ancient vessel, feeling its passage through the warp as though it were her own. Every few seconds, she flinched and shuddered, as though shivering against the touch of a profound cold, making the myriad wires shake and oscillate like tendrils.

Gabriel watched the pain and suffering of the eldar witch. Despite himself, he felt some pangs of sympathy for the frail female, and his mind wandered back to the agonies of the young neophyte, Ckrius, who still laid strapped to the adamantium operating table in the Implantation Chamber of the *Litany of Fury*. So much pain.

The captain's eye-lids twitched involuntarily and closed for a moment, giving his mind a fraction of a second of darkness in which to fill his thoughts full of images of terror and suffering. The vivid memory of Isador's face flickered and vanished, replaced by the rain of melting flesh that fell from the bodies of the people of Cyrene.

A reassuringly firm hand gripped his shoulder, and Gabriel realised that he was swaying slightly. Although his eyes were wide open, his vision was tinged with a wash of silver light. At the touch from Jonas, the light flickered and vanished abruptly.

'Gabriel – are you alright?' asked Jonas, steadying his captain and eying him with concern. He remembered the incident on Rahe's Paradise, when Gabriel had collapsed during the Blood Trials.

'Fine, father. Thank you.' If he had to be deprived of the counsel and companionship of both Prathios and Isador, he was relieved to have the wizened old Librarian at his side.

Standing behind the captain, Librarians Korinth and Zhaphel exchanged glances. They had heard the rumours about Gabriel, but they had not taken them too seriously, and they had certainly not thought that they would witness any of the symptoms so quickly. A moment of physical weakness hardly constituted an act of heresy, but it was highly unusual for a Blood Raven to display any kind of unprovoked frailty. The two Ninth Company Librarians had only been aboard the *Ravenous Spirit* for a couple of hours, but already they were beginning to understand that the Commander of the Watch and Captain of the Third Company was no ordinary Marine.

Bound into the Navigator's throne, Taldeer twitched then spasmed. Her slender muscles tensed and her limbs snapped straight, transforming her into a rigid board. A disembodied moan echoed through the domed chamber, but it did not seem to originate from the eldar's throat.

Immediately, Techmarine Ephraim darted forward, pressing the eldar seer down into the throne with his human arms whilst the mechanical augmetics chattered and whirred between the various couplings and connectors that linked the female alien to the heart of the *Spirit*. It was as though the ancient vessel was trying to reject the alien incursion, like a body rejecting an incompatible organ. But the *Ravenous Spirit* was already deeply immersed in the warp; if the eldar witch were ejected from the seat of the Navigator now, then the entire vessel and all of its crew would be lost. Even if he had to hold the alien in place with the brute strength of his arms, Ephraim would ensure that she could not break loose. Pain wracked her features, and her suffering was obvious to them all, but Ephraim's concern was for the machine spirit of the *Spirit* itself; if safe passage meant the death of the eldar witch, then so be it. Her agonies meant nothing.

In the back of his mind Ephraim toyed with the possibility of throwing the relay and cutting the eldar out of the control circuit – the regular Navigator was already strapped into the back-up station in the *Litany*'s stern. If things got too bad, at least he had this option, although he could not throw the switch without the approval of Captain Angelos, no matter what the circumstances.

'Brother Librarian Korinth,' said Jonas, turning to face the Ninth Company Marine. It was as though the father Librarian could sense the constellation of doubts in the younger Librarian's mind. 'Focus is the key to insight. See whether you and Brother Zhaphel can be of assistance in this.'

The Librarians nodded crisply and strode up the spiral of steps towards the throne, where Ephraim continued to work on the tortured form of Taldeer. They stood to either side of the alien, towering over her twisted and slight body, letting the mechanical arms of the Techmarine twitch and flitter around her head and torso, keeping the connectors tight and secure.

'She is being rejected,' muttered Ephraim, hardly looking up from his work as the two Librarians took up positions beside him. 'The *Spirit* will not accept her presence here, and the interface was not designed with an alien psyker in mind. The connections are flimsy and malformed, and the psychic resonances are off-kilter. I am amazed that she had managed to stay engaged for so long.'

Korinth nodded with understanding. It was bad enough that the vessel had been forced into the warp without a Navigator in the throne; many ships would have rebelled from the very start of this process. But to be made dependent on an alien mind and alien eyes might in itself be enough to bring the cruiser to the point of self-destruction. All over the *Spirit*, through its twisting corridors, antechambers, docks and control rooms, intrusion alarms were pulsing and klaxons were sounding. The ship thought that it was under attack from within, even as it found itself plunged into the dizzying, immaterial mire of the warp itself outside.

Looking down into the alien's contorted and beautiful face, Korinth felt a mixture of emotions competing for his will. He had never been this close to an eldar seer before, and a deep seated hatred and disgust seethed in his heart. A race-memory, hardwired into his being, awoke without provocation. He felt a wave of revulsion and offence flowing over him, and the corner of his lip snarled involuntarily. *Of course the ship is rejecting this wretched creature. She is the damned and the heretic. She is the ancient foe of the Emperor. She is the genesis of cursed erudition, that which leads our disciplined minds into the abyss.*

The thoughts were only half contained in his head, and Zhaphel looked across at his battle-brother, noting the expression of repugnance that scarred his face. *You are not being asked to trust this creature; you are being asked to trust the Commander of the Watch.*

But I do not trust him, Zhaphel. And neither do you. Being asked to trust the untrustworthy is little more than a test of loyalty, and this is no time for games. Korinth looked up from the wretched, broken body and fixed Zhaphel with his uneven dark eyes. *You and I both know why we are here.*

The other Librarian held his battle-brother's red and black gaze for a moment, letting him see the fires that simmered behind his own golden eyes. The delicate metallic emblem of the Order Psykana glinted from behind locks of his long, grey hair like a third eye, just above his left temple.

He nodded slowly. After what had happened in the Sanctorium Arcanum, what choice did they have? Even Captain Ulantus had been forced to let them go, despite his insistence that Captain Angelos had simply gone insane. Korinth and Zhaphel had impressed upon him the urgency and secrecy of their responsibility to the Order Psykana, and they had suggested that they might be released temporarily into the command of Father Librarian Jonas Urelie, who had recently returned to the Third Company. Begrudgingly, Ulantus had conceded this, and he had accepted that the Librarians were unable to tell him the reasons for their actions.

It was not unprecedented for an entire squad of Blood Ravens Librarians to be formed under the semi-autonomous command of a father Librarian; indeed, this was the usual manner in which the Order Psykana deployed its unique power. To some extent, because of its complicated and intricate connections through the Ecclesiarchy and Scholastia Psykana, back even to the grandest halls of Terra itself, the Secret Orders of Psykana resembled an entrenched organisation in its own right: it had its own internal hierarchy and a distinct sense of purpose.

In practice, however, every single Librarian in the Order was a Blood Raven before anything else. Moving from the Ninth Company to join a team under the command of Jonas Urelie was little different from being seconded into the Third Company itself, under the command of Gabriel Angelos. Ulantus had known this, and he had hated being forced to release two of his most powerful Librarians into the service of the unsavoury Commander of the Watch; too many decisions had been taken out of his hands over the course of the last day, and he was furious with indignation and frustration.

A piercing cry cracked through the Navagatorium as the eldar seer's body went rigid, straining up against the tubes, wires, and restraints. She thrashed against the weight of Ephraim as he pressed down on her chest. Despite his massively superior strength, the Techmarine was struggling to keep the slight alien from ripping clear of the throne.

The shrill scream echoed around the chamber, cutting shivers from the spines of the Blood Ravens. Zhaphel planted the palm of his hand on the alien's face and slammed her head back against the adamantium structure of the throne itself, silencing the scream and making her body fall suddenly limp. The warning klaxons stopped abruptly.

Turning in the sudden silence, the Librarian could see Gabriel pounding up the spiral stairs towards the throne.

'What did you do, Librarian?' he demanded.

Before Zhaphel could answer, Gabriel was on his knees at the side of the eldar witch. He gripped her hand in one of his own, and reached for her blood smeared face. Just then, Jonas caught up with him and joined the group around the throne. They all looked down at the tiny form of the alien creature, broken, bleeding and shattered by the agonies of the warp and the hostility of the *Ravenous Spirit*.

'Is she dead, captain?' asked Jonas, giving words to fill the silence.

With an eruption of noise, the incursion alarms suddenly started again, and the witch's eyes flicked open so unexpectedly that the Space Marines started.

Gabriel. It is filled with horror! Her fathomless eyes seemed to contain the warp itself, and Gabriel could see the daemonic tempest that raged around the webway as though it were reflected in the deep black of her pupils.

VAIROCANUM SPARKED AND flared as it collided with the shimmering blades that protruded out of the back of the alien's hands. The eldar Harlequin twisted rapidly, but did not turn away. Instead, the lithe warrior darted inside the arc of my sword, punching forward with its other fist, which was tipped with a long, sharpened barrel. There was no time for me to parry or retreat. As the fleet figure threw its weight into the counter-attack, I dropped my shoulder and let myself fall forward into a roll, flipping over the top of the bizarre weapon.

Rolling back onto my feet, I swung *Vairocanum* back in a wide crescent, turning in time to see the glowing blade slice perfectly through the alien's throat. But there was no blood and there was no deathly scream. Instead, the eldar warrior flickered slightly, like a holographic projection that my sword had momentarily disturbed. At the same instant, I caught sight of a movement to one side. Out the corner of my eye, I saw the same alien warrior lunging at me, its terrible, skull-like face grinning with insane excitement.

Two places at once! The realisation struck me just before the pointed barrel of the Harlequin's weapon. I felt a dull pain punch into my abdomen, and I realised that the weapon had just kissed the surface of my armour but had failed to break through. Glancing down, I saw a fibrous web erupt out of the barrel, sending tiny tendrils questing over the surface of my armour, searching for seams and weaknesses.

But when I looked up again, the Harlequin was not where it should have been. Even though I could feel the scraping impact of the Harlequin's Kiss on the right hand side of my armour, the eldar warrior appeared to be dancing off to the left, leaving a multicoloured blur of light in its wake.

Shaking my head to clear my thoughts, I spun *Vairocanum* vertically, bringing it around in a defensive circle in front of me, ensuring that it would slice through anything that was pressing against me. Although the Harlequin appeared to be several metres away, I felt my blade bite into its gauntleted arm, and I pushed the sword through the resistance offered by the alien's bones. This time there was a shriek of pain. The holographic image of the eldar flickered again and one of its hands faded away. A clattering impact next to my feet told me that I had severed the deceitful creature's forearm.

'They have some kind of holographic camouflage.' I didn't want Ahriman to be taken unawares. I could feel the movements of the sorcerer behind me, as he did battle with others from the Harlequin troupe.

Yes. Holo-suits. Ahriman could give the technology a name. *They mask the fighter and project his image elsewhere.*

Ahriman was a blaze of power. His force staff swirled and spun, spilling lances of warp fire into jagged forks of lightning, which ripped through the mire of misperception that surrounded the two Marines. The holographic images flickered and faded, pulsing with inconsistency as the sorcerer's power interfered with their signal. At the same time, the Harlequin troupe itself wavered and glimmered into intermittent visibility. There were probably twenty of them in the librarium, each leaping and dancing with incredible vitality and menace.

I braced my sword and turned to stand at Ahriman's shoulder. Here and there between the book stacks, I could see the dizzying distortion patterns that had lured me there in the first place. They shimmered and burst into blindingly bright shards of multicoloured light, filling my thoughts with nausea.

Domino-fields. Ahriman gave them a name too, as though sensing my question before I could give it a voice. *It's a blanket light disruptor. The deceitful wretches are hidden in that cloud of light somewhere*. As the thoughts entered my head, I saw a massive javelin of power stab out from Ahriman's staff and pound into the myriad lights. They blinked momentarily as an explosion incinerated several shelves of books, but then they shone even more brilliantly again, as though unaffected by Ahriman's blast.

Several of the oddly coloured Harlequins suddenly stopped their continuous and disorientating movement, turning their hideous masks towards us, letting us gaze upon the steady and unflinching horror of their features. For a fraction of a second, neither Ahriman nor I moved; we just stared at the

face of death itself, recognising in the features of
those alien tricksters the horror of our own condition. It was as though our fears were somehow
amplified and projected by the masks.

A fraction of a second was all that the aliens
needed, and they charged forward in a cacophony of
yells, shrieks and ululations. Somehow their masks
seemed to swell and grow to unnatural sizes, as
though threatening to fill our entire field of vision,
seducing our eyes with their horror and overwhelm-
ing our senses. But under cover of this illusionary
onslaught, powerblades and riveblades slashed and
jousted towards us.

Shoulder to shoulder, Ahriman and I crashed forwards into the tempest of blades, lashing and
thrashing with staff, sword and javelins of warp
power. At that instant, the doors to the librarium
burst open, cracking off their hinges and crashing to
the floor. Without turning, we knew that a squad of
Prodigal Sons had heard the battle and had come to
reinforce us. Battle-brothers. Immediately, volleys of
bolter fire started to whine past my head, punching
into the discombobulating, ever-shifting formation
of Harlequins.

FOR A LONG moment Korinth stood in silence, as
though teetering on the cusp between obedience
and defiance. He had joined the *Ravenous Spirit* with
full knowledge about the reputation of the eccentric
Captain Angelos. After the events that had transpired
in the Sanctorium Arcanum, he and Zhaphel had
agreed that they had no choice but to return to the

place where Rhamah had vanished. The lore of the Exodus of the Summoning was very clear about the necessary responses to anomalies in the ceremony. Captain Angelos and the *Ravenous Spirit* were the only conceivable way back. However, nothing had prepared him for the full scale of Angelos's vision.

'This course of action is insane.' There, it was said. The low resonant tones echoed slowly through the cavernous space of the docking bay, bouncing lethargically off the hulls of the Thunderhawks that lay dormant. The bay pulsed with red warning lights and a steady, mind-dulling siren wailed persistently. Although the alien witch had been severed from the control loop and replaced by the Navigator in the stern-based backup throne, the ship was still suffering the trauma of submersion in the warp and the aftershocks of the violations by the eldar mind.

Nobody offered any response to Korinth's objections. They just ignored him, busying themselves with heavy equipment and supplies, loading them into the nearest Thunderhawk and then bracing them into harnesses for the journey. A gaggle of servitors and serfs milled around the hull, directed by sharp shouts from Techmarine Ephraim. They were making some modifications to the structure of the gunship, adding a series of new sensor-arrays and shield relays.

Korinth turned to Zhaphel, who was standing to one side of the Thunderhawk with his Dorian force-axe slung imposingly over his shoulder. Under his other arm was his helmet. His golden eyes glinted from behind a careless mess of hair, and the mark of the Order Psykana shimmered faintly like a third eye, but he did not turn to meet his battle-brother's gaze. He appeared lost in contemplation, watching the events unfold before him as though quite detached from them.

This is a step too far, Yupres. Surely you can see that. It is one thing to have faith in the captain or even to obey him, but it is quite another to condone foolishness or even heresy.

Very slowly, Zhaphel turned his head towards Korinth, bringing his golden eyes to meet the uneven, red and black gaze of his comrade. He said nothing, but his silence said it all. Nobody ever called him Yupres any more; it was the name that his mother had given him when he was born. It didn't belong to him any more. The galaxy had changed utterly since the last time that anyone had uttered that name, and he had changed even more.

We are explorers, Korinth. We are bound by duty and by nature. And that was it. No arguments, just statements of fact. *There will be no talk of heresy today.*

A rush of movement from the other Space Marines next to the Thunderhawk's ramp drew the Librarian's attention over to the main hangar doors. They rolled open, withdrawing into the ceiling of the docking bay to reveal an unlikely group of figures. Captain Angelos was there with Father Librarian Urelie and Apothecary Medicius. Between them they were carrying a large, heavy throne, in which was slumped the broken and contorted figure of the eldar seer. Even from that distance, Korinth could see the toxic, alien blood coursing out of the wounds that had opened up around the couplings and connectors that had been pushed into the witch's flesh. If she had been human, Korinth would have given her up for dead.

Tanthius and Corallis leapt down from the interior of the Thunderhawk and dashed over to assist their captain, pounding across the metal floor with heavy boots.

As the group approached the gunship, Gabriel and Jonas broke away, letting the others carry the alien up the ramp into the Thunderhawk, trusting that they would take appropriate care of her.

'Ephraim,' called Gabriel, looking up onto the roof of the gunship to find the Techmarine in the eerie pulsing red light. 'You will be needed inside. She is here.'

'As you wish, captain,' replied Ephraim, vaulting down and swinging himself around into the open hatch.

At last, Gabriel turned to face Korinth. 'I am honoured that you will be joining us, Librarian Korinth. Jonas speaks most highly of your abilities. I am sure that you will be an asset to us in the difficult times ahead.' For a moment, the captain was perturbed by the Librarian's mismatched, red and black eyes.

Korinth bowed uneasily. 'Thank you, captain.'

On the fringe of the greetings, Zhaphel nodded his silent assent.

'Captain...'

'Yes, Librarian. Speak your mind. There can be no doubts after this. It is a step with no guarantees of return. Besides,' he smiled weakly, 'questions are what make us Blood Ravens.'

Korinth nodded, acknowledging the captain's integrity despite his prejudices. 'I have concerns about this course of action, captain. Placing the alien in charge of the *Spirit* was further than most servants of the Emperor would be prepared to travel on this road, but I can understand your reasoning. That is why we are here,' he said, implicitly including Zhaphel. 'But this is no longer merely a question of accepting the guidance of an alien. This Thunderhawk is simply incapable of functioning in the warp – it has no warp shields and is too small to have any fitted. Even with the best guidance in the world, I do not think that this course of action is anything other than suicide.'

Gabriel nodded gravely. 'I understand your concerns, Korinth, and I share them. I cannot allay your fears with words of reason; I can only appeal to your faith. I *know* that this will work. My faith is not based on the words of Taldeer, but rather on the certainties of the Emperor's will. I have... I have seen the Emperor's approval.'

Korinth's uneven eyes flashed with shock, and Zhaphel took an involuntary step towards them. Even Jonas looked pained.

'You claim to have seen the Emperor's will?' Korinth made no attempt to disguise his incredulity. He had previously dismissed the whispered rumours about the captain's visions as malicious lies designed to further discredit the Commander of the Watch. Rumours had a tendency to morph and swell, as though they had lives of their own – scholars had to cultivate a healthy scepticism about them. But

Gabriel was not an astropath, not even a sanctioned psyker; to receive any kinds of visions would be grounds for prosecution by the Ordo Hereticus.

'Do not misunderstand me, Librarian,' continued Gabriel, seeing the change in Korinth's eyes and feeling the abrupt increase in tension from the other Librarians. He weighed his words, but there was no apology or doubt in them. 'This is the intuition of a scholar. The greatest advances in our knowledge have been made through leaps of intuition. Rational thought and deduction can take us only so far – using them we can never move beyond the evidence that we have at hand. Yet it would be foolish to believe that we have in our possession all of the possible evidence about any issue. Even the great Librarium Sanctorum on the *Omnis Arcanum* has gaps in its records, holes in the historical archive, entire systems about which nothing is known at all. Ignorance of a thing does not mean that it is not real; it means only that we have not yet discovered it. Is it not the task of the explorer and the researcher to discover the undiscovered… to reach for the unknown with the certainty – the faith – that it is there?'

'This is not a question of faith, Angelos,' said Zhaphel. There was a complicated respect beneath his gruff address. 'Not in you, not in the Emperor. This is a question of technology. The Thunderhawk cannot shield us from the daemonic energies of the warp. At best, we will die fighting.'

'That is always the best that we can hope for, Zhaphel.' Gabriel smiled.

'The problem is that the rupture in the webway is too small for the *Ravenous Spirit* to fit through,' said Jonas, realising that the captain was not addressing the concerns of the Librarians. It was almost as though Gabriel didn't understand the nature of their concerns, which worried the father Librarian. 'The eldar seer has brought us this far, and our trust in her has proven to be justified. Of this much we can be certain, brothers; as you saw, the journey has been at a great personal cost to her. In order to enter the webway and follow it to our destination, we have no choice but to attempt it in a smaller vessel. The Thunderhawks are all we have.' He paused.

Brothers, I would not ask this of anyone, but you are sworn to complete the Summoning of the Exodus – if Rhamah can still be recovered, then this is our only chance. The tear in the webway was probably caused by his fall. All of our fates lie beyond this choice – we should make this stand together. Who better than the Librarians of the Order Psykana should stand against the warp?

'The Thunderhawk has been modified according to the specifications of Taldeer. The eldar have superior knowledge of the warp, and we should not be afraid to acknowledge this,' continued Gabriel, aware that his position on this matter was more than controversial. 'Seer Taldeer says that she will be able to protect a gunship as small as a Thunderhawk for a short period. The *Ravenous Spirit* is close enough to the breach in the webway to ensure only a brief exposure to the warp before the Thunderhawk penetrates the structure. Once inside, we will be shielded by the architecture of the webway itself. She will need your support, Librarians. This is not an impossible task.'

'Captain!' The call came from inside the hull of the Thunderhawk. After a couple of seconds, Corallis appeared at the top of the ramp. 'The alien is in place. Medicius and Ephraim have installed her, and the Litanies of Pacification have been performed to honour the vessel's machine spirit. Medicius is about to return to the Implantation Chamber to oversee the next phase of the young Ckrius's treatment. We are as ready as we will ever be, captain.'

'Thank you, sergeant,' nodded Gabriel, turning back to regard the Librarians, waiting for their judgment. 'Well, brothers?'

There was a long pause. 'It will be as you say, captain,' said Zhaphel finally. He nodded deferentially and then strode up the ramp into the Thunderhawk.

Korinth watched his battle-brother ascend into the gunship and then dropped his uneven eyes back into the blue-green sheen of Gabriel's gaze. For a number of seconds he said nothing, simply staring into Gabriel's eyes, searching for a sign of corruption or of purity. Then he turned slowly to face Jonas. *We will see this done. Knowledge is power.* He was resolved. Bowing sharply he strode up the ramp after Zhaphel.

THE BROKEN AND bloodied bodies of eldar Harlequins littered the floor of the librarium. With their holo-suits and domino-fields destroyed, the aliens looked effete and feeble; their dramatic and menacing visage was reduced to pantomime, and their bright colours were dulled by the ichorous coat of toxic blood. Intermixed amongst the turgid eldar bodies were the magnificent shapes of a handful of Prodigal Sons, each having fallen in the craze of battle in the librarium. A couple of the Marines were still alive, but they had terrible slash-wounds inflicted by the eldar powerblades. Two of the dead Marines were ruined beyond recognition. They had been riddled with fire from the Harlequins' shrieker cannons, filling their superhuman blood stream with virulent toxins that excited the nervous system into overdrive: their armour had cracked and blown apart from the inside as their bodies had exploded from within.

Only a single Harlequin remained alive. It had been backed into a dark corner of the librarium, in amongst the book stacks. A knot of five Prodigal Sons were arrayed in a crescent around it, preventing it from escaping, jabbing it occasionally with their blades and shooting random volleys of bolter shells into the floor, walls and ceiling around it. For its part, the alien looked wracked with fear and panic, but it emitted no sound at all. It merely stared, wide-eyed and maniacal, like a caged animal.

It makes no noise. It looked different from the Harlequins in the rest of the troupe. The colours on its armour were more understated and subtle; its build was even more delicate but its movements were so graceful that they seemed like poetry. Standing in the midst of the corpses, I watched Ahriman stride over towards the prisoner, trampling over the bodies of eldar and Marines without regard.

Distaur.

The word floated easily into my mind, as though Ahriman were answering my unspoken questions once again. He showed no sign of paying me any attention, and his back was to me. I wondered whether he was sharing his knowledge with all of the Marines in the room. *Distaur – it means 'mime.' These are unusual and rare specimens, my sons. We should treat it carefully.*

As Ahriman approached, the formation of Prodigal Sons parted to let him through. With a single stride, the sorcerer brought himself close to the Harlequin mime, watching it squirm and writhe in an attempt to keep some distance between them. For a few moments, Ahriman did nothing; close enough to feel the creature's breath, he just watched the discomfort of the alien, as though he were studying its reactions. Then suddenly, without provocation or warning, Ahriman's hand shot out and clasped around the eldar's throat. He lifted the creature easily into the air, bringing its masked face level with his own unearthly features, feeling its limbs twitching and tensing against the violence being done to its neck.

Distaur – mime – let's see whether you are really mute, or whether there is anything you can tell us about this place.

THE GLITTERING WRAITHSHIP *Eternal Star* flashed into the outskirts of the Lorn system, its wings swept back like a speeding raptor. In close formation behind it was the sleek and dark form of the Ghost Dragon, *Avenging Sword*. The two eldar cruisers decelerated rapidly as they entered planetary space, checking their movement against the complex gravitational forces and suddenly surrounded by chunks of tumbling space debris.

Deep within the shimmering structure of the *Eternal Star*, Farseer Macha sat in focussed mediation. Her Wraithship fluttered and flashed in accord with her will, darting and weaving through the outskirts of the system, sliding in between the asteroids and rolling chunks of junk. The cruiser's movement was organic and fluid, as though it were a living entity, or an extension of the farseer's will.

On the bridge of his Ghost Dragon, Uldreth the Avenger kept his eyes on the ethereal gleam of Macha's vessel. He marvelled at its beauty and elegance. Wraithships were rare and ancient vessels, and Uldreth never ceased to be awed by their bird-like grace – the *Eternal Star* touched something primeval in his soul, speaking to him of the nature of his people. In comparison, his sleek and dangerous Dragon-class cruiser seemed cold and overly technological; it swerved and manoeuvred with perfect precision in the wake of the farseer's ship. For a moment, Uldreth realised that his appreciation of the Wraithship was intermixed in his mind with a sense of the beauty of Macha herself. He realised that his heart was still filled with relief that the farseer was alive.

The *Avenging Sword* snapped abruptly to one side, rolling over on its axis as though in an evasive manoeuvre. Flicking his attention away from the dancing light of the *Eternal Star*, Uldreth suddenly realised what had happened in the Lorn system. The whole system was littered with wreckage and debris. Ruined cruisers and gunships tumbled lifelessly through the void. There were clumsy mon'keigh vessels intermixed with the ruined shapes of shattered Shadowhunters. Massive and unspeakably ugly greenskin hulks bled fuel as they slowly disintegrated. Spinning chunks of rock rained past the *Sword* like asteroids, but they had such velocity that they must have been the debris scattered after a massive explosion.

As the eldar cruisers approached Lorn VII, a monstrous glowering gas giant of a planet, Uldreth's heart sank. Emerging from the far side of the planet, locked into a declining orbit by the gravitational pull of the vast planet, the exarch saw the familiar shape of a Dragon-class cruiser, emblazoned with the iconography of Biel-Tan. The long, slender craft was lifeless. Its majestic starsloop, which projected out of the hull like the dorsal fin of a predatory fish, was torn and holed. The weapons batteries at the prow had been completely blown away, leaving the fuselage ruptured and gaping into the void of space. The entire front end of the once-beautiful vessel had been pummelled into hideousness.

Uldreth recognised the cruiser at once. It was the *Exaltation*; one of the most ancient vessels from the Biel-Tan fleet, built so long ago that not even the oldest of the craftworld could remember its origins. Legend told that its name was given in honour of Khaine himself: it was a weapon worthy of his praise; its violence exalted the Bloody-Handed God. It was Taldeer's ship.

This is not your doing. Macha's thoughts were calm and full of compassion, but they pressed forcefully into Uldreth's mind. She knew him well, and she knew how he would react to these revelations.

Scans of the rest of the system revealed that there was not a single functioning Biel-Tan vessel, other than the two cruisers. However, the sensors indicated the presence of Yngir technology, mostly in the form of fragmented and inconsistent signals.

What have I done? Uldreth's mind recoiled, his sense of guilt overriding his reason until he was unable to engage with Macha's thoughts. Remorse and regret hammered into his head, obliterating the farseer's attempts at reassurance. *The Yngir were here too.*

Taldeer saw this and she embraced her visions. You could not stand in her way, Uldreth of the Dire Avengers. You sent her with a glorious army at her disposal. You were right. Not even I could see the echoes of the ascension in Lorn. Not even I could see beyond the battles of Lsathranil's Shield. We made our choices, and now we are here. You cannot be blamed for a lack of far-sight – if there is guilt here, it is mine alone. But the question is not what we should have done differently in the past; it is rather what we can do to shape the future into our favour. The past is untouchable; the future is yet to be chosen. There was a pause, as though Macha were concentrating. *Taldeer's role in the future has not yet been eradicated. This is not yet over.*

As the cruisers approached the wreckage of the *Exaltation* they cleared the horizon of Lorn VII. In the distance, in a tight orbit around the fifth planet, Uldreth and Macha could see a small, malformed moon, glinting with metallic menace. Automatically magnified by their viewscreens, they could see that it was no moon. The massive, cumbersome and ugly shape was a mon'keigh vessel – recognisable as a battle-barge. It appeared slightly damaged, but scans showed that it was fully operational. Debris and damaged vessels floated in a loose orbit around it, sometimes crashing against its armour or plunging down into the atmosphere of the planet like a rain of fire. A familiar insignia was emblazoned across the hull: a glistening droplet of blood-red was surrounded by broad black wings. Macha had seen that symbol before. *Gabriel.*

Even across the distance of space that separated the two eldar cruisers, the farseer could sense the wave of hostility and suspicion that flooded out of Uldreth's mind as the mon'keigh vessel appeared on their screens.

THE WARP ROILED with curdling energies, twisting itself into a thickening mire of congealing clouds and reaching tendrils. The pristine golden tube of the webway was assailed on all sides, as though the dae-monic forces could sense that it was a possible route out of their limbo and into the material realms. The little breach in its structure was alive with unearthly colours and violence, as though the warp itself were being drawn through it in a massive swirling vortex.

It was an ocean of Chaos being drained through a plug. The rupture seemed to function like a hole in a pressurised cabin, sucking monstrous forms through a gap that was only a fraction of their size, compressing them and tearing them asunder, igniting infernos of warp fire that blazed and licked at the opening. But the daemons poured against the webway, clawing and lashing at each other and the structure itself, in a desperate, thirsty passion for birth into the materium.

Something seemed to prevent them from getting through, as though the breach had been ward-sealed from the inside. A twinkling sheen was collecting around the tear within the golden tube, glittering like a constellation of tiny, crystalline stars – like little warp spiders trying to pull a silken-web over the breach to patch it.

From the control deck of the *Ravenous Spirit*, Sergeant Kohath watched the rugged but diminishing shape of the Blood Ravens Thunderhawk; it was tiny in the fury of the daemonic tempest as it dropped away from the cruiser. The little gunship had no warp engines and only limited manoeuvrability in the immaterial mire – the *Spirit* had ejected it like a drop-pod, setting its path and then jettisoning it like a projectile towards the raging breach in the webway.

From the very first moment that it had emerged from the shielded hull of the *Spirit*, the Thunderhawk had been like a magnet in a sea of molten iron. It was as though the energy flows of the warp itself had suddenly shifted, and a massive current of

Chaotic forms had washed back from the webway, crashing over the tiny gunship like a tidal wave of hate and ferocity. Kohath had never seen anything like it.

The viewscreen began to flicker and the image started to dissolve; whatever the eldar witch had done to the sensor arrays of the *Ravenous Spirit* could clearly not function without her presence.

'Stabilise the picture, Loren,' snapped Kohath, keeping his eyes fixed on the screen as the Thunderhawk was ripped into a spin by the lash of a great, vaporous, snaking tendril of energy.

'There is nothing I can do, sergeant,' answered the serf. 'The image should not be there at all, according to our instruments.'

As the picture cracked and fizzed into incoherence, the last image that Kohath saw was of a giant, ghostly, incisor-riddled mouth emerging out of the chaos of ethereal forms and yawning around the tumbling, uncontrolled shape of the Thunderhawk. The jaw tensed, as though gathering into solidity, and then it snapped closed. The viewscreen hissed, crackled and the went black.

ONE OF THE heavy, stone desks had been dragged across into the pool of red light that flooded through the circular window cavity of the librarium. The Harlequin mime had been strapped to its surface and was pinned by four Marines, each holding one of its limbs in place. The thin, rubbery armour over the alien's chest had been sliced open and peeled back, exposing its porcelain skin. In turn, the skin had been cut, burnt and shredded until it was awash with bloody colours, almost as vibrant as the eldar's armour itself. The alien's mask had been removed, and I could clearly see its startling blue eyes bulge with each incision.

Ahriman circled the table slowly, muttering quietly to himself in a tongue that I recognised but could not fully recall. He was lost in concentration, and seemed to be almost oblivious to the presence of the dying Harlequin on the table next to him. But as he muttered the secret words of his forgotten language, more cuts and gashes appeared in the flesh of the prisoner, each wider and deeper than the last until blood started to ooze out of the joints in the creature's armour, pooling on the table and then on the floor below.

But the Harlequin said nothing. It made no sound at all. Its eyes bulged and widened with each stroke of the invisible knife; it was clear that the alien was suffering terrible pain.

'What do you hope to achieve through this?' I asked, daring to interrupt Ahriman's litanies or spells. 'You haven't even asked any questions.'

The sorcerer showed no signs of having heard me, and continued his circuit around the table. One of the Prodigal Sons glanced up from the prisoner and fixed me with a hollow, cold and ineffable gaze, cautioning me into silence. His features shifted slightly as I looked at them, as though they were not really fixed into place on his face.

'Ahriman! Answer me! What are you trying to do?' I was shouting. My confusion and frustration was building to a head. I felt suddenly and starkly out of place amongst these Marines. 'Ask it a question, Emperor damn you!'

My words echoed in muffled tones around the librarium, murmuring through the sudden and oppressive silence. Ahriman stopped circling the Harlequin and turned his face towards me. At the same time, each of the other Prodigal Sons released the alien and pulled themselves to their full height, looking over at me with vacant eyes. Their faces swam like watercolours in the rain. The hostility palpitated in the air.

Friend of Ahriman, began the sorcerer, a slick smile creasing his ghostly features. *Rhamah of the Sacred Blood, what would you have me ask this creature? Should I ask it for the secrets of the Arcadian Librarium? Should I ask it where they have hidden the broken blade of Lanthrilaq?*

'Ask what you need to know,' I stated simply. If you do not ask, it will tell you nothing. Our power resides in our choice of questions.

'Need?' he laughed. It was a sick, gurgling noise from a distant place. 'What do I need to know from this wretched creature? What could this twisted and broken alien possibly know that I do not know already? Do you know nothing of me, Librarian Rhamah?' *It is not what we need, but what we desire to know that brings us power.*

'If you need nothing from this thing, kill it and be done with it.' *Its very existence is offensive to the Emperor and this ritualistic play merely prolongs its existence.* 'Why must it suffer this way if it need not? We are wasting our time.'

'I am testing a theory. I need not, but I desire to. How else do we learn the secrets that lead us beyond self-preservation and into the grandeur of power itself? Desire is the father of innovation and greatness. Need merely births solutions.'

'What is your theory? What are you hoping to prove?'

'I suspect that this *distaur*, this mime, can speak. My hypothesis is that it will do so when it reaches its pain threshold. This is part of a general theory that I have tested many times before, and it appears to hold true: all life forms change their nature after they experience a certain amount of pain. Of course, the thresholds vary by species and training, but the general theory appears to be sound.'

You are torturing this mute creature to see whether it will become something else? Something that can talk, I asked?

Exactly. You boil water and it becomes steam. Extremes make things change. Remember this, Rhamah, Son of Ahriman: extremes change everything. We must always explore the limits of ourselves and our knowledge; to place limits on exploration is to live a lie.

I watched the sorcerer as he turned away and continued to circle the desk. His Prodigal Sons returned to their positions, stooped over the hapless alien prisoner, clamping its limbs to the corners of the table. For a few more seconds I watched the cuts and the gashes continue to appear across the Harlequin's silent body, seeing its sparkling blue eyes bulge in agony even as the life drained out of them. Just as I turned away, one of the eyeballs ruptured and a wide cut ripped across the eldar's face, covering his features in ocular liquids and blood.

I strode away from the desk and the bloody red light of the triple suns, moving deeper into the librarium, letting the heavy shadows of the book stacks shroud me. Just as I passed out of sight, I heard the mime scream and cry out for mercy.

He can talk after all.

WHEN CAPTAIN ULANTUS strode onto the control deck of the *Litany of Fury* the glittering shapes of two eldar cruisers already loomed large on the main viewscreen. The captain had been summoned back to the bridge by Sergeant Saulh as soon as the alien vessels were first sighted emerging out of the shadow of Lorn VII.

Ulantus had been down in the Implantation Chamber, watching Apothecary Medicius perform the next operation on their most recent and promising neophyte, the young Guardsman Ckrius. Despite or perhaps because of the tumult of war that had gripped the Third and Ninth Companies of Blood Ravens, attention to these ritual details was vitally important for the future of the Chapter.

'What do they want, sergeant?' asked Ulantus, positioning himself in the middle of the deck and gazing at the image of the elegant cruisers as they prowled around the *Litany* like sharks.

'Unknown, captain. We have received no communications.'

Ulantus shook his head in a wave of disbelief. 'Throne damn him,' he muttered under his breath, silently cursing the Commander of the Watch for leaving him to deal with this on his own, again.

'Have you asked them what they want, sergeant?' There was irritation in Ulantus's voice.

'No, captain.'

'Then ask them.' He shouldn't have had to say it.

There was a moment of silence, and then a squeal of feedback cut through the control deck as the servitors struggled to find the appropriate frequencies. A loud whine was followed by the hiss of static and then a click into silence.

'We have no way of reaching them. Their communications arrays appear incompatible with our own.'

'Great,' snarled Ulantus.

As he spoke, the viewscreen flickered and snowed as though a signal were interfering with the image. Gradually, a pale face became discernable behind the interference patterns, but the picture rolled and shivered as though projected from an ancient movie-reel.

'Stabilise that screen,' snapped the captain. 'Locate the origin of the new signal, and stabilise the transmission. Bring us into phase.'

The snow and the rolling stopped suddenly, revealing the porcelain face of a painfully beautiful female eldar, her eyes alive with emerald fire.

'Gabriel.' The tone was bizarre, making the familiar name sound like an alien word. There was no doubt in the voice, and it was not a question. Its uncomfortable assertiveness verged on being a command-tone.

'I am Captain Ulantus of the Blood Ravens Ninth, commander of the *Litany of Fury*. Identity yourself and your purpose,' replied Ulantus, ignoring the farseer's opening word.

'Gabriel?' This time the word was a question, or at least a doubt. The eldar female's face creased slightly, as though she were confused or in pain. At that instant, Ulantus found himself wondering whether she was injured or exerting herself. For a flicker of a second, he felt sympathy for her efforts. Somewhere in his mind, he thought that he could hear the whispering of her voice trying to communicate with him. He shut it out resolutely.

'No, I am not Captain Angelos. I am Captain Ulantus,' he repeated, feeling suddenly that his own identity was somehow inadequate when compared with that of the Commander of the Watch.

'Gabriel.' The word pressed forcefully. It suggested that the alien had understood him, but that she expected Gabriel to be brought before her.

'He is not here.'

'Where?'

'Who are you?' Ulantus was not going to be treated like Gabriel's secretary.

'Macha.' The name meant nothing to Ulantus. 'Farseer of Biel-Tan. Where is Gabriel?' Macha's face twisted with pain as she tried to form the human sounds of High Gothic.

'He is not here, alien. What do you want?' Finally, revulsion settled into Ulantus's mind as he realised that these offences to the Emperor were asking for Gabriel as though they were acquaintances. Anger tinged his thoughts: Gabriel was worse than he had thought.

'What happened here? All dead?'

'The orcs are dead. The eldar are dead. Many of our own are also dead.'

'And the Yngir?'

Ulantus hesitated. 'Yngir?' The sound was ugly and he could not form it properly.

'The... necron?' Macha tried the name like an experiment.

'Yes, the necron are dead too. Your people helped us,' conceded Ulantus, nodding his head in an instinctive show of respect for the deeds of warriors.

'Not dead. There is no dying for the Yngir. You destroyed the portal on the planet. When the Yngir return, things will be worse.'

His argument with Gabriel spun back through Ulantus's mind, and for the first time he began to wonder whether the Commander of the Watch might not be losing his mind. 'It was not us who destroyed the webway portal.'

'But the ruination stinks like humans,' hissed Macha, clearly unconvinced. 'I can smell your minds in the warp even as it spills into the ruptured portal.'

'It was not us. We have reason to believe that there were other humans in this area after the battle – powerful psykers.'

'Why should I believe you, human? You would like to see my people suffer and die.'

'You are right, alien. But this is not our doing.'

'Without the portal, much knowledge is lost. Much hope is lost. The future grows darker.'

Ulantus hesitated, unsure about how much to reveal to this alien witch. He could see her pain and for a moment he realised the potential value of her knowledge. 'Your Gabriel has gone in search of that knowledge.'

Macha's eyes flashed. 'Gabriel?'

'He has taken one of your own – an eldar witch like you – and is searching for an alternative way into the webway.'

'Taldeer is alive?' There was a mixture of relief and concern written across Macha's alien features. 'She is with Gabriel. They must move quickly.'

THE INTERIOR OF the Thunderhawk was groaning with effort. Its structure vibrated and shuddered, like a body immersed in deep cold, and a persistent moan of bending metal filled the compartments. The familiar thunder of the gunship's engines was completely absent – they were not even firing. If there had been any up for them to fall down from in the warp, the vessel would simply be dropping.

'Integrity?' asked Gabriel calmly, looking around the walls of the transportation compartment that dominated the interior of the craft. He thought that he could see the metal warping and bending, as though it had been heated to the point of malleability.

'Holding, captain,' answered Ephraim, his augmetic arms blurring across the dials and switches of one of the monitor-terminals. 'Just.'

'Just is good enough,' replied Gabriel with a faint smile. He glanced over towards the hatch that led into the small control chamber, little more than a cockpit.

It was shut and sealed, but every few seconds Gabriel could see flashes of something that wasn't light bursting within the confines of that tiny space; the brightness pulsed through the armoured hatch as though it were made of paper.

Somewhere in the back of his mind, he could hear piercing cries and screams, but he could not tell whether they emanated from the cockpit or from outside the Thunderhawk. He couldn't even tell whether they were cries from within his own head; perhaps they were the voices of reason rebelling against his actions.

Turning away from the hatch, beyond which Taldeer and the three Blood Ravens Librarians toiled in a secret and terrible Rite of Sanctification, exhausting themselves to preserve the little gunship from the immense psychic pressures of the warp outside, Gabriel looked towards the rear of the compartment. There, in full battle armour with weapons primed and shining, stood the magnificent figure of Tanthius, his legs astride and braced against the rocking motion of the vessel. Next to him, Corallis appeared light and nimble, despite the majesty of his own ancient power armour.

The two sergeants stood sentinel over the main exit-hatchway, unflinching like guardian angels waiting at the gates of hell. As the ship rocked and rumbled, making the hatch-frame shift and warp, the seam around the frame glowed and flashed like the fire of a star probing into the confined darkness.

'And so even the righteous heart is besieged by the blinding light of false knowledge,' muttered Gabriel, only half to himself. The famous lines would be familiar to all the Blood Ravens. 'Falsity is like an ocean that presses around solitary moments of truth, threatening to overwhelm or blind the seekers of knowledge, to eradicate them in an instant of self-deceiving brilliance.'

'Knowledge is power; it guards our souls – guard it well,' chanted the others in response, completing the Prayer of Resolve that had been left to them by the Great Father after he had vanquished the renegade Father Librarian Phraius.

A sharp keening shrilled suddenly through the floor, sending tremulous waves of energy pulsing up through the Space Marines' armoured boots. A roll of thunderous noise crashed along in its wake, rippling through the metallic plating over the floor as though rendering it liquid, firing the rivets out from the edges of the panels like shrapnel.

Gabriel turned just in time to see the cockpit hatchway buckle and shudder. A brilliant flash of deep purple laced through the structure, like radioactive veins. Then the metal hatch bulged like a diaphragm, expanding and contracting as though the cockpit beyond was gasping for breath as it suffocated. Claws, talons and snarling faces began to form in the metal, pressing out into the compartment and stretching the fabric of the hatch-door behind them.

Then nothing. Suddenly the hatch was smooth, cold and grey again. The rest of the compartment had dropped into silence; even the creaking and moaning of the gunship's joints had stopped. The

Space Marines shifted their weight, instinctively checking their weapons with unconscious movements of their fingers. The silence was eerie and unsettling.

Taking a step towards the cockpit, Gabriel felt his boot sink slightly into the metallic deck, as though it had been rendered slightly spongiform in all the chaos. Lifting his foot carefully, he observed threads of metal as they stretched and stuck to the sole. He stepped back, checking the ground around him as it shimmered and rippled faintly, like the surface of pristine, still water. Behind him, he could hear the muffled and squelching sounds of Tanthius and Corallis as they began to fight against the unexpected gravity that seemed to push them inevitably down into the metallic quagmire.

They were sinking into the hull of the ship. Looking back into the liquid deck, Gabriel saw that it was now thick with blood.

A sudden explosion rocked the Thunderhawk as the cockpit hatch blew off its hinges and rocketed through the rear compartment. It didn't spin; it just ploughed through the chamber like a waste compactor. Gabriel and Corallis dove immediately, rolling flat under the accelerating mass. Knee-deep in the swamp-like deck because of the incredible weight of his Terminator armour, Tanthius was unable to dodge to the side. Without pausing for thought, the Terminator sergeant threw his powerfist into the slamming door and brought it to an instant and abrupt halt. It clanked and splashed down into deck at his knees, a massive, fist-shaped dent protruding from the centre of it.

Rolling back to his feet, Gabriel started towards the cockpit, but a shockwave of sound blasted him to a standstill, like the fury of a hurricane funnelled into the narrow fuselage of a Thunderhawk. The sound filled the entire audio spectrum, shrieking through the audible range and screaming directly into his mind, obliterating this thoughts even as its physical force smashed him to a halt.

Framed by the ruined hatchway, Gabriel could see the origin of the torrential onslaught: Taldeer stood bolt upright with her hands pressed against the lintel and her feet braced against the floor. The sinewy muscles in her slender limbs were taut and bulging with exertion. Her neck was knotted with protruding veins and her mouth was stretched into a contorted, rigid and unnatural cave. But it was her eyes that commanded the scene: they had gone. In their place there were simply two gaping cavities, rimmed with a thick, bloody ichor.

She was screaming.

Tearing his own eyes away from the forceful horror of the eldar seer, Gabriel could see the frenzied action that raged behind her. The bizarre throne structure that had been crudely fashioned and jammed into the navigational arrays was engulfed in a blaze of translucent, green flames.

Trails of emerald fire stretched out from the unnatural construction and jabbed into the back of the screaming seer, as the connectors and psychic amplifiers sizzled and spat with unearthly venom. Great blasts of brilliant blue warpfire arced across the cockpit, fizzing and crashing into vaguely discernable forms. From his vantage point, Gabriel could just see the swirling tips of two force staffs and a great axe, hacking through the mire and dispensing sheets of raw power.

Before he could make sense of the scene, a rolling cloud of energy crashed out of the cockpit, blasting into the larger compartment and swamping Gabriel in a wash of pain and nausea. Behind it came the charging figure of Zhaphel, vaulting past the shrieking alien witch with his force axe cutting crescents of purity into the tidal assault, breaking up the force of the wave before it could engulf his brother Marines.

Volleys of fire erupted instantly from Tanthius and Corallis, sending bolter shells hissing through the confined space and punching into the already heaving walls of the Thunderhawk. The daemonic energies swirled and mingled, curdling into the relative density of material form even as the shells and axe-blows dispersed them.

After a sudden, gurgling pause in her screams, Taldeer yelled something incoherent in a tongue that Gabriel did not know. Her voice was shrill and wracked with pain, but there was a new quality to the sound that even Gabriel could recognise. She had been shot.

As the psychic screaming commenced, slightly weaker than before, Gabriel ripped his chainsword into life and whirled it around his head, clearing a moment of clarity in the mists of Chaos for him to assess the situation. A gaping wound had appeared in the side of the alien's abdomen, as though she had been shot at close range by a bolter. Judging from the position of the wound, Gabriel reckoned that the shell had probably ricocheted off the bulkhead and then punched into her kidneys, if eldar had kidneys.

'Jonas!' yelled the captain over the tumult of gunfire, energy discharge and screams. 'Jonas! How much further?'

'Imminent, captain,' barked the father Librarian, hacking out with his force staff and shredding a tendril-like shape as he appeared in the hatchway. 'We were on the cusp of the webway when our shielding failed. The warp pressure was simply too great – the creatures seem to feed on the breach. There are too many of them. Too much energy for us to repel.'

'Trajectory?' asked Gabriel, thrashing his chainsword out in a low sweep to eviscerate the rapidly solidifying, snarling form of a warpbeast.

'Set and fixed, captain,' replied Jonas, reaching Gabriel and turning so that they could fight back to back. 'We should just drop through the hole.'

A loud, resounding crack filled the compartment and shook the structure of the gunship. The ceiling and floor buckled and cracked as though the Thunderhawk were being snapped in two. Jagged dents protruded up through the metal, bending the deck and roof into the imprint of giant teeth, as though the entire gunship had been bitten into the mouth of a monstrous and gargantuan warpbeast.

Gravity failed and the vessel seemed to spin, although it was impossible to tell whether it was the Thunderhawk or the Marines that tumbled hopelessly out of control. As the controlled atmosphere of the cabin ruptured, a torrent of sickly, immaterial force poured into the compartment through the cracks, flooding the vessel with the thirsty, lascivious spirit of purest Chaos.

SILENCE AND DARKNESS. A faint, barely visible, green light pulsed weakly. The air was cold and thin; there was insufficient oxygen to sustain life and the temperature was approaching absolute zero. There was the discernable hiss of escaping gas. Gabriel shook the disorientation out of his mind and realised that the green light indicated a structural breach – the Thunderhawk had lost its integrity. He pushed himself up off the deck, noting that gravity had returned, and surveyed the ruins of his gunship.

The impressive shape of Zhaphel stood in the hatchway to the cockpit. The Librarian usually preferred not to wear his helmet, but now it was firmly secured against the lethal environment. He had leant his axe against the hatch-frame and was stooped over the broken form of Taldeer. A pool of thick blood surrounded the prone alien, hissing with a faint toxicity against the icy metal floor.

In the cockpit beyond, Gabriel could see the back of Korinth as he worked at the controls of the Thunderhawk. The ruins of the eldar's throne-based shield-array had been pushed unceremoniously aside.

The main compartment was in ruins. Techmarine Ephraim was already busy trying to repair some of the worst structural damage; his metallic augmetics chattered and flashed with welding torches and rivet guns, pasting armoured panels back into place like patchwork. The massive form of Tanthius reached up to the ceiling and held the joists and trusses in place for the Techmarine to work on.

The broken and cracked floor was dented with the convex imprints of massive incisors and it was slick with a noxious mixture of alien blood and daemonic refuse. In the extreme cold, the congealing liquids were sickly and viscous, studded with frozen crystals like glittering jewels.

Slumped on the floor were the bulky forms of Jonas and Corallis. They were both beginning to stir from beneath a thick layer of freezing ichor, which coated their armour like a pernicious gloss. Corallis had been tossed into the air and smashed against the ceiling of the compartment just as its structure had been breached; the aging Jonas, recently dragged out of his effective retirement on Rahe's Paradise, had simply fought until he had dropped.

'Sound in,' said Gabriel calmly, realising that everyone was accounted for. 'Korinth,' he added, calling through the hatch into the cockpit as the others confirmed their status. 'What happened?'

'We're in, captain,' replied the Librarian, looking back over his shoulder. 'As we dropped through the breach into the webway, we re-entered material space, leaving the warp violence behind. What a remarkable achievement – a passage of stable, material space through the tempest of the warp,' he said shaking his head. 'And we were just in time,' he added, casting his eyes around the wrecked gunship. 'We could not have survived another moment in the warp without any shields.'

'Captain,' said Zhaphel standing to his feet in the hatchway and cutting off Gabriel's line of sight into the cockpit. 'If you want the alien to survive…' He trailed off, unsure of how to finish the sentiment. 'She has served her purpose by providing a measure of shielding for us.'

Gabriel hastened over to the broken form of Taldeer, who was lying in a frozen pool of her own blood. Her eye cavities trickled with tissue and her abdomen was a shredded mess of flesh and shrapnel. As he knelt at her side, Gabriel could see her mouth moving as though she were trying to form words, but all he could hear was the coarse rasping of her breath and the persistent rattle of blood in her throat. For a moment, Gabriel thought that he was gazing upon the insanity of the warp itself; he had seen Imperial Navigators reduced to wretched and ruined vegetables by tumultuous journeys through the warp, and Taldeer could have been one of them.

'Get her off the floor,' snapped Gabriel. 'Her fate will be the same as ours.'

CHAPTER EIGHT: HARLEQUIN

AND AS THE *Great Enemy* feasted on the souls of the Sons of Asuryan, there was one who stood aside from the feast and laughed like a jester, watching as the newly birthed daemon slaked his thirst with the souls of his kin.

He laughed until the hallowed halls of Arcadia shook, his mirth riddling the magnificent walls with jewels and radiant light.

He laughed as his enfeebled kinsmen fought in vain, falling like wheat before the scythe.

He laughed at the earnest seriousness of Kaela Mensha Khaine, as he swirled and battled the undeniable daemon.

He laughed as his fear-gripped kinsmen took to the skies in their monstrous craftworlds, aiming to flee from their own natures and from the unquenchable thirst that they had loosed on the galaxy.

He laughed as the daemon of Slaanesh turned its hungry and lascivious eyes onto him.

He laughed in the face of damnation, ridiculing the grandiloquence and pomp, finding nothing but amusement in the drama and the death that unravelled around him.

He laughed, knowing that his kinsmen had brought this ruination upon themselves, knowing that this knowledge made him different.

And Slaanesh could find no sustenance in the grinning and mocking face of the Laughing God. As the craftworld eldar fled to the heavens, the Daemon of Passion eyed the Great Jester with cold detachment and disdain, and then threw itself into their pursuit.

And so the Laughing God laughed until his stomach ruptured and his tears fell, spilling his life force over the corpse-strewn floor of his amphitheatre; where each droplet fell, a giggling eldar Harlequin was returned to the living.

Excerpt from *The Mythic Remembrances of Yvraelle*, by Rafaellus Kneg, Heirosavant of the Callidus Temple (901.M41).

A GENTLE MUSIC resounded through the stone amphitheatre. It pulsed and vibrated through the masonry, pushing its way through the legs of the assembly and making itself felt in the hearts of the throng. The rhythm was fluid and without passion; it skipped and stumbled with the aura of childish play. It was uneven, as though intoxicated. It was jilted, as though drunk on its own magic.

With a slow explosion of light, a single figure appeared in the centre of the stage, sparking a susurration of whispers throughout the auditorium: *athesdan*, high warlock, the narrator and grand story-teller. The figure was hazed behind his dathedi shield, shrouded in millions of pin-pricks of light, and his face was utterly featureless, as though a black scarf had been pulled smooth across it. The form of the athesdan was to be formless; he was the facilita-tor of the story, not the story itself.

The music faded out of hearing, but the audito-rium continued to throb and pulse with its uneven rhythms, as though it persisted in frequencies inaudible even to sensitive eldar ears. The silence moved the hall in unspeakable ways.

'Tears fall today as though tomorrow might never be, as though the swift of foot would be lost in the sea, as though Eldanesh were brought humble to his knees, and as though the Laughing God were laugh-ing at thee.'

As the song began, it seemed that stars rose out of the balconies, soaring out above the stage in myriad colours, filling the amphitheatre with radiant light. They revolved slowly in an intricate formation, like a mechanical planetarium or orrery being set to a precise moment in time. Then the colours exploded into showers, falling away from the suspended forms of Harlequin troupers, who spun and flipped and spiralled down to the ground. At the same time, oth-ers sprang out of the stage, leaping from trap doors and dancing into the fray until the stage was awash with colour and motion, like a primordial ocean.

A massive explosion of light obliterated the scene into blindness. As the shadows and colours returned, the stage was transformed: *cegorach*, the Great Harlequin, stood to one side, laughing with a guttural power. His laughter echoed through the silence and obliterated the gentle rhythms that had persisted through the stonework.

The centre of the stage showed a battle. On one side were the silvered host of the Ancient Foe, glittering and white like the stars from which they were born. And on the other stood the noble, eldar kings of old – Ulthanash and Eldanesh flourished their swords with breathtaking grace, while Jaeriela the Thrice-Blessed danced the Spear Thrill with joyous abandon, and Lanthrilaq the Swift knelt in penitence for the flaws that lay in his nature and in his fate, face held up for the audience to see his veil of tears. In the heart of the ancient heroes stood Khaine himself, his shining spear dripping with the decimation of stars and yngir.

On the far side of the stage, opposite the image of the Great Harlequin, Kaelis Ra, the Death-bringer, was stooped over the corpses of his diminishing troops, feasting on their star-birthed flesh. The Great Harlequin could not restrain his mirth, and he pointed and laughed, ridiculing the Star God without restraint, even as he slaughtered its own silvering minions.

Looking up from his unholy feast of star-flesh, Kaelis Ra saw that he had been tricked by the Soul Dancers of the Cegorach: he saw his platinum hordes depleted and dying; he saw that his thirst had been misdirected by the cunning of the Great Trickster. And his fury knew no slaking.

With a great bound, the trouper playing the Death-bringer vaulted into the air. He was lifted high with the assistance of the inertia pivot fitted to his belt, somersaulting into the centre of the stage, scattering the yngir and eldar warriors in all directions, slaying the beautiful Jaeriela with a single venomous glance.

Suddenly the motion on the stage stopped. It was as though the moment in time had been frozen: warriors were held in mid strike, and dancers were caught in mid air as they spun and flipped. The silence of death gripped the auditorium, and even the laughter of the Great Harlequin was gone.

From the front of the stage, the narrator sung once again.

'At the turning of the tides came the Swords of Vaul, the Blade Wraiths of the Smith God held death in their thrall. But the flaws of one became the doom of them all, with Lanthrilaq the Swift's inevitable fall.'

Life returned to the stage as the performance lurched back into motion. The battle roiled and raged for a few minutes, as the troupers on both sides demonstrated their effortless prowess with blades and projectiles. But suddenly Lanthrilaq fell to his knees at the front of the stage, holding his Vaulish blade before him like an offering to the audience. It was chipped and dripping with death, but the tip had been snapped off, making it blunt and worthless.

Tears of blood streamed down the Swift's face as he realised what this failure would mean. Behind him, their formation broken, the eldar heroes fell in swathes. Eldanesh was the first to die, and the audience watched in horror as his soul was freed from his body only to be consumed by the Bringer of Death. Then it was Ulthanash that fell, sliced in half by the scythe of Kaelis Ra.

The trouper playing Khaine let out a terrible roar, repelling the silvered hordes with the sheer force of his fury. In desperate hate and anger, he lowered his shining spear and charged at the Star God, refusing to concede defeat, refusing to be beaten by the treachery of Vaul's blade.

The stage turned instantly black. All the lights were extinguished, and each of the Harlequins deactivated the glittering projections from their dathedi shields. The audience never saw Khaine's spear pierce the chest of Kaelis Ra. The only figures left illuminated were Lanthrilaq at the lip of the stage, staring up in beseeching despair, and the Great Harlequin himself, grinning broadly at the back of the stage.

There was complete silence as the image of the Great Harlequin began to fade into blackness, gradually vanishing from the stage as the trouper dimmed his shield. At the same time, almost imperceptibly, the lonely image of Lanthrilaq started to change. It was subtle at first, just a slight creasing of the lips. Soon it was a smirk, and then a grin. Out of the utter silence emerged a barely audible chuckle. The audience heard it without knowing it; it seeped into them, transforming the desperation of the scene into a tragic comedy without anyone understanding why. After a few more seconds, the image of Lanthrilaq had been transformed into that of the Great Harlequin himself, clutching the broken Blade Wraith in his hands and laughing without restraint or fear.

THE LIGHTS IN the auditorium came up, revealing the troupe in a ceremonial formation on the stage. The performance was over, and they received the rapture of the audience like plants soaking up the sun. The troupe's Great Harlequin, Eldarec the Mirthful, remained kneeling at the front of the stage, turning Lanthrilaq's blade in his hands, gazing at its shattered splendour with a faint smile.

The Dance of Lanthrilaq was the only way to summon the blade from its place of rest, and it had been a long time since Eldarec had felt its touch against his skin. The dance was like an elaborate combination lock, opening up the immaterial vaults in which the Harlequins sequestered the ancient treasures over which they stood sentinel.

It didn't matter where in the galaxy the dance was performed – the troupe travelled widely through the domains of the craftworld eldar and their darker cousins – it would always open the vault to the flawed Vaulish blade; time and space moved differently on the Harlequins' stage. Here on Arcadia, where the audience was entirely comprised of inanimate, grinning mannequins and the handful of Harlequins not involved in the dance, the rite was comically easy.

'The mon'keigh are here,' said Eldarec, rising to his feet to address the audience, seeing the living masks of troupers shifting amongst the inanimate faces of the mannequins. The amphitheatre was instantly transformed into a council hall. 'We knew that they would come one day, that the sacred ground of Arcadia would eventually be sullied by their ugly, earnest boots.'

'Why are they here?' a voice called from the balcony. A grim-faced Harlequin rose to his feet, standing out of an immobile and sinister row of grinning mannequins. 'Do they know where they are?'

'The young races have no sense of the value of things, but they act with such passionate confidence. Although the old races know this value too well, their fear of its power leads to impotence,' answered Eldarec, smiling in pleasure at his circular response.

There was silence. None knew how to reply.

'There are many things in this place that the mon'keigh know nothing about. We must ensure that these things remain hidden. There are other things here that they may have come to find.' The Great Harlequin turned the Blade Wraith in his hands, admiring its flawed form. 'And we must deny them these things.'

'We are few. They are many.' Murmurs of discussion rippled around the auditorium, as though even the life-sized mannequins were enjoined in the conspiracy.

'Not so many that our numbers seem small,' countered Eldarec, his lips curling into a playful smile.

'And we are not alone.' The voice was low and resonant, echoing around the amphitheatre with profound drama. It was an expert projection by a powerful trouper, but its origin was lost in its pervasiveness.

Eldarec's smile fixed for a moment, losing its sincere vitality. He glanced around the hall, taking in the faces and masks of each of his troupe. They appeared suddenly worried and tense, their expressions becoming fixed like those of the mannequins. They knew whose voice this was – he could be the mannequin next to them. They knew as well as Eldarec did. Discomfort and fear fell over the theatre.

'Show yourself, Karebennian!' commanded the Great Harlequin from the stage. 'This is no time for your tricks.'

'Quite wrong,' echoed the reply, as though from everywhere at once. 'This is the perfect time for tricks. It may be the time for nothing else.'

The voice of the Harlequin Solitaire rumbled and rolled around the theatre, tumbling with playful menace, making the Harlequins in the audience shuffle and eye-check the dolls around them. Then there was a flash of darkness and shadow, and Karebennian faded into visibility next to Eldarec. It was as though he had just climbed out of the webway itself, emerging onto the stage through an immaterial trapdoor.

Eldarec recoiled slightly, edging away from the newcomer with an obvious mix of disdain, awe and fear. The Solitaire was well known to the Harlequins of Arcadia; he had passed through the Ritual of Laughter with them long ago, emerging on the other side of that rite of passage free from the temptations and clutches of Slaanesh. But there had been something different about him even then, something dark and depthless that set him apart from his kinsmen in the masque. There had been whispers that his spirit had been touched by the essence of the Laughing God himself. In the Great Dances of the Mythic Cycles, he was drawn towards the forbidden roles until eventually his mask began to take on the terrible, daemonic visage of Slaanesh.

Shunned by his troupe and shunning them in return, Karebennian had condemned himself to the wilderness, plunging into the webway and vanishing from Arcadia for a hundred years. He lived the life of a solitary wanderer and a troubadour, dancing the matrix of the webway and losing himself in the infinite complexities of time and space, becoming one with the ancient structure itself. It was said that he even found his way to the Black Library.

Then, one fateful day, he had felt a force calling into his soul, screaming and singing and laughing at his solitary existence, drawing him back onto the stage of his people. He had flashed through the labyrinthine webway and reappeared on Arcadia in the midst of a performance of the legendary tale of the Birth of the Great Enemy, the most dangerous of all Harlequin masques. He had sprung out of an unknown and hidden portal onto the stage, immediately and naturally taking on the role of Slaanesh itself – the one role that even the Great Harlequin could not adopt without being driven into insanity. It was then that the Harlequins of Arcadia realised that Karebennian was a Solitaire – the vagabond troubadour, the lonesome traveller, the wandering warrior poet of legend.

Since then he had appeared from time to time to bring news of the other sons of Isha, and each time he had struck the souls of his kinsmen with awe and fear. Whispered legends told of how he flitted between the craftworlds and exodite colonies, how he stood guard over one of the myriad portals into the Black Library itself, and even of how he made no distinction between the eldar and their darkling cousins, performing for each in their appropriate time and place. It was said that his name was known by the leaders of every eldar and dark eldar cluster in the galaxy.

'Karebennian,' said Elderac, watching the shifting pleasures cycle over the Solitaire's mask. 'Your presence here is unexpected, as always.'

'Thank you, Elderac the Mirthful.' The answer was almost a song, turning the respectful language back on itself, and producing a uncomfortable lilt.

Karebennian bowed with such ostentation that it resembled pantomime. There was the show of deference, but there was nothing earnest in it. Everything was a performance.

'There will be no further masques today, Solitaire.'

'I do not come to dance with you, cegorach,' he replied, using the ancient term for the Great Harlequin, playing with its syllables as though it were a puzzle. 'I come with news. There are mon'keigh feet in the sands of Arcadia.'

'We know this,' answered Elderac. 'We are taking precautions to keep those things that are secret hidden, and to hide those things that appear to be plain to see.'

Glancing down at the Blade Wraith in Elderac's hands, a flicker of emotion wisped over the Solitaire's mask. He nodded. 'The blade of Lanthrilaq is not to be surrendered to these animals. But I suspect that the mon'keigh seek other treasures. They will take what knowledge they can, for knowledge is pleasure and knowledge is power. We must guard it well. They must not be permitted to find the portal to the Black Library.'

'The mon'keigh are strong. There is a sorcerer amongst them that is known to us. A powerful and ancient soul, rich in knowledge that should have been forbidden to it. It thirsts for more and it is hard to resist.'

'Yes, Ahriman. We have met before.'

'You have defeated him before?'

'We have met, and we both dance the webway yet.' The Solitaire's answer was ambiguous. 'We are not alone in this fight, cegorach. I have met with a seer of Biel-Tan, and she has promised to send aid. Her *Bahzhakhain* – the Tempest of Blades – was in ruins, but her soul spoke of other defenders of truth; she will bring them to our side. The sorcerer and his mon'keigh soldiers may have found their way to Arcadia, but we will ensure that they do not leave. If the exits are clear, then they must be obscured. Knowledge is power, and it is not to be shared with these mammalian primates.'

The troupe remained in silence, always unsure of how to respond to the elliptical speech of the Solitaire, never wholly convinced that his words contained less artistry than truth. For the Harlequins, life was a performance art.

'It will be as you have said,' announced Eldarec with grave seriousness, shaking his head forlornly and looking down at the ground. Then suddenly he erupted into mirth as a broad grin cracked across his mask. The mock earnestness vanished and laughter rolled around the auditorium; the dramatic atmosphere was broken once again. With a hint of theatrics, the Great Harlequin reached out and embraced Karebennian like a long lost friend.

The Solitaire did not laugh; it was a cheap trick.

THE DESERT SHONE red in the reflected light of the triple suns, as the Thunderhawk dropped through the atmosphere. It was a smoking ruin of dull metal, dripping flames out of its burners and scattering hull fragments in sparking rains. Entire sections of the fuselage ruptured and buckled as the gunship ploughed through the stratosphere, flaring into brilliance before breaking free and tumbling down to the ground. The Thunderhawk was falling apart even as it descended towards the barren surface of Arcadia.

'Engines?' asked Gabriel, his voice hissing with static as the vox-beads in the squad's helmets crackled through the ionosphere. Blasts of air and waves of pressure crashed through the shredded compartments, throwing equipment and shattered parts of

the structure against the Space Marines. Flames
licked out of gashes in the terminals and deck, filling
the interior of the gunship with an inferno of heat,
smoke and flickering light. Gabriel stood in the middle of the main compartment, letting the tempest
rage around him as though unwilling to acknowledge its force.

'Failing.' Ephraim was lying on his back at the rear
of the compartment, his abdomen half-hidden
under a torn and exposed bulk-head. His multiple,
metallic arms were chittering and working in the
cavity above his head, and jets of simmering oil were
venting across his armour.

'How long?'

'Seconds.' Ephraim pushed himself clear of the
wrecked engine block and clambered to his feet, fires
burning intermittently over his arms and chest,
where the oil was rendered incendiary by the harsh
wind.

Only Korinth remained in the cockpit, trying to
restore some element of control to the plummeting
gunship. He struggled with the controls, but to no
effect; the stabilisers and thrusters had failed completely as the Thunderhawk had punched into the
fiery atmosphere. It was little more than a massive,
flaming dead-weight crashing towards the ground.

'Distance,' demanded Gabriel, unmoving in the
centre of the deck.

With one arm clamped around a bent structural
truss in the wall, Corallis hung out of the ruined side
of the Thunderhawk, catching himself at an angle so
that he could assess the distance of the vertical drop

beneath the plummeting gunship. 'Two thousand metres.'

Something on the distant but rapidly approaching ground caught Corallis's enhanced and well trained eyes, glinting like a treasure under the ocean. 'Captain – there is another gunship in the desert. It looks like a Thunderhawk. Not one of ours…' He hesitated for a second. 'And the ground… it's incredible.' Corallis strained his eyes to work out the intricate cracks, valleys and patterns that had been carved into the surface of the planet below. He couldn't work out whether the work was the result of natural or artificial processes, and he couldn't even work out what he was looking at. 'It's incredible,' he repeated.

Before Gabriel could react, an impact shook the craft suddenly, sending the remaining equipment skidding across the deck and making the Marines check their balance. It was followed in rapid succession by two more hits.

'Tanthius?' asked Gabriel, remaining in the centre of the burning deck.

'Some kind of projectile – non-explosive. Could be a primitive cannon or an advanced cluster cannon of some kind.' The Terminator sergeant peered out of the other side of the Thunderhawk, trying to catch a glimpse of what had hit them. 'I cannot see the source.'

They come… The thoughts were weak and feeble, hardly even discernable in the chaos of the plummeting gunship.

Gabriel's immovability faltered as the rasping thoughts made themselves felt. 'She's still alive,' he snapped, striding through the flames towards the broken shape of Taldeer, who was strapped and restrained in one of the crash-harnesses.

For a split second, Zhaphel and Jonas exchanged glances, then Jonas moved to help the captain as he stooped down over the bleeding body of the alien. Zhaphel watched them for a moment and then moved over to one of the brutal gashes in the cabin wall, staring out into the rush of red air outside.

'Nightwings,' he said, identifying the sleek, swift fighters that spiralled through the atmosphere around the dropping dead-weight of the Thunderhawk. The ruby radiance of the triple suns burst around the speeding shapes, rendering them into silhouettes. The swept wings of the fighters were slowly pushing forward as the crafts slowed to engagement speed. Blasts of dark projectiles hissed out of the dual-pronged noses, and lines of lasfire streaked out from under their fuselages.

'Eldar fighters?' Corallis swung himself back inside the compartment and hurried over to Zhaphel to confirm the identification. 'Captain,' said the veteran scout, peering out of the holed hull. 'Four Nightwings, but they are not alone.'

Intermixed in the formation of the curved and smoothly shaped Nightwings were two other vessels. Their design was not wholly different, with wide, elegant, sweeping wings around a central fuselage. But the outlines were not smooth like those of the Nightwings; instead they were barbed and bristling with spiked features. There was something brutal and menacing about their shape that set them apart from the other fighters.

'Ravens,' said Corallis with foreboding.

They come for me. Taldeer's thoughts were weak.

Stooped over her blind and bleeding body, Gabriel looked back at Corallis.

'You're sure?' His voice betrayed his confusion and concern. Ravens were dark eldar fighters; to see them in formation with eldar Nightwings was unprecedented. Although a number of theories suggested that the two alien races were distant kin, Gabriel had never heard of any sightings of them co-operating. It had always been supposed that the two species were mortal enemies, opposed in nature and ideology.

As though to answer Gabriel's question, a hail of splinter fire from one of the Ravens rattled and crashed against the crumbling fuselage of the Thunderhawk, followed by the sizzling and explosive impact of a Nightwing's bright lance.

The alien fighters screamed past the Thunderhawk, ripping through the air over and under the ruined gunship, sending Corallis and Zhaphel rushing to the other side of the compartment to see the fighters peeling out of formation and turning back for another attack run.

With the light of the triple suns no longer behind them, the fighters leapt out of silhouette and into bizarre multicoloured glory. The usually black Ravens were coated in brilliant colours, daubed across their barbed yet elegant hulls in an ostentatious and vaguely comic display. Similarly, the sleek Nightwings, which were usually painted into the intricate, disciplined and uniform patterns of a craft-world army, were splattered with eclectic and brightly coloured patterns. The unlikely squadron appeared to cohere in its random and colourful abandon.

They come for me, Gabriel. I can hear them calling. The rillietann – they are singing in my mind!

'Rillietann?' asked Gabriel, distracted from the impacts and the quaking Thunderhawk by Taldeer's thoughts. The word seemed familiar to him, but he could not place it.

'What did you say?' asked Jonas, looking up from the dying seer as debris and sparks rained down over the captain next to him. 'Rillietann?'

'Yes. Does that mean anything to you, father?'

'It's an eldar word. Harlequins,' answered Jonas, rising to his feet and striding over to Corallis and Zhaphel. 'They are Harlequin fighters. That explains why there is such a mixture of gunships. Conventional wisdom suggests that the Harlequins maintain relations with all of their various kin, both the eldar and the dark eldar. It seems that evidence now bears out the theory.'

As he spoke, lances of fire speared through the already shredded Thunderhawk, blasting chunks of hull and armoured panels clear out the other side of the gunship. A second later and the gloriously rag-tag squadron roared past the dropping Thunderhawk once again, banking up into the largest of the suns before turning for another run.

The coughing engines started to splutter and falter, then they simply cut out, leaving the Thunderhawk in complete freefall. At the same time another barrage of fire punched through the increasingly flimsy armour around the hull, dragging blasts of wind into the compartment and whipping the flames into new levels of intensity. The whistle of wind resisting the acceleration of gravity began to fill the cabin.

They come for me.

'Instruct them to stop,' said Gabriel, taking the prone and almost lifeless body of Taldeer by her shoulders.

They do not obey me. They are the rillietann and answer only to cegorach. They are outside the society of eldar. They come for me, but they do not come at my bidding.

Suddenly the attack ceased. Aside from the crackling of fires and the whistling of the wind, silence abruptly embraced the interior of the Thunderhawk.

'They've broken off the attack,' said Tanthius, watching the fighters as they held their position about a thousand metres away. 'They're matching our velocity – keeping pace with the fall.'

'Korinth?' asked Gabriel, letting Taldeer's body slump back into the harness as he hurried into the cockpit. 'Can you land this thing?'

The Librarian looked back over his shoulder at the captain, his visor reflecting the flaming ruin that wracked the main compartment behind Gabriel and his helmet obscuring the look of incredulity that flashed over his face. 'No,' he said.

THE BODY OF the Harlequin mime went suddenly limp. Its feet swung back and forth in the stream of ruddy light that pushed in through the circular window of the librarium. The noose of rope around its neck was looped up over the lintel that ran over the top of the window cavity. Thickening blood coursed down its cut and violated body, dripping into a growing pool beneath its feet. If it hadn't been dead when it was strung up, it was dead now.

Sitting at the stone desk next to the alien's feet, the great sorcerer Ahriman leant casually over an open book. He had been staring at same page for some time as though reading and re-reading the same passage over and over again, undistracted by the hanging eldar corpse that swung gently in the breeze next to him.

The rest of the surviving Prodigal Sons had already left the librarium, clearing the worst of the carnage away so that their venerated leader might study the secrets of the ancient eldar tomes in peace. Ahriman had sent two of them on an errand, directing them down into the lowest vaults of the librarium, hidden within the foundations of the tower, where he thought that they might find the fabled Arcadian web-maps, allegedly drawn up by the Harlequin troupes as they flittered and darted throughout the galaxy.

You wish to know what I am reading?

Standing in the heavy shadow of one of the bookstacks, hidden from the ruby light of the suns, I had said nothing and Ahriman had not looked up.

You cannot resist the question can you, friend of Ahriman? I can feel the interrogation in your mind. Why do you not ask?

I stepped out of the shadow, letting the blood-drenched light of the triple suns flood over me and transform my armour into an imperial purple. 'Why did you hang the mime?'

It was of no further use.

He didn't move, but just carried on studying the page. It was as though my question meant nothing at all. I felt a wash of disapproval and disappointment flow out of the great sorcerer. *That is not the most interesting question, friend of Ahriman.*

'You wish me to ask about what it said?'

No. The content of its speech was never the point of this experiment. You know this. Ahriman lifted his head slightly, showing me the wide-eyed, vacant horror of his shifting mask. As I looked, the patterns on his face seemed to swim and then whirl abruptly back into a conventional shape, resembling human features once again. He smiled faintly, as though aware that it might be an appropriate expression. *Knowledge is its own goal, my friend. Once it is achieved, its means become irrelevant.*

Looking up from the ghastly visage of the sorcerer, I watched the eviscerated and ruined shape of the half-stripped mime as it swung gently, blood still running down its body and dripping from its toes. I felt no sympathy for the alien creature – its very existence felt deeply offensive in ways that I did not feel needed to be rationalised. There was not even anything particularly repulsive about the violence that had been done to the creature's body; although I could not remember the details, I was sure that I had seen far more terrible mutilations of life-forms for which I had some measure of sympathy in the past. However, something in my soul rebelled against the scene.

'Knowledge is power, Ahriman, and power brings responsibility.' *Your actions show the mark of arbitrariness, not responsibility.* I realised that this was what I found discomforting. 'Your experiment served no purpose. Knowing that the mime can speak but asking it no questions is an exploitation of your power, not a use of it.'

The formulaic smile cracked a little wider, as though genuine amusement had suddenly worked its way into the sorcerer's expression. *Exploitation depends on your point of view, friend. Your exploitation is my use, it seems. Power and knowledge intermix and co-substantiate each other: knowledge is power, as you, of all people, know very well. Power is the employment of knowledge – of what use is knowledge if it remains passive and unexercised? It withers into impotence. We must test our knowledge with our power at every opportunity; how else will you know the truth of your theories? Your exploitation is my science.*

'I am not sure that I appreciate this science of exploitation, Ahriman.'

Your uncertainty demands a test of its own! This is precisely the point – your questions define your quest for certainties. Which brings us back to the matter at hand: what is it that you want to ask of me now?

I hesitated, unsure that my concerns had really been addressed. 'I assume that your book is *The Legend of Lanthrilaq*. I further assume that you are searching for clues about the possible location of the lost blade-wraith. My question, naturally, is whether you are having any success?'

Success is the result of tests, my friend, not of theories – as we have just been discussing. But I have the suggestion of a theory; it is beginning to take shape into something that can be tested. Ahriman's smile broadened.

GABRIEL PUSHED HIMSELF out of the sand and rose to his feet, turning immediately to see the wreckage of the crashed Thunderhawk erupt into flames. The nose of the once-glorious gunship was buried in the desert, and its rear stuck up into the air, venting fire and flame. A deep channel had been cut into the surface of the desert where the Thunderhawk had ploughed down into the sand, skidding and digging its way to a gradual, fiery standstill.

Sweeping his eyes around the surrounding terrain, Gabriel could see the glints of red armour that identified Corallis, Ephraim and the massive form of Tanthius, their shapes obscured against the radiance of the triple suns that were dropping towards the horizon behind them. The blue of the Librarians, purpled by the red suns, shone from various points in the desert. The squad had bailed out of the gunship just as it hit the ground, tumbling and rolling through the sand. Now they were dispersed along the impact trail of the flaming vessel.

'Report,' said Gabriel, punching the side of his helmet as the vox-bead whistled and hissed in protest. 'Ravens, report,' he repeated.

The only response was the crackling and howling of static.

A series of dark specks appeared on the horizon, like sunspots on the surfaces of the three local stars, distracting Gabriel for a moment. He stared into the blinding, ruddy light of the suns, watching the tiny movements of shadow shift slightly. They grew almost imperceptibly larger as he watched. Whatever they were, they were speeding towards the crash, low and fast over the desert, coming out of the suns as though to hide their approach. They were too low to be the Nightwings or Ravens returning.

Dropping his eyes back into the desert, Gabriel saw that the other Blood Ravens had also spotted the skimmer vehicles on the horizon. Tanthius, Corallis and Ephraim had already formed a firing line, with the towering form of the Terminator armour looming up behind the Scout and the Techmarine.

Over to the east, the cadre of three Librarians had shaped up into a loose formation; Gabriel could see traces of crackling blue energy enshrouding the group like an aura of power. He nodded silently to himself, realising how privileged he was to have three Librarians of the Order Psykana with him. It was not unusual for Blood Ravens combat squads to include one or more Librarians, and there were even occasions on which the Chapter could field entire squadrons of these magnificent psykers.

Gabriel himself had once authorised a strike force of Psykana Librarians to raid an immobilised dark eldar cruiser on the edges of the Circuitrine nebula – the then youthful Jonas Urelie had led the mission.

However, concentrations of Order Psykana Librarians very rarely formed within normal combat groupings – their mysterious and secretive order reserved the right to organise itself into battle formations when the need was dire. It was no secret that the Order defined dire need in slightly different terms from the rest of the Chapter. Hence, Gabriel felt the privilege of their presence and the awe of their co-ordinated and glorious power.

Gabriel… The thoughts died almost as soon as they entered his head.

Taldeer! She was still alive. Turning his attention to the downed wreckage of the Thunderhawk, Gabriel saw the flames licking out of every crack and gash, and thick, black smoke billowing out of the engines. They had left the eldar seer strapped into a crash harness as the gunship had dug down into the sand, thinking her dead.

Gabriel. There was hardly any strength in the thought at all, and Gabriel found himself unmoved. He gazed over at the smouldering wreck and performed a mental calculation. Although he was no Techmarine, he was reasonably certain that a Thunderhawk that had sustained that much damaged, including a critical impact to the engine block, would explode within a few minutes. He reasoned that they had abandoned the gunship nearly two minutes before, which meant that the explosion was probably imminent.

As the sound of Tanthius's storm bolter barked through the desert air, followed by the distinctive rattle of Corallis's Ephraim's bolters, Gabriel realised that even he had to draw a line somewhere. He had spent so long trying to convince his battle-brothers to follow his unconventional instincts, and therefore to follow this eldar seer, that he had almost forgotten his own disdain for the alien.

The battle cries of the rest of the Blood Ravens broke through into Gabriel's helmet, crackling and hissing with intermittency and static as his vox-bead spluttered unreliably. He could hear the thunder in Tanthius's voice and he could imagine the fury of power being unleashed by the knot of Psykana Librarians. In the background, he was also aware of the sleet of tiny shuriken projectiles being loosed by the speeding Vypers as they flashed out of the suns. But he did not look round; his eyes were fixed on the inferno that was gathering in the downed Thunder-hawk, enshrouding the dying eldar seer in a thick death-mask of smoke and toxins. In a moment of self-knowledge he realised that he was not going to save the alien witch, and that he would be wrong to try.

'Venoms.' The word hissed and whistled through the vox, and this time Gabriel turned in time to see a squadron of skimmers pass between the two groupings of Blood Ravens, splintering off into two streams, one banking to the left and the other to the right, each circling around to get behind their targets and to separate their fire.

The skimmers looked similar to eldar Vypers, except that they were daubed with the vulgar, multicoloured patterns that had distinguished the Nightwings and Ravens, marking them out as

Harlequin vehicles. As he watched them speed through the gusts of sand that blew across the desert, Gabriel realised that it was hard to calculate exactly where they were. Despite the garish colours, their outlines seemed vague and hazy, as though they were indistinct or improperly resolved.

Volleys of bolter fire from the Blood Ravens sliced through them, making the Venoms flicker like projections but failing to make any impact on the skimmers themselves. The sleek vessels obviously employed some kind of holo-field to disrupt their shape.

A spluttering eruption turned Gabriel's attention back towards the downed Thunderhawk and the helpless, dying thought of Taldeer.

Gabriel.

It was little more than a rasping whisper at the back of his mind as the engines finally detonated, blowing the exposed rear of the gunship apart and drilling its prow even deeper into the sand. Massive chunks of metallic debris were thrown out of the wreckage, like molten rock from a volcano, and smaller shards of red-hot shrapnel were sent sizzling through the desert air, radiating from the blast in the midst of the concussive wave of pressure.

As the debris rattled against his armour, Gabriel silenced his mind for a moment half-wondering whether Taldeer's thoughts would still be there. But there was only a faint silvering voice in the silence – it was a gentle and angelic tone, and Gabriel had heard it many times before. He closed his eyes for a second, letting the soaring, pristine tones of the silver choir fill his soul. Just as the immaculate light rose into his eyes, the voices turned to screams and the silver started to run with blood.

Gabriel snapped open his eyes, wild and fierce, immediately clamping them onto the tempest of flames, smoke and molten metal that was once his Thunderhawk. Somewhere in that inferno, the eldar seer had died, having been rendered bloodied and ruined to bring the Blood Ravens to this place. He had left her for dead: death to the alien. Something in his soul rang hollow as his thoughts gave voice to the ancient and indisputable mantra.

WITHOUT ANOTHER WORD, I turned away from the grinning sorcerer and walked back into the heavy shadows of the aisles between the book stacks. For several minutes, I walked in silence letting the fecund atmosphere of erudition gradually overcome the confusion and anger that Ahriman had instilled into my mind. Something deep within me stirred and arose in opposition to the sorcerer's manner and his reasoning, but I could not find the words to express my opposition. And without the right words, a scholar's opposition is meaningless – I would be left merely with my sword, which is nothing but a vulgar and primitive substitute, a rearrangement of words. Yet I was the sword of Vidya, and *Vairocanum* felt reassuringly solid on my back.

I knew that I could confront Ahriman's logic. I knew it with the kind of certainty that could only have been born out of rehearsal and accomplishment. The flaws in his thinking jabbed at my mind, prodding my subconscious to remember the appropriate retorts and rebuttals. I had been trained to combat this approach to knowledge; the synapses in my brain had become hardwired into adamant opposition. But I simply could not remember what to say. Memories stirred without ever really reaching resolution; they shifted and swam, falling in and out of focus like the Harlequin troupers that had danced and died amongst these very books.

At random, I stopped and pulled down a book from the shelf nearest to me. It was the action of indolence, little more than a reflex in the presence of books. I didn't even look at the cover, but just stood turning the book in my hands, as though it were a prop to help me think.

Knowledge is power. The Harlequins guard it with their lives, and Ahriman seeks it at the cost of their lives. The Harlequins die, knowledge is transferred, but at what cost to Ahriman? What does he trade for his knowledge and his power? Surely he must sacrifice something for this gain?

What is loss and what is gain? Turn it on its head again and again. Both will result in agony and pain.

The thoughts came from everywhere at once, whirling around my head and making me spin on my heel. My eyes twitched and scanned the bookstacks, searching for a Prodigal Son Marine, or even for Ahriman himself. But something told me that the thoughts were not human – even less human than the thoughts of Ahriman.

Can you see without looking and know without thought? You spin and turn like the kinsmen you fought. In a web of confusion I see you are caught.

'Who are you?' I hissed, trying not to raise my voice for fear that I would be overheard.

Who are you? That's a better question.

I turned again and again, sweeping my eyes through the shelves and pouring my consciousness down the shadowy aisles, searching for a shape or a movement. But there was nothing. Instinctively, I reached over my shoulder and clasped the hilt of *Vairocanum*, pulling it gently and silently over my head.

With a sword in one hand and in the other a book, like a vision of justice and valour you look. Did your Emperor look thus when the galaxy he shook?

'Enough riddles. Show yourself.' My patience ran into frustration, but something told me that I should not call for assistance from the other Marines. *My Emperor. I am an Angel of Death – Adeptus Astartes. I am the sword of Vidya.*

Why are you here, Angel of Death?

As the thoughts appeared, so a figure stepped out of the shadows into the faint light between the stacks. It was a Harlequin, but unlike any of those that I had seen. Its face swam like a prehistoric ocean, cycling through primeval emotions and projecting them into terrible expressions. It swayed and moved, as though constitutionally unable to remain still. If anything, it showed even more grace and innate elegance than the other Harlequins I had killed that day.

I slid *Vairocanum* out in front of me, letting its faintly glowing blade define the space between us, keeping the alien at a distance while I weighed up its intent.

Ah, Vairocanum. I have not seen this blade in many centuries.

The thoughts startled me and I felt my eyes widen.

How sad to see it broken now, like the blade of Lanthrilaq himself. I remember when it was glorious and whole, slicing through the silvering hordes with untempered fury. I remember it in the hands of Lavena the Joyful… before she fell into tragedy.

'Who are you?' The question was the most powerful demand I could make.

Who are you? Who am I? I have many names amongst the sons and daughters of Isha. The rillietann call me Karebennian, so here on Arcadia that will suffice as my name.

The name set bells ringing in my ruined memory. When I had first seen Ahriman in the desert, he had been performing some kind of rite using a book. My mind's eye scanned back through the images stored in my short-term memory: *The Tome of Karebennian.* It was a legendary guidebook, supposedly containing a description of one of the routes to the fabled Black Library itself. Ahriman had found it and used it to get to Arcadia. *Was this the author of the Tome of Karebennian?*

You have heard of my book, Angel of Death? I had thought it lost long ago. Many of your lifetimes have passed since it was taken from me by a sorcerer who is not unknown to you. I thought that it would have taken him longer to understand it well enough to find his way here.

'You speak of Ahriman?'

That is what I called him then and I believe it is his name still. Are you a friend to this Ahriman?

The words were rich with suggestions, leading my suspicions in many directions at once. I could not fathom the motives of this quizzical and dire alien. Its question brought my own doubts home to me.

Am I a friend of Ahriman? He had called me that so often that part of my mind had made its peace with the idea. Yet the prodding of this alien awoke me to my credulity. 'I do not remember knowing him well enough to call myself his friend.'

Do you stand with him, Sword of Vidya?

As I considered the various possible implications of the question, I heard heavy footfalls approaching through the aisles behind me. Keeping *Vairocanum* outstretched before me, I turned to glance back over my shoulder. There was nobody there, but the footsteps grew louder and closer. Turning back again, Karebennian was gone. I stood with *Vairocanum* held forth at nothing more than a patch of shadow.

What are you looking for, friend of Ahriman?

It was the great sorcerer himself.

Flipping my blade into its sheath, I turned on my heels to face Ahriman as his heavy footsteps brought him striding up the aisle towards me. Instinctively, I flicked open the book that I had been gripping in my hand, and I looked up from its pages in affected surprise.

'There is much of value and interest in this place, Ahriman. I am an explorer of knowledge, just like you.'

Just like me? The thoughts were tinged with mirth and scepticism. *Indeed. So, my young friend, what have you found in this labyrinth of treasures?*

Without waiting for an answer, Ahriman reached forwards and flipped the cover of my book so that it closed in my hand. He turned his head, as though to read the upside down title. *Very interesting. I wondered whether you might find this.*

I suddenly realised that I had no idea what the book was; I hadn't even bothered to read its title since I pulled it down off the shelf earlier. As Ahriman's hand closed around its spine and started to pull it away, I snapped my eyes down to its cover. What I saw there made my heart jump. There was a picture of an ancient heraldic crest: wide, black raven's wings flanked a bead of blood, which appeared to be represented by an encrusted ruby. The script was runic, probably of eldar origin, and I did not have time to decipher the meaning before Ahriman had the unlikely treasure in his hands. He cracked open the ancient covers and leafed casually through the pages. *I have seen a copy of this before*, he conceded. *I owned one for a long time; it was in my personal librarium. I wonder what its meaning might be for you, Angel of Vidya. As I recall, I took my copy off a seer from Biel-Tan. She seemed to have an unusual fascination for these things.*

My mind was racing. I had seen that icon before. A variation on it was inscribed into my own armour. The sight of it made something spark and kindle in my soul, as though a tidal wave of memories were poised behind a massive dam, waiting to break through. And I had given it up so easily. I had picked it up in complete ignorance and then surrendered it without so much as a word. At that moment, I realised that I hated Ahriman and his intense, smug presumption. *Is he testing me again? Why must everything be a test?*

Because everything is a test. Ahriman's eyes widened into depthless cavities, daring me to look into his soul.

THE VENOMS FLASHED over the desert, whipping up plumes of sand into tunnels of mist and haze that obscured their outlines even more. They banked and peeled away from predictable formations, screeching in between the knots of Blood Ravens and then returning to attack them from behind. Hails of shuriken fire erupted from the twin-linked catapults on either side of the skimmers' fuselage. As the vehicles closed, Gabriel could see five or six Harlequin troupers on the open-topped gun-deck of each, all of the garishly colourful aliens brandishing long blades and rifles.

Watching carefully, Gabriel realised that he couldn't make a precise head count: he concentrated his attention on one of the Venoms as it wove and threaded its way through volleys of bolter fire from Tanthius, Corallis and Ephraim. The gun-platform phased and shimmered, partially obscured by the sand-haze and the burst of red sunlight from behind it, but Gabriel focussed on the dancing figures that rode on its back. He counted four armed troupers. Then the Venom banked, twisting in mid flight to bring its main canons back round. Looking again, Gabriel could see six Harlequins on the gun-deck. It bobbed and skidded through three hundred and sixty degrees, spraying shuriken fire in a full circle before continuing to charge the Blood Ravens. Gabriel saw only three troupers on the gun-deck. It was entrancing and horrifying all at once.

Meanwhile, the Blood Ravens were in retreat. They had held their ground with fierce determination, but only long enough to reach a proper understanding of their enemy's tactics. It was not the way of the Blood Ravens to stand and fight in an unsustainable position, and it had not taken Tanthius long to realise that they would not last long in the open desert against a squadron of Venoms.

Several hundred metres away, the phalanx of Librarians had reached the same conclusion. For a few moments, they had wondered whether retaining two separate firing points might serve to dissipate the Harlequins' attacks, but it had become quickly obvious that that eclectic and wild attacking style of the aliens actually favoured multiple targets. The Harlequins whooped, sung and cackled as their Venoms charged through the desert between the two target groups – they were enjoying themselves.

Almost at the same moment, Tanthius and Father Urelie had signalled the retreat. The two groups moved diagonally across the sand, maintaining their firing solutions while they closed on each other and on Gabriel's position near the smouldering and ruined Thunderhawk. They both realised that the wreckage was the only type of cover available to them, and they both suspected that a single concentrated bank of fire would be more effective against the Venoms than their split fire power.

'How many do you count?' asked Gabriel as Tanthius took up a position at his shoulder. The four Marines had clambered into the wreckage of the Thunderhawk and were using its ruined hull to protect their flanks and rear. Flames rose up around them and licked against their armour, half-hiding their blood-red shapes in the heat haze.

'Six Venoms with four in each,' answered Tanthius, tracking one of the skimmers and unleashing a constant barrage of fire from his storm bolter. His voice was tense with anger; his hit ratio was incredibly low, which was not something to which he was accustomed.

Gabriel nodded, sharing the Terminator sergeant's frustration. 'I make it five, with between three and six occupants per Venom. Corallis?'

'They seem to change, captain. I can't decide on a fixed number. And I can't track their trajectories either – my shells either fall short or fly past. It's as though they are not where they appear to be, captain.' The veteran scout, who had been elevated directly out of the scout company into the command squad because of his prodigious talents and impeccable service record, was reaching the brink of his patience.

'These cursed holo-fields,' grumbled Ephraim, yelling his frustration into the wake of a volley of bolter fire. 'Their armour may be feeble, but it doesn't matter if you can't hit the wretches!'

'This effect is not only the result of holo-fields, brothers,' said Jonas as the Librarians found their way into the gunship's wreckage. 'There is some kind of warp charge held in those skimmers – I can see it. It cycles, building to a crescendo every few seconds. Then the Venom actually dips fractionally into the warp and re-emerges into a slightly different point in space. The movement is slight, but for a second the gun-platform is literally nowhere at all, and then it reappears on a fractionally different trajectory, which throws off our aim.'

'Phase fields,' confirmed Korinth, turning his staff in a slow spin to deflect a flurry of shrieking shuriken that perforated the weakened armour of the wreckage around them. Next to him, the unflinching figure of Zhaphel stood engulfed in flames, his ancient force axe slung casually over his shoulder.

As the Blood Ravens watched, the Venoms swept into a single attack line in the middle distance and then accelerated towards the downed Thunderhawk. The Harlequins opened fire the instant that they came into range, sending sheets of shuriken hissing along in front of them, drilling them into the remnants of the gunship's armour. Their velocity did not seem to slow, but they flickered and lurched, as though rendered in strobes of light, leaping closer with each phase shift.

The Space Marines waited for the Venoms to veer away, knowing that their most vulnerable points lay at the rear, in the engines themselves. But this time the Venoms showed no sign of turning or slowing. They ploughed relentlessly towards the Thunderhawk, as though they were going to ram it, unleashing torrents of fire in ever increasing intensity as they closed.

Suddenly they stopped. They stopped dead, less than twenty metres from the edge of the wreckage. There was no deceleration and no wavering. They just stopped and their weapons fell silent. Lithe, colourful figures sprang out of each of the four Venoms, arraying themselves in front of their vehicles in various theatrical poses. They held a range of bladed weapons and a number of rifles, but none of them moved to attack. They appeared as though frozen in time.

Wind blew through the space that separated the aliens from the Space Marines, and red dust clouds passed between them.

As the gust of wind died down, a single figure could be seen walking through the no-man's land. It was a slight, female form, staggering and stumbling as though walking required an incredible effort of will and balance. It was walking out of the lapping flames at the edge of the wreckage and towards the alien lines.

'Taldeer!' Gabriel gasped with genuine emotion. He had thought she was dead. He had thought that he had let her die, that he had killed her – another death on his conscience.

As though hearing his call, the eldar seer stopped and turned. She gazed back into the flames and ruination of the Thunderhawk, her eyeless cavities black and cavernous in her elegant, blood-stained face. It was the face of death itself.

Gabriel.

She dropped to her knees in the sand, unable to maintain her blind balance any more. Gabriel lurched forwards, vaulting over the armoured panels that provided his cover and rushing forwards through the flames.

'Gabriel!' yelled Jonas in disbelief. 'Gabriel, what in Vidya's name are you doing?'

The Commander of the Watch ignored the father Librarian and strode on through the flames and the clouds of sand. Out in the desert, he could see a leaping figure dart out from the Harlequin line and dance towards the fallen seer. It flipped and tumbled, moving with exquisite ease over the sand as though it were weightless. Gabriel ploughed through the desert, raising plumes of sand from the impacts of his heavy boots.

Before he reached her, Gabriel saw Taldeer fall forwards onto her face in the desert. By the time he knelt at her side and rolled her onto her back, she appeared dead. There was a shimmer of light, like a corona around her body, and then she simply faded away.

You have done this, human. The thoughts were cold and heavy, like ancient ice.

Looking up, Gabriel saw the contorted and terrible features of death projected on the rictus mask of the Harlequin Shadowseer staring down at him. There was pure hatred and terror held in that expression, as though it had been conjured as a weapon in itself.

As he rose to his feet, towering over the slender form of the Harlequin, Gabriel could not wrest his eyes from the alien's mask. But the mask swam and shifted as he watched. Then it seemed to split into two, cracking the Shadowseer down the middle as though he were multiplying by fission or mitosis. Two Shadowseers split into four and then four into eight, until Gabriel thought that he would be surrounded. He shook his head, knowing at some level that this was a trick, but it was not being played on his eyes. Somehow, the Shadowseer was playing tricks directly on his mind.

Ripping his chainsword from its holster against his leg, Gabriel roared and thrashed it into a crescent, pushing it through the multiplying images. His head was beginning to throb and pound. Glittering lights swam in front of his eyes, but he couldn't tell whether they were actually dancing in his head. His spluttering chainsword hacked through a couple of the Shadowseers, making them flicker and falter, but they sprung backwards with the others, leaping out of range.

Roaring again, trying to force the intrusion out of his mind by sheer power of will and volume, Gabriel lurched forwards again, thrashing at the leering faces of the menacing aliens. At the same time, volleys of bolter fire lashed past his head, shredding the multiple images, which flickered but remained in place. Behind him, Gabriel could faintly hear the stampede of boots as the other Blood Ravens broke cover and stormed to support their beleaguered captain. But he heard them as though they were in another world. Ahead, behind the growing wall of Shadowseers, Gabriel could sense the movement of the other Harlequins dashing towards him. Clusters of grenades detonated all around, sending sparkling fields of colour and spiralling images erupting through the desert, like hallucinations.

'For the Great Father and the Emperor!' he yelled, struggling to focus his mind and bring his roiling thoughts under control. As he charged towards the central figure in the line of Shadowseers, conscious that he was leading his Marines in their attack, a grenade fell through the alien's immaterial body from behind. It detonated in the air just in front of Gabriel and he dove to the ground, throwing himself flat. But he never hit the sand. In place of an explosion of fire, a wave of gravitational disruption crashed over the captain, leaving him struggling to maintain his balance and holding him fractionally above the ground. His mind swam, riddled with sparkling lights and a single, silvering voice that he thought he recognised. For the first time in nearly a century he felt helpless and lost, and his mind reached for the security of the silver tone.

For a moment it was like he was swimming in the air, and then the Harlequins were upon him.

CHAPTER NINE: ASCENSION

A VOLLEY OF bolter fire punched into the rear of the rapidly retreating Venom. Its holo-field flickered and crackled intermittently, as though it were shorting out as it pitched and shook through the desert, weaving erratically through the smoking remains of the other skimmers. The triple suns of Arcadia started to dip below the horizon in front of it, and a sudden blast of cold air rippled through the desert.

Korinth lowered his staff and yelled into the wake of the fleeing skimmer, sending a jagged spear of warp energy cracking into its rear vents, making the image splutter and flash violently. It pulsed and convulsed, as though bursting into darkness, and then vanished completely as the warp field ruptured and exploded.

The Blood Ravens were surrounded by the smoking ruins of Venoms. Behind them was the wreckage of their Thunderhawk, which had crashed into the desert, utterly ruined. Fires blazed uncontrollably in its carcass, sending shimmering heat waves pulsing over the surface of the desert, even as the Arcadian suns vanished and a hideous cold descended on the planet.

The corpses of Harlequins were scattered over the sand, broken and wretched, riddled with bolter holes and warp scars. In the midst of the battle, Zhaphel had noticed that unlike their eldar brethren, the Harlequins had made no effort to recover the waystones from their fallen kinsmen. Stooping down over one of the corpses, the Librarian rolled it onto its back and inspected its ruined armour: there was no waystone set into the chest. The Harlequins obviously had some other way of protecting their souls from the lust of their daemons.

Staring after the vanished Venom, Gabriel saw the suns dip below the horizon and felt the blast of icy night roll over him. His sealed armour adjusted to the terrible cold in an instant, but the fractional delay was enough for him to realise the extent of the climatic change that had just engulfed his team.

Looking down at his feet, the Blood Ravens captain saw the indentation in the sand where wretched and ruined body of Taldeer had fallen, before it had vanished. Her body had looked utterly violated and lifeless. The cavities that had once held such radiant eyes had been dark and vacant. Surely she had died? But Gabriel had thought that of her once before.

As he watched, a sudden blast of icy wind whistled over her imprint in the sand, and froze it into the surface of the desert, coating the indentation in an instant, delicate and glittering array of crystals.

'Which way?' asked Gabriel, turning and stomping through the sand towards Corallis. 'We have to get moving.'

Sitting on the twisted remains of a skimmer, the scout sergeant nodded, looking up from his damaged augmetic arm. One of the Harlequin blades had punctured his forearm and forced its way through the bionics until it was hilt-deep. After the encounter with the eldar of Biel-Tan on Tartarus, Corallis had lost most of his right-hand side. Now the Harlequins of Arcadia had ruptured his replacement, augmetic arm as well. The sergeant inspected the wound for a moment longer and then gripped the hilt of the blade with his other hand and ripped it out of his arm. An electric crackle and spark danced in the suddenly open wound momentarily.

'The rock aberrations were to the south,' explained Corallis. 'If there is a settlement in this region of the desert, then it will be there.'

'And the other Thunderhawk?' asked Jonas, his voice tinged with a dark concern.

'I don't think that it lies between us and the settlement, father,' replied Corallis, trying to remember the exact scene that he had seen from the plummeting gunship. 'Do you want to investigate it, captain?'

Gabriel appeared to ignore the question. He pulled himself upright and turned to scan the horizon. 'No,' he said, finally, as though struggling against his naturally inquisitive tendencies. 'The important thing is what those Space Marines are doing now – the Thunderhawk itself is of little concern to us. If we need to know about the occupants of that gunship, we will find them soon enough – probably in the settlement you speak of. The urgencies of time must provoke leaps of faith in us all, sergeant. South, then.'

Without waiting for responses from the others, Gabriel strode off through the icy desert, the flickering light of his burning Thunderhawk lapping against his blood-red armour.

THE FROZEN DESERT held crisp indentations that suggested a dozen footprints. Corallis stooped and inspected them in the near darkness.

'There are three groups of prints, captain: perhaps a squad tracking an individual of similar size and weight.' He paused and looked up at Gabriel. 'They look like the prints of Space Marines.'

The captain nodded, staring ahead into the outskirts of the stone city that had gradually emerged from the labyrinthine matrix of rock formations in the desert. He realised immediately that whatever intelligence had designed this city, it was a military mind: the entire city was immaculately camouflaged into its environment, and the approach through the rocks was narrow and twisting – the perfect defensive formation.

Not for the first time, Gabriel found himself struck with admiration for the ingenuity of the eldar.

'You mentioned three sets of prints, sergeant?' he asked finally, looking down at the crouching form of the scout.

'Yes, captain. But the third is are completely different: much smaller and lighter – they hardly leave any prints at all. Their trail is intermittent and broken, as though they were leaping or vanishing completely from time to time.'

'Harlequins?'

'Very likely, captain.'

'What are they doing?'

'It appears that they are tailing the individual Marine. They are not distracted by the trail of the squad, which suggests that they moved ahead of that squad or that they were able to differentiate between the hunters and the prey.'

An unspoken question hung in the air.

'It is Rhamah?' Zhaphel broke the moment of silence and gave voice to the idea that was lingering in all the minds of the Librarians of the Order Psykana.

'It is possible,' confirmed Corallis, rising to his feet. 'Whoever they are, they all went into the city.'

THE PICTURE FIZZED and then died into black, but Macha left her eyes fixed on the blank screen for a few more seconds. Her mind was racing and her spirit was ill at ease. For a moment she had thought that there was hope: the mon'keigh captain that had

appeared on the screen had looked just like Gabriel.
She had been sure that it was him, and had
struggled to understand why his mind had become
so closed to her. But then she had realised that it
was not Gabriel at all – this 'Ulantus' was a quite
different creature. Although she had always known
that the primitive mammals displayed certain
amounts of individuality, she had become
accustomed to seeing them as an undistinguished
mass of animals.

Except for Gabriel. He had been different from the
start. The farseer had seen the distant echoes of his
mind reflected in myriad futures, and she could hear
its clumsy resonance in many lines of the past.
Gabriel and his Blood Ravens had a significance that
was not shared by others of his species. Now that
Macha had finally realised how to recognise and differentiate between the mon'keigh warriors, she
found that Gabriel had already vanished into the
warp with Taldeer – *with Taldeer!*

That young seer could not know the significance of
the mammal that she accompanied. She had not
been there on Rahe's Paradise. She had not even witnessed the events on Tartarus. Whilst her soul was
pure enough, her mind was not yet fully formed. For
her, Gabriel was little more than another generic
mon'keigh: either she would underestimate him and
suffer the consequences, or she would glimpse his
potential and bring an even worse fate upon herself.

Finally turning away from the viewscreen, Macha
folded herself back into her meditation posture on
the podium in her chambers. Around her, she could

feel the pulses of anxiety and readiness that flashed around the wraithbone infrastructure of her cruiser. Nothing happened aboard the *Eternal Star* without its echo or feedback reaching the mind of the farseer in her chamber.

She nodded inwardly, satisfied that her crew were alert to the possible dangers represented by the massive but cumbersome Astartes battle-barge that loomed in space directly before them. They knew that the humans could outgun them, especially at this range, but they also knew how to prevent the situation from deteriorating to the point when a point-blank exchange would become necessary.

For her part, Macha infused the *Star* with calm – she did not believe that this Ulantus would want another battle. His mind was exhausted with anger and accusations, but they were not levelled at the Sons of Asuryan. If she had read his alien features correctly, Macha believed that the captain's ire was directed towards Gabriel himself, which she found mysterious and impossible to fathom.

Even though she knew that the mon'keigh found the eldar enigmatic and difficult to understand, Macha often found herself amused by the irony of the fact that she found those simple mammals so very difficult to comprehend as well. Their base emotions and primitive urges had been abandoned by the children of Isha many millennia before. Gazing into their volatile, vulgar and violent souls was like gazing back in time, to the very origins of the eldar species, when the Old Ones had first called them into being.

Without touching them, with merely a movement of her glittering, emerald eyes, Macha cast her rune-stones out before her and closed her eyes. In the darkness behind her eye-lids, she could see the image of the stones as they began to levitate off the shining wraithbone surface and spiral into a vortex. They spun faster and faster, dragging the air in the chamber into a whirl as they began to glow with an unearthly green. The farseer could feel the distur-bance they caused in the material and immaterial space of her circular chamber as they flashed past her face, aspiring for the apex of the sweeping, con-vex ceiling.

Something jabbed into her mind, jogging her concentration suddenly like a single raindrop into a desert. A flicker of feedback from the *Eternal Star* splashed into her thoughts: one of the sensor arrays had picked up a disturbance in the local star. A sunspot had appeared without warning, and great fountains of radioactive solar flares had been dis-charged, spouting out of the yellow inferno like eruptions.

She put the thoughts aside. The sensors of the *Eternal Star* were interlaced into the capillaries of space itself: they picked up any and all shifts in the material realm. The ancient vessel was organically fused with the space through which it sailed, just as it was effectively an extension of Macha's own being. It served to mediate her experience of the world. Had the solar flares failed to make their pres-ence felt in the farseer's mind, then there would have been something wrong.

With a last effort of concentration, Macha flicked open her eyes and sent the runes scattering through the space before her. They snapped suddenly into motionlessness, as though some kind of stasis field were suddenly activated to freeze their movement. Some of them hung suspended in the air, while others lay prone on the wraithbone deck. Some of them glowed green with energy and life, while others were dull and without lustre.

Cocking her head slightly, Macha inspected the patterns, mentally discarding the dead stones and those that had clattered impotently to the ground. If the runes themselves had no power, then the futures they emblemised in the present lacked all potency; this was not the time for her to be worried about the most unlikely of eventualities.

Rillietann. Vaul. Cegorach. Arebennian.

The runic symbols for the ancient words glistened and revolved slowly. As Macha let her mind rest on each of them, they started to swirl and swim, intermingling and mixing with each other in complex patterns that it had taken her centuries to master. It was as though they were dancing for her, enacting one of the great mythic cycles: in the elegant and smooth motions, Macha saw the unfolding of the Myth of the Birth of Fear – only the tragic hero Lanthrilaq was missing from the scene.

As she watched the display, letting the movements and ideas slip easily into her consciousness, two more stones started to shimmer and click against the wraithbone deck where they had lain dead. They vibrated rapidly, as though willing themselves back into life, until one of them burst into green and flew up into the spiralling pattern of the other runes.

Mon'keigh.

Macha raised an uneasy eyebrow. It was highly unusual for stones that had fallen dormant in the casting to return into the formation. Although the runes always formed a multi-dimensional pattern, often spread through a discreet period of time, it was nearly always the case that all the active stones were active from the start. A late comer was a disruption – it was an unwelcome fate.

Just as she had processed the intrusion of the humans into the ancient mythical cycle, the second regenerating stone sprang up into the pattern. It burned more brightly than all the others, flaring and colliding with the other stones as though seeking to eradicate them all or drive them from the ritual space.

Shafts of physical pain stabbed into Macha's eyes as she watched the new stone burn and crash, scattering the others out of her concentration and sending them skidding and clattering to the ground. After a few seconds, only it and the *Mon'keigh* remained. It flashed before her eyes and then stopped in space, spinning on its vertical axis like a gyroscope, burning its runic symbol into the farseer's pupils.

Yngir.

Macha's eyes widened.

Farseer! Uldreth's mind was angled and sharp; his thoughts carried an edge of urgency.

Disoriented for a moment, Macha's mind raced and tumbled. She struggled to drag her thoughts out of the runic future and return them to the present. Finally, snapping her eyes shut, she heard the last of the runes sizzle and then drop to the ground. When she opened them again, all of the stones lay motionless and dormant before her knees. She sighed heavily.

Yes, Uldreth Avenger, she replied at last. *You are concerned about the activity in the star? You are right – the yngir are returning. The mon'keigh were presumptuous in their claims to have killed them. Their energy is reforming, and the star will give them birth once again.*

How long do we have, Macha, asked Uldreth?

The farseer looked down at the stones. They were cracked and shattered, some of them beyond recognition. The *Mon'keigh* rune was chipped, and a single crack ran through the middle of it, as though splitting it into two. Only the *Yngir* remained undamaged.

Not long enough, my Avenger. Not long enough. We should inform the mon'keigh. They will not be aware of these developments. They may yet be of use in all this.

As THE SQUAD of Blood Ravens emerged out of the labyrinth of rock formations that surrounded the unusual and circular stone city, Gabriel drew his Space Marines to a halt. The outskirts of the settlement were comprised of low-rise, stone dwellings, standing in sharp contrast with the massive cliffs that defined the circumference of the city, but the roofline steadily heightened towards the city centre, giving the impression of town planning around a conical theme. Many of the roofs actually sloped to match the gradient. The effect was truly breathtaking, making the city appear as though it had been cut down into the ground rather than built up out of it.

Because of the sloping, conical design, the Blood Ravens could see the street plan reflected in the layout of the roofs, and they noticed immediately how the stone streets wound in intricate and complicated patterns, as though designed deliberately to confuse and disorientate an attacking force.

'This place was all but invisible from the air,' muttered Corallis, his mind leaping back to the scene that he had seen from the plummeting Thunderhawk. 'It just looked like an unusual rock formation.'

'That is clearly the idea,' replied Korinth, scanning the townscape with admiration.

'And yet you recognised it as a possible settlement, sergeant,' smiled Gabriel, unsurprised by the competence of his scout sergeant. It was not for nothing that Corallis had been elevated to his current rank directly out of the scout company.

'Look at this place, Gabriel,' began Jonas as he unclasped his helmet and gazed at the vista before them. 'Do you know where we are?'

Gabriel saw the look of wonder on the Librarian's face and recognised the spark of excitement that had appeared in the old veteran's eyes.

'You know this place, father?'

'I have heard of places like this, Gabriel, but I never thought that I would live to see the day when

I would walk in the streets of such a city. It makes the excavations on Rahe's Paradise seem pathetic.'

'Taldeer said that it was an ancient world of knowledge – she called it Arcadia,' nodded Gabriel, unclipping his own helmet to share the moment with his old friend. 'She led me to believe that it contained... sensitive information.'

Jonas shook his head and a smile crept across his face. 'I suspect that is a masterful understatement.' He opened his mouth as though to speak again, but then closed it. A moment of silence hung between them.

This is Arcadia. Zhaphel and Korinth showed no signs of having heard the thoughts of the father Librarian, but they were the only ones who could.

Yes. They agreed.

'I have heard of this place,' continued Jonas at length, without looking into Gabriel's eyes. 'The architecture is unmistakably eldar, as you can see. And the temple roofs,' he continued, pointing distinctly to the domed rooftops that punctuated the unusual sky-line, 'appear to indicate that they were built to honour the mythical Laughing God of the ancient ones. Do you know what that means, Gabriel?'

The captain shook his head. 'Tell me, father. Your knowledge is superior to mine.'

'This is a Harlequin settlement – a world of knowledge that is hidden even from the eldar of the craftworlds. The Order Psykana have being searching for such a place for centuries; it is said that the Harlequins possess knowledge of rifts in the time-space continuum – they can travel both through time and space, utilising the timelessness of the warp. An influential thesis in our Order suggests that this knowledge will provide the key for the recovery of the Fated Fifth.'

As he spoke, Zhaphel and Korinth turned to face Jonas, clearly surprised that the Librarian father was revealing so much, even to the Commander of the Watch.

Gabriel nodded, accepting the wisdom of his old friend without questions or doubt. He had complete confidence in the old Librarian's scholarship and erudition. 'Is this the reason why the Chaos Marines would be interested in this place? Or why Taldeer would be so adamant that we should get here?'

There was a pause. 'I doubt it, captain, but it is possible.'

'Other reasons?'

'It seems likely that a lost eldar world of knowledge would house many technologies that could be used as weapons by the unscrupulous or undiscriminating. This is exactly the kind of place that traitors to the Emperor could find assistance in their dark quests. It seems unlikely that the degenerate Marines of a Chaos Legion would realise that there were things of even greater value here.'

'Taldeer spoke of a sword.'

Jonas looked at Gabriel, searching his eyes for a sign. 'The Sword of Vaul, yes.'

Korinth and Zhaphel shifted in visible unease. They had not expected the father Librarian to be so forthcoming to anyone outside the Order Psykana, not even to Captain Angelos.

'It is a mythical blade. A rare and forbidden volume recovered from the ruins of one of the smaller Callidus Temples in the outskirts of the Orphean sector contains a record of the myth: *The Fall of Lanthrilaq*. Evidently, one of the Callidus heirosavants, Rafaellus Kneg, extracted the tale from a captured Harlequin mime called Yvraelle.'

'Mime? I thought that the mimes were incapable of speech,' interrupted Ephraim, taking an interest in the possibility of technical knowledge being revealed to them on this planet.

'Yes, that is the standard, orthodox position,' agreed Jonas nodding. 'It seems that the agents of the Callidus Temple suspected that this position was flawed, and they sought to test their theory. As it turns out, it transpired that they were right. By the end of the interrogation, Yvraelle had divulged details of a number of the mythic cycles over which the Harlequins appear to stand sentinel. One of them was the Fall of Lanthrilaq.'

Tanthius leaned forward, bringing the massive bulk of the Terminator armour into close proximity. 'Just tell us about the sword, Jonas. This is not the time for legends and myths. Just tell us about the sword so that we can get off this alien, forsaken rock.'

'It is said that Lanthrilaq once bore a heavenly blade – one of the fabled Blade Wraiths constructed by the eldar smith-god, Vaul. Whilst the other blades were destroyed in the ancient battles with the necron, it is rumoured that Lanthrilaq's blade fell shattered from his hand, never to be found.'

'Never to be found? Then why should we believe that it is here?' Tanthius was growing impatient, standing on the edge of a tangibly real alien city and having to listen to children's stories about eldar gods and their broken swords.

Jonas glanced over towards Korinth and Zhaphel, as though looking for support, but they showed no signs of reaction.

'We have reason to believe that brother Librarian Rhamah may have been drawn to the location of the last Sword of Vaul,' he conceded, as though confessing something terrible.

There was a long silence as the others waited for Jonas to continue. As they waited, the first of the triple suns crested the horizon and sent a sudden, soft sheet of red light unfurling through the streets of the stone city, apparently flooding it with blood.

'Brother Rhamah has an eldar blade of his own – the *Vairocanum*. It is an ancient and famous sword, once wielded by the Harlequin warlock Lavena the Joyful. But one day Lavena fell under the onslaught of a force more glorious than anything she had encountered before: the Great Father, Vidya himself – the Seeker of Truth – fell upon Lavena and clove her life force in two, ending the Harlequin raids of Qulus Trine. After his victory, Vidya gave the wealthy Qulus system to the Eighth Company and took *Vairocanum* as his own prize.'

'Rhamah has the sword of Vidya himself?' Tanthius was stunned.

'In a manner of speaking,' offered Korinth. If Jonas was going to reveal so much, he would at least seek to rectify any misunderstandings. 'In fact, the Great Father never wielded *Vairocanum*. We are not sure why, and Vidya left no records to explain his reasons, as far as we know. Instead, he left the blade in trust to the Order Psykana.'

'And we stood as its guardians for many centuries,' interjected Zhaphel, removing his helmet at last, letting his long grey hair fall loosely in front of his golden eyes. 'It was held in the...' He trailed off, apparently unwilling to finish the sentence.

'It was held in the Psykana Armorium, hidden in one of the psychically shielded subchambers of the Sanctorium Arcanum aboard the *Litany of Fury*,' said Jonas, meeting Gabriel's eyes levelly and watching the reaction of the Commander of the Watch carefully.

Gabriel raised an eyebrow at the mention of a secret armoury hidden in the bowels of his own battle-barge, but he said nothing to interrupt the father Librarian.

'This armoury contains only force weapons, most of which have been procured throughout the ages by Blood Ravens Librarians in encounters with the eldar. Some, in fact, have been bequeathed to us voluntarily.'

Gabriel shook his head. 'Does Ulantus know about this place?' He smiled broadly at the sudden realisation that the straight-laced captain was currently in command of potentially the most heretical battle-barge in any Chapter of the Adeptus Astartes.

The three Librarians exchanged glances. 'No, captain,' answered Korinth firmly. 'Ulantus knows nothing of this. Nobody except the initiated of the

Order Psykana have ever been permitted this knowledge.'

'Knowledge is power, but ignorance is safety,' murmured Tanthius under his breath. He didn't like this at
all.

'Why?' The abrupt question came from Ephraim.

'Why what?' asked Jonas.

'Why was the sword committed to that Armorium?
We have a number of force weapons in the other
armouries in the fleet.'

'The Psykana Armorium is more than merely an
armoury, brother Ephraim. It acts as a conduit for the
psychic potentials of the weapons it holds, chan-
nelling them into the Beacon Psykana itself,
amplifying the psychic signal that pulses in the heart
of the Blood Ravens.

'After a certain period, the weapons become psychically fused with the beacon. When new Librarians are
initiated into the order, they are free to select one of
the weapons as their own. Carrying this weapon with
us ensures that we retain a permanent connection with
the beacon at all times – this means that we can draw
on its power at times of need, but it also means that
the beacon can draw on us. This is partly how the
Summoning of the Exodus functions.'

Gabriel nodded. He felt that he had known this
already. For an instant, his mind flashed with half misremembered images of the Astronomican, and he
wondered whether there was any connection between
these dubious moments of unsanctioned psychic
awareness and the secret beacon held in the core of his
battle-barge. With so much psychic energy confined

within the structure of a space vessel, surely there would be some unexpected or uncontrollable consequences?'

'What does this have to do with Rhamah coming to this planet?' asked Corallis, his clear headedness bringing the conversation back on track.

'In the legend of the Fall of Lanthrilaq,' began Jonas, turning to address the sergeant who had once trained under him on Rahe's Paradise, 'Lanthrilaq's blade is broken in combat with the necron. Afterwards, Lanthrilaq is slain and his imperfect blade falls to the ground on an unknown planet. However, the fragment that broke off his blade has a story of its own. It was found shortly afterwards by Lavena the Joyful, who had it re-forged into a new blade: the touch of death.'

'*Vairocanum,*' realised Corallis.

'Exactly. Rhamah's blade contains part of the essence of the last Blade Wraith.'

'Its nature is now divergent – it is tied both to our Beacon Psykana and to its origins as part of the imperfect blade of Lanthrilaq. It is perhaps because of this that the Great Father chose not to wield the blade himself – he was aware of the dangers,' explained Korinth.

'But Rhamah chose the blade?' asked Tanthius, his concern for the moral choices of the Blood Ravens coming to the fore once again.

'The blade chose him,' answered Zhaphel simply.

'When he plunged it down into the deck of the *Litany of Fury* while we were struggling through the warp, perhaps *Vairocanum* saw a chance to return to its source,' said Korinth.

'It can be no coincidence that *Vairocanum* snapped in exactly the same way as Lanthrilaq's blade. Coincidences are for the weak-minded and the ignorant,' continued Zhaphel. 'Even the remaining fragment of *Vairocanum* was so potent with psychic power that it overwhelmed the beacon when we attempted the Summoning of the Exodus. Neither Rhamah nor the rest of the sword are lost. If anything, their powers have grown since their fall.'

'We can only assume that this is because they are drawing close to the psychic home of *Vairocanum*,' concluded Jonas. 'That is why we think that Rhamah is here on this planet, and why the Sword of Vaul is here too. The presence of the Harlequins supports our theory, and the interest of the Traitor Marines is also circumstantial support.'

Gabriel looked his old friend directly in the eyes and saw the constancy of his purpose. The explanation had been an act of trust and confession; Gabriel had never asked and would never have asked Jonas to betray the details of the Order Psykana. As scholars, the Blood Ravens were fully aware of the value, importance and power of secrets.

Shifting his attention to the other two Librarians, he realised that they were taking a big risk. They had never served under him before, and he was fully aware that their opinion of him was probably shaped by the rumours that circulated through the Ninth Company under the command of Ulantus. Now, it seemed, they were on even ground.

As he looked from one to the other, the last of the Arcadian suns broke the horizon and a blinding blast of red light and heat swept across them, bathing them in a shower of burning sand. At that moment, Gabriel found himself wondering whether Taldeer had known all of this from the start.

Clicking his helmet back into place to protect his eyes and face from the harsh elements, Gabriel activated the vox bead. 'It's getting late. Let's find out what other secrets we can explode in this city.'

DOZENS OF FAKE grins glared down onto the stage. It was almost impossible to differentiate the Harlequins in the stands from the mannequins that simply made up the numbers when the audience appeared overly thin.

It was thin today.

'They have come, Eldarec. The mon'keigh have come in greater numbers.' The voice echoed down from the highest balcony in the amphitheatre, bouncing around the acoustics until it appeared to have no origin at all. It might even have come from one of the lifeless, smiling mannequins. Such was how it should be for the voice of the chorus: impersonal but insightful.

'They tried to kill the farseer, Eldarec!'

'She was alive on the surface of Arcadia – and then they tried to kill her!

'We were there!'

'We watched her fall before the ugly and clumsy violence of the mon'keigh!'

'Karebennian was wrong, Eldarec! He is not to be trusted. The seekers of truth bring death not assistance in our fight.'

'The mon'keigh are all the same – they have no place on Arcadia!'

'The arebennian is deceitful – he is a trickster. The mon'keigh must die.'

'We must prepare for war, Eldarec! We must purge the surface of Arcadia!'

'The Solitaire takes the role of the Great Enemy and leads us to our doom!'

The lights in the theatre flickered and flashed then a controlled explosion detonated in the middle of the stage. As the smoke cleared, the lithe yet solid shape of Karebennian was revealed.

'Oh cegorach,' he began, 'it is true that the mon'keigh have landed in greater numbers. But it is not true that the newcomers are the same as those who have taken up position in the ancient repository.'

'They tried to kill the farseer, Karebennian,' countered Eldarec.

'It is true that the farseer suffered, but the cause of her injuries is not unclouded, cegorach. She was not killed – I saw to that. She led the mon'keigh here, and I believe that she did so willingly. Her mind spoke of the seekers of truth – we have encountered such creatures before. Lavena the Joyful once danced with their leader.'

'And she was killed, a fate that may yet befall this Taldeer of yours.' Eldarec's tone was grave despite the sudden grin that cracked across his mask.

'How can you tell them apart, Solitaire?' The shout echoed out of the audience; it carried accusations as much as interrogations.

Swirling to face the audience, Karebennian swooped into a leap and then a bow. 'One of them carries the *Vairocanum*.' His words were like song and his movements seemed to enact the drama of the Blade Wraith all over again. 'I have seen it.'

There was a hush of silence.

'They come for our resources, as once they came for the sword!' The call ricocheted and bounced around the stands. 'There is no trust amongst such animals. The farseer was wrong to bring them here.'

'Whatever differences you see between them: they are all the same! They come for our power!'

'Knowledge is power!'

'We should rid Arcadia of their stench!'

'We go to battle!'

'Commence the Dance of War!'

The call to arms echoed with the support of dozens of voices, as the sound whirled around the amphitheatre, gathering volume and power.

'I will not dance this dance with you,' said Karebennian, walking to the front of the stage and slumping, cross-legged to the ground. 'There is no harmony in this move. All great symphonies contain moments of rest and calm: this should be such a moment. We should wait before we act rashly: the mon'keigh may surprise us yet.'

Eldarec watched the Harlequin troupe spring to its feet in the stands, flipping and leaping their way down to the stage, leaving the grinning mannequins immobile and sinister in their seats. As the troupe started to assemble on the stage behind the Solitaire, Eldarec threw his head back and laughed, filling the arena with the rattling, guttural sound of mirth.

'If you will not join us, you will be alone, Karebennian.'

'Such is the path of the Solitaire.' There was no joy in his voice as he faded slowly out of visibility.

The Great Harlequin took up the centre of the stage and raised the Sword of Lanthrilaq above his head in a dramatic pose. As he did so, the rest of the troupe fell into position around him, each striking a combat stance that seemed frozen in time, as though the theatre had suddenly been thrown back into the dimness of history to the point at which Lanthrilaq and Eldanesh had mustered their greatest heroes to confront the soulless evil of the yngir. Gradually, the troupe's dathedi-shields powered up and their images were actually transformed to resemble the mighty host that once laid waste to the silvering minions of the star gods.

A series of dull impacts reverberated through the theatre and then a distant explosion shook the stage. Immediately, the rattle of gunfire and the hiss of warp discharge filled the background of the performance on stage. For a moment, the troupers wondered whether this was a new trick of the Great Harlequin, designed to make their posturing even more dramatic. But then cracks began to appear in the ceiling of the amphitheatre, sending dust and debris raining down onto the stage. More explosions sounded, and the theatre rocked.

In a sudden plume of flame, Karebennian reappeared at the edge of the stage, still cross-legged on the floor, facing up into the mannequin-filled audience.

'The mon'keigh have engaged each other. They are in the plaza in front of the main repository.'

THE COMMAND DECK of the *Litany of Fury* was silent. Captain Ulantus stared at the blank viewscreen as his mind raced to try and make sense of what was going on. It seemed like only hours before that he had been engaged in the simple and unambiguous affair of war: the *Litany of Fury* had proven itself once again in battle against the orks and even the necron. It now hung massively in orbit around the devastated spoils – Lorn V.

However, life was more complicated than war, even for a captain in the Emperor's Adeptus Astartes. The presence of two fully-armed eldar cruisers in tight formation just off the stern of his battle-barge was not something that Ulantus was comfortable with. Although he was relatively confident that they would be no match for the awesome firepower of the *Litany*, especially from such close range, the mere presence of the aliens made him feel uncomfortable. In a moment of insight, Ulantus realised that his discomfort was proof of his steadfast spirit: he was not Captain Angelos, and the presence of the eldar *should* fill him with righteous revulsion. His discomfort was his shield against heresy.

But the alien witch had confirmed many of the things that the errant Captain Angelos had claimed before he had gone gallivanting into the warp with the other eldar seer. The coincidence was simply too striking, and Ulantus was too much a Blood Raven to let such a coincidence pass unmarked.

'Coincidences are for the weak-minded and the ignorant,' he muttered to himself, echoing the words of the Great Father himself, still staring at the blank blackness of the viewscreen.

He considered the facts: it was true that there had been a webway portal on the surface of Lorn V. This had been confirmed by General Sturnn independently of Gabriel and the alien seer. It was further confirmed by the covert arrival of an Ordo Xenos inquisitor, the furtive Tsensheer, who had been summoned by Sturnn when the Cadians first discovered the site of the portal.

Tsensheer had studiously avoided all contact with the Blood Ravens since arriving in the Lorn system, which made Ulantus both suspicious and angry: Gabriel's reputation tarnished everything he touched. It would not be appropriate for Ulantus to contact the inquisitor himself – to do so would be to suggest that his lines of communication with the Blood Ravens Commander of the Watch were obscured in some way, which would fuel rather than dispell any rumours about the current state of the Blood Ravens. It was undoubtable that the direct and straight-forward Sturnn would have informed Tsensheer that Captain Angelos had already been down to the surface with an eldar seer in tow.

Not for the first time, Ulantus cursed the Commander of the Watch under his breath.

It was also true that the portal had been disabled in some way, but that neither the Blood Ravens nor the Cadian Guard had done anything that could have achieved this result. Gabriel had spoken about the presence of a Nova-class frigate out near Lorn VII, and had implied that it might have been a Chaos vessel that had somehow ruptured the portal from a distance. Leaving aside the question of who those Traitor Marines might have been and why they might have wanted to disable a webway portal, Ulantus had ordered the scan-array servitors to go back through the records of the mid-range scanners for the last day, and they had indeed shown the abrupt presence and sudden disappearance of a frigate-sized vessel around Lorn VII at about the time the *Ravenous Spirit* had entred the system.

The biggest hole in Gabriel's account of events, however, had been the leap from these factual observations to the assertion that the destruction of the webway portal was simultanously an opportunity for the unidentified Traitor Marines to find a way to an ancient, lost eldar planet of forbidden knowledge and power.

Gabriel had made this leap on the basis of information gifted to him by an alien witch who, until merely hours before the appearance of the necron menace, had been assaulting the *Litany of Fury*.

Ulantus turned away from the viewscreen and strode towards the exit of the control deck, deciding that he should go and check on the progress of the young neophyte, Ckrius, in the Implantation Chamber. He needed to see something material and controllable, something that spoke of the future of the Blood Ravens in a more affirmative manner.

Something uncomplicated by the affairs of Gabriel
Angelos.

As he walked he realised that Farseer Macha had
basically confirmed Gabriel's story. He wasn't sure
what to make of the realisation. Thinking back to his
conversation with the alien, Ulantus realised that he
had referred to Captain Angelos as 'Your Gabriel,'
when speaking to the farseer. It had been an unconscious move, but he wondered whether it revealed
something deep-seated about his views concerning
the commander.

The farseer had implied that the destruction of the
portal would bring doom to Lorn. She had said that
Gabriel and the other seer had to move quickly. But
she had not said why.

As the blast doors hissed and clunked closed
behind him, Ulantus found himself wondering
whether he should try to re-contact the eldar farseer
to find some answers to this question: with the orks
and necrons defeated, what could possibily be the
threat to the Lorn system now?

Behind him, Ulantus heard the blast doors unpres-
surise and hiss open once again.

'Captain Ulantus,' called Sauhl, stepping out of the
control room after him. 'You should see this.'

Ulantus stopped at the end of the corridor and
turned back to face his sergeant. 'See what, Sauhl?'

'The sun, captain. It's… it's changing.'

THE SOUND OF gunfire drew me through the sweeping, circular window cavity in the wall of the
librarium and out onto the balcony beyond. The

light of the three red suns streamed into my face as I emerged out of the shadow of the countless book stacks housed within the great reading-room. I held my hand to my face to shade my eyes from the glare and stepped up to the stone balustrade that ran in a beautiful arc, matching the crescent-shaped sweep of the balcony's floor.

It took a while for my eyes to adjust – the brilliant sunlight jousted through the long, thin streets and emerged into the plaza below the balcony like the beams of a laser, bursting into blinding radiance against every polished or metallic surface. I could see two groups of figures moving around the piazza: one group was growing as reinforcements stormed out of the gates that led into the building below me. The other group, on the far side of the square, was smaller and more isolated.

What is happening here? Who are those soldiers?

Good questions, friend, answered Ahriman. He was leaning against the wall of the librarium at the far edge of the balcony, watching the developing battle and bathing in the radiance of the bloody suns. In the startling light, his face seemed almost translucent.

Those are not Harlequins. The newcomers were much bigger than the eldar warriors and their movements were heavier. Even against the bursting light of the suns, I could see that their armour was not characterised by the multicoloured patterns of the Harlequins, but by solid colorations in red and gold. Two or three of them appeared to be in blue. And the armour was much more solid than anything employed by the Harlequins. Their weapons coughed and barked with a familiar gravity and resonance. *They look like Space Marines.*

Yes, young friend. They look like Space Marines. All of this knowledge acts like a beacon for the thirsty and for the seekers of power. If there is anything worth dying for, it is knowledge. Ahriman leant over the edge of the balcony for a moment, watching a volley of shells crash into the wall below and blow great chunks of masonry down into the piazza. Then he turned and peered back into the librarium through the circular arch. *If nobody else wanted this, how could we be sure of its value?*

I stared down into the blaze of sunlight, which was now hazed with smoke from the explosions and fires that had erupted around the plaza. Something about this scene felt wrong. *Ahriman is not surprised by this battle. He expected it. He needed it to happen – it is like an affirmation of his success.* 'You were expecting them?' I asked.

We did not start this fight, young sword of Vidya. My Prodigal Sons are merely defending themselves. Those Blood Ravens drew the first blood. The great sorcerer had stepped back through the archway into the librarium, as though the unravelling battle was already boring him.

Blood Ravens? The words struck me like daggers and then worked their way deeper in my mind, cutting through my thoughts like a chainsword.

We are merely defending ourselves and the knowledge that has fallen into our keeping. Knowledge is power, young Blood Raven, and we must guard it well. The great sorcerer paused for a moment, as though to let the significance of his words sink in. Then he stooped over the desk in front of the window, with his back to the balcony, and proceeded to inspect one of the books that he had left there before the battle had drawn him outside. *You must understand, friend of Ahriman, that I am doing no more nor less than they would have done in my position: I am protecting this knowledge from agents that will not understand it, or who will use it for the wrong purposes. In protecting it, I am protecting myself. What else could you expect me to do?*

Blood Ravens? The Sword of Vidya? My mind span with the words, as though I had heard them for the first time, or as though a fever had dredged them out of my deepest being and thrown them sizzling into my consciousness. Half remembered images of the red Space Marines charging towards me in the daemonic corridor flashed through my mind. *Blood Ravens*.

I staggered slightly, catching my weight against the stone balustrade. *Who am I? I am the sword of Vidya.* My eyes dropped to the heraldic icon etched into my own blue armour: black raven's wings with a pristine droplet of blood in their heart. My mind raced to the image on the cover of the book that I had found in the librarium.

Coincidences are for the weak-minded and the ignorant.

The maxim came from nowhere, as though I had known it forever.

Instinctively, I pulled *Vairocanum* from its sheath and held it up before me, as the battle for the courtyard continued to rage below. Its broken blade glowed an eerie green. I stared at it, letting my mind embrace its image. Something shifted in my thoughts, drawing my spirit down towards the blue-clad Blood Ravens in the piazza – it was as though the blade itself had some connection with them.

I am a Blood Raven...

Yes, friend of Ahriman, you are a Blood Raven. The sorcerer was leaning back against the desk, letting the flood of red sunlight wash over him as he turned a book over and over in his hands. *But we are not so different, you and I.*

I lowered *Vairocanum* so that it pointed directly at the great sorcerer, but I did not move. Instead, I looked down into the plaza and watched the battle rage for a few more seconds. The Blood Ravens and the Prodigal Sons were exchanging fire across the courtyard, but both groups were in heavy cover and most of the damage appeared to be to the beautiful stone structures of the city itself. *Such a waste.*

Looking back up at Ahriman's smiling, calm, unearthly face, I had no idea who I was at all. With my memory still shot to pieces, I could not deny that I felt some affinity for this seeker of knowledge. Something inside me thrilled at his esoteric power; it spoke directly to my being. Did I really need to make an enemy of this Ahriman? We had stood shoulder to shoulder against the Harlequins.

No, friend of Ahriman, there is no need for us to fight. Except in the mind – for it is in the mind where the most important battles are always fought. The Prodigal Sons are always open to new seekers of knowledge – how else can we survive? We are not so different, you and I, Librarian – you simply deny that part of you which I embrace happily. You need not fight with your own nature, Rhamah, just as you need not fight with me: the only meaningful fight is in your head.

As his words slipped easily into my mind, Ahriman rose from the desk and took two strides towards me. Drawing to a halt at the tip of *Vairocanum* he reached out his hand. *We were not always so different, friend of Ahriman.*

In his outstretched hand was the book that I had found in the librarium, with the Blood Ravens insignia on the cover.

There was a time, long ago before the Change, when the Thousand Sons of Magnus the Red wore the blood-red armour of their primarch. But times change. Everything changes. We have changed. This is one of the constant laws of our chaotic times. The key is to learn how to control the changes, how to master them and transform them to your own advantage. Do you think that it is coincidence that the Librarians of your Blood Ravens wear the blue armour of the Prodigal Sons and the Rubric of Ahriman? We are the seekers of truth, friend of Ahriman. We need only ever confront each other with our minds.

Keeping *Vairocanum* between us, I took the book from Ahriman's hand.

CHAPTER TEN: CONTESTATION

ON THE FAR side of the piazza was a grand, domed building. Arising out of its smoothly curving roof was a conical spire, like a giant finger pointing into the heavens. To one side was a high-rising tower, bristling with balconies and elegantly circular windows. The sheet of red light from the triple suns washed over one face of the tower, transforming it into a ruddy, reflected blaze. Somewhere near the top, Corallis could just about make out two figures on one of the balconies. They appeared to be clad in blue power armour, marking them out as Space Marines.

When he turned to inform the others, Corallis found that the three Librarians of the Order Psykana were already staring up at the figures.

A dark opening in the base of the domed hall, at the top of a flight of white, stone steps that rose out of the plaza, marked an entrance into the complex. The stairs were strewn with the bloodied and broken bodies of Harlequin troupers, some slumped into piles and others lying prostrate down the steps. At the top of the steps were a series of statues and monuments, some of which resembled humanoids – humans, eldar and dark eldar, all intermixed together – but most of them appeared to depict creatures of the warp, vile and snarling with vicious beauty. Like the other artistic structures that decorated the pristine streets of the unusual alien city, these inspired a mixture of awe and disgust from the Blood Ravens.

Hidden in amongst the statues and gargoyles outside the great hall was a squad of Space Marines. It was almost impossible to determine how many there were, since the statues provided more than ample cover for them, and they never attacked all at once. When the Blood Ravens had first emerged into the plaza, they had seen two of them standing sentinel in front of the entrance to the hall. However, as the first shots had been fired, those two had thrown themselves into cover and a flood of blues and golds and washed out of the dark entrance, flowing behind the monuments. There might have been one or two squads.

However many there were, there were more than enough to frustrate the attempts of the Blood Ravens to cross the plaza. Instead, the two sides were exchanging sporadic fire, most of which seemed to inflict damage only on the stone monuments behind which they had adopted cover.

'Jonas,' called Gabriel, leaning his back against a statue of a giant deathmask, which was grinning in the bloody sunlight even as chunks of it were blown off by occasional bolter shells. 'Jonas? Tanthius? Can you hear me?'

The father Librarian nodded from behind the wreckage of some kind of stone animal. He was crouched with Zhaphel and Korinth as the three Librarians attempted to assess the situation. 'Yes, captain. I hear you.' As he spoke, Korinth broke cover and unleashed a javelin of warp fire across the plaza, smashing it into the image of a leaping warp beast and blasting its head into shrapnel.

'Assessment?' asked Gabriel. 'Do we need to go around?'

'Stalemate, captain,' replied Tanthius, who was standing between two statues of dramatic eldar heroes, each of them with swords outstretched to the skies. He held his storm bolter before him and was unloading a relentless tirade of explosive shells towards the Traitor Marines at the top of the steps. He did not believe that a Terminator sergeant should be seen to take cover. 'We need to flank them before they flank us.'

As he spoke, the whistle of a grenade cut through the air. He watched it arc out from within the shadows of the hall's entrance, rising and then falling in a steep parabola before it clinked onto the ground in front of one the statues next to him. He stepped calmly to one side and watched as it detonated only a fraction of a second later, blowing most of the statue's base into rubble and revealing the crouching figure of Corallis behind it. As though this presented them with a new opportunity, Corallis and Tanthius open fire together, sending hails of bolter fire sleeting back across the plaza.

Gabriel nodded. 'Who are they, Jonas? Who are we fighting?'

'The yellow and blue markings are reminiscent of the Thousand Sons, captain,' offered Korinth as lightning poured from his staff to provide cover for Zhaphel, who was storming towards the huge, ornate, stone fountain in the centre of the plaza. 'That would also explain their interest in this world: who other than the Thousand Sons would go through all this trouble for a lost eldar library?'

'We would,' said Gabriel, with forced amusement.

'It is possible,' responded Jonas, ignoring the captain's tone, 'that these Marines were once Thousand Sons. But look at them more closely: they have no helmets. According to the most ancient records, the Thousand Sons became fused into their armour in the days after the Rubric of Ahriman. Only a small group escaped the devastating effects of that great and terrible spell. Only they can remove their helmets. These Marines must descend from those who were the children of Ahriman himself.'

'The Rubric of Ahriman?' asked Gabriel, his memory stirring faintly at the mention of the ancient spell.

'Yes, aboard the *Omnis Arcanum* we are fortunate enough to have one of the few remaining copies of the *Grimoire Hereticus*, in which the Rubric is described as a spell of such unimaginable power that even daemonic horrors fled before the singular roaring tempest of magic unleashed by Ahriman and his cabal,' explained Jonas.

'Ahriman was so desperate to escape the mutating touch of Tzeentch that he cast a spell which rendered his battle-brothers into little more than hollow automata – beneath their power armour the bodies of the Thousand Sons withered away into dust. Without bodies, what could there be to become mutated or corrupted,' added Zhaphel as he skidded to a halt under the cover of the great fountain.

The vox channel hissed with sudden static. 'They became pure consciousness?' asked Gabriel.

'Perhaps that is a rather too generous way to phrase it, captain,' replied Jonas cautiously. 'Better that we should call them inorganic abominations.'

'Of course. But this Ahriman – he escaped the effects of the spell?'

'Yes, so the *Grimoire* reports. Ahriman escaped the effects of the spell, but was banished from the Planet of Sorcerers by Magnus the Red himself, condemned to wander the Eye of Terror seeking clues as to the nature of Tzeentch.'

'He searches for knowledge of magic,' concluded Gabriel, recalling some of the rest of the story from his time in the Librarium Sanctorum. 'As I recall, he refuses to acknowledge that he is a servant of the Chaotic Powers – is that correct? He claims, rather, that he is a servant of knowledge itself – searching for it in its purest and most unadulterated forms across the galaxy.'

'We need not acknowledge our nature in order to be who we are, Gabriel. Such acknowledgement is an act of truth with which not all seekers of knowledge are comfortable.' Jonas's voice was suddenly grave. 'Do not confuse this seeker of knowledge with our own Great Father's search for truth. Truth is something with boundaries in the moral and the real. Knowledge is not always so bounded, especially knowledge of the power of Chaos. The Emperor himself decreed this division in the Edicts of Nikaea – remember that. Ahriman may not acknowledge his service to Tzeentch, but his very existence does violence to the memory of our Great Father and to the word of the Emperor of Man.'

'Enough preaching, Jonas,' snapped Gabriel, suddenly angry as he realised that he had only ever permitted Prathios to speak to him in this way before. 'You are not our chaplain.' He regretted his words as soon as he spoke them. 'Tell us what you know of the tactics of these Sons of Ahriman: what do they want here?'

'The *Tactica Adeptus Chaotica*, which has been assembled in the Librarium Sanctorum, contains very little on the Thousand Sons, except to indicate that they are well known for seeking to avoid direct fire-fights at close range, presumably because this nullifies the advantages offered by their impressive sorcery skills. It notes, I believe, that we should expect illusion, misdirection and feint. If possible, they will avoid armed conflict altogether: their objectives are rarely mere destruction.' Jonas's tone was efficient and clipped.

'Objectives?'

A sudden silence descended on the plaza as the bolter fire stopped abruptly. Without hesitation, Gabriel stepped out from his cover and stared across the pot-holed piazza towards the statues around the top of the steps that led into the grand hall. There was a blur of motion, and flashes of blue and gold streaked between the monuments.

'They're moving out?' suggested Corallis. 'Perhaps trying to get around to our flanks?'

'Or perhaps trying to make us think that,' replied Gabriel, raising his bolter and taking careful aim. He squeezed the trigger and watched the shell screech across the plaza and slide between the legs of one of the heroic eldar statues, behind which the Traitor Marines had been encamped. There was a metallic chink followed by a small explosion as the shell impacted against ceramite armour. Then a bank of fire erupted from the top of the steps, raining back down towards the exposed Blood Ravens.

'Objectives?' asked Gabriel again, stepping back behind cover.

'Two are possible – one is likely. One is the generation of followers. Because of the Rubric of Ahriman, it is unknown how the Thousand Sons are able to replenish their ranks. They seem to seek to foster cults on dozens of worlds at the same time, cultivating magi who can contribute in some way to the power of the Legion. This network is called the Prodigal Sons of Ahriman – and the name is also used by the Space Marines closest to the terrible sorcerer.'

'Unlikely to be the objective in this case,' agreed Gabriel.

'Agreed. The most likely is that these Prodigal Sons are searching for a specific artefact or artefacts. It is reputed that Ahriman himself conducts raids on museums, librariums, scholaria and reclusia all over the galaxy, searching for items of power and knowledge.'

'The Sword of Lanthrilaq,' concluded Gabriel swiftly. 'Taldeer was right. So these Marines are not trying to kill us, they're just trying to buy some time for their brethren to find the Blade Wraith? They are a diversion.'

'Corallis – see if you can get around behind that hall and find another way in. If we can do this without fighting, we will. In the meantime, we will provide a diversion of our own. Tanthius, if you please.'

As Corallis sprinted back out into the plaza, Tanthius strode forward towards the fountain behind which Zhaphel had taken cover. Korinth stepped out of cover and dashed to flank the massive Terminator sergeant, letting his force staff spit and hurl warp flames in a continuous barrage against the statues as he ran. By the time he reached Tanthius, Zhaphel had taken up a position on the other side of him. The three of them formed a short, blazing, firing-line in the very centre of the plaza. Storm bolter shells whined in a relentless tirade while lashes of warp fire crashed out of Korinth's staff. Zhaphel raised his force axe above his head and then drove it down into the flagstones. As the axe-head struck, it sent a crackling line of lightning jousting through the ground and up the steps, exploding the legs from one of the statuesque warp beasts that served as cover for the Prodigal Sons.

'Gabriel. There is another possibility,' said Jonas, catching the captain just as he broke cover and started to advance to join the others.

He paused and turned. 'Yes?'

'Have you ever heard of the Sacking of the Etiamnun Reclusium?'

'No, Jonas. Should I have?'

'The story is not shared with many outside the Order. Etiamnun III was a small, distant world on the edge of the Eastern Fringe – a barren and inhospitable planet. Not wholly dissimilar from Rahe's Paradise, in some ways.'

'Father, is this really the time for a history lesson?'

Bolter shells whistled past them, and the battle cries of Tanthius, Ephraim and the other Librarians could be clearly heard as they unleashed the fury of the Blood Ravens against the Prodigal Sons.

'This is important, Gabriel. You need to be aware: I am not your chaplain, but I am your Librarian.'

Gabriel nodded. Jonas was right. They were Blood Ravens, and they were nothing without knowledge.

'The population of Etiamnun III was limited to a few recluses in the reclusium, which was established in the ancient and forgotten past on a site... on a site bequeathed to the Imperium by the eldar of Altanzar, before that craftworld was lost to the Eye of Terror.

'For a number of decades now, the world has fallen under the direct protection of the Order Psykana. It appears almost completely insignificant, but its worth is immeasurable.'

'The Order Psykana has a force sufficient for the defence of a world?' Gabriel's astonishment was obvious. In front of him, he could see and hear the destruction being wrought by Korinth and Zhaphel together, and he wondered how many such Librarians would be needed to stand sentinel over a small, backwater world.

'That is not the point of this story, Gabriel. Another time. About a century ago, the reclusium was attacked by a force of Thousand Sons Marines, apparently led by a terrible sorcerer lord. They conquered it easily, since it had no defences other than its obscurity.'

'I don't understand why I need to know this, Jonas. If there is a point, get to it.'

'The sorcerer lord led his Marines deep in the mountain complex that lay under the reclusium. In its heart he found what he had come for: the central chamber housed a long hidden and all-but-forgotten portal into the eldar webway.

'The Order Psykana was summoned to expel the sorcerer, but by the time we arrived the sorcerer was gone, vanished into the webway. Left behind in the hurry was a handwritten copy of a book, *The Tome of Karebennian*. You have probably heard of that book, Gabriel? It's supposed to show the various routes through the webway to the Black Library of the eldar. That is what the Thousand Sons are looking for, Gabriel.'

'What happened to the book, Jonas? Is this also hidden away in some secret chamber of the Order Psykana?'

'We destroyed it, of course, Gabriel.' Jonas's voice betrayed genuine surprise at the question. 'Why would we keep such a thing? The quest for knowledge of alien sorcery was explicitly forbidden by the Edicts of Nikaea, as you know. We are not sons of Ahriman, Gabriel, we are the children of Vidya. We seek truth, not merely knowledge for its own sake.'

'I see,' nodded Gabriel, not entirely convinced by this logic. 'Then the book is gone.'

'I said it was a copy, Gabriel. It was a hand-written copy. Another sorcerer from the Thousand Sons, possibly Ahriman himself, must have one of the originals. Whoever found Arcadia knew that the webway portal on Lorn V would lead them here. Whoever these Prodigal Sons are, it seems likely that they have seen a copy of *The Tome of Karebennian*, and they are probably here for more than the Sword of Lanthrilaq.'

STEPPING BACK INSIDE the librarium and forcing my shoulder past Ahriman, I flipped *Vairocanum* back into its holster on my back. Sitting into one of the stone chairs, I pushed aside the other books that Ahriman had collected onto the desk in front of the window, sending a couple of them fluttering heavily down to the ground. The sorcerer did not protest against my actions, but he watched me carefully with an amused and patronising smile playing about his face.

Gazing down at the cover of the book, I saw the now-familiar insignia of the Blood Ravens emblazoned on the ancient boards. As I had noticed before, the script on the cover was eldar in origin, and it sported a number of runes that I could not recognise.

As I stared at them, wracking my brain for memories that could be of help, Ahriman drew up a chair and sat down opposite me, casting a heavy shadow over the book and rendering himself into a stark silhouette against the red light of the suns outside. *Quezul'reah*.

'What?'

'The runes,' he explained, as though teaching a child how to read. 'They say *Quezul'reah*.'

I looked from the sorcerer to the book and back again.

'It means the *Un-Founding*. I'm sure that you have heard of it.' Ahriman's smile was fixed. 'As I recall, your Azariah Vidya once held a copy of this book. If I remember correctly, he even wrote a commentary on it. What was it called?'

'The *Apocrypha of the Un-Founding*,' I replied, remembering the name as soon as the sorcerer asked the question. *I have seen that book. It is one of the foundational texts of the Order Psykana.* 'How do you know this?'

'Ahriman knows all things, son of Ahriman. I knew Vidya better than you might expect, young sword of Vidya.'

I held the sorcerer's ghostly eyes for a moment, trying to see through them into whatever semblance of a soul resided within. Something inside me rebelled against his words. *He's lying to me. He can see fragments of my memory and he's playing with me.* But I couldn't work out why. *What does he want from me?*

Just as I was about to speak, the heavy doors to the librarium crashed open and three Prodigal Sons rushed through them. Their armour was scratched and carbon-scarred. One of them was clutching a large, oversized tome, which he slammed victoriously onto the desk in front of Ahriman, utterly obscuring my book beneath it.

'You will forgive our intrusion, my lord,' muttered the book carrier as he sank into a smart bow.

'Will I, Obysis?' But Ahriman had already forgotten about the sorcerer-Marine. He was running his fingers over the cover of the book, feeling every crease and crack in its ancient covers, his eyes burning with excitement.

'It was precisely where you said it would be, Lord Ahriman,' continued Obysis, unphased and still hopeful of reward.

'Of course it was,' muttered the sorcerer lord, without any great attention.

'There was some resistance. We lost two battle-brothers.'

'Indeed,' replied Ahriman, cracking open the cover with intimate care. A broad smile cut across his face as he saw the first page of the book. 'Still, some things are worth dying for,' he said, looking up at the bowed Prodigal Sons at last. 'Signal to the others, Obysis. We are moving out.'

'Yes lord.' The three Marines bowed briskly and then ran back out of the librarium.

I watched the scene unfold before me, the thought of the *Quezul'reah* gradually and reluctantly fading from my mind. These were the Marines that Ahriman had dispatched to find the webway navigational charts, which were alluded to in the *Tome of Karebennian*.

Judging from the size of the tome with which they had returned, and looking at the expression that hazed over Ahriman's face, they had found the book of charts. Despite my animosity towards the sorcerer and my frustration about the *Quezul'reah*, I was gradually overwhelmed by the desire to see the book. *It has probably never been graced by the attention of human eyes.* In the back of my mind there was another thought, silent and secret in my soul: *I am the eyes of the Emperor.*

'You are right, friend of Ahriman – never before have we seen a book like this. It is for knowledge such as this that Ahriman has scoured the galaxy for unspoken centuries... for millennia. Even the riddles of that Emperor-cursed Karebennian could not keep me from this forever.'

Pushing my chair back, I rose and walked around behind the sorcerer, leaning over his shoulder to view the open pages of the book, our eyes gazing onto the same images, as one. There was a slight ripple of tension in Ahriman's shoulders, as though my presence there repulsed or worried him. Whether he was unaccustomed to allowing people behind him, or whether he was simply unused to sharing the content of his books, the tension dropped away quickly as we pored over the text and charts together.

THE RATE OF fire from the Prodigal Sons dropped suddenly and Gabriel held up his fist to indicate that the Blood Ravens around the fountain should cease fire. The air was thick with dust, debris and smoke, which wafted through the blood-red atmosphere, reducing visibility to only a few metres. In between wafts of noxious clouds, Gabriel could catch glimpses of the ruined statues that once stood in defiant magnificence before the entrance to the great hall. Little flecks of colour told him that there was movement: moments of blue and gold flashed and dashed between the statues, but their density was diminishing. After a few seconds, he could see no colour at all, just the white of the stone and the dirty pock marks of explosions. By the time the dust had begun to settle, it looked as though the Prodigal Sons had gone.

Gabriel opened his fist and flicked two signals: one sending Korinth dashing out into the square to the east, curving round and up the steps on that side; the other sending Zhaphel on a mirrored path to the west.

Once they were in position on either side of the dark entrance into the grand hall, they nodded their readiness and the rest of the Blood Ravens broke cover and charged up the centre of the steps, with Gabriel the first to crest the stairs. Without pausing, the captain burst through the open entrance, dropping his weight into a roll as he crossed the threshold and coming up with his bolter trained into the darkness around him. Behind him, he could hear the solid footfalls of the other Blood Ravens moving in support.

'Light,' snapped Gabriel as he realised that the darkness was too dense even for his enhanced eyes. There was a single shaft of red light in what he assumed was the centre of the chamber, piercing down out of the ceiling. Immediately, Gabriel assumed that it was running down the heart of the unusual conical spire that protruded out of the roof of the dome. Despite the danger of his situation, he made a mental note about the incredible architectural achievements demonstrated in this alien city.

There was a murmured whisper from one of the Librarians behind him, and then a faint bluish light hazed into the grand, domed hall. It revealed a wide, circular chamber, with an ambulatory running all the way around the circumference, shrouded in the shadows of the pillars that divided it from the main part of the chamber.

With the benefit of the faint light that glowed off the tip of Korinth's staff, Gabriel could make out the shape of a figure crouched in the shadows on the far side of the cavernous chamber. As soon as his eyes alighted on the figure, it seemed to realise that it had been seen and rose to its feet, bowing slightly.

'They ran straight through here, captain,' hissed the voice of Corallis into the vox. 'There is a smaller entrance through a passageway to the north,' he explained, pointing a faintly visible arm to one side.

'I made it inside just as they were retreating through this chamber, and I decided to wait for you to follow.'

'Very good, sergeant. How many were they?' Gabriel rose to his feet and began to stride out across the floor towards the scout sergeant.

'I'm not sure, captain,' replied Corallis. 'They moved strangely, making it difficult to assess their numbers precisely. But not many. No more than a squad.'

'And where did they go?' asked Captain Angelos, reaching the shaft of red light in the centre of the room and passing his own red, gauntleted hand back and forth through the beam.

'There is an entrance to the tower over there,' pointed Corallis, indicating an area of deeper shadow on one side of the cavernous hall. 'They filed through the doors and then bolted them from the other side. I presume that they anticipated that you would attempt to follow them.'

'They anticipated correctly,' answered Gabriel, smiling weakly. Hunting Traitor Marines was devoid of ethical dilemmas for him, and he enjoyed the rare moment of certainty. 'Tanthius. Ephraim,' he added, turning back to the rest of the Blood Ravens as they began to fan out around the chamber to secure it. 'See what you can do about the doors. Quietly is better, but open is better than closed.'

The Techmarine and the Terminator sergeant broke off their sweep, nodded, and then strode purposefully across the chamber towards the large, black doors that barred the way into the tower.

'Father Urelie,' said Gabriel formally. 'Any ideas about this place?'

Jonas was walking around the circular chamber in a decreasing spiral, his head scanning all of the beautiful architectural features that specked the massive domed ceiling, the pillars that supported it, and the ambulatory that swept simply around the perimeter. 'It is breathtaking, captain,' he concluded.

Despite himself, Gabriel smiled a little. Jonas Urelie had once requested a secondment to the backwater world of Rahe's Paradise so that he could lose himself in the search for the truth about the origins of the Blood Ravens; he had willingly given up the life of an Angel of Death, arguing that he had grown too old for tearing around the galaxy in pursuit of divine vengeance and righteousness.

How ironic that his first mission since Rahe's Paradise was destroyed found him here, surrounded by more archaic knowledge than he might ever have seen before in his long and exalted career as a Blood Ravens Librarian. Of course he would find this breathtaking, reflected Gabriel; his awe was somehow reassuring. It *was* breathtaking – to take this place lightly would be to fail to appreciate its value.

'Have you noticed, Gabriel?' continued the Librarian, pointing up at the domed ceiling. 'Have you noticed how they have constructed this remarkable roof?'

Gabriel smiled again and stepped away from the shaft of vertical, red light so that his eyes would not be dazzled as he looked up. As his vision adjusted to the dim, bluish light that lit the curving ceiling, Gabriel's heart leapt.

'It's full of books, Gabriel! This is part of a massive librarium. This is the great hall that leads into the legendary Arcadian Librarium!' The father Librarian's excitement was undisguised.

Sure enough, the massive dome was comprised of thousands of concentric rings of book shelves, each packed with so many books that they would defy any attempt to count or catalogue. They were so densely and perfectly organised that a casual observer would not even notice that their spines were anything other than intricately patterned ceiling tiles.

'How are they prevented from falling?' asked Korinth, who had abandoned his sweep of the huge chamber in favour of sharing the wonder. 'The angles are all wrong. The books should fall.'

The shelves at the very top of the dome – the ones that ran most tightly around the hole through which shone the shaft of red light – were effectively vertical, and the books on those shelves appeared to defy gravity.

They are held in place because they are in their correct place. Everything tends towards its home, human, as you know. Things can be summoned back to their rightful place, even after an exodus. This is because the galaxy dislikes the out-of-place. It wants returns and homecomings.

Many things are bound to others – just as wills and souls can be bound into brotherhoods or cabals.

These books are at home here, and here they stay, whether gravity seeks to relocate them or not.

The Librarians and Gabriel turned as one, each drawing their weapons and spinning into combat readiness. The thoughts had not come from any of them; they were unfamiliar, cold, insidious and powerful thoughts.

Standing casually in the shaft of red light, as though spot-lit on a stage, was a figure that Gabriel, Jonas and Corallis had seen before. Although it didn't appear to be moving, it somehow seemed to swim and shift as they looked at it, giving it the impression of being a hologram or a trick of the red light.

The last time I saw you, Gabriel, you were in more auspicious company.

'The seer has gone,' said Gabriel bluntly. He recognised Karebennian from the ice cave on Lorn V, but he had not realised that the Solitaire could communicate in words. It had danced for Taldeer.

'Captain?' queried Corallis, looking from Gabriel to Karebennian with his bolter drawn. He could only hear Gabriel's words but was conscious that the Librarians were waiting for something, poised.

I saw her fall, human. You tried to kill her.

'No!' Gabriel shouted. 'It was not our doing. We brought her here, and your Harlequins attacked us. They attacked her in the desert. You killed her, Karebennian!'

She is not dead, Blood Raven – no thanks to you. But her fall speaks ill of your intentions, Blood Raven. She fell because you came here. Karebennian's answer was elliptical and indirect. Gabriel could not tell whether it was a concession or a further accusation. The Solitaire began to shift its weight, as though it was uncomfortable remaining still for so long. The movement made the Ravens twitchy.

'Her fall speaks ill of your judgement,' retorted Gabriel, hearing echoes of a familiar conversation in the back of his mind. 'My intentions are not the issue here.'

Then why are you here, Gabriel, friend of Macha?

'We came out of trust, and we ask for the same from you.' Gabriel deliberately said nothing about the appellation. How did this Solitaire know Macha, and what did he know of her relationship with him? A thought struck him. 'Is Macha… dead?'

The Solitaire spun with a sudden release of energy, and then froze into an abrupt and elegant position.

No, not dead, human. She is waiting for you at Lorn.

'Macha is in the Lorn system?' Gabriel's mind raced with the possible implications. 'Has she made contact with the Blood Ravens?'

She has spoken with your servants, Gabriel of the Hidden Heart. They all await your return. Many things are bound to others.

'Why do they wait for me?' asked Gabriel, myriad possibilities cycling through his confused mind.

The yngir have returned to Lorn. The souls of the Biel-Tan and the radiance of your infinity pool have drawn them back into material space. They seek to finish their Great Task. Macha awaits your assistance, Gabriel. They need your help.

What do you mean by our 'infinity pool,' alien? Korinth's thoughts interrupted the exchange with an edge of hostility and suspicion. A visible tension gripped Jonas and Zhaphel.

'What does she expect me to do?' asked Gabriel, ignoring his Librarians.

She hopes that your intentions are pure, human. Then you will do what is required of you.

There was a pause as Karebennian cocked his head to one side and looked quizzically at the Commander of the Watch.

What do you want from this place, Gabriel?

Gabriel unclipped his helmet and laughed. He looked up into the towering dome of knowledge that swept over their heads. It was almost as though he could see the knowledge and power seeping out of the bindings themselves.

He sighed. A place like this was a Blood Raven's dream – Gabriel himself had led countless expeditions into the Eye of Terror and into the bowels of ancient, abandoned planets looking for lost artefacts and forbidden or hidden knowledge. It was through such enterprises that the magnificent Librarium Sanctorum on the *Omnis Arcanum* had been assembled; it was now one of the finest and most celebrated librarium anywhere in the Imperium.

The Blood Ravens revelled in their scholarship – in the absence of a clear and concrete story of their own origins, they prided themselves on their knowledge of all other things: knowledge of the other had gradually become a substitute for knowledge of self. It was an unquenchable thirst.

He looked back down at the shifting and deceitful mask of Karebennian. 'We have come for our battle-brother. He was lost to us, and we have reason to believe that he is here.' Gabriel realised that this was the truth. 'We are also here because your Taldeer impressed upon us the importance of our coming to this place. There are others here whose wills may not be as trustworthy as ours.'

I have seen the others. One of them is known to me. His will is simple and clear. I understand it well – I have been aware of him for longer than you can imagine. Are you really so different from these others, I wonder? One who is with them resembles you more closely than you might want to realise.

'We do not hide from our natures, Karebennian. Those Prodigal Sons want nothing but power from this place. They do not care about the consequences. And they certainly do not care about the plight of Macha or of Lorn. If you see no difference between them and us, then you should stand aside and detain us no longer. You suggested that we were in a greater hurry than even we ourselves had realised.' Gabriel racked his bolter and turned to move away. 'Ephraim! What progress on those doors?'

Wait. There is something that you must know.

SAULH POINTED AT the main viewscreen on the control deck of the *Litany of Fury* and said nothing. Words were redundant.

'By the Throne, sergeant,' muttered Captain Ulantus. 'What in the Vidya's name is happening to that star?'

A constellation of sunspots was clustered near the star's equator. They were black against the radioactive radiance of the sun, but they appeared to shift and shimmer, as though possessing their own power. Massive fiery storms were raging around the perimeter of the star, spilling fountains of thermal radiation and superheated hydrogen through the orbits of the inner planets of the Lorn system. Lorn I was already beginning to die, as its atmosphere started to bleed away under the onslaught, leaving the rocky surface of the planet exposed to the rain of fire and radiation. Its colour was gradually shifting towards an inferno of orange, even as the star began to swell and its colour darkened towards red.

'It's dying, captain.'

'I can see that, Saulh. But how, why?'

'We can't tell. All the probes indicate that it is well within the average lifespan for a star of this size and constituency. Something appears to be draining it of energy, literally bleeding it dry.'

'What about the aliens?' Ulantus's mind leapt immediately to suspicion.

'The eldar? Their vessels have not moved, captain. And we can detect no connections between them and the star.'

'Where is the energy drain focussed?'

'On the far side of the sun, captain. We should be able to see it shortly, when the orbit of Lorn V swings us around the next sector of the ellipse.'

'I'm not sure that we should wait that long, sergeant. Bring the engines on line. Let's take a look.'

'As you wish, captain,' replied Saulh, nodding a signal to one of the serfs at the main control bank.

As the image on the viewscreen began to move, reflecting the sudden motion of the *Litany of Fury*, the picture began to snow and disassemble.

Interference patterns hissed across the image, breaking up the picture until it was hardly discernable.

'Sergeant?' prompted Ulantus, waiting for an explanation or a solution.

'Working on it, captain. It looks as though–'

Saulh's voice was cut off by a loud squeal of static and feedback that resounded around the control deck. At the same time, the image on the viewscreen flickered and then snapped into focus, showing the porcelain face of the eldar farseer once again.

'Captain Ulantus,' nodded Macha, making a visible effort to remember and pronounce his name.

'Alien,' replied Ulantus, his irritation obvious. 'Your timing is terrible. You are interfering with the *Litany*'s viewers. Desist at once.'

Macha's face was untroubled by the captain's words. She ignored him as though his protests were utterly insignificant. 'You must realise your failure, human. The yngir are returning. Look to the star. They draw its strength into themselves, waiting to be reborn into the materium.'

'We destroyed the necron fleet, alien. Had any of them survived, your own kin would have confirmed this.'

'No, not destroyed. The yngir are not a foe that can be destroyed with the weapons of mon'keigh. The silvering hordes return and return until they are put to death by the spear of Khaine, or by the wraith blades of Vaul himself. Where is Gabriel?'

Ulantus growled. 'Sergeant, kill this connection. We have more important things to worry about than the rantings of an alien witch. Captain Angelos may place his faith in these creatures, but I will place mine in the Great Father, in the Emperor's light, and in the righteous bombardment cannons of this battle-barge.

'Kill this connection and bring us around to the far side of the sun; let's see what is really happening with our own eyes.'

SNAPPING THE OVERSIZED book of charts shut, Ahriman rose abruptly to his feet as the rest of the Prodigal Sons burst through the doors into the librarium. Quickly scanning the piles of books that had been discarded onto the floor by the side of the desk, he reached down and extracted one other tome before turning to address his Marines, who had rapidly arrayed themselves into formation before him.

I stood to one side, watching the scene unfold like an observer of a piece of theatre.

'Brothers,' he began, with a broad smile playing over his shifting, ghostly features. 'This is a reckoning day. We have searched for this world for many centuries, following the leads left for us by the treacherous and devious minds of the aliens in their vulgar and misconceived tomes of poorly directed knowledge. And now we are presented with an embarrassment of riches as reward for our diligence and intellectual labour. Here, in this hand,' he said, raising the large book of webway charts, 'I hold the key to our final destination. And here, in the other hand,' he added, holding up the *Legend of Lanthrilaq*,

'I hold the encrypted directions to the location of the last of the Blade Wraiths of Vaul.

'This is the day when Ahriman and his Prodigal Sons will finally take the knowledge and the power for which we have been searching, for which we have been dying, for which we have been killing. Neither the effete Harlequin guardians nor the misguided Blood Ravens can prevent this now.' The last words were directed towards me, and I nodded in affirmation, believing them to be true.

'My lord,' asked one of the sorcerer-Marines. I recognised him as Obysis, the one sent by Ahriman to recover the book of webway charts. 'Do we have time to achieve both goals? Should we not merely choose the greater and concentrate on that? Once we have found the Black Library, will not the blade of Lanthrilaq pale into insignificance? The Blood Ravens draw near,' he added, casting a furtive and untrusting glance at me.

'It is always good to ask questions, Obysis,' smiled Ahriman with menace glinting off his phantom teeth. 'Questions are the ground-spring of knowledge, after all. But it is usually unwise to question *me*. Do you question me, Obysis, sorcerer of Ahriman's cabal?'

'I… I do not question your intentions, Lord Ahriman. I merely ask about the possibility of success.'

'So you question my judgement? Is that it?'

Obysis hesitated visibly, unsure whether this was the kind of contestation that Ahriman would reward or punish. He decided, wisely, to err on the side of caution. 'No, my lord. Your judgement is superior to

my own, which is why you are Ahriman and I
remain Obysis.'

'Yes, Obysis, greater power is the result of greater
knowledge. Let that be your lesson for today, and let
mine be the recovery of the Blade Wraith and the
discovery of the Black Library. We have come too far
to let either of these slip through our fingers now.
When there is power hidden in knowledge, then I
will make it mine: the sword of Lanthrilaq will be in
these hands before we leave Arcadia!'

If knowledge is worth anything, it is worth dying for.
The thoughts came unbidden to my mind.

*I will not be dying today – but a few other deaths would
be a price that Ahriman could afford to pay.*

'And it is worth killing for,' grinned Ahriman,
glancing at Obysis with mock subtlety. Then he
turned and strode out of the librarium, with the
Prodigal Sons falling into formation behind him.
Before I could think about what to do, I found
myself being swept along with them.

An explosion from far below told us that the
Blood Ravens had broken through the security doors
at the base of the tower.

THE GRAND AMPHITHEATRE of Arcadia was alive with
motion. In the centre of the stage, Eldarec, the Great
Harlequin, had established a podium on which he
had prominently displayed the sword of Lanthrilaq,
so that it could be clearly seen from even the very
highest of the balconies.

A gentle music had already begun to resound reassuringly through the stonework of the ancient arena,

and the chorus troupers were already in place in the pit under the stage, singing and chanting the earliest stages of the mythic cycle, *The Death and Re-Birth of Hope*.

The stage itself was teeming with Harlequins, each rushing to prepare the props and trap-doors that would be required for their individual performances in the forthcoming play. The *margorachs*, Death Jesters, dashed for their emplacements, letting their dathedi fields cycle and flicker through the various masks that they would have to don during the performance, settling eventually into the visage of death itself. The *distaur*, the mimes, flipped and somersaulted around the back of the stage, preparing their supple bodies for the contortions and exertions that would soon be required of them.

At the same time, the *athesdan*, the high warlock, flicked his mask to the image of the great story-teller, a distant echo of the face of the Laughing God himself, and positioned himself in amongst a cadre of *esdainn*, the warlocks who would support his telling of the story with resonating voices to fill out the sound, and with moments of magic to show the wizardry of the theatre.

Only Eldarec himself sat in silence and inactivity. He had positioned himself at the very front of the stage, with his legs hanging down into the chorus pit below. He had never played the Laughing God in this mythic cycle before, and he was mulling the risks in his mind. Any performance that involved so many of the *rillietann* was potentially hazardous for his sanity, since he had to hold the entire play in his mind, directing the action as it unfolded. But *The Death and Re-Birth of Hope* involved players from outside his control – creatures from beyond the reaches of Arcadia, mammals that had no sensitivities for the artistry of the sons of Isha or the spawn of Cegorach. The risk was considerable, but death was a price worthy of high art.

Up in the balconies, more troupers had positioned themselves in amongst the mannequins, giving the impression that the amphitheatre was full of eyes. They had adjusted their dathedi-fields to project images of the mannequins themselves, so that the living and inanimate members of the audience were indistinguishable – each of them grinning in sinister anticipation. At some point during the performance, Eldarec knew that the troupers in the audience would have a role to play. It was the way with all the best shows: the audience doesn't realise that it is part of a fabrication until it is too late to escape from it. Art, reality and death are the perfect blend.

'They are coming!' The voice echoed down from one of the highest balconies as one of the look-outs spotted the approaching mon'keigh.

'And so begins the play of our time,' said Eldarec, springing to his feet and turning in a slow circle so as to address every soul in the amphitheatre. 'And like the best of all beginnings, this one commences in darkness.'

With that, the stage blinked into emptiness, as though all of the troupers had suddenly vanished. All that was visible was the slight electric shimmer of dozens of dathedi fields shielding the Harlequins from the light. In the audience, only the mannequins were still visible.

With Eldarec apparently alone at the front of the stage, the house lights went out.

KAREBENNIAN'S MOVEMENTS WERE slow and deliberate compared with those that Gabriel had seen in the ice cave on Lorn V. It was as though he were speaking very slowly, for a foreigner or a slow-witted fool. His body shifted and flowed under the radiant, red spotlight in the ornate and breathless hall, twisting into impossible contortions. Then suddenly his body seemed to explode, shedding fragments of light in all directions, like a rain of silver, making the Blood Ravens step backwards, instinctively moving out of range.

Each of the silvered fragments planted itself like a seed into the flagstones, before taking root and growing into recognisable shapes. After only a few seconds, a dozen silvering necron warriors shimmered into being, each of them swaying in sympathy with the movements of the Solitaire. But then Karebennian swirled into a vortex, transforming his image almost beyond recognition. His shape cycled through the appearances of several eldar heroes, with every one of them hacking out towards the silvering horde with blades and spears, until his form finally fixed on that of Lanthrilaq the Swift.

At the same time, the cavernous space within the great hall shifted and pulsed, as though the Solitaire's performance were eliciting sympathy from the building itself, drawing in the inanimate surroundings with the magical captivation of his solitary performance. The walls appeared to move and morph, taking on the shape of tiered seating, stands, and balconies, until the great hall appeared transformed into an intimate amphitheatre, with Karebennian alone on the stage in the midst of a battle with the silver host.

The Blood Ravens reeled, turning on their heels, struggling to make sense of the shifting sensory data around them. But Karebennian continued to draw their attention, holding them in his thrall while he flipped and swooped through the combat postures of the legendary, tragic hero.

Finally, having slain a number of the ancient enemies, Lanthrilaq lay dying on the flagstones, bathed in the blood-red shower of light. His blade fell dramatically from his hands as he collapsed to the ground, turning over and over in slow motion, as though art were working against the force of gravity.

It clattered against the stone, chipping and splintering its already imperfect shape, splashing into a pool of Lanthrilaq's blood.

The Blood Ravens stared at the fallen sword, momentarily unable to take their eyes from it. Enchanted by the power of tragedy, and by the sudden on-rush of hope that the existence of the flawed blade represented for the future.

'The Blade Wraith of Lanthrilaq,' muttered Jonas.

His words shattered the illusion, bringing the other Blood Ravens back into the cold, stone, great hall. The amphitheatre was gone, as had the silvering hordes of the necron.

Looking up from the image of the broken blade, Gabriel searched for Karebennian, his mind riddled with questions and awe, but the Solitaire had vanished too. When he looked back down into the pool of red light at the base of the shaft, Gabriel saw that the sword had gone. The Blood Ravens stood alone in the cavernous hall once again.

An explosion from the shadows to one side of the hall told them that Ephraim's attempts to open the doors had failed, and that Tanthius had succeeded. 'Quietly is better, but open is better than closed,' mused Gabriel to himself.

Collecting his thoughts, Gabriel turned to his squad. 'We need to find that amphitheatre,' he said, striding off towards the tower of the librarium.

CHAPTER ELEVEN:
DEATH AND REBIRTH

THE STAR WAS bleeding.

As the *Litany of Fury* powered around a tight solar-orbit, it rapidly brought the far side of the sun into view. Tendrils of gleaming matter were questing out from its gyring form, and the rotation of the massive sun was slowing visibly. Huge sunspots speckled its fiery surface, but each appeared to be riddled with tiny stars, as though they were actually holes through the substance of the sun itself, revealing the space beyond. Infernos of solar storms erupted from the star's surface, throwing radiation and fire out into the Lorn system, bathing the floating wreckage and debris with heat and reactive energy.

The snaking tendrils of starlight whipped and lashed into the vacuum, filling it with streaks of

silvering light. After a while, the questing tendrils
seemed to latch on to flecks of debris, cracking into
them and filling them with iridescence. Even as
Ulantus watched, the main viewscreen on the
control deck of the *Litany of Fury*, he saw the
apparent debris flare and catch, reforming into
recognisable shapes, as though flicking back into
life. After a few more moments, he could see the
distant specks flash with power as their engines
came back online. The immobilised necron vessels
seemed to be drawing power directly from the sun,
bleeding it dry so that they might live again.

With the viewscreen magnifying the distant
image, Ulantus checked the images against the ves-
sel-categorisation charts just to be certain, and he
could see that perhaps ten or fifteen of the smaller,
Dirge-class raiders were already back in motion. A
couple of slightly larger Jackals had come online,
and all the raiders were spiralling around a group of
crescent-shaped Shroud-class cruisers, which
remained dark and lifeless, despite the arcs of lightning that poured energy into the pyramidal
structures that encrusted their surfaces.

'Sergeant,' said Ulantus with a calmness that
belied his internal turmoil. 'See whether you can
contact the *Ravenous Spirit*. Tell Captain Angelos
that his presence is required in the Lorn system.
Code your message "imperative".'

'As you wish, captain,' answered Saulh, nodding
briskly and turning to leave.

'And Saulh,' continued Ulantus, as though reluctant to voice the next sentence. 'If you can match

their frequency, try to raise the eldar vessels. We may
need their help.'

'Yes, captain.'

'Then get back to the *Rage of Erudition* and prepare
it for battle. Let us hope that repairs have been completed since our last encounter with these cursed
necron. We will need all the firepower we can
muster.

'Gunnery. Target torpedoes and bombardment
canons onto one of the Shrouds. Fire when ready.
And keep firing until there is nothing left.

'Helm. Keep us on this course. The closer we can
get, the more damage our heavy weapons will do.'

THE AMPHITHEATRE WAS shrouded in darkness and
quiet as we entered. Ahriman paused for a moment
at the side of the stage, keeping us arranged behind
him, and looked up around the balconies. He muttered a few words of power and a reddish glow
erupted from his Black Staff, filling the arena with a
moody and bloody light.

All around the stage, tiers of seats and balconies
rose up towards the invisibly distant ceiling. There
must have been room for an audience of tens of
thousands.

Staring up into the stands as my eyes adjusted to
the dim light, I thought I could see hundreds of eyes
staring back at me. Hundreds of half-hidden figures
sat in the balconies, their eyes glinting and their
teeth sparkling in the suggestions of grins. Before I
could process the image properly, a bank of spotlights clunked and then hummed into life, blasting

bright white light down onto the stage and dazzling us, forcing us to turn away from the audience and shade our eyes for a moment.

'And so begins the play of our times, in which hope will die and be reborn anew!' The voice echoed and bounced around the stage, as though it were being chanted by dozens of mouths, fractionally out of synchronisation. 'In the beginning there was darkness, but into that darkness from the realms beyond shone light.'

Whispered murmurs pulsed around the audience, invisible beyond the brilliance of the stage lights. Then a low, throbbing music arose out of the stone beneath our feet, beating through the ceramite of our boots with an odd, syncopated rhythm.

A shaft of red light came down from the ceiling striking the very centre of the stage like a magnificent column. Held on a podium within the light was a glittering but broken sword, sparkling with jewels of crimson, like droplets of blood. The rest of the stage remained empty, but the murmurs of the invisible audience grew slightly louder and a single note of an alien melody joined the rhythmic undertones of the background music. It was a pristine and silvering note, like a fleck of starlight on a cloudy night.

Ahriman took a step forwards towards the blade, gazing around himself cautiously. In all the long centuries of his search for knowledge, he had never encountered anything like this before.

I watched him take another step towards the Blade Wraith in the centre of the stage, and noticed that the other Prodigal Sons did not follow him. They remained at the edge of the stage, as though waiting in the wings for a signal.

Looking out towards the audience, squinting my eyes against the light, I thought that I could see sporadic, eager faces dispersed throughout the stands. They were grinning, as though anticipating something unexpected.

When Ahriman took another step, a figure shimmered into being at the front of the stage. The crested and vividly coloured Great Harlequin had his back to the sorcerer lord, his arms held out before him, as though beseeching the audience.

Ahriman turned his head and a look of momentary confusion crossed his ghostly face. He didn't understand what was happening. Looking from the Great Harlequin to the Blade Wraith and back again, I could see that Ahriman was trying to work out whether the aliens were attempting the defend their treasure or not.

Is this performance just an exercise in illusion and misdirection? Is it supposed to compensate for a lack of real defences? Are the Harlequins so few that they dare not confront the power of Ahriman? The questions were in my head just as they were in Ahriman's.

Finally, his patience exhausted, Ahriman's face gnarled into a grimace of frustration and anger. He drove his Black Staff down into the surface of the stage and sent a crack of lightning pulsing through the ground towards the Great Harlequin. At the same time, a lance of energy lashed out of the top of his staff and smashed into the spotlights that dazzled the stage area, shattering them and plunging the amphitheatre into relative darkness.

As the curtain of shadow descended onto the stage, the Great Harlequin sprang into the air, turning an impossibly slow flip as Ahriman's blast passed beneath him, as though gravity had been partially suspended for a moment. When his feet touched the stage once again, a troupe of Harlequins appeared around him at stage-front, glittering into visibility like a host of multi-coloured stars. They each snapped into combat poses, blades and barrels held with dramatic poise.

A cheer erupted from the audience, filling the amphitheatre with audio waves that pulsed and vibrated powerfully through the air and the stonework. The grinning faces on the balconies remained eerily immobile, as though fixed into place. But here and there in between them appeared the menacing smiles of Death Jesters with tripod-mounted shrieker cannons and brightlances.

Ahriman swept his eyes around the unfolding scene and laughed. *Is this the best defence that the Laughing God can muster?* He howled with dramatic rage, spinning his Black Staff over his head and letting arcs of raw warp power pour out of its tips, spraying it around the theatre and into the stands. As though on cue, the rest of the Prodigal Sons charged forwards on the stage, bracing their weapons and training them up into the audience to confront the Death Jesters.

'And so it is that hope is killed!' The invisible narrator's voice echoed powerfully around the arena, tinged with a mixture of amusement and menace.

At precisely that moment, an explosion fired on the far side of the amphitheatre, blowing masonry and debris across the stage. Even before the smoke had cleared, a squad of Space Marines came storming out of the rough hole where once a stage door had been, spilling out onto the far side of the stage, on the other side of the spot-lit Blade Wraith.

Drawing *Vairocanum*, I charged forward to join the Prodigal Sons in their stand against the decreasingly favourable odds. I felt the hum and pulse of power course into my blade, and I saw the faint green glow from its runes diffuse into the shadow-thickened air.

Almost instantly, volleys of bolter fire erupted from the red-armoured Blood Ravens as they established themselves on stage-left. Three blue-clad Librarians lashed out with arcs of blue energy. The Prodigal Sons, on stage-right, returned fire at once, reducing the stage instantly to a hail of shells and a mire of warp power. Meanwhile, the Great Harlequin and his troupe quietly faded out of sight once again as tremendous cheers crashed down out of the auditorium.

I know those Space Marines. The thought hit me like a bolter shell.

I know those Space Marines. It cycled round and around in my mind, blinding me to all other thoughts and impulses. Something moved in my soul, shifting my will and binding me to forgotten oaths. *I know those Space Marines.*

I stopped half way across the stage, in the middle of a charge with *Vairocanum* brandished above my head, my mind racing with sudden and profound indecision. I stood between the Ahriman and his Prodigal Sons on one side and the Blood Ravens on the other, centre stage before the Blade Wraith of Lanthrilaq itself.

My head was suddenly assailed with competing voices and thoughts: *Come home to us, lost son of Vidya; we are more similar than you know, friend of Ahriman; this is the death of hope; coincidences are for the weak-minded and the ignorant; I am the sword of Vidya; knowledge is power; friend of Ahriman... eyes of the Emperor... come home... everything wants to return home... Vairocanum... Lanthrilaq...*

Bolter shells and energy blasts scorched past my face as I dropped to my knees in the centre of the stage, staring up into the insane, maniacal grinning faces of the audience. As I stared, a troupe of Harlequins shimmered into being at the front of the stage. In the fore was the Solitaire that I had seen in the librarium, his mask shifting through numerous guises and expressions, as though searching for the most appropriate visage of death.

Karebennian!

Screaming projectiles and javelins of brightlance fire started to sizzle down from the Death Jester emplacements on the balconies, raining toxins and laser heat onto the stage. Cheers and screeches of excitement resounded around the arena, as though the acoustics amplified the sound itself into deafening weapons.

As the flagstones beneath my knees trembled and cracked under the relentless onslaught from all sides, I watched Karebennian's mask slide into a seductive abhorrence as he adopted the guise of Slaanesh – the role of power that was reserved only for Solitaires. As the images of the troupers behind him began to morph and shift into inconstancy, I saw them leap and dance towards me in patterns of breathtaking beauty and unpredictability. In a matter of seconds, I found myself gazing into the face of Slaanesh itself, and saw the laughing reflection of my addled soul staring back at me.

THE AVENGING SWORD flashed around the sun with the *Eternal Star* in close formation behind it. The message from the mon'keigh vessel had been garbled and incoherent, but Macha didn't need to understand the ramblings of primitive mammals to know that the yngir were regenerating on the far side of the local star. Uldreth, the exarch of the Dire Avengers, had needed little more than a hint of shifting chemical and thermal patterns in the sun to recognise the danger.

As the eldar cruisers swept around to the other side of the star, the exarch and farseer saw exactly what they had feared. The energy of the sun was bleeding out into space. It was being conducted through the crystalline prisms on the decks of the dormant yngir vessels and then focussed into their energy circuits. The effect was not dissimilar from that seen on terrestrial battlefields when the yngir deployed the so-called 'resurrection orbs,' which were basically micro-scaled star-fusion devices. The only difference here was scale.

Assessment? Macha's thoughts crossed the vacuum of space between her *Eternal Star* and the *Avenging Sword* instantaneously. It was precisely such phenomena that drove the yngir into their ancient and endless frenzies of hatred.

I can see twenty raiders and four cruisers already online, replied Uldreth, his mind sharply angled and focussed on the battle to come. He had already sent hundreds of Biel-Tan eldar to their deaths in the Lorn system, and he was not about to lose any more to the ancient enemy. The Dire Avengers were not noted for their penchant for mercy or forgetfulness.

I concur.

There is something else, added Uldreth as a series of explosions detonated over the shimmering surface of one of the Shroud cruisers. The Avenger tracked the line of fire back on a curving trajectory in a tight orbit. Judging from the nature of the explosions, he assumed that the mon'keigh battle-barge had commenced bombardment of the cruisers before coming properly into range. From his position, the battle-barge was not yet even visible around the sun.

I can see it too. Macha's mind was full of concern.

Uldreth concentrated and stared through the dazzling threads of lightning and starlight that interlaced across the face of the rapidly re-energising yngir fleet. Behind the cruisers, shrouded in the dark of the vacuum and constructed out of a mysterious and utterly non-reflective metallic substance, he could just make out the outline of another ship. It was bigger than the others, much bigger. It resembled a massive cross, bristling with gun batteries and the distinctive emplacements for gauss particle whips and lightning arcs. Protruding from the sharpened nose was the vaguely visible suggestion of a star-pulse generator. *It's a Harvest Ship.* The realisation filled Uldreth with horror and determination simultaneously. *Scythe-class, I think.*

Agreed. Confirmed Macha without emotion. *It is not yet online.*

I am deploying the Sword's complement of Shadowhunters to engage the Dirge and Jackal raiders.

Concentrate on the Jackals, Uldreth. They are equipped with portals – We do not want to be caught up in boarding actions.

Understood.

Macha watched the flotilla of escort vessels spill out of the *Avenging Sword* and accelerate off towards the startling collection of yngir ships. For the first time she allowed her thoughts to move from the questions of whether and when the threat of the yngir would arise and she started to wonder why they would arise so closely together in time and yet so far apart in space. The coincidence of the ascension at Lsathranil's Shield and this one in the Lorn system was simply too great to be ignored: coincidences are ignored only by the weak-minded or the ignorant, she reminded herself.

There was something deceptive and deliberate about the coincidence that made her suspicious. Uldreth had focussed his passions on the mon'keigh, blaming them for awakening the long-dormant enemy. And he blamed himself for decisions that he had been given no choice but to make. But Macha had to see beyond these intimate emotions: the ancient enemy was not petty or vindictive on this small scale. The yngir's ambitions were grand to the point that their realisation would mean the end of the sons of Asuryan altogether. Their hatred was focussed against living, organic matter itself, but especially against the psychic race of the eldar.

Macha could not discount the possibility that the ascension at Lsathranil's Shield was a diversion designed to split the forces of Biel-Tan so that the Swordwind might be defeated: the whole psychic strength of a united Biel-Tan would be awesome to behold, and perhaps not even the yngir could stand against it. At least not yet.

But if this were the case, the implications were terrible. Macha had heard rumours of the return of the Deceiver – Mephet'ran – the star-god that had once tricked Kaelis Ra into turning against his own silvering hordes, convincing him to feast on the flesh of the yngir themselves. She had seen the Harlequins of Arcadia perform the Masque of the Deceiver, and listened to Eldarec narrate the many myths of his return.

The Harlequins, sons of the Laughing God, had mixed and complicated emotions about the Deceiver – admiration and terror gripped their souls at the mention of his name, and only Eldarec himself was able to perform his part in the masques. Sometimes they told stories of the Deceiver's exploits as though they were the deeds of the Laughing God himself.

Of all the lords of the yngir, only the Deceiver might have the wit for this kind of galaxy-spanning performance.

Together with the Solitaire, Karebennian, Eldarec had once performed the *Dance of Mephet'ran and Vaul* in the grand amphitheatre of Biel-Tan. In that dance, the Deceiver took on various organic forms to lure the living into his service. In the dance, the Deceiver's objective was to convince the living to destroy or banish all of the weapons and talismans that had been constructed by Vaul, the smith god, to prepare the way for his return. He found the psychic resonance of the Vaulish artefacts offensive.

It was certainly true that the talismans had been lost, and all but one of the Blades of Vaul had also fallen out of the memory of the children of Isha. As the numbers of the eldar dwindled throughout the galaxy, Macha felt sure that the Deceiver would be plotting his return and testing the water. The yngir could taste the cross-pollution of materium and immaterium; it was like poison to them. But as the light of the eldar faded from the galaxy, so the interflow of the warp into real space would begin to dwindle, providing a more conducive environment for the return of the ancient foe.

But somehow she could not make all the pieces fit. There was not quite enough for her to be sure of anything, and the frustration drove her to the point of anger. The yngir were without souls, and this made them almost impossible to see clearly in the myriad unfolding futures and pasts of the present. She hated them, and hated that she could not master them or even fully grasp them.

As she sat in her mediation chamber, watching the viewscreen that was trained on the emergent, shimmering yngir fleet, she noticed the massive form of the *Litany of Fury* crest the outline of the dying sun, with its cannons and torpedoes firing relentlessly.

In her mind's eye, she could see the radiance of the psychic presence in the heart of that ugly vessel, and she wondered whether the Blood Ravens were really aware of the value of the beacon that they so industriously and studiously maintained there. Even Gabriel did not really seem to understand, despite her persistent efforts to reveal the truth to him.

There had been a mon'keigh warrior once, long ago, who had understood the need for psychic radiance in the galaxy, especially in a galaxy from which the eldar were rapidly fading. But those primitive mammals lived such short lives, even the most promising of them.

Whether the humans understood their power or not, Macha was certain that the regenerating yngir could see the brilliance of the psychic pool in the *Litany of Fury*, and that they would seek to extinguish it as quickly as they possibly could. In comparison with the cumbersome and heavy mon'keigh battlebarge, her virtually immaterial, glittering Wraithship, *Eternal Star*, seemed fleeting and ethereal.

Gabriel, hurry home.

As THE DOORS into the amphitheatre blew, Gabriel charged forward through the smoke and the scattering debris. The dance of the Solitaire had been clear and unambiguous about the location of the sword of Lanthrilaq, and Gabriel was determined that it should not fall into the hands of the Prodigal Sons. Such a weapon could do untold evil in the wrong hands.

Storming out of the smoke, Gabriel found himself emerging onto the stage of a massive amphitheatre. The stands were dimly lit but riddled with the grinning faces of eldar Harlequins. The stage was alive with motion and action. A terrible sorcerer lord was standing on the other side of it, with a squad of Prodigal Sons behind him. He was spinning his staff in a blaze of fury, sending sheets of warpfire lashing out around the stage. Over to the right, at the front of the stage, Gabriel caught a fleeting glance of a troupe of Harlequin warriors before they quickly faded from view, leaving the stage to the Space Marines.

Flashing a couple of rapid hand signals, Gabriel deployed the rest of his squad into a firing arc behind him. The engagement was unexpectedly sudden and furiously intense at short range. Tanthius stomped up towards the back of the stage, his storm bolter coughing and spluttering with discharging shells. At the same time, Korinth and Zhaphel peeled down to stage-front, hurling crackling blasts of warp energy across towards the Prodigal Sons. Jonas strode up to Gabriel's shoulder, adding the fury of his own force staff to the repeated rattling of Gabriel's bolter, concentrating his fire on the sorcerer lord himself.

Gabriel – It's Ahriman!

Meanwhile, Corallis and Ephraim took up support positions behind them, loosing relentless volleys of bolter fire across the stage.

Return fire, projectiles, bolter shells and energy blasts pinged and ricocheted off their armour, scarring the ceramite and cracking through the reinforced panels. At this range with virtually no cover neither the Blood Ravens nor the Prodigal Sons would last long.

In the tempest of combat, Gabriel noticed that heavy weapons fire was raining down from the balconies. Through the smoke, recoil flashes and explosions of light, he could just about discern the shapes of Death Jesters, laughing and grinning at gun emplacements in the stands. It seemed that the Harlequins were helping him.

Pulling a grenade from his belt, Gabriel hurled it across the stage and watched it detonate behind the formation of Prodigal Sons, throwing one of them off his feet and raining shrapnel over the backs of the others.

Suddenly, Jonas's staff fell silent and the father Librarian staggered slightly, taking half a step forward before catching his weight. In a moment of concern, Gabriel lurched to the side and caught his old friend's shoulder, steadying him in the face of the enemy, worrying that he had been hit. But Jonas shrugged his captain's hand away.

'Gabriel. It's Rhamah.' There was a sinking horror in the Librarian's voice.

Without knowing where to look, Gabriel scanned the blue and gold Prodigal Sons. Charging out of their formation was a single Space Marine. For a moment, Gabriel failed to recognise the difference in his insignia and markings; the smoke and commotion of combat obscured more than proximity revealed. But after a second of stunned concentration, Gabriel realised that the sword-wielding Marine was a Blood Ravens Librarian. He was brandishing the broken sword of *Vairocanum* and charging directly at him.

Another second passed before Korinth and Zhaphel realised who it was, and they also froze in shock and horror, letting their force weapons die in their hands, unable to process the scene before them.

In the lull, Sorcerer Lord Ahriman brayed with laughter and lashed out with renewed violence against the Blood Ravens, coating them in an agonising wave of warp fire. His ghostly features were alive with the pleasure of power and combat. He seemed to thrill in the confusion that wracked his foes.

At the same moment, Rhamah broke his charge, coming to a standstill in the centre of the stage with *Vairocanum* still held aloft. He froze, as though suddenly wracked with indecision, staring at Gabriel and Jonas, then shifting his eyes to Korinth and Zhaphel. His body trembled, as though he were fighting with his own instincts and struggling to control himself. Then, all at once, it seemed as though his strength deserted him and he sank down onto his knees.

'Brother Rhamah!' yelled Gabriel, taking a step towards the desperate and immobile Librarian. 'Brother Rhamah, we have come to take you home!'

A dramatic melody rose suddenly from under the stage, echoing around the arena with psychic resonance. And, as though conjured by the music, Karebennian shimmered into being at the front of the stage, flanked on both sides by a gaudily coloured troupe of Harlequin warriors. They struck theatrical poses then advanced up the stage directly towards the kneeling Rhamah, spinning and rolling and ducking around the hail of fire that continued to rain down from the balconies behind them.

Rhamah stared into Karebennian's face, as though transfixed, rising to his feet as the Solitaire closed on his position. With a movement of dramatic grandeur, the Librarian raised *Vairocanum* over his head and poised himself ready to strike, but it was not clear in which direction his blade was going to drop. His face scanned slowly from side to side, taking in Ahriman on one side and Gabriel on the other, before returning it to the hideous visage of Karebennian himself.

Without missing a step, the Solitaire sprang past Rhamah, spinning into a whirl as though rolling around him on his way to confront Ahriman. But there was a flash of metal in the roll, and Karebennian left death in his wake. Before Rhamah had the chance to move, one of the Solitaire's arm-mounted riveblades had sliced into his stomach and the other had parted his head from his neck.

As Karebennian bounded on without looking back, Rhamah's decapitated body slumped to the ground and his head rolled gorily off the front of the stage, leaving a trail of thickening blood behind it.

A great cheer arose from the stands and a rhythmic beating started to thunder and resonate through the stonework as the audience thumped its feet in appreciation and awe.

Seeing one of his Blood Ravens cut down, Gabriel roared his fury into the performance and charged forwards, casting his bolter aside and ripping his chainsword into life. Jonas, Korinth and Zhaphel responded simultaneously, each storming towards the centre of the stage to engage the Prodigal Sons at close range.

However, by the time that Gabriel had taken the few steps needed to place him stage-centre, Karebennian had already leapt into the path of Ahriman, placing himself between the sorcerer lord and the Blade Wraith. His troupers had deployed around them, separating them from the rest of the fray as though defining a distinct and exclusive theatre of combat for the great heroes.

Gabriel paused, unsure about how to proceed. The Solitaire's actions seemed to make no sense. First it had led the Blood Ravens to this stage, then it had killed Rhamah with breathless ease, and now it was engaged in a duel with the Sorcerer Lord Ahriman. The Commander of the Watch could not understand the alien's motivations.

Looking down at his feet, Gabriel saw the broken and cracked form of *Vairocanum* lying in a pool of Rhamah's blood, fallen just out of the dead Librarian's grasp. Instinctively, the captain stooped and picked up the sacred weapon, closing his grip around the hilt and feeling its power flow into his being. The blade ignited into a fierce green glow as Gabriel cast his spluttering chainsword aside and raised the force weapon into both hands.

As he held the broken blade aloft, Gabriel could vaguely hear the rapture of the audience in the stands. He could hear a swell of music erupt from under the stage, and he could make out a single, silvering note piercing the harmonious cacophony. The sound seemed to carry him away from the stage and the battle. It was a sound that he had heard before, a pristine and silvering tone that had riddled and guided his thoughts many times before. He opened his mind to the music, and let the silver note become a flood of platinum light in his head.

There was a time when he had thought that the Astronomican was reaching for him and offering him guidance, but now he didn't know whether it was the Emperor's light or the light of Vidya that gave him direction, calling him home and guiding his judgement.

'And so it is that hope is re-born!' The narrator's voice was dim and almost inaudible against the din.

'CAPTAIN, THERE IS a communication from General Sturnn on Lorn V. He reports that necron warriors are on the ground. He requests support.'

'I think the general is on his own for the time being. Send my apologies.' Ulantus smiled without humour.

Warning claxons wailed and red lights pulsed all throughout the *Litany of Fury*. While the space battle raged outside, with the eldar cruisers and the *Rage of Erudition* attacking the Shrouds while the Shadowhunters and Cobra fighters spiralled in dogfights with the impossibly rapid flecks of darkness that were the Dirge and Jackal raiders, the cross-like Harvester ship had pulled into closer proximity with the *Litany*.

'Concentrate all fire on the Scythe-class Harvester – torpedoes and weapons batteries,' bellowed Ulantus from the bridge. He was ignoring the proximity warnings, assuming that there was some kind of malfunction in the distancing cogitators. The Harvester was still several thousand metres away, and he could see no danger of collision or boarding from that range. Besides, given the huge mass superiority of the *Litany*, a collision could only possibly be to their own advantage. The main disadvantage of the closing range was that they were now too close to employ the bombardment cannons without risking damaging the *Litany* with explosive concussion.

Torpedoes and lasfire pummelled against the surface of the necron vessel, but somehow it managed to escape serious damage. It appeared to perform no evasive manoeuvres, and yet the punishing tirade of fire just slipped off its armour, like light bouncing off a mirror. Its hull was immaculately black, to the point of virtual invisibility; it seemed to wrap space around it, reflecting vision back on itself or bending it around the vessel so that a clear conception of its shape and size was almost impossible. Just as sensors could not quite grasp the vessel's dimensions, so weapons failed to find much purchase against its unusual, metallic skin.

'Any word from the *Ravenous Spirit*?' snapped Ulantus, cursing the absent Commander of the Watch yet again. 'Where in Vidya's name are you, Gabriel?'

'They are closing on the fringes of the Lorn system, captain. Sergeant Kohath is in command. Captain Angelos is not with them. Estimated arrival: fifteen minutes.'

'Kohath is coming without the commander?'

'Yes, captain.'

Ulantus paused for thought. If Gabriel was not aboard his strike cruiser, then where the hell was he? An electric crack blew the question out of his mind as the control deck rocked violently.

'Throne! What was that?'

'Some kind of particle whip, captain, amplified to incredible power. The necrons appear to be drawing their fire-power directly from the sun.'

Another blast punched into the prow of the *Litany*, this time with a thunderous explosion that sent reverberations rippling throughout the massive vessel's infrastructure.

Ulantus watched as the huge column of dark light pulsed out of the nose of the Harvester and drilled into the *Litany*. It was a weapon unlike any he had ever encountered.

'Bring the planetary bombardment cannons to bear!'

'Captain, we're too close–'

'This is not a request!'

A huge roar erupted from the turret-mounted linear accelerators as a salvo of heavy, magma-bomb warheads powered through the intervening space between the *Litany of Fury* and the Harvester. As they impacted against the deceptively spindly necron vessel, they detonated into massive infernos, coating the entire craft in roiling magma and blasting it several hundred metres back away from the *Litany*. A couple of seconds later, the backwash from the explosion crashed into the prow of the *Litany* itself, throwing superheated radioactivity across the thick shields and making the massive vessel pitch slightly. For ten seconds the viewscreens snowed into blackness.

'Damage reports!' snapped Ulantus, pushing one of the control deck serfs aside and studying the read-outs that chattered up on his terminal. 'Damage?'

Then the screens clicked back on line and Ulantus bit down on his teeth, clenching his jaw. The Harvester had moved even closer, and it appeared to have suffered only cosmetic damage.

'Captain! We have a hull breach in the prow. Sector 17.a.392. Captain – we are being boarded!'

AHRIMAN LAUGHED AT the slender and sinister Solitaire as it flipped and danced around him, flourishing its riveblades with unspeakable elegance. The great sorcerer did not even bother to turn and track Karebennian's movements; he simply stood unmoving and implacable, leaning slightly on the absolute lightlessness of his Black Staff. The two figures dominated the centre of the stage, ringed by a troupe of Harlequins that framed them as a dramatic focus and separated them from the ongoing fury of the exchange between the Blood Ravens and the Prodigal Sons. The battle between the Marines seemed to have been reduced to a sideshow, and the audience's unmoving eyes appeared transfixed by the epic clash between sorcerer lord and Solitaire.

Have you forgotten already, Karebennian? Ahriman's spectral face twisted into a mirth-ridden sneer, but the Solitaire's only response was a spiralling leap that the sorcerer blocked easily with his staff. *Do you not remember how this ended last time we met?*

I remember that we live to fight today. Karebennian's answer was accompanied by a feint and a lunge which slipped past the Black Staff and stabbed into the covers of the book of webway charts that Ahriman held in his off hand.

Ahriman sneered in indignation. *You are not worthy of me, web-walker.* He hefted the book into the air and then kicked out at the Solitaire, crunching his boot into the Harlequin's abdomen and sending him skidding off over the stage. The book, still impaled on Karebennian's riveblades, was shredded into tatters by the violence of the movement, and scraps of paper billowed up into the air like confetti.

The audience gasped.

I will not be frustrated by you again, Karebennian! Ahriman shrieked, spinning his staff and then jabbing it out towards the crumpled Solitaire, focussing all of his hatred and resentment into one strike. A vicious and intense blast of warp lightning lanced out of the Black Staff and engulfed the fallen alien.

Karebennian screamed in ways that Ahriman had never heard before. His agony cut all the Marines and Harlequins to the bone, bringing the battle to a standstill and arresting the music that had throbbed throughout the performance. Wisps of smoke and gas rose from the charred remains of the Solitaire's body, as though his soul were seeping away into the shadows.

Finally. Ahriman turned away from the corpse of the alien and started back towards the shaft of red light in which he had seen the Blade Wraith.

But in place of the sword, sitting on the podium under the blaze of red was Eldarec, the Great Harlequin himself. A wide and jovial smile played over his features and, as the terrible lord of sorcery approached, his smile cracked into a broad grin, and he threw his head back to laugh. The Blade Wraith was gone.

CHAPTER TWELVE: MOCKERY

'Casualties?' barked Ulantus as the warning sirens continued to sound. Fires had ignited under a number of terminals and monitors on the control deck, and several of the viewscreens were either cracked or malfunctioning.

'Fourteen battle-brothers in the prow section, captain. They fell before we could seal off the quadrant. The blast doors into the next hull segment are holding, but will not hold forever. The boarding action has stalled, it has not be repelled.'

'And out there?' The captain turned his head to indicate the main frontal viewscreen on which the space battle was raging.

'Eleven Cobra fighters.'

'And the eldar?'

'Unknown, captain. The two cruisers are sustaining heavy damage, and a number of their Shadowhunter escorts have been destroyed. We have unconfirmed reports that one of the cruisers may have been boarded.'

'And what about the necron, officer? Are we taking them with us?'

'Many of the smaller raiders have been immobilised, captain.'

'That's it? "Many immobilised." That's it?'

'Yes, captain.'

'I see. And where is the *Ravenous Spirit*?'

'On route.'

'Distance?'

'She is just clearing Lorn III, captain. Arrival is imminent.'

Ulantus sighed and looked around the bridge of the venerable battle-barge. He had never thought that any enemy could reduce the pride of Vidya to a smoking wreck, especially not on his watch. Part of him rebelled against the responsibility, and Gabriel's face swam into his mind. If anyone was to blame, it was the erratic and unreliable Commander of the Watch. He had told Angelos not to go. He had attempted to force him to stay. But the famously cavalier captain had pulled rank and insisted that he should be permitted to take his strike cruiser on another of his secret eldar trysts. One day he would make Gabriel answer for his actions. If the *Litany of Fury* were to fall, he would make sure that the Chapter Masters knew that it was Gabriel who had abandoned it in its moment of greatest peril.

'There is nothing more I can do here,' he murmured, half to himself. 'You, Sergeant Abraim.' The
Marine standing sentinel by the blast doors nodded
his acknowledgement. 'The bridge is yours. I am
needed in the prow.' Nobody will be able to accuse
me of shirking my duty in the face of the enemy, he
vowed to himself. 'Maintain fire against the Harvester. If that blows, then this is over.'

With that, Ulantus strode purposefully off the control deck of the *Litany of Fury* and rushed off towards
the embattled prow.

As THE LIGHT and the music faded, a pulse of laughter flooded over the stage, as though the entire
auditorium were united in mockery or amusement.
The house lights came up slowly; it was as though
the performance had ended and the Harlequins
expected everyone to leave.

Gabriel blinked the silvering light out of his eyes
and lowered the sword from above his head, bringing it down in front of him. In the newly constant
glow of the house lights, he inspected the blade and
realised that it was no longer broken. The cracked
and chipped form had become whole, and the missing shard from the tip had somehow been recast.

'Hope is reborn as the sword is made whole once
again. Vaul bowed with a flourish and the Laughing
God, Cegorach the Wise, chuckled with mirth. It is
always as it would be.'

A voice inside his head muttered familiar words: *I
am the sword of Vidya.*

That sword is mine, Blood Raven.

Gabriel tore his eyes away from the glimmering, enchanting blade and turned on his heels. The thoughts were harsh and abrasive, unlike any that he had experienced before. They hurt him.

If you give it to me, then there will be no problem between us. You can save us all much suffering, friend of Ahriman.

The sorcerer lord stood further upstage, in front of the red spotlight, in which sat the Great Harlequin, rolling with laughter. Gabriel could see immediately that the Blade Wraith was gone from its podium, and he realised in that instant that he was holding it in his hands. Something had happened during the Harlequin masque, some kind of transference or homecoming; the Blade Wraith and *Vairocanum* had been made whole.

Everything tends towards its home, human, as you know. The thoughts were not Ahriman's, though they were no longer Karebennian's.

Some sort of mockery of their dance had seen the performance unite what had been broken and bring perfection out of what had once been flawed. It was as though the dance had itself been part of the forging process for the incomplete blade. It all began to make sense to the Blood Ravens captain.

'I am not your friend, Ahriman of the Prodigal Sons. I am Gabriel Angelos of Vidya's Blood Ravens – between us is the problem of truth.'

A snigger cackled around the audience.

The sorcerer's ghostly face was a fury of fiery eyes and fierce hostility. There was insanity flickering over his wild features as he glowered at the captain. For a moment, Gabriel thought that Ahriman was simply going to launch himself into the attack and he tested the weight of the ancient blade of power in his hands, but then a sudden calm shifted over the sorcerer's spectral features.

We are not so very different, you and I, Gabriel. We are the same. Why must we fight when there is so much knowledge here to go around. We can share it. The real enemy here is them. Ahriman smiled smoothly and spun his Black Staff to indicate the Harlequins that were gradually appearing into a wide ring around them on the stage. He pointed up into the stands where the Death Jesters pointed back with their heavy weapons and the mannequins grinned inanely.

Gabriel swept his eyes around the scene, as though following the direction of the sorcerer. He saw his own battle-brothers standing ready around him, all of them poised on the point of righteous fury, each of them ready to die if he gave the word. He saw the Prodigal Sons arrayed to one side of the stage, formed into a solid and implacable firing line, their ghostly faces set into concentrated outrage. Two of them lay motionless at the feet of their comrades.

Before Gabriel lay the mutilated and broken bodies of Rhamah and Karebennian, and the stage was speckled with the corpses of Harlequins that he had not even noticed before.

'No,' said Gabriel slowly and firmly. 'We are nothing alike, you and I. I seek knowledge only in the service of the Emperor, only for the protection of the Imperium, for the glory of the Golden Throne, and in the name of Vidya.

'There will be no sharing today, Ahriman. I want no part in this.'

Gabriel hefted the Blade Wraith in one hand, feeling its ineffable lightness, as though it were actually weightless, as he gestured towards the slaughter around him.

There was a slow murmur from around the auditorium, and a gentle music glided into the range of human hearing. At the same time, dozens of Harlequin troupers shimmered into visibility around the stage, surrounding the Marines with rings of bristling blades. In the audience, hundreds more faces seemed to appear between the grinning faces of the mannequins, as though the sons of the Laughing God had been merely in hiding during the performance, so as not to interfere with the show. Now they were showing themselves and their appreciation. Applause thundered around the arena. Hundreds then thousands of Harlequins were staring down onto the stage.

Ahriman's smile set fixedly and then slowly transformed into a scowl of anger. His eyes flared with fury and his Black Staff began to burn with unspeakable powers. His mouth worked silently, spilling out incantations that had not been heard for centuries, calling out for assistance from the minions of the warp, dragging his daemonic servants towards the materium and attempting to press them into service. The air around the stage started to condense and whirl, making the Harlequins suddenly nervous. This was not in the script.

* * *

THE WRAITHSHIP TREMBLED and convulsed under the relentless assault, and Macha flinched in physical pain with each of the critical strikes against her *Eternal Star*. Although she was hidden away in her meditation chamber, she could feel each crack of a Shroud cruiser's lightning arc, and each attempt of a Jackal's portal projectors to open up a space for a boarding movement. She could even feel the tread of each footstep as her crew ran through the maze of wraithbone corridors.

She ducked and twisted violently, throwing the *Star* into a spin and plunging it down under the anticipated lash of a lightning arc. Pulling the nose up, Macha gasped suddenly and squinted her eyes in intense concentration, pouring her will and her fury into the massive discharge from the prow-mounted pulsar lance exactly as she loosed the keel-launched torpedoes.

The barrage punched and punched again into the already weakened armour of the Shroud, finally rupturing its hull and sending it spinning out of control. Its momentum carried it crashing into its sister ship, which had been deployed in a tight formation on its wing.

Screaming with lust for the kill, Macha loosed another volley of torpedoes, which plunged through the holes in the armour of the first Shroud and detonated inside. The vessel convulsed and then exploded from within, shredding its sister ship in the spray of superheated, metallic debris. Whatever the necron made their spacecraft from, it seemed that it was also the best material to use to attack their vessels.

Twisting again, her eyes wild with passion, Macha sent her Wraithship spinning into a wide sweep, trying to flank one of the remaining Shrouds that was engaging Uldreth's *Avenging Sword.*

Uldreth Avenger! Have you been boarded?

Farseer – yes. A small boarding party made it through a portal before we could disrupt its phase variance. My Aspect Warriors have engaged the enemy and the compartment has been sealed, she replied

Farseer, continued Uldreth. *You must engage the Harvester. The mon'keigh will not be able to defeat it on their own. Once the Harvester falls, this battle is won. Without it, the yngir lose their leadership.*

Macha nodded in silent assent. She knew that the Avenger was right; she had never doubted his military good sense. The Scythe-class Harvester was indeed the key to this battle. The ancient eldar had named it after the scythe of Kaelis Ra, the bringer of death, because although its appearance was fearsome, its removal constituted the hobbling of a yngir attack.

Clicking her viewscreen, Macha saw a second Blood Ravens strike cruiser blazing around the sun, its prow cannons already firing on the Harvester that continued to pummel the *Litany of Fury.*

Gabriel? she called, but there was no answer.

She scanned through the mon'keigh frequencies. 'Gabriel? Is that you?'

A whistle of static echoed incongruously around her mediation chamber. Then an ugly human voice. 'This is Sergeant Kohath of the Blood Ravens strike cruiser *Ravenous Spirit.* How may we be of assistance?'

Then a second voice. 'Sergeant Kohath. Glad you could make it.'

'Abraim? Where is Captain Ulantus?'

'We have been boarded, Kohath. The captain is leading the counterstrike.'

'I understand. Where do you need us?'

'The captain ordered that all weapons be focussed on the Harvester, sergeant.'

'As you wish.'

Macha listened to the alien conversation, letting its ugly and painful tones pollute her meditation chamber for reasons of expedience. At least the humans seemed to know the right tactics for this battle, she thought, reassuring herself. But she also realised that the yngir were indeed aiming to extinguish the psychic beacon hidden within the *Litany of Fury*: they had been boarded already. She wondered for the second time whether the presence of the Blood Ravens at both Lsathranil's Shield and Lorn was more than coincidence. The time-lines of the future-past were riddled with possible coincidences, some more powerful and pregnant than others. Perhaps the Deceiver or the Laughing God himself was smiling in the background to all this?

Shaking the thoughts out of her head, she banked the *Eternal Star* and threw it into the approach towards the Harvester vessel. At exactly that moment, a barrage of living energy tendrils latched on to the bottom of her hull and ripped the Wraithship apart.

As THE CURRENTS of warp power began to swirl and eddy around the stage, focussed on the central figure of the terrible sorcerer lord, Ahriman, the Great Harlequin vaulted up and out of the shaft of light on stage-centre. He flipped up over the head of Ahriman and landed before him, directly between the sorcerer and Gabriel, a wide grin still etched into the elaborate mask.

He spoke loudly in a tongue that even Ahriman had never heard before, making his troupers stamp their feet and throw their own voices into a chorus. Soon, the amphitheatre was flooded with a thunderous, rhythmical alien noise that drowned out all other sounds, swamping even the incantations of the sorcerer lord. Tendrils of Harlequin magic threaded around the area, intermixing and interlacing the minds of the troupe into a giant web of psychic energy that served as a containment field around the stage.

Ahriman's own chanting turned into a howl of frustration.

Eldarec stopped his song, and the other Harlequins let it drop into the background, chanting quietly without ever letting a gap or hole appear in the blanket of psychic noise.

In between Ahriman and Gabriel, Eldarec bowed flamboyantly.

With all things in the future, we cannot see beyond our choices. We may hear the music, or listen to the voices. But the future is forged through our own devices. And in our choice of the future, the present is retold. We learn about the deeds of the foolish and the bold. We know whose heart is true, and which one is cold.

And so a choice.

As the thoughts made themselves felt in the minds of Ahriman and Gabriel, the Harlequins on the stage started to leap and dance, tumbling and twisting through a series of closely orchestrated movements. They sprang and jumped, climbing up on top of each other, balancing like acrobats. In a matter of seconds, they had formed two vertical circles, one on each side of the stage, each comprised of a ring of Harlequin troupers.

At a word from Eldarec, the rings suddenly pulsed and flooded with a sheen of warp energy, transforming them into portals, framed by the laughing features of dozens of Harlequin masks.

Now choose. Eldarec gestured for Ahriman to look into the portals, offering him a way off Arcadia and out of the terrible Harlequin theatre, offering him his life.

The sorcerer lord looked at Eldarec for a moment, narrowing his eyes with suspicion and hatred. It seemed that the Harlequins had knowledge and power beyond even the comprehension of Ahriman. Then he nodded, as though in acknowledgement.

In one of the portals, Ahriman saw the great Black Gates of the fabled Black Library. They morphed and shifted uneasily, as though not really existing in the conventional or material sense. Within their mythical structure Ahriman could see myriad stars glittering, as though the library held the entire galaxy within its glorious and ineffable gates.

The sorcerer's eyes widened with lust, but something made him turn to inspect the other portal. If the Harlequins could tempt him off their planet with a webway route to the Black Library, what else could they be offering him? He could think of nothing that could possibly match the value of this gift, but something in his dark soul told him that they might know of something even more glorious that had remained hidden to him for all this time. There was always something better.

It took several seconds for Ahriman's ghostly eyes to make sense of the image in the other portal. It was muddled and spluttering with lights. It was a confusion of fire and lashes of electric blue. He inclined his head slightly, trying to decipher the movements, as though they were some form of alien script. But then he realised that he was gazing on a space battle. Looking more closely, he could see the flickering and flitting forms of eldar escorts spiralling into dogfights with necron raiders. He could see an embattled Blood Ravens battle-barge beginning to list and break apart under a barrage of fire from a necron Harvester.

He grinned and then laughed. The irony was almost too much for him. He laughed a loud and powerful laugh, letting his voice reverberate dramatically around the auditorium, enjoying the moment of theatre.

'There is no choice,' he said. 'Knowledge is power.'

He flicked a quick signal to Obysis, indicating that the Prodigal Sons should follow him, then stepped into the first portal. The rest of his Marines charged in after him, splashing through the warp field and vanishing from the face of Arcadia.

And we guard it well. Eldarec's thoughts were full of mirth as he finished the maxim for Ahriman. Despite appearances, the portal did not lead to the Black Library.

A great cheer arose around the auditorium. It was loud and thunderous at first, and Gabriel thought that he could hear the rapture of thousands of celebrating souls. But the sound thinned quickly, tumbling into a skeletal clapping. Looking up around the balconies, the Blood Ravens could see the Harlequins in the audience vanishing quickly, as though they had never been there. Their numbers reduced from thousands to hundreds, to dozens, to merely a few Death Jesters sitting amongst the sinister echoes of their kin – the fixed grins of the mannequins.

At the same time, the troupers on stage thinned to a handful, and Eldarec slumped suddenly, clearly exhausted by the effort of maintaining the charade. The Great Harlequin had projected an elaborate show and drawn a sorcerer lord into his play, but now he was hard pressed even to maintain his balance. As the apparently healthy holographic troupers faded away, so too the corpses of dozens of dead Harlequins began to appear all over the stage. The scene of carnage was terrible. The Harlequins of Arcadia had paid a terrible price.

Gabriel looked around him in confusion and concern. He could see his Librarians and Marines doing the same thing – they were amazed by the scale of the deception and appalled by the reality that lay hidden behind it.

Eldarec laughed weakly, a trickle of blood gurgling in his throat.

Choose, Gabriel of the Hidden Heart. Show us that the mon'keigh are not all the same.

Gabriel smiled faintly and nodded. He did not turn to beckon the other Blood Ravens – he knew that they would follow him. He sheathed the Blade Wraith, bowed briskly, with controlled theatricality, and strode directly into the faltering, fading portal.

ON THE MAIN viewscreens of the *Ravenous Spirit*, Sergeant Kohath saw the beautiful and familiar Wraithship explode. He watched the rain of light that it left in space scatter and fade until there was not even the memory of it left. He had no love for the alien farseer that he had learnt to associate with that vessel, but this was not the time to welcome the destruction of allies, however temporary and untrustworthy they might be. Besides, Captain Angelos had trusted her, and his judgement had always been good enough for Kohath.

'Concentrate the prow cannons on the Harvester, Loren,' he said, standing firmly in the middle of the bridge in his usual position of authority and confidence. 'How many Thunderhawks do we have operational?'

'Four, sergeant,' answered Loren instantly.

'Let's get those out there to run guard duty before we get boarded by these sly undead aliens. Inform the port and starboard batteries to be alert. That Harvester is spilling Jackals all over the place.'

'Yes, sergeant,' snapped Loren crisply.

'And, Loren?'

'Yes?'

'See about putting me in touch with the *Rage of Erudition*. Let's see what Saulh has been up to in our absence.'

Kohath could see the *Rage* performing a slow axial roll off to the port-side of the Harvester. It was bleeding energy out of its prow-mounted weapons and it appeared that its engines had failed. Port and starboard batteries were firing intermittently, but largely to repel the persistent attentions of the smaller raiding craft that flitted around the cruiser like scavengers around a dying animal.

Several Jackals were circling tightly around the powerless but venerable vessel, and Kohath knew enough about the tactics and abilities of the necron to be aware that this probably meant that the *Rage* had been boarded. The Jackals packed portal projection arrays that acted as unusually precise teleporters. Dozens of necron warriors would already be aboard.

'Loren. Any word from Saulh?'

'Nothing, sergeant.'

Kohath exhaled through his nose and clenched his jaw. He hated space battles. He hated not having solid ground beneath his feet. He hated not being able to see, hear and feel the crunching death of his enemies. But most of all he hated the impotence that came with distance: although he could see what was happening to the *Rage of Erudition*, there was almost nothing that he could do about it. His own rage, his righteous anger and his will to impose vengeance on all those aberrations to the Emperor's sight, these things had to be held in check. He could not storm over to the *Rage of Erudition* and throttle the damned necron with his bare hands, much as he would have liked to.

Instead, he had to stand on the bridge of his own strike cruiser and let its frontal cannons pound away ineffectively at an alien vessel that was steadily taking the Third Company's battle-barge apart. Meanwhile, Captain Ulantus was the only one in the front line, actually taking the fight to the necron warriors themselves, fighting them hand to hand in the bowels of the *Litany of Fury* herself.

Further away from the sun, just beyond the point where Macha's Wraithship had been ripped apart, Kohath could see the valiant struggle of an eldar Dragon cruiser as it twisted and spun around the multiple assaults of two Shroud cruisers. Its weapons were ablaze with fire, and sheets of rockets spilled continuously out of all of its launchers. It appeared as the very incarnation of fury and vengeance, but Kohath could see that it would be no match for the two Shrouds in the end. Not even the eldar could maintain such ferocity forever, and the soulless necron could absorb the punishment until the eldar crew exhausted itself.

Surveying the theatre of battle into which he had just thrust the *Ravenous Spirit*, Kohath realised that this was not a battle that the Blood Ravens could win. They simply did not have the weaponry or the numbers to overcome the necron menace.

THE BLAST DOORS of the sealed prow section of the *Litany of Fury* were glowing red-hot. They would not hold much longer.

When he had arrived at the barricades, Captain Ulantus had found his men and Space Marines in disarray. The remnants of two Devastator squads had formed up into a single firing line across the main corridor. They had been reduced to seven battle-brothers, and an entire third squad had already been lost in the attempt to repel the boarders.

The regular, pledged human crew of the *Litany* had mustered themselves for her defence. They had dragged fixings and furniture, bed-frames, doors, old cogitators, ammunition canisters, equipment crates and anything else they could lay their hands on and they had thrown them all into the main corridor in front of the blast doors in an attempt to slow down the advance of the necron warriors. Then the guards and sentries of the prow sections had assembled into militias and manned the make-shift barricade with rifles, pistols and grenades. It was not only the Space Marines of the Blood Ravens Ninth Company who could fight for the survival of their venerable ship. The pledged workers of the *Litany of Fury* had families to defend.

When Ulantus had strode down the corridor, his heavy boots clanging against the metallic floor, the men and Marines had been staring at the slowly melting blast doors in utter silence, waiting for the necron to break through. The sight of the captain, down in the bowels of the ship, ready to the face the boarding action along side his men, filled the ad hoc force with a sudden hope.

Without pausing, Ulantus had ripped his chainsword into life in one hand and drawn his bolt pistol with the other. He had vaulted over the makeshift barricade and marched to the front of the Devastator line. The pledged workers on the barricade cheered, and the surviving Devastator sergeant nodded his acknowledgement.

As the blast doors finally ruptured, Ulantus roared with defiance, triggering the first volley of fire from the Devastators. An immense bank of bolter fire lashed out of the firing line, shredding the remnants of the doors and the first of the necron warriors that emerged through the smoke. A hail of grenades bounced and rolled into the breach, where they detonated and filled the lost prow sections with blazing infernos of shrapnel.

When the firing stopped, another cheer arose from the barricade. Smoke plumed and billowed out of the ruined blast doors, but no necrons emerged from the devastation. Hope washed over the defenders in a cruel wave.

An almost inaudible scratching noise started to scrape through the structure of the corridor. It grew louder and louder, scraping and rustling until it became a metallic din. Little flecks of black appeared on the floor in front of the blast doors. They looked like beetles or roaches, scurrying across the ground. There were dozens of them, then hundreds spilling out into the corridor. Hundreds rapidly became thousands, pouring out of the breach towards Ulantus and the Devastator Marines. Then a thunderous cacophony of beating wings erupted from the breach and a great cloud of flying scarabs burst out of the smoke, like a solid black, gleaming cloud of sharpened metal.

Flamers erupted into life and bolters spat shells relentlessly, but the scarabs swarmed around the attacks and engulfed the firing line, flowing up, over and through the barricades. Ulantus hacked out with his chainsword, smashing hundreds of the alien beetles and swatting them away as they tried to gnaw through his armour. Behind him, he could hear the screams of the unarmoured fighters on the barricade as they were eaten alive. Dropped grenades suddenly detonated, blowing sections of the barricades away and mercifully killing the militiamen that no longer had arms with which to throw them.

Ulantus yelled into the swarm, defying it with his own fury. The remaining Devastators were ablaze with fire, pouring flames and shells into the metallic cloud in disciplined volleys and then undisciplined tirades. The fight was desperate and brutal.

As the swarm swept over them and passed through into the corridors beyond, Ulantus keyed his vox bead and ordered the next section of the hull sealed behind them. He could hear the next set of blast doors close and seal further down the corridor, and then he could just about make out the metallic scurrying of scarabs as they clattered up against them in frustration.

Heavier metal thuds brought the captain's attention back to the breached doors before him. Diffuse clouds of scarabs were still flying out of the rupture, but Ulantus could see several sets of burning red eyes approaching in the darkness beyond. As he watched, momentarily transfixed, the skeletal form of a necron warrior strode out of the shadows and placed its first foot in the brightness of Ulantus's corridor. Its soulless eyes burnt with hellfire as it fired its long-barrelled weapon from its hip.

The gauss flayer struck the Devastator at Ulantus's shoulder and for a moment it seemed to have no effect. There was no pressure behind the strike and the Space Marine held his ground. But then the vox was suddenly filled with screams as the Marine's armour fizzled and then dissolved away, exposing his raw skin and muscles, which were consumed atom by atom. After less than a second, even his bones were suddenly rendered into dust.

'For the Great Father and the Emperor!' yelled Ulantus, loosing a tirade of fire from his bolter and charging forward at the warrior with his chainsword spluttering thirstily.

'SERGEANT KOHATH. WE have an intrusion,' reported Loren, poring over a faintly glowing terminal on the bridge of the *Ravenous Spirit*.

The sergeant nodded, actually relieved that he would not simply have to stand on the bridge and wait for his cruiser to be exhausted of ammunition and then destroyed. 'Location?' he asked, already striding towards the door.

'The Apothecarion.'

Kohath paused in the doorway, just as the blast doors slid open in front of him; he was surprised by this report. But then he shrugged and stepped through the doors, letting them hiss closed behind him again. He clicked the vox bead in his helmet as he sealed it into place, breaking into a run along the corridor.

'Loren – you have the bridge.'

'Me, sergeant? Yes, sergeant.'

That's what comes of being the only serf whose name I can remember, thought Kohath, permitting himself a smile as the elevator doors slid open and he ran out towards the Apothecarion.

He paused for a moment outside the sealed doors and checked his bolter. This was so much better than a space battle, he thought, and then he punched the door release.

The doors clicked and then hissed as the medical facility beyond depressurised and released a cloud of sanitising gases. Without hesitating, Kohath strode through the doors, snatching his bolter from side to side to cover the wide room inside.

It was empty and white. Nothing moved.

He waited, keeping his gun braced.

Nothing.

Then there was something. It was not a noise, but it was more than a silence. He quietened his breathing and concentrated on his hearing.

Nothing. But there was definitively something. It was a weak, non-noise.

Gabriel.

There it was again.

Gabriel.

With his bolter held out before him, Kohath stalked through the deserted Apothecarion, searching for the source of the disruption. As he pulled back one of the white curtains that had been swept around one the treatment tables, the sergeant froze.

Gabriel.

It was the farseer, Macha. She was bloodied and scarred. Her emerald eyes ran with tears and her diaphanous clothes were torn and shredded. She looked up at Sergeant Kohath with desperation in her eyes. She was pleading with him.

Gabriel?

Kohath unclipped his helmet and looked down at the farseer, his heart racing with mixed emotions. Overriding everything was the feeling that he had somehow been cheated of his last great battle. He had not come running down into the depths of the *Ravenous Spirit* in response to an intrusion alarm merely to play nurse-maid to an injured alien, no matter how beautiful she was. She was beautiful. But even her beauty made him angry – it was an uncomfortable, forbidden, alien beauty that filled him with as much disgust as appreciation.

'You survived, then.' That much was clear. He recalled that the other seer, Taldeer, had also managed to escape from the destruction of her ship into the relative safety of a Blood Ravens Apothecarion. He didn't know what else to say. 'Captain Angelos did not return.'

Macha gazed at him as though showing him her soul in the depths of her emerald eyes. Then she nodded. Perhaps she understood. She stood to her feet and gestured that she would follow the sergeant.

'Gabriel,' she said. This time it was a statement of fact.

As THEY WERE approaching the blastdoors that separated the control deck from the corridor, Kohath clicked his vox again.

'Loren. I'm returning to the bridge. You may return to your station.'

'I am already in my station, sergeant.' The reply confused him. Perhaps he had been wrong to expect the serf to take command of a strike cruiser?

The doors hissed and slid open, and Kohath strode onto the control deck, with Macha walking along behind him.

'Greetings sergeant,' said Gabriel calmly, turning from his position at the main viewscreen to face Kohath and Macha. 'Good of you to join us. And Farseer Macha – I might have expected to find you here too.'

'Captain… I… I don't understand.' Kohath looked from the captain to the other familiar faces on the bridge: Tanthius, Corallis, Jonas, Ephraim, Korinth and Zhaphel. They were all back.

'It is of no importance at the moment, sergeant.'

Gabriel. You survived the tests of the rielletann. Do you bring the Blade Wraith? Macha pushed past Kohath and walked directly up to Gabriel, staring directly into his blue-green eyes.

'Yes, farseer, I have the Blade of Vaul.' Gabriel unsheathed the legendary blade and laid it across his palms for Macha to inspect. 'But I confess that I have no idea what to do with it.'

It is a sword like any other, Gabriel, and yet like no other. It must be wielded as no other blade. She was gazing at it without looking up at him, but she paused suddenly. *Gabriel, it is whole again.*

'What do I need to do?' he asked, genuinely willing to do as the farseer told him. For the first time in his life, he realised that there was some knowledge, some genuine and essential knowledge, that was only possessed by aliens. In his search for truth, he would have to accept that he could never possess it all for himself.

The others waited, each of them willing to listen to the guidance of the farseer.

Macha nodded and smiled, lifting the blade out of Gabriel's hands and turning it easily in her own. She rotated it fluidly, spinning it and flourishing it with practiced ease. *It is a beautiful blade.*

She looked up at the viewscreen behind Gabriel and saw the destruction and devastation. Although it was still firing, the *Litany of Fury* was beginning to list to one side under the onslaught from the necron Harvester. The *Rage of Erudition* appeared to have lost all power, and was being picked apart by a shoal of raiders from the outside and a knot of necron warriors from the inside. The *Avenging Star* was still fighting, but its fury was diminished and the two Shrouds were gradually beginning to assert their superiority.

It is time to end this, Gabriel. The Dance of Lanthrilaq the Swift is the masque of the death and rebirth of hope.

Today we have seen its rebirth. She smiled again, the familiar expression seeming utterly alien on her blood-riddled, porcelain face. *We are the children of Lanthrilaq, and it is to us that this blade must pass. I will see the dance completed. This is the Blade Wraith of Vaul, and the yngir will cower before it.*

With that, Macha stepped back from Gabriel and held the sword to her chest. She folded her arms around it and whispered something inaudible in a tongue that none of them recognised. The blade burst suddenly into green flames, but they did not burn her. She muttered some more indiscernible sounds and the flames flared still more brightly, expanding into a radiant aura that swept around her figure, transfiguring her into a being of pure psychic energy.

Thank you, Gabriel. The thoughts did not feel like hers any more.

An explosion of light ripped through the control room, dazzling the Blood Ravens momentarily. When it faded, Macha was gone. Turning to the viewscreen, they could see a pulse of green warpfire unlike anything they had ever witnessed before, like a gash torn through into the immaterium itself, as though the blade had somehow ripped through the boundaries between realms. The tear stretched out of the prow of the *Ravenous Spirit* all the way to the hull of the necron Harvester, where it was joined by a fork of similar energy arcing out of the heart of the *Litany of Fury*.

As soon as the energy touched the hull of the Scythe cruiser, its armour buckled and folded, as though the merest touch of that force was enough to repel the

pristine and perfect material technology of the
necron. The Harvester folded and crumpled, collaps-
ing back in on itself as though it were being reduced
into a two dimensional form. Then, in a sudden
explosion of darkness, the Harvester imploded, sucking the great rips of fire into a massive vortex that
spiralled momentarily, dragging the Dirge raiders, the
remaining Jackals and the Shrouds into a tempest of
immaterial fury that consumed them in a single gulp.
After a second, there was nothing left but the gently
floating wreckage of Blood Ravens vessels and the
limping shape of an eldar cruiser. All vestiges of the
necron were gone.

APOTHECARY MEDICIUS EMERGED from the Implantation Chamber and moved quickly between the
patients in the *Litany of Fury*'s Apothecarion. He
found Captain Angelos standing at the side of a fallen
Space Marine and stood a short distance away, waiting for the appropriate moment to approach the
Commander of the Watch.

Gabriel looked down at the battered and bloodied
form of Ulantus. His body had been recovered from
the forward sections of the prow sector after the
boarding action had finally been repelled. It was
broken and ruined, but it would not be beyond the
expertise of Medicius to bring the straight-laced
captain back to full operational strength.

Gabriel watched the unconscious Ulantus for a
moment then nodded. He had done the right thing –
Gabriel would leave the *Litany* in his hands again, if
he had to.

'Captain Angelos,' said Medicius as Gabriel turned away from Ulantus. 'There is someone I think you should meet.'

The captain followed the bustling apothecary through the cluttered and overfull Apothecarion. There had been many casualties over the last few days, and Medicius had his work cut out for him. They paused momentarily next to the sarcophagus that still held the body of Chaplain Prathios in stasis. Gabriel placed his hand onto the casket and whispered something that Medicius did not hear.

At the far side of the Apothecarion was a flimsy, white door which led through into a consultation chamber. Medicius paused in front of it and waited for Gabriel to catch up. Then he clicked the release on the door, turned, and hurried back to see to his patients.

The door slid open and Gabriel stepped inside.

'Captain Angelos. Scout Ckrius Qurius reporting for active duty.'

Gabriel looked at the stranger for a few seconds, not recognising the scarred and wizened face that was protruding from the immaculate and highly polished armour of the scout. 'Ckrius?' he said eventually, suddenly realising who this was. 'Ckrius, is that really you?'

As he gazed at the new Blood Ravens scout, he felt a wave of relief wash over his soul. As long as strong new warriors were surviving the implantation process, even in such an accelerated and suboptimal form, there was hope for the future of the battered and beaten Chapter. Recruits like the young

Ckrius, plucked out of the smouldering remains of Tartarus, held the fate of the Blood Ravens in his hands.

Looking down at the new scout's hands, as though ready to shake one of them, Gabriel's eyes widened in horror. In place of hands, Ckrius had grown strange fleshy stumps with a series of intertwining tendrils protruding where fingers should have been. The tendrils swayed delicately and interlaced into a sequence of solid forms that approximated hands.

'Scout Ckrius,' snapped Gabriel, recoiling automatically from the sight of the mutation, as he realised that the rapidity of the implantation process had clearly exacted a cost on the former Guardsman. He hesitated, weighing up the possible alternatives in his head. He thought back through the incredible pain and suffering that the neophyte had endured, all the tests that he had passed, and finally thought back to the spirit that the youthful fighter had shown against the orks when he had first encountered him on Tartarus. Finally, he thought of the empty berths that were scattered throughout the *Litany of Fury*, and he reached a decision. 'Find some gauntlets for those immediately.'

ABOUT THE AUTHOR

C S Goto has published short fiction in *Inferno!* and elsewhere. His work for the Black Library includes the Warhammer 40,000 Dawn of War novels, the Deathwatch series and the Necromunda novel *Salvation*.